SPELLFIRE

ED GREENWOOD

SPELLFIRE

Distributed in the United States by Holtzbrinck Publishing. Distributed in Canada by Fenn Ltd.

Distributed to the hobby, toy, and comic trade in the United States and Canada by regional distributors.

Distributed worldwide by Wizards of the Coast, Inc., and regional distributors.

Cover art by Jon Sullivan
Cartography by Rob Lazzaretti
First Printing: April 2002
Library of Congress Catalog Card Number: 00-190894

9 8 7 6 5 4 3 2 1

UK ISBN: 0-7869-2837-9
US ISBN: 0-7869-1874-8
STOCK NUMBER: 620-88777-001-EN

U.S., CANADA,
ASIA, PACIFIC, & LATIN AMERICA
Wizards of the Coast, Inc.
P.O. Box 707
Renton, WA 98057-0707
+1-800-324-6496

EUROPEAN HEADQUARTERS
Wizards of the Coast, Belgium
P.B. 2031
2600 Berchem
Belgium
+32-70-23-32-77

Visit our website at **www.wizards.com/forgottenrealms**

INCUDI REDDERE

This one's for all who've brought the Realms to life over the years:

To Jenny, Andrew, Victor, John, Ian, Jim, Anita, Cathy, Dave, Ken, Tim, Kim, Jeff, Kate, Eric, Steven, George, Grant, Bryan, Julia, Michelle, Elaine, Bob, Mel, Carrie, Mary, Karen, and Bruce.

A special salute on this one to Rob, who's riding the other saddle of this horse.

It's also for newfound friends who've joined the ride as the years have passed; well met and welcome!

It hasn't always been easy being Elminster . . . but it's always been worth it.

So let us return to the Rising Moon . . .

VETERIS VESTIGIA FLAMMAE

FOREWORD

by Ed Greenwood

When TSR, Inc., went looking for a new fantasy world setting for the Second Edition of the DUNGEONS & DRAGONS® game, I'd piled up many articles in *Dragon*® Magazine featuring the FORGOTTEN REALMS.

The Realms was born in 1967. When ongoing D&D play began in the Realms a decade later, I didn't feel it was fair to clobber players with new spells, monsters, or magic items until they'd been published, and so the Realms was introduced to a wider public.

When TSR launched the Realms as a game setting, they asked me to "show us all the Realms" in a novel, and *Spellfire* was born.

The plan was for me to pen a novel every year. I wanted the first one to show a lot of spectacular scenery, introduce every interesting character I could find an excuse for including, and demonstrate the depth of detail the Realms offered. Humor and Three Musketeers-style swashbuckling, not just fate-of-the-world-hanging-on-the-heroes high fantasy quests. Gold Rushes and city intrigues and crooked merchants as well as dragons and roaring monsters and endless dungeons.

Just for fun, I also wanted to blow holes in fantasy clichés. Let's see a heroine save the hero. Show a swaggering band of heroes do something recklessly stupid and (for once) get killed off as a result. Ever notice villains get attacked while asleep or in their homes–but not heroes? Well, I wanted to fix that. Ever notice how heroes stride or gallop across a continent on scant sleep, never having to relieve themselves? I wrote scenes of blundering exhaustion and embarrassed searches for concealing bushes. I also included wizards hurling mighty spells and missing their targets, and grand charges that ended in spectacular pratfalls.

I made my heroes weep, gasp, curse, slip and cut themselves. Often. Every time an evil guard fell over dying, I let the reader know about his fading dreams and his family back home. I tried to show "good sides" of every bad guy, and vice versa. I shoehorned in scores of monsters and characters I wanted other authors to use, later . . . and ended up with a novel that was, ahem, more than a third longer than was now wanted with scant time to fix things.

Out came editorial axes, some hasty stitching covered the worst resulting holes, and *Spellfire* was hurled forth. Many, many readers loved it, but I winced at the published version because many surviving characters now "looked and sounded wrong," and because the Malaugrym had disappeared completely from the novel, making it seem as if Elminster and the Knights heartlessly abandoned Narm and Shandril to certain death, rather than fighting covertly to protect them. Now the chance has come not to restore the full original novel (that would take the by-now-standard fantasy trilogy!), but to bind some wounds and sharpen some points and clean up *Spellfire*. I hope you'll all still love it as I do. Hearken, then, to a romp that tries to be more than its surface blast and bluster.

Thanks for reading.

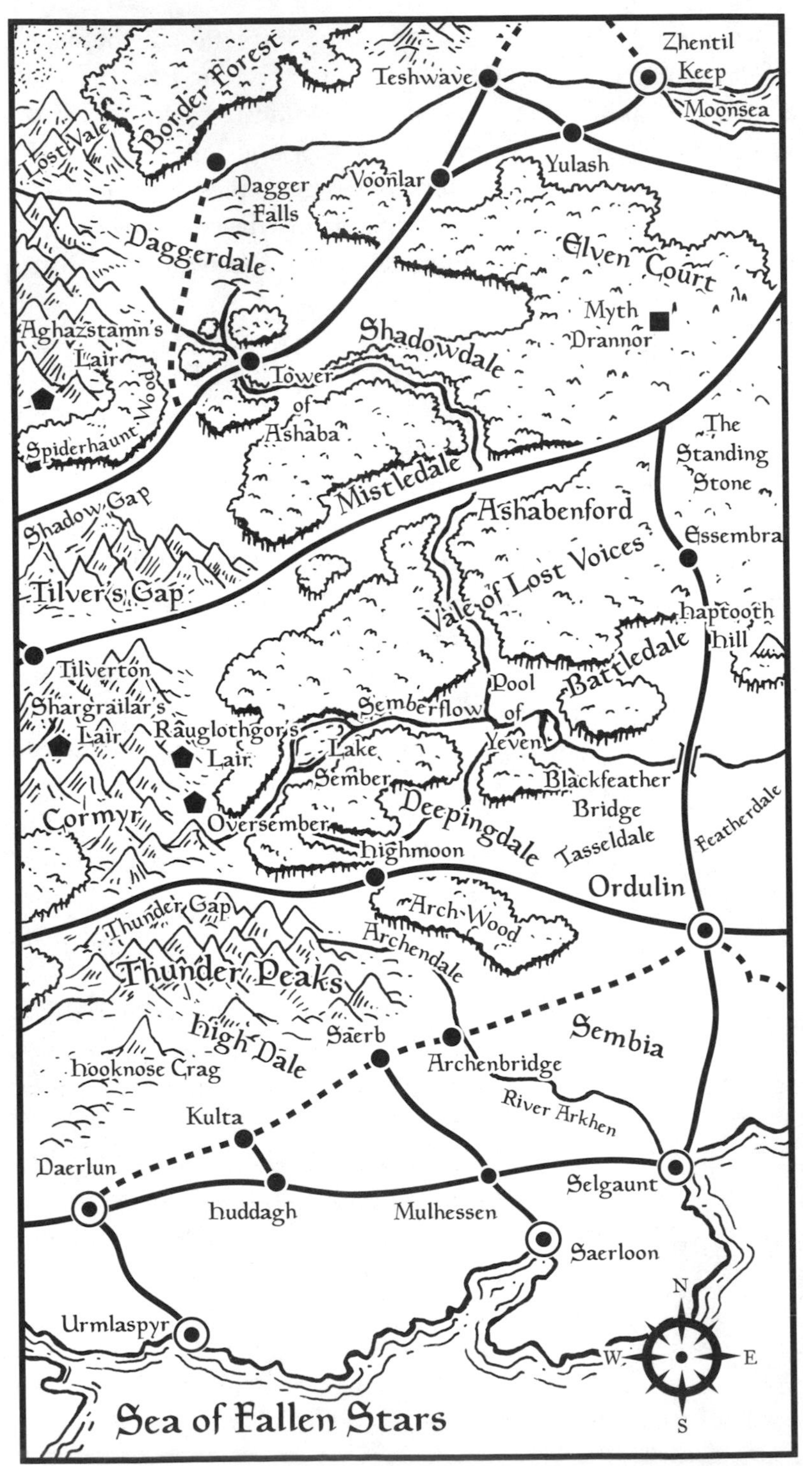

Zhentil Keep
Teshwave
Moonsea
Border Forest
Lost Vale
Yulash
Dagger Falls
Voonlar
Daggerdale
Elven Court
Myth Drannor
Aghazstamn's Lair
Shadowdale
Tower of Ashaba
Spiderhaunt Wood
The Standing Stone
Mistledale
Shadow Gap
Ashabenford
Essembra
Vale of Lost Voices
Tilver's Gap
haptooth hill
Tilverton
Battledale
Pool of Yeven
Shargrailar's Lair
Rauglothgor's Lair
Semberflow
Lake Sember
Blackfeather Bridge
Deepingdale
Cormyr
Oversember
highmoon
Tasseldale
Featherdale
Ordulin
Thunder Gap
Arch Wood
Archendale
Thunder Peaks
high Dale
Saerb
Sembia
hooknose Crag
Archenbridge
River Arkhen
Kulta
Daerlun
Selgaunt
huddagh
Mulhessen
Saerloon
N
Urmlaspyr
W
E
S
Sea of Fallen Stars

1

At the Sign of the Rising Moon

Neglect not small things, for all ruling and war and magecraft are naught but small things, one built upon another. Begin then with the small, and look close, and you will see it all.

Seroun of Calimport
Tales of Far Travels
Year of the Rock

It was a good inn, but sometimes Shandril hated it—and this was one of those times. She cried at the pain of her scalded hands, tears running down her chin and arms into the suds as she washed a small mountain of dishes.

It was a hot Flamerule noon. Sweat stood out all over her like oil, making her slim arms slippery and glistening. She wore only her old gray tunic, once Gorstag's. It stuck to her here and there, but only the cook, Korvan, would see her, and he would slap and pinch even if she were bundled in furs.

She blew out sharply. Lank blonde hair parted reluctantly in front of her eyes. Tossing her head to fling the drenched tresses aside, Shandril surveyed the stack beside her and concluded with a sigh that three hours' worth of dishes remained.

More than she had time for. Korvan was starting the roasts already. He'd want herbs cut and water brought soon. He was a good cook, Shandril allowed grudgingly, even if he was fat and stank and had hot and sticky hands. Some folk stopped at the Rising Moon just because of Korvan's cooking.

Korvan had once been a cook in the Royal Palace of Cormyr in fair Suzail. There'd been some trouble (probably over a girl, Shandril thought darkly, perhaps even one of the princesses of Cormyr), and he'd had to leave in haste, banished upon pain of death.

Shandril wondered, as she eyed a soapy platter critically, what would happen if she ever managed to get Korvan drunk senseless or knocked cold with a skillet and somehow dragged him through the Thunder Gap into Cormyr. Perhaps King Azoun himself would appear out of thin air and roar to the Cormyrean border guards, "*Here* he is!" and they'd draw their swords and hack off Korvan's head. She smiled. Perhaps he'd have time to plead for mercy or cry in fear as the blades flashed up. Perhaps.

Shandril snorted. Great chance of *that* ever happening! Korvan was too lazy to go anywhere, and too fat for most horses to carry him. No, he was trapped here, and she was trapped with him. She scrubbed a fork fiercely until its twin tines gleamed in the sunlight. Yes, trapped.

It had been a long time before she'd realized it. She had no parents, no kin—and no one would even admit to knowing where she'd come from. She had always been here, it seemed, doing the dirty work in the old roadside inn among the trees.

It was a good inn, everyone said. Other places must be worse, but Shandril had never seen them. She couldn't remember having been inside any other building—ever. After sixteen summers, all she knew of her town of Highmoon was what she could see from the inn yard. She had thought of running away but was always too busy, too behind with her work, or too tired.

There was always work to be done. Each spring she even washed the bedchamber ceilings, tied to a ladder so she wouldn't fall off. Sharp-eyed old Tezza did the windows, all those tiny panes of mica and a few panels of blown glass from Selgaunt and Hillsfar. They were far too valuable for Shandril to be trusted with.

Shandril didn't mind most of the work, really. She just hated getting bone-tired or hurt while the others did little or, like Korvan, bothered her. Besides, if she didn't work or fought with the others—all of them more necessary to the running of the Rising Moon than Shandril Shessair—she'd upset Gorstag. More than anything (except, maybe, to have a real adventure), Shandril wanted to please Gorstag.

The owner of the Rising Moon was a broad-shouldered, strong man with gray-white hair, gray eyes, and a craggy, weathered face. He'd broken his nose long ago, in his days as an adventurer. Gorstag had been all over the world, swinging his axe in important wars. He'd made quite a lot of gold before settling down in Deepingdale, in the heart of the forest, and rebuilding his father's old inn. Gorstag was kind and quiet and sometimes gruff, but it was he who insisted that Shandril have a good gown for feast days and when important folk stopped at the inn, though Korvan said she'd serve them better by staying hard at work in the kitchen.

Gorstag also had insisted she have a last name. Years ago, the chamber girls had called her "a nameless nobody," and "a cow too runty to keep, so someone threw it away!" The innkeeper came into the room and said in a voice that had made Shandril think of cold steel and executioners and priestly dooms: "Such words—and all others like them—will never be spoken in this house again."

Gorstag never hit women or spanked girls, but he took off his belt, as he'd done when he thrashed the stable boy for cruel pranks. The girls were white-faced, and one started to cry, but Gorstag never touched them. He closed the door, set a chair against it, and walked over to the whimpering girls. Saying nothing, he swung the belt high and brought it crashing down on the floorboards. Dust curled up, and the door rattled. Then he put his belt back on, took the shocked Shandril gently by the shoulder, and led her from the room, closing the door behind him.

He led her to the taproom and said thickly, "I call you Shandril Shessair, for 'tis your true name. Do not forget. Your name is precious!"

Shandril asked, voice quavering, "Was I so named by my parents?"

Gorstag shook his head slightly and gave her a sad smile. "In the Realms, little one, you can take any name you can carry. Mind you carry it well."

Yes, Gorstag had been good to her, and the Rising Moon was like him: kind and good, well-worn and bluntly honest, and lots of hard work. Day after day of hard work. It was her cage, Shandril thought fiercely, reaching for another dish while the sweat ran down her back.

She saw with surprise that there were no more dishes. In her anger she'd washed and scrubbed like a madcap and now was done. . . . It was early yet, time enough to change to her plain gown and peek into the taproom before cutting the herbs.

Before Korvan could come give her extra work, Shandril vanished. Her bare feet danced lightly up the narrow loft stairs to her trunk.

She washed her face and hands in the basin of cool water she'd left for Lureene, who waited tables and shared the sleeping-loft with her, save for nights when she had a man and Shandril was banished to the cellar for her own safety. She changed swiftly in the familiar gloom and crept downstairs to the deserted taproom. The flagstones felt cool under her feet.

Gorstag had started the evening fire, ready for a party of adventurers from Cormyr. The taproom was warm and smoky. Light blazed on the crackling hearth and on torches mounted on the walls, hooded with grim black iron. Shadows leaped along the great beams that ran low overhead, bearing the floors above on their mighty backs. In the ever-shifting play of light, the scenes on faded, flaking paintings seemed to live and move—high deeds of heroes and glories of battles long past. Massive oak tables crowded the room, surrounded by plank benches and stout chairs covered in worn leather.

Over the bar hung a two-handed broadaxe, well-oiled and sharp. Gorstag had borne it in far-off lands in days long gone and adventures he would not speak of. When there was trouble, he could still toss it from hand to hand like a dagger and whirl it about as if it weighed nothing. Shandril imagined it in Gorstag's hands on sun-drenched battlefields or amid icy rock crags or in dark caverns where unseen horrors dwelt. It had been places, that axe.

The bar boasted a small, gleaming forest of bottles of all sizes and hues, kept carefully dusted by Gorstag. Some came from lands very far away, and others from Highmoon, not half a mile off. Below these were casks, gray with age, that yielded drink to thirsty Moon patrons by means of brass taps. Gorstag was very proud of those taps. They'd come all the way from fabled Waterdeep.

Above the bottles and the axe hung a silver crescent moon: the Rising Moon itself. Long ago, a traveling wizard had enspelled it to never tarnish.

The house was a good inn, plain but cozy, its host respected, even generous, and Highmoon was a beautiful place.

Yet to Shandril, it seemed more and more a prison. Every day she walked the same boards and did the same things. Only the people changed. The travelers, with their unusual clothing and differing skins and voices, brought with them the idle chatter, faint smells, and excitement of far places and exciting deeds. Even when they came in dusty and weary from the road, snappish or sleepy, they had at least *been somewhere* and seen things. Shandril envied them so much that sometimes she thought her heart would burst right out of her breast.

Every night folk came to the taproom to smoke long pipes, drink Gorstag's good ale, and listen to gossip of the Realms. Shandril liked best when the grizzled old men of the dale told of their youthful feats and the legendary deeds of older heroes. If only she were a man, strong enough to wear coat-of-plate and swing a blade, to send foes staggering back with the force of her blows! She was quick enough and fairly strong, but not like these great oxen of men who lumbered, ruddy-faced, into the inn to growl their wants at Gorstag. Even the long-retired veterans of Highmoon, shrunken with age, seemed like old wolves—stiff, slow, and hard of hearing, but wolves nonetheless. Shandril suspected in their huts, old blades hung in places of honor, too.

If ever I get to see any other house in Highmoon, 'twould be a wondrous thing, she reflected sourly.

She sighed, her scalded hands still smarting. She dared not smear goose-grease on them before getting the herbs, or Korvan would fly into a rage. His aim with kitchen steel was too good. Smiling ruefully, Shandril took the basket and knife from behind the kitchen door and went out into the green stillness of the inn garden.

She knew what to cut, how much to bring, and what was fit to use, though Korvan made a great show of disgust at her selections. He always sent her back for one more sprig of this and chided her for bringing far too much of that. Still, he used all she brought and never bothered to get more himself if she was busy elsewhere.

Korvan was still absent when she returned. Shandril fanned the herbs out neatly on the board. Turning, she lifted the wooden yoke and its battered old buckets.

I'm used to this, she realized grimly. I could be forty winters old and still know nothing but lugging water.

Korvan was coming down the passage, grumbling loudly about the calm thievery of the butcher.

Shandril slipped out the back door and darted away, holding the yoke-ropes with practiced ease to keep the pails from banging together.

She felt eyes on her and glanced up. Gorstag had come around the corner of the inn. Trotting head down, she'd nearly run into his broad chest. He grinned at her startled apologies and danced around her, making flourishes with his hands as he did when dancing with grand ladies of the dale. She grinned back and danced to match him. Gorstag roared with laughter, and Shandril couldn't help giggling.

The kitchen door banged open, and Korvan peered out angrily. Opening his mouth to scold Shandril, he closed it again with an audible snap as the innkeeper leaned over to smile at him.

Gorstag turned back to Shandril and asked, for Korvan's benefit, "Dishes done?"

"Yes, sir," Shandril replied, giving a slight bow.

"Herbs cut and ready?"

"Yes, sir." Shandril bowed hastily to hide her growing smile.

"Going straight out for water. I like that . . . I like that indeed. You'll make a good innkeeper someday. Then you will have a cook to do all those things for you!"

Korvan sniffed, and the kitchen door slammed.

Shandril struggled to swallow a fresh flood of giggles.

"Good lass," Gorstag said warmly, giving her shoulder an affectionate squeeze.

Shandril smiled back through the hair that had fallen over her face. Well, at least *someone* appreciated her.

She hurried off down the winding path of beaten earth and exposed tree roots. Tonight would be busy. If Lureene did not bed with one of the travelers, she'd have much to tell as Shandril hissed questions in the dark loft: Who came from where, bound where, and on what business? News and gossip . . . the color and excitement of the world outside.

Gratefully Shandril waded out into the cool stream, her bare feet avoiding the unseen stones. She filled the old wooden buckets. Grunting with the effort, she heaved them up onto the bank and stood for a moment, hands on hips. She looked up and down the cool, green passage of the stream, through Deepingdale's woods. She could not stay long or swim or bathe, but she could look . . . and dream.

Past her feet, the Glaemril—Deeping Stream, some called it—rushed laughingly over rocks. Farther on, it joined the great river Ashaba, which drained the northern dales and then turned east to slip past rolling lands, full of splendid people and wondrous things . . . lands she would see, someday!

"Soon," she said firmly. A heave, a momentary stagger under the great weight, and she began the long climb up through the trees back to the inn. Soon.

Adventurers were staying at the Rising Moon this night; a proud, splendid group of men hight the Company of the Bright Spear. Lean and dangerous in their armor and ready weaponry, they laughed often and loudly, wore gold rings on their hands and at their ears, and drank much wine.

Gorstag had been busy with them all afternoon, for as he told Shandril with a wink, "It pays to keep adventurers happy, and it can be downright dangerous if you do not!" They'd be in the taproom now, Lureene flirting and flouncing saucily as she brought them wine and strong cider and aromatic tobacco. Shandril promised herself she'd watch them from the passage while Korvan was busy with the pastry.

Shandril kicked the rusted pot by the back door so the cook would hear and let her in. The chain rattled as Korvan threw the half-bar and snarled, "Get *in!*"

The expected pinch and slap came as she staggered across the uneven floor. "Don't spill any of that! Dishes await, sluggard! *Move* that shapely little behind!" Korvan rumbled, ending with his horrible, barking laugh.

Shandril set her teeth grimly under the yoke. Someday she'd be free of this!

The evening grew cool, as it often did in the dale after a hot day, mist gathering in the trees. The Rising Moon's taproom filled quickly; townsfolk had done business with the Company of the Bright Spear, and veterans had come to take their measure and perhaps swap some tales.

Shandril managed one quick peek and saw the adventurers holding court, all boisterous jests and laughter, at the central tables. A scattering of local veterans sat nearer the bar, and at the small tables along the wall were other visitors. Shandril noticed two lady adventurers nearby—noticed and stared.

They were beautiful. Tall, slim . . . and free to do as they pleased. From the shadows, Shandril gazed at them in wonder. Both wore leather and plate half-armor without colors or blazon. Long, plain scabbards at their hips held swords and daggers that looked to have seen heavy use. Their cloaks were also plain, but of the finest cloth and make. Shandril was surprised at the soft beauty of the two and the quiet grace of their movements—no red-faced oxen, these. What struck her most was their calm self-assurance. They were what she longed to be.

Shandril stared at them until Korvan came out of the kitchen with a roar. He grabbed a fistful of her tunic and roughly hauled Shandril down the passage and into the kitchen.

"Do *I* stand and gawk? If I did, what would the guests eat *then?*" Korvan snarled in a fierce whisper, his stubbled face an inch from hers.

Shandril feared for her life. If there was one thing Korvan cared about, it was his cooking. For a wild moment, as he thrust a bowl of potatoes at her, Shandril considered attacking her tormentor with a kitchen knife, but that wasn't the sort of "adventure" she wanted.

Under Korvan's hot glare, she washed and cleaned out three hares. She'd had more than enough of this treatment. She was going to do something to get out of here. Tonight.

"A good place, I've heard," said the mage Marimmar in the last blue light of dusk. Ponies carried them through the trees toward the lanterns of Deepingdale. "Mind you, say nothing of our business or destination, boy. If asked, you know nothing. You are not even all that interested in Myth Drannor."

Narm Tamaraith nodded in weary silence.

His master turned on him sharply in the gloom. "Do you hear, boy? Answer!"

"Aye, Lord. I . . . nodded, not thinking you would not see. I beg full pardon. I'll say nothing of Myth Drannor."

Narm's master, Marimmar "the Magnificent" (Narm had heard him called other things occasionally, but never to his face), snorted. "'Not thinking!' That's the problem, boy. Well, *think!* Deep but sharp, boy, deep but sharp—don't let the world around escape your notice, lest it stick a blade in your ribs while your wits are off considering Xult's Seven Sigils! Got that?"

"Aye, Lord," Narm replied, sighing inwardly. It was going to be one of *those* evenings. Even if this inn was nice, he'd scarce have the chance to enjoy it, with Marimmar holding forth on Narm's many shortcomings.

Narm could see now why the Mage Most Magnificent had so readily agreed to take on an apprentice. Marimmar needed someone to belabor, and few stayed long to listen. His master's Art was good; Narm had learned enough magic to be certain of that. But Marimmar ruined the delight of any adventure—or even daily chores, for that matter.

Narm turned into the yard of the Rising Moon pronouncing

silent curses on his master. Perhaps there'd be pretty girls inside. . . .

After the hares and four pheasants and too many carrots and potatoes to count, Shandril stole away for another look at the guests. The adventurers might talk of their deeds or even show off some treasure. Moreover, she might learn who the two ladies were. In her greasy tunic, Shandril flitted barefoot down the passage and peered out into the noise and bustle.

Across the smoky taproom sat an imperious man in fine gray robes. His fat fingers waved a thin pipe to emphasize the words he imparted to his companion, a much younger man. This one was handsome, even in overlarge gray robes. He was dark-haired and slim, with a very serious face. His eyes stared intently at the cup of wine he clasped on the table.

Shandril was turning away when his gaze suddenly met hers.

Oh, his eyes! Belying that stern face, they were dancing. They met hers merrily and did not ridicule her wild-tousled blonde hair and greasy garb, but winked at her as an equal—one lucky to be in shadows and not facing a barrage of questions.

Shandril flushed and tossed her head . . . and yet could not go. Snared by his gaze, by being regarded as a—a person and not a servant, Shandril stood watching, mute, hands clenched in the folds of her apron. Abruptly, the youth's gaze was jerked away as a hooked fish is pulled from the water regardless of its will to stay. The older man had snapped his fingers.

Shandril stood alone in the shadows, trembling with excitement and hope. These folk who traveled about the world outside were no greater than herself. Oh, they were rich enough, and had companions and business of import, and experience . . . but she could be one of them. Someday. If ever she dared.

Shandril turned back to the kitchen, railing at the fear that held her there, despite the endless pots and scalding water . . . despite Korvan.

"Get *in* here!" Korvan rumbled, red-faced, as she returned to the kitchen. "There's onions to chop! I can't do it all!"

Shandril nodded absently as she walked to the chopping board. Korvan pinched her bruisingly and roared with laughter, but she hardly noticed. The knife rose and fell in her hands, twinkling.

Korvan stared at her. Shandril had never before hummed happily while chopping onions.

It was hot and close in the low-beamed room. Narm blinked wearily. Marimmar showed signs of neither weariness nor relaxation in the cozy warmth.

I suppose all inns are the same, more or less, Narm thought, but to take this—his gaze strayed again around the noisy camaraderie of the room—all for granted!

Before Marimmar snapped at him to mind his studies and not the drunken locals, Narm noticed that the girl who'd stared at him from across the room was gone. The darkness didn't seem right without her. She belonged in that spot, somehow, and yet . . .

"*Will* you heed?" Marimmar snapped, really angry now. "What's snatched your senses, boy? One drink and *this?* You'll have a short life indeed if you gad about like this in the wilds! Some creatures'll see you as a quick meal and not wait for you to notice them!"

Obediently, Narm faced his master and dragged his attention back to queries on casting spells: casting in the dark, casting when the proper components were lacking, casting (Marimmar added acidly) when drunk. Narm's head swam with the vision, his forever, of the girl gazing into his eyes from the shadows. Longingly. He almost looked to see if she was there, but his master's eyes were stern.

One of the adventurers had chanced to spill a platter of food, so Shandril was there when it happened. The Company of the Bright Spear numbered six, led by an important, square-bearded young giant of a man named Burlane. Gold gleamed and winked in the firelight at his ears and throat, fingers and belt. He belched and chuckled and reached vaguely for his tankard.

To his left sat a real dwarf, the worn and baggy leather of his breeches not a foot from Shandril's bent head as she scrubbed beneath the table. The breeches smelled of wood smoke. The dwarf was called Delg, "the Fearless," as one of his companions added mockingly, to everyone's amusement. Delg wore a dagger strapped to his leg just above his boot; its hilt shone enticingly inches from Shandril's face. Something rose within her. Trembling, but with infinite care, she reached out. . . .

One of the veterans of the dale, Ghondarrath, a stern-eyed old warrior with white fringes of beard edging his hard jaw, was telling of the treasures of the ruined City of Beauty, Myth Drannor.

Shandril listened, scarcely daring to breathe. She took hold and pulled ever so gently. The dagger came free, cold and hard and heavy in her hand.

". . . So for many long years, the elves kept all others away, and the woods grew over the ruins of Myth Drannor. The Fair Folk let it alone; not a harp or spellbook or gemstone did they take. There it all lies in the wood still, not a week's ride north. Waiting for the brave—or foolish—to try for it, for 'tis guarded by devils . . . and worse!"

The old man paused, his audience intent on his every word. He raised his tankard. His free hand suddenly darted across his chest like a striking snake.

One of the adventurers, a thin man with short blond hair and a ratlike face, had been passing behind him, but paused.

Old Ghondarrath grunted, set down his tankard, and raised his other hand. All could see the adventurer's wrist clasped within. In that captured hand was Ghondarrath's purse.

"Well," Ghondarrath said dryly, "Look what I've found."

The room fell silent, save for the crackling fire. No one moved.

Shandril clutched the dagger fiercely. She knew she should creep away, lest the dwarf reach for his blade . . . and yet, she couldn't miss this!

With his free hand, the thief whipped a slim dagger out of a sheath behind his neck and stabbed down.

Ghondarrath jerked him coolly sideways to crash helplessly

onto the table. Ghondarrath's free hand came down on the back of the thief's neck with a solid crash, like a tree falling.

"Dead?" asked a daleman in a hoarse whisper.

For a second, there was silence. Then with a roar the Company of the Bright Spear were on their feet.

"Get him!"

"Sword the graybeard!"

"He's killed Lynxal!"

The dwarf nearly took Shandril's nose off as he kicked back his chair and sprang to his feet. Chairs overturned and men shouted.

Adventure, Shandril thought ruefully as she scuttled on hands and knees beneath the table, is upon me at last.

"They'll kill you, Ghondar!" said one of the old warriors, face white. Beside him, Ghondarrath stood defiant, his chair raised. He had no other weapon.

"I was never one to back down," he said roughly. "I know no other way. Better to die by the blade, Tempus willing, than grow old shamed and craven!"

"So be it, graybeard!" said one of the company's warriors viciously, striding forward, blade out.

"Stop!" the old man bellowed with sudden force, startling all there. "If there's to be a fight, then let us go outside. Gorstag's a good friend to us all—I'd not see his house laid waste!"

"You should have thought of that a breath or two earlier," sneered another company member through the mocking laughter of his fellows. They surged forward.

Shandril reached her feet just as Gorstag and Korvan pounded past her. The cook swore, a cleaver in his hand. Two more blades flashed in the firelight as, catlike, the lady adventurers leapt in front of the old man. One of their swords glowed and shimmered with blue-white fire.

A rumbling gasp of wonder shook the room.

"I apologize to this house and to its master for drawing steel," said its silver-haired owner in a clear, lilting voice. "But I will *not* see butchery done by young fools with quick tempers. Put up your blades, 'company' "—her voice twisted that into a shaming quotation rather than a rightful name—"or die, for we shall surely slay you all!"

"Or," her companion added pleasantly over the point of her own ready blade, "this can be forgotten, and all keep peace. The thief was caught and drew steel. The fault is his and his alone, and he's paid. That's an end to it!"

With an oath, one of the adventurers plucked at his belt, meaning to snatch and throw a dagger. The man grunted and then cried out in fury and frustration, but his hand was gripped by another as unmoving as iron.

Gorstag said quietly, "Drop your blade. All others, put away your weapons. I will not have this in my house."

At the sound of his voice, everyone relaxed, the dagger clattered to the floor, and blades slid back into scabbards.

"Have I your peace while you stay at the Rising Moon?" the innkeeper asked.

The company members nodded, said "aye" in reluctant chorus, and returned to their seats.

Across the room, the silver-haired bard sheathed her glowing blade and turned to Ghondarrath. "Forgive me, sir," she said simply. "They were too many. I would not shame you!"

The chair trembled in the old man's hands.

"I am not shamed," he said roughly. "My friends sat all around, and when it came to the death, I was alone, but for you two. I thank you. I am Ghondarrath, and my table is yours. Will you?" He gestured toward a chair.

The two ladies clasped hands with him. "Aye, with thanks. I am Storm Silverhand, a bard, of Shadowdale!"

Her companion smiled, too. "I am Sharantyr, a ranger, also of Shadowdale. Well met."

Gorstag passed them wordlessly, reached the bar, and turned. "The night has turned hot," he said to the crowd, "so the house gives you all chilled wine from far Athkatla." There was a general roar of approval. "Drink up," he added, as Lureene hastily started around with flagons, "and let this incident be forgotten." He lifted the limp body of the thief, its head dangling loosely, and carried it away.

Across the room, Marimmar removed a restraining hand from Narm's arm. "Well done, boy," he said. "Continue to hold your peace, and life will be far easier for you."

"Aye," agreed Narm dryly. His master had certainly given him much practice in holding peace.

All around them laughter and the clink and clatter of eating built up again. Tempers had been restored, and it was too soon to talk of the near-brawl. The company seemed in fairly good humor, as if the thief hadn't been liked much anyway.

Narm looked about for the girl he had locked eyes with earlier, but she was nowhere to be seen. There was something about her. . . . Ah, well . . .

The Company of the Bright Spear drank much and went up to their room late. Rymel, his lute left upstairs with their travel gear, had led the locals in a score of ballads with his fine voice alone. Delg the dwarf had lost his favorite dagger somewhere and was moody and suspicious. The burly fighter, Ferostil, was very drunk and traded coarse jests in a slurred voice. The wizard Thail, grim and sober, guided him up the stairs with many a jaundiced look.

"Lend me a hand, Burlane," he pleaded, as Ferostil nearly fell atop him. "This lout is nearer your size!"

"Aye," their leader said good-naturedly. "We've lost enough tonight!" He leaned back to grab Ferostil's shoulder. "Come then, Lion of Tempus," he said, hauling hard. "Now, where's that room?"

"This one," the wizard said, and threw the door wide.

Within, all was as they had left it: packs strewn about, cloaks thrown over racks. A single lantern had been lit.

"My spear!" Burlane roared suddenly. "Where is the Bright Spear?" They peered all about, alert, but no place in the room could have concealed its flickering radiance. Their greatest treasure was gone.

"By all the gods!" Burlane bellowed. "I'll have this inn apart stone by stone if need be! That thieving bastard of an innkeeper! Delg—quick, run to demand it of him! Thail, look to our horses! Is anything else missing?"

"Aye," said the wizard thickly. His hands trembled above his opened pack. "My spellbooks!" His face was ashen; he sat suddenly on the bed and stared at nothing, dazed.

"Thail!" Burlane roared, shaking him. "Come, we must—"

"My axe also," the dwarf's sour voice cut through Burlane's rage. "Moreover, I see no sign of our charter from the king, nor Ferostil's shield. Rymel?"

The bard was standing sadly by his pack. His shrug and empty hands told them his lute was gone as well. The men of the company stared at each other mutely. Everything dearest and of most value was gone.

Into the shocked silence came a knock upon the door.

Delg was nearest. Dourly he flung the door wide, expecting trouble. Over his shaggy head they all saw the pale, solemn face of a young girl with large, dark eyes. In one hand, she held their charter from the king of Cormyr. In the other, she gripped a spear that flickered with a pale blue light.

She stepped calmly into the room past the astonished dwarf, cleared her throat in the tense silence, and said softly, "I understand you need a thief."

2

Wandering in the Mist

If discomfort and danger be always at hand, why adventure? Something in mankind leads folk to such foolishness, and the rest of us benefit by the riches and knowledge and dreams they bring us. Why else tolerate such dangerous idiots?

Helsuntiir of Athkatla
Musings
Year of the Winged Worm

The Company of the Bright Spear numbered six. The tall leader, Burlane, bore the enchanted Bright Spear. With him rode a younger swordsman, the fierce Ferostil. Delg, the dwarf, was also a warrior. His constant companion was the merry bard Rymel, brightest of them all. The wizard, Thail, deferred to his younger, louder companions. Last and least was the thief, one Shandril, a bright-eyed, soft-spoken waif in ill-fitting breeches and a much-patched tunic.

They had nearly slain her when she appeared with their missing gear. After their rage had subsided (under Rymel's laughter), only Delg had protested her joining. The younger warrior was enthusiastic, wearing the same avid look that Korvan got. Thus far, though, Ferostil had not bothered her.

Leaving only a hastily scribbled note for Gorstag, Shandril had slipped out of the inn that same night to wait in the trees on the edge of Deepingdale. She'd spent anxious hours in the dark, with small forest creatures scuttling unseen around her. Had the company changed their minds and ridden off without her? Shandril's heart had leaped when they had come into view through the dawn mists, leading Lynxal's empty horse. She had trembled so with excitement that she could hardly speak, but climbed into the saddle somehow. She had never before ridden a horse. The dead thief's weapons and gear had been strapped to the saddle. Shandril had no idea how to use them, but would just have to learn . . . and fast!

She'd taken nothing from the inn but the clothes she wore, and her single nice gown. Robbing Gorstag seemed a poor way to repay his kindness, and Shandril was not a thief at heart.

She wondered if she'd be any good at thievery, with the company's eyes on her in judgment. Her arms grew stiff from gripping the reins. Her legs ached even worse. Places on her thighs rubbed raw. Soon it rained, and cold winds lashed, and Shandril wondered why she'd ever left the safe warmth of the Rising Moon.

The next morning, her heart light and free, she knew why she'd left. All around her lay the green gloom of deep woods, where only elves walked scant summers ago. Everywhere she looked she saw new, wondrous things. Burlane changed their course after a discussion in which Rymel and Thail spoke most, and Shandril was thrilled at the simple freedom of choice.

There was another reason she'd left. For the first time ever, she had friends around her. Oh, Gorstag and Lureene had been her friends, but they were always busy, always rushing off to work. Now she had friends who rode with her and would fight beside her and be there all the time.

Even in the taproom, when it might have meant gruff old Ghondarrath's death and the company had been loud and mocking, even then it had thrilled her: the belonging, the trust. One of their number had been attacked, and as one, they sprang to defend him, daring all, heedless of rules or cost. Above all in the world they were companions. Each one raised his blade to defend the others, no matter how weak.

That's what she was, the weakest of the company, the one with the least experience, no magical weapons, no magery. She was not even truly a thief. The weakest of the company.

But she was *of* the company, a full and proper member. The next night in wild country, she darned her socks with the rest of them by the fire. In the gray, misty morn that followed, they all washed themselves, fully clad, in an icy stream. Shandril had given up on her snarled, greasy hair, pulling it back into a simple tail with a broken strap of Delg's. Even if she was the only female and jests hailed her as she scrambled, red-faced, out of the deep brush after relieving herself, she *belonged.* They were her companions, her family, and she would die for them.

The company had left Deepingdale and turned north into the woods, heading for Lake Sember. From old records in Suzail, the wizard, Thail, had learned that elves had lived on the shores of the Sember for two thousand years. Even if nothing of value remained, Lake Sember lay along their path to Myth Drannor, and scouting it would serve as practice for exploring the ruined city. The company had come upon good trails in the woods, and for days had ridden steadily north. Game was plentiful. The forest chattered around them, and they saw neither men nor large, dangerous creatures.

At last the trees thinned, and they looked out over Lake Sember. Its waters were deep blue and very still. Clouds overhead reflected in the lake. By the shore, the water was crystal clear. Beneath it, they could see the bottom of the lake fall away, a drowned tree's limbs long, dark, and silent, and the scuttling of tiny crayfish bound for the deeps.

The company fell silent as they looked upon Lake Sember. They knew why it had been so special to the elves. Far away, down the long lake, a great gray heron rose from the shore and winged silently across the water. It vanished into the trees.

The air grew cool, and Shandril shivered.

Burlane looked up abruptly. "We must move east. I hope to make camp this night where the Semberflow leaves the lake. Let's go!"

The company turned east along the shore, weaving around trees but keeping the water in view. It would not do to get lost and stray south. Mist gathered in white curls along the water's edge. The air grew colder. Wisps drifted in under the trees, and the sky fell to silver-gray. Burlane hurried them on.

Shandril found a cloak in the saddlebags and thankfully drew it over chilled arms and shoulders.

Ahead, a bird called amid the trees. The call did not echo, but faded. In the gathering darkness, Ferostil quietly drew his sword. The trees grew dense and the footing uneven, so they continued on foot.

"Sharp watch," Burlane commanded quietly.

Blades were drawn all around. Shandril drew her own slim long sword and clutched it firmly. Made for Lynxal, it was a trifle too heavy. The mist closed in.

Suddenly there came a high, weird, unearthly call, as if from a great distance.

The horses snuffled and shifted uneasily. The companions halted, puzzled by the sound. Shandril was not the only one frightened. By unspoken agreement, the Company of the Bright Spear waited in tense silence, but the call was not repeated. Shandril breathed a silent prayer of thanks for the kindness of Tymora, goddess of good fortune.

With a silent jerk of his head, Burlane ordered the advance. Glad to be moving, they shifted damp grips on weapons and reins and led the horses on through the thick white mist.

"We should tarry until this mist passes," Rymel said, his bard's voice and gray eyes serious for the first time in Shandril's memory. Droplets of mist hung in the curls of his short beard.

"Aye," Ferostil replied, his voice low and wary. "Yet, that cry . . . if we wait, who knows what might hunt us? We'd not even see it until too late."

His words left a deafening silence.

Shandril met Burlane's eyes, trying to look calm. A trace of a smile crossed his lips, but his calmness was an act, too. Shandril felt grateful and suddenly less afraid.

Delg growled, "I agree. I cannot abide waiting a whole night in this damp, doing nothing. I say, push on, and we'll be the sooner out of it!" The light grew dim. A horse snorted and shifted. Delg went to it and spoke soothingly.

"What say you, Thail?" Burlane asked quietly.

"It would be more prudent to wait for morning and the lifting mist," the wizard replied calmly. "But I, too, would hate to."

"Shandril?" Burlane asked in the same voice.

Shandril looked up in surprise, thrilled to be considered an equal. "I'd rather stumble into danger than wait for it," she answered, as calmly and steadily as she could. She heard several vigorous murmurs of agreement.

Burlane said simply, "We go on. Better to be all awake and expecting the worst than to be all asleep but two."

Nearby, something slithered softly and then plopped into the lake. Shandril's skin crawled.

The company could see nothing. Cautious minutes later, they moved on. Soon they came to a place where the long grass lay in a wide swath as it crushed by the passage of some great bulk. Trails of green-white slime flecked the ground. The horses shied and had to be pulled across, snorting and rolling their eyes and lifting their feet as though surrounded by snakes. The company hastened on.

Later they heard something scuttle away from their path, but again met no creature. They went on as night drew down.

At length, they heard wide waters moving before them.

Thail, probing with his staff, barred their way. "Open water," he said in a low voice.

"We've reached the Semberflow," said Rymel, "where you intended to camp." He looked to Burlane.

In the gloom, their leader replied, "Aye, likely. I'll look."

Pale light flared as he unwrapped the Bright Spear and bore it past them. The bard went along, putting the reins of his horse wordlessly into Shandril's hands. She clung to two sets, pleased to be so entrusted and yet apprehensive. If something startled the horses, she lacked the strength to hold them.

The two were a long time looking. Even Thail began to step about anxiously before the Bright Spear's radiance pierced the violet and gray mist. Burlane stepped back into their midst, looking pleased.

"The Semberflow," he announced. "We camp here. We cannot see to cross."

"A fire? Lanterns?" asked Delg.

Burlane shook his head. "We dare not. Double watch, the night through—Shandril and Delg, then Ferostil and Rymel, and Thail and I to see the dawn. Make no needless noise. Don't let the horses lie down. It's too damp; they'll take the chill."

The band quickly unburdened and fed the horses, shared cold bread and cheese, and rolled themselves into cloaks and blankets.

Shandril found Delg in the darkness. "How can we keep watch if we can't see?"

Delg grunted. "We sit down in the middle of everything, back to back, d'you see? We give each other a pinch or an elbow now an' then to keep awake. Three such or more, quickly, means: 'Beware!' You look, yes, but mostly keep still an' listen. Mist does funny things to sound. You can never trust where and how far away something is. Listen hard to us and the horses first, an' get to know those sounds, an' then listen for sounds that aren't us!"

Shandril stared at his red, gnarled face. "All right," she said, drawing her blade. "Here?"

The dwarf rumbled affirmatively. He sat on his cloak, legs outstretched. A fold of fabric warded dew off the axe in his lap.

Shandril sat down against his rounded, hard back, feeling the cold touch of his mail. She laid her own blade across her knees and said no more. Around them, the camp settled down into steady breathing, muffled snores, and the occasional faint, heavy thud of a shifting hoof. Shandril peered into the night, blinking dry eyes.

A long while passed in silence. Shandril felt a yawn coming. She tried to stifle it, and failing, tried to yawn silently. Delg's axe butt drove immediately against her flank. Grinning in the darkness, Shandril elbowed him back and was rewarded with a gentle squeeze.

Shandril could visualize his stubby, iron-strong fingers pressing on the point of her elbow and was reassured by the veteran's presence. His eyesight was far better than hers in the darkness . . . and he'd had years of calm experience. She could trust in that.

An hour later, he squeezed her elbow gently again. She extended it in firm reply and grinned again. So they passed the night.

Suddenly Delg shifted. "Sleep now," he said into her ear. "I'll wake Rymel and Ferostil." Shandril nodded as the gruff warrior clasped her shoulder—and was gone.

Sleep now? she thought. Just like that? What if I can't?

Shandril rolled over, pulling her cloak up, and stared into the dank darkness. Where were they? How would she know which way to walk if she awoke and her companions were gone?

Suddenly she felt lonely and homesick. Shandril felt the sting of threatening tears, but bit her lip fiercely. No! This was her decision, for the first time—and it was right!

She settled her head on her pack and thought of riches and fame . . . and if not, an inn of her own, perhaps?

A gentle hand on her shoulder shook her slowly but insistently awake. Shandril blinked blearily up at Rymel. The bard smiled a wordless greeting and was gone. Shandril sat up in the dripping grass and looked around.

The world was still thick, white, and impenetrable. Her companions were gray shadows moving past a larger bulk that must be one of the horses. By all the gods, was there no end to this mist?

The patient, gray-white cloak of vapor stayed with them as the Company of the Bright Spear followed the Semberflow. Thail recognized a certain moss-covered stump and directed them to cross. The wizard stepped down into the dark river confidently, the water swirling around his ankles and then rising near his boot-tops. Rymel followed readily, leading his horse, but kept his blade ready and looked narrowly at the waters. Ferostil went next, and Burlane waved Shandril after him.

The water was icy. Shandril's boots leaked at one heel. Once she stepped into a deep place and nearly fell. Her grip on the reins saved her; her horse snorted his displeasure as her weight pulled at his head. She recovered and went on.

The far bank was no different from the one they'd left: tall, drenched grass and thick mist. The company rubbed dry the legs of their mounts and peered about. The mist brightened as the unseen sun rose, but did not break or thin. Burlane strode ahead a few paces and listened intently.

Three warriors in chain mail suddenly advanced out of the fog, weapons ready. They bore no badge or colors, and behind them a fourth man led a mule, heavily laden with small chests. Something within the chests clinked at the beast's every step.

There was an instant of surprise, and then the three strangers sprang to attack the company. The fourth turned the mule to flee back into the mist.

Abruptly, the Bright Spear hurtled through the air to pierce him at the back of the neck and bear him down. "At them!" Burlane hissed. "Look sharp!"

Ferostil pushed roughly past Shandril to take a stranger's blade on his own. He shoved hard to rock the man back on his heels. With ringing, teeth-jarring slashes, he battered his way past the man's blade.

Shandril was shocked at the savagery of their hacking blows.

Delg trotted past and calmly launched himself into the air with a grunt. At the height of his leap, his axe cut hard at the side of the man's helm. There was a dull *crump* as the blade bit home. The warrior reeled and tumbled to the ground. Delg had already reached the next warrior.

The burly man roared a warning back into the mist. He retreated before the eager blades of Rymel and Ferostil.

Burlane grunted in pain as the third warrior's blade bit into his shoulder. The man also swung a war hammer, but Thail caught it on his staff before their attacker could drive it through Burlane's guard.

Shandril released the reins of her mount and ran toward the Bright Spear, which flickered and glowed in a tangle of grass. She heard a strangled cry behind her but dared not look as she rushed over the uneven ground. Metal skirled and clashed. Shandril reached the spear.

Menacing shapes loomed out of the mist. More warriors! One of the newcomers snarled at Shandril, his eyes glittering. His long blade reached for her as he charged.

She jerked the spear free and ran, ducking low and turning, trailing the enchanted weapon point-down in the grass. A sword sliced empty air behind her.

Delg grinned at her as he rushed past to meet the newcomers. Beyond him, Shandril could see the company advancing. All of their opponents had fallen.

She looked to Burlane, raising the spear.

He shook his head, clutching his shoulder. "I cannot use it. Wield it well! More come!"

Turning, Shandril saw Ferostil and Delg closing with five warriors. Beyond, more newcomers loomed out of the mist, weapons gleaming. The company was overmatched. Shandril hurried to Burlane's side, to guard his injured flank with the spear. It felt awkward in her hands, but he'd be close enough to shout directions.

From Thail's hands burst bolts of light, streaking through the air to strike at three foes. One stiffened and fell; another staggered but came grimly on. The third gasped and then roared a warning back into the mist, in a harsh, hissing tongue.

Then a warrior rushed her. He had burst past the company warriors and closed quickly, a great sword overhead. With sick fascination, Shandril saw that its edge was dark with blood. It came toward her so smoothly, so quickly, swinging down, down—

Burlane shoved her roughly from behind.

Shandril fell helplessly forward, dropping the spear as she crashed into the man's legs. He toppled and came down hard on her shoulder.

Red pain exploded in Shandril's arm. She fought for breath. She sobbed and rolled desperately away, her shoulder burning. Below it, her arm felt numb.

Shandril came dizzily to one knee and saw Delg calmly hew another foe into the grass. She turned. Burlane regarded her gravely across the body of the warrior she'd faced. Burlane had cut his throat.

The Bright Spear blazed in Burlane's grasp. He held it out to her. "Never freeze in a fight," was all he said. As he lifted his head to look past her, Shandril noticed the white line of an old scar on his neck.

The mist lifted enough to reveal, trampled in the grass, the still bodies of many fallen foes—as well as far more enemies who were still alive and angry. Before them stood the company warriors, leaning on their weapons and panting.

Thail looked worried as he turned to Burlane. "Perhaps I can use the Art to drive some to slumber, but too many remain . . . far too many."

Shandril knew he was right. The strangers had drawn back to gather and attack as one—nearly twenty men in leathers or chain mail. None bore any sigil or blazon; all were armed. Their leader was a stout warrior who wore a dark helm. At his gesture, his men spread out in a long crescent, curving around the company, advancing.

Shandril turned to Burlane to warn him to pull back, to run, but as she saw his face—calm and bleak and a little sad—the cry died on her lips. Where was there to run to?

She looked at their foes. So many, so intent on her death. Beyond their grim line, more men held the reins of a score of mules, all laden as the first had been. There was no escape.

Shandril, her shoulder throbbing, gripped the Bright Spear, determined to please the war god Tempus even if Tymora, the Lady of Luck, had turned her face. She should never have left Gorstag and the Rising Moon. . . . But she had, and she was going to see this through. She hoped she would not run.

"Clanggedin!" Delg roared hoarsely, as if to the ground at his feet. He flung down his axe. "Battle-Father, let this be a *good* fight!" He drew the war hammer at his belt and brought it down hard on the axe. Metal rang—a knell that thrummed and echoed around them before rolling away. Delg began to sing. The axe at his feet glowed and shimmered and lifted slowly into the air.

The company and their foes alike stood amazed.

Delg, his weathered face wet with tears and his voice cracking as he sang on, extended one stubby hand. The axe rose into it, winking with light. Delg seemed to grow and straighten. His beard jutted defiantly, and the war hammer he held began to glow faintly. Its radiance pulsed and grew as he sang, until it matched the sheen of the axe in his other hand.

The dwarf stepped forward, singing old ballads in his rough voice. Pride and awe and gratitude rang in his songs as Ferostil and Rymel stepped forward to join him.

Shandril looked to Burlane and whispered, "Does he do this every time? I mean—"

Burlane roared his laughter aloud and clasped her to him.

She felt foolishly happy. "Ah, if one is to die," she said, quoting a wandering priest of Tempus who once stopped at the inn, "it is best to die in a good cause, fighting shoulder to shoulder with good friends."

That brought a sudden chill. Shandril raised the Bright Spear's glowing point and tensed.

Across the trampled grass, the enemy warriors exchanged a few barked commands and trotted forward, blades raised to slay.

Delg sang on. The gleam of his weapons grew dazzling and then died away as the mist momentarily parted.

In the sudden morning, two newcomers strode between the warring bands. One was tall and handsome, clad in forest green. A great sword was scabbarded at his hip, and a gray hawk rode on his shoulder. He strolled slowly to match the stride of his companion.

That companion was an old and long-bearded man whose eyes shone with keen intelligence and good humor. He wore plain brown robes with a tattered gray half-cloak. Stains of spilled food and wine were dry but copious down his front. He spoke in a voice of aged, crotchety distinction. As the two stepped nearer, Shandril could make out the words:

" . . . Silverspear distinctly *told* me, Florin, that if there were elves left to meet us anywhere in the Elven Court, they'd meet us *here*, and I've never known elves . . ."

His companion had noticed the two groups of combatants. Darting swift glances about, he reached to draw his sword.

The old man walked serenely on. ". . . to be untrustworthy, nor forgetful. Never. I doubt they've been either this time, say others what they may. Many hundred winters I've known them, and . . ."

The tall warrior plucked gently at his companion's shoulder. "Ah, Elminster . . ." he ventured, hand on hilt, eyeing the score of warriors on their left and the six on their right. "Elminster!"

". . . though that be but a short time to an elf, 'tis long enough for *these* eyes and ears to take the measure of—eh? Aye then, what?" Irritated, the old man peered about, following the warrior's swiftly pointing finger right and left.

He peered at the Bright Spear in Shandril's hands and paused to nod at Delg. Stopping, Elminster gestured to his right.

The warrior Florin obediently turned to face the company, half-drawing his blade. It glowed with its own blue-white light. He did no more but stood, wary eyes raking them all.

Shandril swallowed, staring. Here was a man other men would follow to the death and obey with loving loyalty.

The company stood unmoving.

The mage Elminster chanted as he drew two small items from his robes and brought them together, his hands moving with a curious, gentle grace. He drew them violently apart. Light pulsed—and the items were gone. Elminster faced the charging warriors, flung his hands wide, and spoke a last quiet word.

The warriors came to a halt just short of the old mage. They wavered and backed away, trotting awkwardly. They turned, roared out their bafflement, and gathered speed. In wonder, Shandril watched mules, warriors, and all charge away as fast as they could, crying out in rage and frustration. The mist swallowed them long before their cries died.

Elminster glanced again at the Bright Spear, made a "move away" gesture at the company, and strode on unconcernedly into the mist. "Now, as I was saying, I was told to expect them on the banks of the Sember, and I've never known Silverspear to speak falsely. There's many a time . . ."

Florin cast a long look at the company. The green eyes of the hawk on his shoulder had never left them. He turned and strode on to catch up with his friend. As the mists swallowed them both, the tall warrior calmly gazed at them once more, and Shandril could have sworn that he winked.

The company stood in shocked silence.

Burlane dragged Shandril with him to where the others stood. "Come on!" he hissed, "Delg! Enough! Clanggedin has heard! Let us go, before they return!"

"Who *was* that?"

"Go? Where?"

"Aye, while we can!"

"Did you see that? A wondrous thing!"

"Later!" Burlane said sharply, and the company fell silent. "Thank you, Delg—let us not waste the good fortune Clanggedin has given us! You check the bodies! Thail and Rymel, collect the horses! Be back here before I count six. Then we flee!"

"What? Af—"

"Later," Burlane said, and they went. He sheathed the Bright Spear's glowing blade while the others searched. Ferostil and Shandril bound Burlane's shoulder with strips of cloth.

No coins were found on the bodies, and the weapons did not measure up to their own. A few extra daggers and one good pair of boots was their booty. Rymel and Thail arrived back in haste with the horses, which had not strayed far.

Burlane pointed ahead and to the right. "We go this way," he said. "Quick and—at all costs—quiet. They'll expect us to flee. Men so strong in numbers and so quick to slay will not expect us to pursue them." He strode forward.

"What?" Ferostil hissed angrily. "Slink away with nothing to show for it? There was coin on that mule, maybe on all of them! Wha—"

"Later," said Burlane again, almost mildly, but Ferostil flinched as if a sword had struck him. "I've no wish to let slip treasure, nor let pass those who draw our blood without so much as a greeting. Our skulker can trail them. We'll follow and strike when death is not such a close and certain answer."

He smiled down at Shandril as they pressed on over the grass. "Ho, little skulker. A task for you . . . most dangerous. Will you?" Faces turned to her, curious.

Shandril flushed under Burlane's smile and replied firmly, "Yes. Tell me what and how, and I'll do it."

"Well said." Burlane's smile was grim. "A simple thing, and yet difficult in this mist. Hide—belly down was Lynxal's usual way—and lie near where we fought. Not close to the bodies, mind; they'll check those. Keep close and quiet. Follow us this way only if they haven't come back before you get hungry. I think they'll be back soon, and expecting us. If they hunt us, come to us and cry alarm. Otherwise, follow them, unseen. Return to us if they camp or night falls, or they go where you cannot follow. We'll try to keep near, but I can promise nothing in this mist. No fighting, mind—just eyes and ears. Understood?"

Shandril's nod brought another pain-twisted smile to his face. "Good; enough talk. Pass me your reins and wait here. May Tymora and he who watches over the shoulders of thieves smile on you." Burlane did not name the god Mask. To any who did not worship the patron of thieves, utterance of the god's name brought ill luck.

Shandril shivered at the thought of what the evil god's aid might be. She stopped and watched the company hasten on until the mist swallowed them all. Better to trust in Tymora, Lady Luck, capricious though her luck might be.

Finding a likely hiding spot, Shandril sank to her knees in the wet grass, ignoring the pain in her shoulder. The dew made the grass glisten silver-gray. Shandril slipped the tail of her cloak in front of her and lay down. The unseen sun brightened the mist, revealing the ground nearby. Wet grass tickled her nose.

Shandril peered intently all around. She had not yet escaped death today . . . and there would be no Elminster to rescue her this time if the twenty warriors saw her. She lay very still.

With heart-stopping suddenness, a familiar-looking warrior loomed out of the mist, perhaps forty paces away. Another followed, and another; the men returned, free from the magic that had driven them back. They advanced carefully in the wet grass, weapons ready, close together, and unspeaking.

Shandril tried to keep count. She did not want to creep out at their backs only to find others behind her. If I am caught, she thought with a sudden chill, a quick death would be a kind end. Adventure? Aye, adventure.

She counted warriors. Like creeping shadows they passed in front of her . . . sixteen, eighteen, twenty-one. Then came the mules laden with chests and canvas sacks. Shandril counted fifteen before the procession ended. She waited for the space of two long breaths, fearing a rearguard.

Her caution was rewarded when six silent swordsmen stalked into view, swords drawn. One seemed to stare at her all the while they passed. Shandril lay still, hoping he'd not be too curious or diligent.

He was not. The gods were with her. She drew a trembling breath and waited until she had drawn two more before she eased herself up and crept after them.

The mysterious warriors headed roughly west, close to Lake Sember. They moved warily but rapidly, as if they still had a long way to travel. An occasional tree loomed darkly out of the mist as Shandril followed. On higher ground, she worked her way closer, but in wet areas, where one slip and splash might bring them down on her, she dropped back. Soon she was soaked and shivering.

So this is what Gorstag meant when he said adventure was pain and weariness conveniently forgotten later, Shandril thought, recalling a fireside talk. Grinning, she crept closer. She'd seldom felt more alert, more alive, more excited. He never told me it was this much fun.

She came to the crest of a little rise and dropped to her belly in the tall grass. It was well she did. The mist rolled briefly away—revealing six warriors standing just below the brow of the hill. The rearguard. Beyond them, mules labored up the next hill, into rising land.

Shandril could hear the low mutter of the rearguard but could not make out the words. She dared not crawl nearer; three peered her way. The mist began to close in again. They were waiting here to deal with anyone following them. It would mean her death to go over the ridge, even with the mist.

Shandril lay still on the damp ground. What should she do?

Without warning, a man strode out of a white wall of fog two steps away. He stalked past her, the wet grass whispering around his boots, and was gone, walking back the way she had come. He held a strung bow and a shaft ready, and wore a long knife at his belt but no armor. He looked young and bleakly confident. After a moment, another archer followed, passing farther away. Shandril gasped in horror. They were going back to slay the company!

In her mind she could see arrows leaping from the mists to bring down Delg, Burlane, Rymel, Thail—one by one, convulsed and writhing in the grass, their slayers quickly gone. Any chase would run straight into a storm of arrows.

How to warn the company? Shandril doubted she could get around the archers without being killed. There was only one thing to do.

Fighting down a sick, sinking feeling, she rose out of the grass and drew Lynxal's blade—her sword, now. Fun, she reminded herself wryly, as she went off to war.

She hurried as quietly as she could, picturing the faces of her companions as she strolled up to them and tossed two heads at their feet. Her stomach lurched at the thought. She stared at the sword, cold and heavy in her hands, with real revulsion.

She looked around in the mist, feeling suddenly lost and helpless. A sharp blade is little comfort when you know you can't use it, and even less comfort once anyone else knows.

Shandril stopped to lean against a gaunt, bare tree. She carefully sheathed her sword. The tree was dead but damp; when she tugged at one branch, it broke with a dull sound, not the sharp crack she'd feared—leaving her holding a curved, twisted, and surprisingly heavy bough. Shandril hefted it a few times and stalked on through the mist.

She came upon him quite suddenly. The archer who'd passed close to her was standing alone, bow ready, listening. He heard her and half turned. His eyes met hers, and his mouth opened in surprise.

Shandril leaped forward, heart pounding, and brought the tree limb down as hard as she could across his throat.

The force of the blow numbed her hands and knocked her off balance. Slipping in the wet grass, she slid right under him, getting tangled in his legs. The archer fell, making a horrible gurgling noise. His knee hit her forehead hard.

Dazed, Shandril lay staring up at the mist, the breath knocked from her lungs, her back and bottom aching.

Sudden footsteps thudded nearer.

"Bitch!" a man snarled nearby.

Shandril rolled to one side and looked up.

The other archer charged her, a gleaming knife drawn up to strike.

Shandril screamed in helpless terror as the knife leaped at her throat, so bright and quick. She flung up her hands—the branch gone, her sword too slow to draw—and tried to jump aside.

Too late. The archer's grasping hand caught her left shoulder with cruel force, spinning her sideways as his biting blade repeatedly stabbed her shoulder and back.

Shandril screamed at the slicing pain. She tripped, and they fell together on top of the first archer's sprawled body. Her shoulder felt wet and afire.

Her attacker's furious, glaring face was inches from her own.

Shandril struggled furiously to avoid his clutching hands and block the knife—clawing, biting, and driving her knees viciously into him. Somehow she got both hands on his wrist and forced the knife past her . . . but he was stronger, and pulled it slowly back to menace her again.

Suddenly the snarling face inches from her own gasped, eyes darkening. Blood dribbled from slackening lips. The archer's strength ebbed away, and strong hands lifted his weight off her. Through tear-blurred eyes, she saw the bright and terrible tip of a blade growing out of a dark, spreading stain on the archer's chest. His head lolled as he was lifted aside.

Anxious faces looked down on her. Shandril smiled weakly as she met Rymel's eyes, and saw Delg, Thail, and Burlane behind him. She caught a shuddering breath, steadied her shaking hands, and managed to say, "My thanks. I . . . think these two were . . . sent back . . . to slay you all with their arrows . . . I . . . had to stop them."

She winced as gentle hands touched her shoulder to raise her. Burlane murmured something comforting as Thail's fingers probed cautiously. With crimson fingers, the wizard took a flask from his belt and said simply, "Drink."

The liquid was thick and clear and slightly sweet. It soothed and refreshed, sending a delicious warmth through Shandril's stomach.

"My thanks," she said roughly, as the pain started to fade.

Her eyes sought Burlane. "I followed them," she said. "They went west . . . the land rises. Two hills away the rearguard split. Four swordsmen followed up the mules, and these two came back to slay any who pursued!"

The pain was almost gone now, and her sick, dizzy feeling with it. "What was in that vial?"

"A potion," Thail said simply. "Can you walk?" He raised her gently to her feet.

Surprisingly, she did not fall. As she took a few cautious steps and turned, reaching a wondering hand to her shoulder.

Delg patted her hip and growled, "Well done, ladymaid!"

Shandril gave him a smile and looked at the others. Ferostil seemed relieved that her eyes no longer misted in pain. Rymel wordlessly held out to her the knives of the two archers.

"Can you use a bow?" Burlane asked quietly.

Shandril shook her head, but took the knives and slid one down either boot. Rymel nodded approvingly.

Burlane laid a gentle hand on her shoulder. "Let's go," he said. "I would have this treasure we've bled for."

With a general rumble of agreement, the Company of the Bright Spear moved forward.

Shandril glanced over her shoulder at the twisted bodies of the archers. She had killed a man. It had been so quick . . . so frighteningly easy. She stumbled, almost falling despite Burlane's steadying arm, and halted to throw back her head and draw a shuddering breath.

"Shandril," Burlane asked quietly, "are you—well?"

"I . . . ah, yes. Yes. Better now!"

Shandril shook her head and strode on, trying not to look down at the tunic that clung to her damply. It glistened with the blood of the man who'd nearly slain her. Her skin crawled. She hoped it would not begin to smell.

⊠ ⊠ ⊠

Far to the east, the mist was thinner. Wisps curled about Marimmar's pony as the Mage Most Magnificent led his apprentice through thickly grown trees. "This way, boy! Just ahead, and you'll lay eyes on what few but elves have seen for four lifetimes of men! Myth Drannor! Who knows what Art may wait here for you and me? We could wield magic unseen in these lands for centuries, boy! What say you?" The pudgy mage trembled with anticipation.

"Ah, Master . . ." Narm began, looking ahead.

"Aye?"

"Well met, lord of the elves," Narm said hastily, "and lady most fair. I am Narm, apprentice to this Mage Most Magnificent, Marimmar. We seek Myth Drannor."

Marimmar blinked in surprise and beheld a tall, dark-haired male elf who bore both wands and sword at his belt. Beside him stood a human lady of almost elfin beauty—dark eyes, a gentle mouth, and a slim, exquisite figure—who wore plain, dark robes.

They blocked the old, overgrown trail Marimmar had been following and showing no signs of moving aside. Both wore polite expressions, however, and had nodded courteously at Narm's salutation.

Marimmar cleared his throat noisily. "Ah—well met, as my boy has said. Know you the way to the City of Beauty, good sir?"

The elf smiled thinly. "Yes, I do, Mage Most Magnificent." His voice was low, musical, and faintly sarcastic. His eyes were very clear.

Narm stared in wonder. This seemed an elf lord like the old tales told of.

"However," the elf continued, gently and severely, "I stand here to bar your way to it. Myth Drannor is not a treasure-house. It is a sacred place to my people, though most of my kin have gone from these fair trees. It's also very dangerous. Evil men have summoned devils to the ruined city. They patrol the forest not far beyond where we stand."

"I am not a babe to be frightened by words, good sir," Marimmar snapped, urging his pony forward. "We have come far to reach Myth Drannor before it is plundered, its precious magic lost!

Stand aside. I have no quarrel with you and would not harm you!"

"Back to your mount, mage," the lady said calmly, "for *we* have no quarrel with *it*." She stepped forward. "I am Jhessail Silvertree of Shadowdale. This is my husband, Merith Strongbow. We are Knights of Myth Drannor. This is our city, and we bid you politely begone. We have the Art to drive you back, Marimmar—or destroy you utterly. Force us to wield it at your peril."

Marimmar cleared his throat again. "This is ridiculous! You dare to tell me where to pass and where not to pass? *Me?*"

"Nay," Merith mocked the mage's florid speech. "We but inform you of the consequences of your choice. Your destiny remains in your hands." He smiled at Narm, who had backed his pony away.

Marimmar looked around and discovered he stood alone. With a hasty "harrumph" he turned his mount. "Perhaps there is something to your warnings. I shall direct my quest for knowledge elsewhere for now. But know this: Threats shall not stay me—nor others who even now seek this place with greedier intent than I—from exploring Myth Drannor. When the opportunity proves more . . . ah, auspicious, my Art may open me a way you cannot gainsay!"

Merith smiled. " 'Tis said a man must follow where his foolishness leads."

"Safe journey, Narm and Marimmar, both," Jhessail added, her eyes alight with amusement. Narm could see no less than three wands at her belt—just beneath her waiting hands.

Marimmar saw them too, and nodded curtly to the Knights as he wheeled his pony. "Until our paths cross again." The Mage Most Magnificent spurred his mount into a canter, tearing past Narm like a whirlwind.

Narm turned and saluted the elf and the lady mage with a smile ere he trotted off in his master's wake.

The Knights watched them go. "The old one is too much the fool," Jhessail said thoughtfully. "He'll turn about and come by another way . . . and meet his doom."

Merith shrugged. "One less arrogant fool to swagger his Art, then. He was warned. I hope he doesn't drag the young one down with him."

Jhessail nodded. “If not for the devils and the beasts, Myth Drannor’s population would have grown to rival Waterdeep’s. Why are these magic-seekers such idiots?”

Merith grinned at her. “Adventurers and idiots are one and the same.”

Jhessail’s coldly succinct reply consisted of a silent, level look.

Merith smiled again and swept his wife into an embrace.

It’s rare for elf and human to love so deeply and so simply without high tragedy, Jhessail thought, as she kissed him. *Marimmar Oh-So-Magnificent would not appreciate this, but his young lad might. . . .*

“Here, then,” said the Mage Most Magnificent, a short time later. “I can see towers through the trees . . . this must be that part of the old city where the mages dwelt.”

The confident words had scarcely left his mouth before a dark and grinning face rose from the underbrush just ahead.

Narm, heart sinking, had not time for even a cry of alarm before the devil leaped, clapped batlike wings, and flew unhesitatingly at them. Its fellows rose dark and sinister from the brush.

Marimmar’s voice quavered as he babbled a hasty spell.

After that terrible instant of realization, they were fighting for their lives.

3

The Gates of Doom

My fires ring my foe around, and my fangs and claws strike at her while she flees. Cruel, am I? Nay, for until now she has ne'er really lived, nor known the worth of the life she has used so carelessly. She should thank me.

Gholdaunt of Tashluta
in a letter to all Sword Coast ports
on his hunting of the pirate
Valshee of the Black Blade
Year of the Wandering Waves

Mist rolled about them as the Company of the Bright Spear hurried quietly and warily over rising hills. Bare rock appeared more frequently. Somewhere ahead, hidden in the mist, the Thunder Peaks jutted skyward in a great wall. The warriors who'd attacked them hastened on, unseen but trailed by trampled grass.

Burlane frowned. "What do you think, Thail? If their bowmen don't return, will they be warned? Are we rushing into a trap?"

Thail nodded. "Aye. Yet we dare not turn aside and approach the peaks another way. In this mist, we'd lose their trail and stumble into any number of traps. Best we continue close on their heels or turn back altogether!"

Burlane looked at them all. "Well?" he asked. "Do we press on, turn back to Myth Drannor, or seek fortune elsewhere? This chase could mean our deaths, and soon!"

"We face death every day," Ferostil said with a shrug, "and treasure's guarded the world over."

There were nods of agreement.

"We go on, then," Burlane said. "Weapons ready, and pick up the pace; we slow only where attacks seem likely."

They urged their reluctant horses into a trot. The hills climbed more steeply. Still the company saw no warriors or laden mules. The trail led through scrub, up into the mountains, leaving the mist behind. Loose stones soon forced them to dismount. Slip-hobbling their horses, they proceeded on foot, Ferostil and Burlane setting a brisk pace.

"Who d'you think we're following?" Delg grumbled, running hard to keep pace.

Burlane spread his hands; each bore a weapon. "Who can say? No blazon displayed, blades a-ready and not slow to use them—outlaws, surely, but from where? Whence such booty, and where do they lair?"

"Cheery speech," Ferostil grunted sourly. "So we hasten to meet gods-only-know how many bandits, all well-armed and expecting us. And me without fresh bandages on my wounds!"

Rymel chuckled, and Burlane snorted.

Delg grinned wolfishly. "If it's fresh bandages you seek, long-jaws, I could provide fresh dressings—an' fresh wounds to go under them!"

"Ahead!" Thail snapped sharply. All fell silent and looked.

The trail led up a rocky rise between two pillars of stone. The land on all sides looked bleak and uninhabited. Between the pillars, the company could see a high, green valley, climbing to the right and out of sight. Mountains rose on either side.

Burlane nodded. "A place to be wary. Yet I see no danger."

"Invisible, by magic?" Ferostil suggested.

Delg gave him a sour look. "Waste all that Art to hide from six adventurers? You are a king among fools."

"No, he's just a gloom-thought," Rymel said, grinning. "Yet if we climbed one wall of that valley as soon as we pass yon pillars, I'd feel safer. This is a spot for ambush."

Burlane nodded again. "Once within, climb the right-hand slope, the first good place you see—and look sharp! I want no foes sounding an alarm or rolling rocks down on our heads. Understood?"

With nods of agreement, the company hurried into the cleft between the pillars.

Delg peered narrowly at the rock faces to either side. He wore a thoughtful frown, as if old stone could tell him things. The valley beyond seemed quiet and empty.

Ahead, the grass grew shorter, broken by bare rock, moss, and weeds. Even Shandril could see where unshod mule-hooves had sunk into the mud.

In the clear light of highsun, the vale before them lay small, green and rugged, walled in by mountains. Scraggly trees huddled along the base of a steep cliff that formed the northwest wall of the valley. Water gleamed in little pools to the company's left, and rocks rose brokenly to their right. Nothing living met their eyes save a lone hawk, circling high above. There was no sign of warriors or mules except the trail running on.

The company swung to the right and began to climb, Burlane waving Delg to the fore.

The dwarf nodded, swarming up the rock with swift ease that gave way to slow, wary movements . . . and finally to a pause. Delg stood like a statue among the rocks above. Slowly he turned his head. "Does something about this place feel . . . wrong?"

Mounting a rock, Burlane nodded, "Yes, and until—"

A man in maroon robes seemingly stepped out of thin air and onto a rock farther up the slope. He was broad, stout, and thin-bearded. Though he bore no staff or weapon, he did not look friendly.

"Who are you," he called angrily, "and why have you passed the gates without leave? Speak! Show me the sign forthwith or perish!" The man held up his hands like a wizard and glared at them, his eyes black and glistening.

Shandril had never before seen a man who looked so cruel and . . . *evil*.

“What gates?” Burlane called, climbing nearer.

Though Shandril crouched behind a rock, the rest of the company advanced with weapons out. They shifted apart.

Their challenger watched them, his black eyes darting coldly back and forth. “The Gates of Doom,” came his cold reply. His fingers moved as if they were crawling spiders. He chanted a rising phrase, and lightning leaped from the empty air before his fingers in a spitting, crackling bolt.

In its blue-white flash, Ferostil raised his sword in a convulsive, jerking dance. The warrior’s roar of agony died away as his body blackened, tottered, and fell. The corpse dropped out of view between two rocks.

Rymel threw a dagger as the company leaped to attack. The short blade flashed end over end toward the dark-eyed mage. In midair, the knife struck an invisible barrier and bounced to one side.

The mage pointed at the company and said something clipped and cold. Nine streaks of light blossomed from his finger. Glowing missiles darted down with frightening speed, turning to follow the adventurers. Thail and Burlane were struck by two bolts each before there was a flash of light around the edge of Shandril’s boulder. Something cold and burning and almost alive hit her. Very hard. Such pain . . .

Shandril twisted in agony, crying out as she hugged herself. She wrapped her arms tightly around the searing fire in her gut. It burned into her chest and nose and brought tears to her eyes. At last, it died away, leaving her empty, weak, and sick.

Shandril found herself on her knees leaning against the rough rock, her hands shaking uncontrollably. She knew she should draw her blade and attack, but the world spun around her in gathering darkness. . . . Stone scraped cold and hard against her cheek as she slid down it.

Down . . . down . . . gods above! What had the wizard *done* to her?

From somewhere dark and increasingly chill, Shandril tumbled back to the Realms again, rising, drifting . . . here.

Where was here? She slumped against stone, stiff and torn. From somewhere above her, cold laughter came.

She should have stayed at the Rising Moon. . . .

Groaning, Shandril looked up over rising, broken rocks to where the dark-eyed wizard stood, his hands twisting in spell-casting. Rymel was only a few feet below him, climbing grimly. Not far below Rymel, the radiance of the Bright Spear bobbed into view. Burlane leaned in pain on his enchanted weapon as he climbed. On the rocks below lay the still, twisted form of Thail. Delg, obviously hurt, crouched beside the fallen mage.

Rymel was not going to reach the dark-eyed wizard in time. A spell was going to tear open his face while he was still half a spear's length away.

The wizard snarled and brought his hands down with a flourish, as if thrusting a great sword at Rymel. The bard sprang into the air like a child playing at being a frog, caught at the top of a higher rock, and desperately swung himself onward and upward, shoulders rippling.

Shandril tasted blood. She spat it out angrily and started her own grim climb, knowing that long before she could reach the wizard he'd have doomed the company with his spells—but also knowing she had to do *something*.

Rymel whirled. His outstretched sword bloodied the mage's hand and ruined another spell that might have slain them all. The bard drew back his sword to strike again, fighting for balance.

The wizard stepped back and shouted one thunderous word in desperate haste.

An instant later Rymel stood alone on the high rock. His sword glittered as he spun, searching for his foe.

Air trembled above a rock in front of Shandril but behind the rest of the company. Suddenly the dark-eyed wizard stood there, very near.

With a cry of rage and terror she snatched out her sword, knowing she was too weak and unskilled to do any harm.

Burlane heard her cry. He turned and threw the Bright Spear in one smooth motion.

The mage stood grinning down at Shandril, his hands moving again. A flicker came behind him. He glanced back a moment too late.

Suddenly the spear's long shaft was standing out of the mage's side. Its strike hurled him sideways off the rock. Crumpling around the spear, he fell out of sight.

Shandril clambered over the rocks toward the spot, peering anxiously. Even as hope rose in her, the mage's shoulder and drawn, furious face appeared again.

He thrust a fist into the air. On one of his fingers was a brass ring that flashed with sudden light.

Shandril ducked hastily behind a rock, praying aloud to Tymora that whatever the ring unleashed would spare her. Two long, ragged breaths after her prayer had ended, with no cries or flashes, Shandril dared to rise again, sword ready.

The mage hadn't moved. He stood against a rock, clutching his side where the spear was still lodged. Burlane climbed over the rocks toward him, brow bristling in fury, sword drawn. Rymel also clambered to the attack, moving faster among the rocks but coming from farther off.

The mage raised bloody hands to cast another spell. Burlane cursed and flung his blade. The mage ducked and stepped back a pace, but did not cease his weaving of Art. The whirling sword missed, clanging on the rocks before it slid out of sight.

Burlane cursed horribly, staggering as he came down off a large rock. He drew the long knife he carried at his belt and hurried to the next rock.

Shandril remembered the knives in her own boots. She plucked one out, sheath and all. Carefully she judged the distance, drew off the sheath, and threw the dagger.

She was too slow.

The mage finished his spell, and Burlane was suddenly shrouded in a dark, sticky web of strands that held him fast among the rocks, shouting in helpless rage.

A moment later, the mage cried out and cursed. He glared at Shandril in hatred, clutching the back of his left hand where her dagger had cut him.

Cold fear settled in her, but she raised her sword and climbed toward the wizard. Only a few rocks separated them, but Rymel was even nearer, springing rock to rock in angry haste.

The wizard backed away, the spear quivering. Its end caught

and scraped on a rock. The mage gasped and stopped, sinking briefly in pain. He staggered to his feet and turned away from them, his ring flashing as he lurched between two rocks, seeking to flee.

"Oh, no, you don't!" Rymel roared, leaping wildly over Burlane's webbed form and landing precariously on the rocks beyond. He drew back his arm to hurl his own sword—

A deep roar shook the rocks. The wizard turned with a triumphant laugh. The light of his ring seemed a bonfire on his hand.

The roar filled the valley, echoing off the mountains around—and no wonder. In the sky above, turning ponderously as it emerged from between two frowning crags, was the vast, scaled bulk of a green dragon. Its huge, batlike wings beat once. It dipped its great serpentine neck and dived at the company.

Vast and terrible, it was, as long as seventy Rising Moons or more.

In its glittering gold-and-white eyes, Shandril saw her death. Paralyzed with dragon fear, she could not even scream as the dragon spewed a billowing cloud of thick, greenish yellow gas.

Rymel's hurled blade flashed past the laughing wizard, company members cursed or screamed—then, amid racing, whirling green mists, the shadow of the flying wyrm fell on them.

Shandril couldn't breathe. Her lungs burned, her eyes smarted. Choking and coughing, Shandril fell to her knees, a searing pain racking her lungs. Darkness closed talons around her, and she fell. . . .

Drifting through shifting, blood-red mists, Shandril dreamed of dragons dancing. . . .

It was cold. Shandril lay on something hard and rough. The chill air smelled of earth, old dust, damp mold, and decay. She opened her eyes, tensing against the pain—and realized, astonished, she felt none. She was no longer hurt—healed by magic, most likely, but whose and why? Even her shoulder felt whole.

Shandril lay on stone and against stone. From somewhere nearby on the other side of that rock, two human male voices rose in converse, coming nearer. . . .

". . . No, your men shall not have her! Her blood is too valuable—valuable, mind, only so long as she is inviolate!" The voice was excited and imperious.

"How can you be sure of that?" an older, deeper, and more sour voice snarled. "These days—"

Shandril listened no more. In frantic haste she scrambled up and searched for an escape. The stone was cold under her bare feet. Bare—?

Someone had taken her sword, dagger, the remaining knife from her boots . . . and the boots themselves. She'd been lying against a large stone rolled across the mouth of the cavern. It was a small cave, narrowed at one end into a crack too small to pass through, bereft of other visible doors, clefts, or side passages. She was imprisoned.

Her cell was lit by a pale violet glow. It came from the center of the cavern where a carved stone block stood, as long as two tall men and breast-high to Shandril. A seam ran around its top, the edge of a lid. . . .

In breath-snatching horror, Shandril realized the glowing stone must be a casket. Two lower, unlit caskets lay on either side.

With growing despair, she wondered how, gods willing, she would get out of *this.*

She listened at the door stone again but heard only silence; the men must have left. She pushed vainly at the stone, and then felt around its edges for a lever or catch or handle but found nothing. With all her strength, she heaved, kicked and, in hysterical desperation, leaped at it. Nothing.

Gasping, she slumped against the stone. She was trapped, and she was going to die. She shuddered, recalling the voice: "your men shall not have her! Her blood is too valuable—"

"*No!*" she hissed. "I *have* to get out of here!"

The cavern wasn't large, and she felt, beat upon, and ran her hands over the floor and all of the walls she could reach. The cavern ceiling looked just as solid. She'd looked everywhere.

With a sighing groan, she slumped against the cavern wall, staring in despair at the three blocks of stone, so large and still, like—

She had not looked in the caskets.

Shandril stared at the glowing one, massive at the heart of the cold gloom. It was huge, featureless, and silent. There were no runes cut into or painted on it; it had been smoothed with great skill and left unmarked. Dwarven work, most likely.

Now that she'd thought of opening it, she hardly dared do so for fear of what she might find. A fresh corpse, horribly mutilated and crawling with worms, or one of those terrible undead creatures—vampires, or ghouls, or skeletons. Her skin crawled.

She had nowhere to run if something in the casket reached for her. Why did this one glow? Would a spell be unleashed on her if she opened it? Did something enchanted lair—or lie imprisoned—within?

For a long time Shandril stared at the caskets, trying to master her fear. Nothing stirred. No voices spoke. She was alone and unarmed.

Trapped. At any moment the stone covering the portal might grate open, and then it would be too late . . . for anything. Shandril swallowed. Her throat was very dry. She heard her own faraway voice saying softly, "I understand you need a thief."

Are they dead? Burlane, Rymel, Delg . . . ? Shandril wondered. Thrust such thoughts aside. The casket is your concern. Nothing else. But what if my friends, dead and bloody, are inside, shut in here with me?

She screamed inwardly, though all that came out was a whimper.

Into her mind came Gorstag's kind, weathered face, smiling. Gorstag must have been in worse straits once or twice, and he was still around to tell tales. . . .

Shandril drew a deep breath and faced the lit casket. Swallowing a dry lump, she strode forward and laid a hand on the lid. There was no flickering in the radiance, no change.

Nothing happened. She was not harmed. Silence reigned.

Shandril pushed. The stone lid was massive and old and did not move. Steeling herself, she crouched beside the casket and put her shoulder to the lid, feeling nothing as the radiance played about her. Snarling with the effort, she gathered her strength into a heave, bare feet slipping. She drove the lid sideways. It scraped and shifted. She caught herself before her arm or head could dip into the open tomb.

Within, nothing moved, nothing stirred. Bones . . . yellow to brown, were scattered about inside—a human skull, a jawbone . . . nothing more.

Shandril sighed, looking at the tangled bones. Someone had ransacked this casket already; anything of value had been carried away. Why then the radiance?

Shandril wondered who lay buried here—or rather, unburied—bones scattered like rotten twigs on the forest floor. Idly she looked for certain bones. There, the thighbone; he must have been tall. There, the skull—

She noticed something odd. There were three skeletal arms in the casket.

Just the one skull, and only bones enough, give or take a few, for one body. But three arms? One crumbled into separate bones. Another remained intact, strips of withered sinew clinging to the wrist and holding all together. The third was larger. . . . Curious, she reached into the tomb and touched the hand that did not belong.

Idiot! she thought, too late. What have you done?

She froze, waiting for some magical doom to befall, or the old bones to take her hand in a bony grasp, or a stone block to fall from the ceiling—*some*thing!

Nothing.

Shandril peered around the cavern warily. She shrugged and lifted the skeletal arm. It dangled limply at the wrist, small finger bones pattering back into the casket as she peered curiously at it. Something had caught her eye a moment ago, something different—

Faint scratches caught the light along the bone, writing of some sort!

Shandril peered at it closely, wrinkling her nose in anticipation of a rotting smell that wasn't there. The writing was a single word.

Why would someone scratch a word on a bone and leave it here? Squinting, Shandril made out the word.

"Aergatha."

Suddenly, she was no longer in the cavern. Still clutching the bones, she stood somewhere dimly lit and smelling of earth. Cold air moved against her face.

Cold claws reached for her. She barely had time to scream.

⊠ ⊠ ⊠

White with fear, Narm desperately swung his staff. The skull faces of two bone devils grinned at him as he backed away, trying to keep their hooks at bay and flee Myth Drannor.

They stalked him lazily, with horrible, throaty chuckles, entertained by his struggles. Thunder rolled, and it was growing dark under the trees.

Narm backed away, gasping. Thrice they'd tried to outflank him, and only frantic leaps and acrobatics had saved him. By turns, they faded into invisibility. He'd swing wildly at the empty air, hoping to deflect an unseen bone hook swinging for his throat. Once, his staff crashed into something, but the devil reappeared unaffected, grinning just beyond his reach.

Twice he'd been wounded, hook slashes that stung under his sweat. The glistening sheen drenched him and left him nearly blind. His feeble Art was useless against these creatures, even if he'd had time to cast anything. Far stronger magic hadn't saved Marimmar.

The pompous mage was overwhelmed after a few spectacular spells, then slowly torn apart with bone hooks—the same bloody weapons that even now tormented the screaming ponies.

The elf and his lady had given fair warning, and Marimmar had scoffed. Now the Mage Most Magnificent was dead, horribly dead. One mistake, only one, and now it was much too late to undo their fates. . . .

He was going to die here, in agony, as cruel devils laughed.

Suddenly Marimmar's severed head appeared before him in midair, dripping blood, eyes lolling in different directions. Narm screamed as those eyes focused on him. The blood-bearded mouth opened in a ghastly smile.

Frantic, Narm swung his staff. It cut empty air. The head was gone, gone as if it had never been! Illusion, Narm realized in helpless anger, as devils hissed laughter around him.

Around him—they'd gotten on both sides! Desperately, Narm turned and charged one, swinging his staff to batter it down. It danced aside, its barbed tail curling at him. Narm stumbled and sprawled in the dry leaves and dirt.

Rolling over, heart pounding, he found his feet and flailed about with his staff. . . . He was dead anyway. He'd never escape. If only he and Marimmar had turned back!

Then, amid a blinding flash, the world exploded.

Narm hit something, hard. Putting out a hand, he felt bark. He hauled himself along the tree until he was upright. Something hampered his grasp. He came slowly and dazedly to the realization that he still held his staff.

A dry female voice spoke, close by. "He lives, Lanseril. If your bolt had been a couple of hands closer . . ."

"Your turn, remember?" a lilting male voice replied, pointedly. Then both voices chuckled.

Narm blinked desperately. "Help," he managed to say, almost sobbing, "Help! I can't *see!*"

"Can't think either, if you planned on storming Myth Drannor armed with nothing but a sapling," the female said to him, and then hissed a word.

Something brightened to Narm's left and raced off as many moving lights. He could see nothing more in the white fog that cloaked his eyes.

A hand fell on his arm. He stiffened and swung his staff up.

"No, no," the male voice said in his ear. "If you hit me, I'll just leave you again, and the devils'll have you. How many companions had you?"

"I—just one," Narm choked, letting his arm fall. "Marimmar, the—the Mage Most Magnificent."

"I take it that he's no more," the female voice said gently. A hand took his sleeve, and Narm was being led rapidly over uneven ground.

"Aye," the man said. "I've seen pieces of him, mixed up with two ponies. Can you ride, man?" Insistently he shook Narm, who managed a violent nod. "Good. Up you go."

Narm felt a stirrup, and then was thrust up onto the back of a snorting, shifting horse. He clutched its neck thankfully.

The female hissed something, and the man said, "Tymora spit on us, they're persistent! There's another flying at us now! *Ride!* Illistyl, lead him, will you?"

Narm heard a sudden flutter of wings. He struck out at it wildly, blindly, with his staff.

"Mystra give me *strength*," the woman snarled, and Narm was jerked roughly to one side. "Strike down Lanseril? *Idiot!*"

A small, strong hand clouted him under the jaw and jerked the staff from his grasp. Narm heard it clatter to the ground.

"I beg pardon!" he stammered, clutching at the horse's straining neck as it gathered speed. "I meant no harm! Devils flying, he said!"

"Aye, they are, and we're not out of the woods yet, either," Illistyl replied tartly. "You might help by letting the horse breathe and turn its head. Loosen your hold on its neck."

Finding the raised edge of his saddle, Narm did so.

"I am Illistyl Elventree," his guide added. "Lanseril Snowmantle flies above us. He *may* forgive you by the time we reach Shadowdale."

"S-Shadowdale?" Norm asked, trying to remember what Marimmar had told him of the dales. He could see dark things moving . . . no, he was moving past them—trees! His sight was coming back!

"What—how did you save me? I was—was—"

"Trapped, yes. Lanseril nearly caught you in the lightning he called—wouldn't have been the first time. Can you see?"

Narm shook his head, trying to clear the white mists. "Trees, a bit, and the head of my horse." He turned his head toward her voice. "I can't see you, yet." Hearing his voice shake, he drew a deep breath. "How came you to find me? And—and—"

"We are Knights of Myth Drannor. Those who venture here for treasure often meet with us. The unlucky, such as yourself and your master, find the devils first."

"We . . . we met an elf first, good lady. Strongbow. He stood with a lady mage, and they warned us back. My master was angered. He was determined to find the magic that remains, and so went around another way. He is—was—proud and willful."

"He stands in large company in life and death. You were apprenticed to him?"

"Aye. I am but new come to the Art. My spells are not of any consequence. They may never be, now."

"What's your name, wise apprentice?"

"Narm, good lady."

"Nay, that I'm not. A lady, yes, when I remember, but I fear my tongue prevents my being called 'good' overmuch. Slow your mount, Narm. This next stretch is all roots and holes."

"Yes, but . . . the devils?"

"We're largely clear. They seem under orders as to how far they may venture. If we are beset now, I've time enough to call on Elminster."

"Elminster?"

"The Sage of Shadowdale. He's seen hundreds of winters, and used them to become one of the most powerful mages in Faerûn. Mind your manners before him, Narm, if you'd see the next morn as a man and not a toad or worse!"

"As you say, lady. This Elminster . . . ah, is he in need of an apprentice?"

Illistyl chuckled. "He enjoys having a 'prentice as much as coming down with a plague. But you may *ask*. . . ."

Narm managed a grin. "I know not if I dare, good lady."

"A man who fights bone devils with a stick of wood, afraid to ask a question of Elminster? He'd be most flattered." She chuckled again, the full, throaty chuckle few women allow themselves, and leaned over to lead Narm's horse by the bridle through a narrow passage and around a large pit.

Narm could see her clearly at last. To his astonishment, she was a tiny wisp of a girl, no older than he, wrapped in a dark cloak over the earthen-hued tunic and breeches of a forester. Her boots were fine leather, but their swash-topped cuffs were plain.

She felt his gaze and gave him a smile. "Well met."

Narm smiled back as she spurred down a slope in the path. How powerful were these Knights, that one so young might, with but one companion, calmly contend with devils? What would become of Narm in the hands of ones so powerful?

With dull despair Narm realized he'd lost all of his books of magic—worse, all he owned but a knife, a few coins, and the clothing on his back. He had no home, no master, and no means of earning coins anew. What need would Shadowdale have of an apprentice worker of the Art with the likes of Elminster and Lady Illistyl in residence? Narm set his jaw and rode on with a heavy heart.

Illistyl saw and said nothing, for some things must be faced and fought alone.

They rode on. The day waned and grew dark beneath the trees. Suddenly a great eagle swooped down from the sky to join them in a clearing. Writhing before their eyes, it rose into the shape of a lively-eyed man in the simple robes of a druid.

Narm bid grave greeting to Lanseril Snowmantle.

Lanseril returned it and asked if he cooked meals or washed up afterward. There was laughter, and the darkness within Narm lightened.

Nothing disturbed their camp that night, but in his dreams Narm died a thousand times and saved his surly master a hundred times and slew ten thousand devils. Often he awoke screaming or weeping. Each time Illistyl or Lanseril sat close to reassure him. As Narm rolled himself into his cloak once more, he'd shake his head wearily. It would be a very long time before his dreams would be free of grinning, hissing devils.

The next day, riding with the Knights west through the vast wood, Narm knew he must return to Myth Drannor. Not to avenge Marimmar or to try to recover lost spellbooks, but to be free of the taunting devils of his dreams. Half-asleep, he slumped in his saddle and wondered if he'd live long enough, next time, even to glimpse the ruined city.

They rode at last into a beautiful dale of busy farms and gardens and well-loved trees. Beyond stood a keep on the banks of the river Ashaba, at the base of a bald knob of rock known as the Old Skull.

Illistyl nodded to the guards. She turned their mounts out

onto a meadow in the care of an old and limping master of horses and three eager youths. She then led Narm into the Twisted Tower.

More guards waited within. They nodded to Illistyl as she strode to a pair of massive arched inner doors. They opened under her hands into a vast chamber where an expressionless man in elegant finery sat on a throne. Two farmers stood before him, arguing about a broken fence and the ownership of hogs.

Lord Mourngrym's mustache hid his mouth, but one of the lord's forefingers repeatedly traced a sinuous design of stags and hunters on the gold scabbard of his long sword.

Illistyl led Narm to a bench at the front of the nearly empty hall, ignoring the expressionless scrutiny of the guards flanking the lord's throne. Huge tapestries hung behind that throne. High above, on Narm's right, a balcony curved across a corner of the room. A guard stood there, too, and the prow of a loaded crossbow rested casually on the balcony rail.

"Enough," the lord said suddenly, and the argument stopped in midword. "I'll send men to repair the fence this day. You are to obey them as you would me. They'll see you divide all hogs on both farms into two equal groups, one for each of you. You'll eat together this night, both families, with my men and the wine they'll bring—and let all hard feelings be put behind you both. See to it."

He gave each man a level stare and added, "Be true friends again. If any trouble over fences or anything else brings you before me again, it will cost you a hog each."

He nodded in dismissal, and both farmers bowed and walked out wordlessly. No sooner had they passed into the hall, however, than their voices rose in argument again.

Narm thought he saw a smile steal across the lord's handsome face.

Illistyl rose and tugged at his arm. "Come." She led him to stand before the throne.

Narm started to bow hesitantly. Illistyl's grip on his arm jerked him upright. "Narm," she said, "this is Lord Mourngrym, of Shadowdale. He will ask questions; answer him well, or I shall regret having aided you." Smiling, she turned to the man on the throne. "We found him beset by devils in Myth Drannor, Grym."

Lord Mourngrym nodded. The eyes he turned on Narm were very clear and very blue. Their gaze held the apprentice as if at the point of a gentle sword. "Welcome. Why came you to Myth Drannor, Narm?"

Narm was silent a moment. His words came out in a rush. "My master, the mage Marimmar, sought the magic he believes—believed—the city holds. We rode out of Cormyr and up through Deepingdale seeking the ruins, just the two of us."

The Lord of Shadowdale arched one eyebrow, but his expression did not change.

Narm drew in a deep breath. "There we met Merith Strongbow and Jhessail Silvertree of the Knights, who warned us back. My master was angry. He thought they were trying to keep him from the magic, so we went southeast and turned again to reach the city. We were beset by devils, and my master was killed. I would have died, too, had not this good lady and the druid Lanseril Snowmantle come to my rescue. They brought me straight here."

Mourngrym nodded. "Their patrol was ended. Here you stand; what will you do now?"

Narm paused. "A night ago, Lord, I'd not have known. But I am resolved: I'll go back to Myth Drannor, if I can." He saw devils in his mind and shuddered. "If I run, I shall be seeing devils forever."

"It could be your death."

"If the gods Tymora and Mystra will it so, then so be it."

Mourngrym looked to Illistyl, whose eyebrows had risen in faint surprise. "What say you? Let a man go to his death?"

Illistyl shrugged. "We must do as we will, if we can. The hard task, Grym—decreeing who can do as they will—is yours." She grinned. "I look forward to observing your masterful performance."

Mourngrym's mustache curled in a tight smile ere he turned back to Narm. "You now lack a master. Do you also lack spells?"

"Yes, Lord," Narm replied. "If I return again from Myth Drannor, I would seek a mage of power to study my Art. I have heard of Elminster. Are there others here who might welcome an apprentice?"

Mourngrym smiled openly this time. "Yes," he said. "The lady who stands beside you, for one."

Narm looked at Illistyl. She smiled faintly, eyebrows and gaze raised to the rafters.

Mourngrym continued, "Her mentor, Jhessail Silvertree, for another. Other, lesser workers of Art in the dale may also welcome you. I try to make welcome only those who mean Shadowdale no harm. Do you yet serve anyone—the Dragon Cult, perhaps, or anyone of Zhentil Keep? Have you accepted coin from anyone to observe and report what you see?"

The air around Narm suddenly tingled. "*No*, Lord," he said firmly, letting a little more anger into his voice than he should have. "I swear I work for no one, and mean no ill to Shadowdale. You have my word on it."

The lord of the dale looked at Narm with interest. "And is your word good?"

Narm's face flooded bright red. "It is. Believe it."

"I do," Mourngrym said thoughtfully, "and yet I ask myself why. Perhaps you'll tell me."

"I . . . I must keep it good," Narm told him grimly, "because it is all I have."

The lord inclined his head. "Illistyl trusts you," he said gently, and the smile that followed was as dazzling as it was sudden. "Wherefore you have the freedom of the dale and are welcome, here in the Tower, to our table and a bed. May the gods smile on you when you return to Myth Drannor."

Narm bowed. "Thank you, Lord." Turning, he offered his arm to Illistyl. "My lady?"

Illistyl nodded, winking at Mourngrym. "Adventurers and fools walk together, eh?"

"Yes," Mourngrym agreed. A sparkle glimmered in his eye as he added, "But which is which?"

4

Many Meetings

Always we hurry through our lives, we who travel. Only folk tied to the land wait for danger to come to them. All others blunder ever onward, swords at the ready, through many meetings. Each may be the last, for in the wilds the wolf, the orc, and the gorgon hunt and smile when they meet dinner. What is more dangerous even than these? Why, any man you meet.

Jarn Tiir of Lantan
A Merchant's Tale
Year of the Smoky Moon

Shandril desperately flung herself aside. The fearsome thing of stone wavered once more and toppled past her, shattering flagstones with a thunderous crash. Broken jaws and claws bounced and skittered, making the girl from the Rising Moon—she who should never have *left* the Rising Moon, by all the gods!—cough amid rising dust.

So, statues *could* break. She'd always wondered. . . .

She'd landed on her knees and forearms in an old, deserted room. It was a large dark hall, its corners and ceiling lost in gloom. Dim sunlight crept in from somewhere off to her right, across a stone floor littered with dust and rubble.

Shandril rolled over and got up hastily to look behind her. She was alone. In the dust beside the toppled statue, she could see the marks of her landing. She'd simply *appeared* here, wherever here was.

Shandril had no desire to explore. She sank to the floor, cursing softly at the pain of many minor bruises, and sat still, catching her breath. The inscribed bone remained clutched in one hand, though the smaller bones had fallen off. Shandril dropped it in her lap and sighed.

Here she was, lost and alone, penniless, unarmed, barefoot, in pain, somewhere unfamiliar that she'd reached by Art she neither understood nor controlled. Moreover, she was thirsty, hungry, and badly in need of relieving herself.

Shandril sighed, brushed tangled hair out of her eyes, and got up. Adventure, hah. Unending pain, fear, and discomfort are nearer the mark. That—she reflected, looking warily about as she loosened her breeches—and never relaxing, not even for an instant.

All too soon, something moved high up in the darkness at the far end of the hall, flapping toward her. Three somethings, ugly creatures with curving beaks, barbed claws, and bat wings covered in dusty brown feathers. Small yellow eyes glittering nastily at her. . . .

Shandril cursed, struggled to her feet, laced and belted her breeches, clutched the bone that had brought her here, and ran across the hall in the direction of the daylight.

It's not like this in travelers' tales, she thought ruefully as she slipped on loose stone and twisted her knee. "Come to think of it, I've not seen a single gold coin yet." She ran on.

Sunlight came from two tall, narrow windows ahead of her, set high in the wall. Beneath them she could make out the arch of a small doorway, a wooden door carved with a beautiful design. Then she realized in horror that she saw no pull ring, knob, or even keyhole. Wings flapped close behind her.

She reached the door, ran desperate fingers around it, tugged vainly at the ridges of the carving and the edges, and finally hurled her shoulder against the thick, polished wood, gritting her teeth against the impact.

There was a dull crash, and she was through the door. Its rotten wood collapsed into splinters and pulpy dust around her as she . . . fell!

Shandril twisted helplessly in the air, falling through daylight, down, down toward a well. Around her were huge trees and vine-covered stone towers. Where was she? She laughed wildly, shaking her head at her helplessness. Adventure, aye!

Colder laughter answered. From a nearby stone spire, a woman with wings sprang into the air and flapped in Shandril's direction. The maid from Highmoon had a brief glimpse of dusky naked flesh, cruel eyes, and a dagger flashing as the wings beat. Then she struck cold water with a crash that shook her very bones.

She plunged deep. Only the icy water kept her from passing out. Numb, Shandril feebly struggled to the surface.

"Lady Tymora!" she gasped as her face broke water. "Please! No more!"

Overhead, the winged woman gleefully swooped and darted. Her dagger flashed and struck, gutting the three little horrors who'd flown after Shandril. From the tales she'd heard, they were probably stirges, and the woman . . . the woman was some sort of devil.

A devil. Devils lurked in ruins . . . and the nearest ruins she remembered from talk in the Rising Moon were those of Myth Drannor.

"Gods preserve me!" Shandril groaned, teeth chattering.

She splashed to the edge of the well and clawed her way out. Her arms felt leaden. The enchanted bone was gone in the dark water. At least, she thought slowly, crawling away, there was nothing waiting for me in the well.

Something splashed behind her. Great tentacles reached up from the waters. A cluster of eyes goggled about on one dripping stalk. Other tentacles slapped at the winged devil and then coiled about it hungrily. . . .

The she-devil was overmastered. Breast heaving and feathers flying, she struggled. Her fangs sank into one tentacle, but it swiftly drew her down. She struck feebly with her dagger as the tentacles dragged her under, leaving only bubbles and darkening water behind.

Shandril turned away, feeling sick, and crawled toward some bushes growing up the side of the hall. Perhaps she could hide there, and rest—

The stones beneath her gave way, and Shandril fell into musty darkness. She was too weary to care.

Tymora, it seemed, had answered her prayer. Shandril sank into oblivion, wondering what she had landed on that was so hard. Whatever it was shifted under her metallically, for all the world like coins. Perhaps she'd die a rich adventurer, after all. . . .

⊠ ⊠ ⊠

"Have a care, sot," Torm said affectionately to Rathan, kneeing his horse to urge it closer, "else you'll be right off your beast and headfirst in the mud!"

The florid, red-eyed cleric clamped large fingers on the rim of his saddle and fixed Torm with baleful eyes. "Tymora love thee for thy ill-placed concern, bootlicking dog!" He belched comfortably, adjusted his paunch to settle a disagreement it had with the saddle, and wagged a finger at the mischievous thief. "So I like to drink! Do I fall from the saddle? Do I disgrace the Great Lady whose symbol I bear? Do I yip and yap incessantly in a double-tongued, fawning, untruthful manner, like certain nameless-but-all-too-near thieves? Aye?"

Narm, between them, wisely said nothing. They were in deep woods, riding east to Myth Drannor. The horses evidently knew the trail, for the two Knights spared little attention for guiding them. Since departing Shadowdale days ago, the sharp-tongued Torm had spent his time needling Rathan, and the big cleric had spent his emptying skin after skin of wine. The pack mules that followed his mount resembled huge ambulatory bunches of grapes. Those behind Torm carried all the food.

Mourngrym had lent Narm the mount that snorted and grumbled beneath him. He'd also suggested that Narm ride back to the ruined city in the company of two Knights of Myth Drannor leaving for a patrol there. Overwhelmed by a magnificent feast and a canopied bed in the Tower of Ashaba the night before,

Narm had accepted. Several times since, he had questioned the wisdom of that decision.

Torm's thin mustache quirked in a smile. "Lost in thought, good Narm? No time for that, now you're an adventurer! Philosophers think and do nothing. Adventurers rush in to be killed without reflection. A single thought as to what they're facing would no doubt have them fleeing!"

"Not so," Rathan rumbled, wagging that finger again. "If ye worship the Lady Luck, Tymora the True, luck will cloak thee and walk with thee. Such thoughts but mar thy daring."

"Yes, if you worship Tymora," Torm returned. "Narm and I are both more prudent men."

"Ye worship Mask and Mystra between ye and speak to me of prudence?" Rathan chuckled. "The world rears strangeness anew." He leaned forward suddenly to point into the dimness. "Look, ye loose-tongues! Is that not a devil in the trees?"

Narm froze in his saddle, his hands suddenly icy. He tried not to tremble. Torm turned his mount, slim long sword out. "Do they wander so far, now? We may not be able to wait for Elminster's or Dove's return before we raise all against them, if they're grown so bold!"

"It's but one, oh bravest of thieves," Rathan said dryly, standing in his stirrups to get a better look. "And there's something awry. See how its flame scorches not? It passes through brush without so much as a leaf crunching or a twig cracking. 'Tis an illusion!" He swung about to fix Narm with a stern eye, the silver disc of Tymora shining in his hand. "This would not be your work, Narm Not-Apprentice?"

"No," Narm said, spreading honest hands. The Knights could see he was white with fear.

Both turned to peer at the woods suspiciously.

"Why an illusion, but to draw us away?" Rathan asked.

"Yes," Torm replied softly, "into a trap or away from someone who wants to pass?"

"Hmmph," Rathan said and rose in his saddle again, holding his holy symbol aloft. His free hand traced empty air around the disc, following its shape. "Tymora! Tymora! Tymora!"

The disc began to glow, faintly at first and then more brightly, until it shone with a bright silver radiance. Torm scanned the woods, blade ready. Abruptly Rathan released his hold on the glowing disc. It did not fall, but hung silently in midair, as the priest sang to it:

By Tymora's power and Tymora's grace,
Be revealed now wherever I face,
All lives and things that evil be
Unveiled truly now before me!

The disc flared blindingly as Rathan's words ended. He plucked it from the air and held it out before him. Its glow slowly faded, and he peered down the path, eyes keen.

"Aha!" he said. "Six creatures on the trail, headed this way!" Dragging a heavy mace from his belt, he whacked his armored knee lightly and swung his arm to limber his shoulder. "Ready, Torm?" he asked. "Narm, watch the rear, will ye?"

Narm blinked. "Six? What if they're devils?"

Rathan Thentraver stared at him for a breath and then shrugged. "I *do* worship the Lady of Luck," he explained, as if to an idiot child. "Torm?"

The slim thief slipped back into his saddle and grinned. "It's your head, oh smeller-of-evil. The mules are hobbled."

Rathan nodded briefly and jerked his horse's reins, thrusting his mace into the crook of his arm. His mount reared, pawing the air. With practiced ease, the priest clipped the disc onto his shield. When the horse came down, his mace was back in his hand. "For Tymora and victory! The Knights of Myth Drannor are upon ye! *Die!*"

Narm gulped as the horse and the roaring man atop it tore away through the trees at full gallop. Torm rode right at Rathan's heels, waving his long sword in circles.

From far ahead yells echoed in the forest, followed by the slash and skirl of steel on steel. There was a short shriek, quickly cut off, much thudding of hooves, more clangs, a few scattered yells . . . and then silence.

Narm wondered uncomfortably what he should do with the mules if the two were slain. He had no wish to be thought of as an enemy of Shadowdale, or a thief, but . . .

Something rustled along the trail ahead, nearer than the battle. Nervously, Narm drew his dagger.

"Ho, Narm!" Torm's voice came floating through the trees. "Haven't the mules eaten all the leaves on that stretch yet?"

With a cheery wave, the thief rode into view, eyed the dagger Narm was sheathing, and swung lightly from his saddle to see to the mules. "Adventurers out of Zhentil Keep—priests of Bane and an illusionist out to make a name for himself."

"Dead?" Narm asked.

Torm nodded. "They weren't willing to surrender or flee," he said mildly, holding the reins of the mules. He thrust the hobble ropes through his belt and swung up into his saddle.

Narm shook his head in disbelief.

"Eh? Why so?" Torm asked.

Narm grinned weakly. "Just the two of you, and Rathan bellowing war cries . . . and three breaths later you come back and tell me they're dead."

Torm nodded. "It's what usually happens," he replied, deadpan.

Narm shook his head again as they rode forward. "No, no," he said. "Mistake me not . . . how can you attack like that, knowing you face six foes, at least one a master of Art?"

"The war cries and all? Well, if you're risking death, why not have fun?" Torm replied. "If I wanted to risk death without having fun, I'd be a tax collector, not a thief. Come on—if we're much longer, Rathan'll have finished *all* the food and wine, and we're not even there yet!"

When her sensibility returned, the light overhead was much brighter. Shandril lay at the edge of a huge mound of coins, feet up on the slithering riches, head down and aching. She felt weak and dizzy. It seemed days since she'd dared to open that tomb.

Slowly, she got up and looked around. The coins—rusty-brown with age and damp—looked to be copper. Sigh. Above her, atop the heap, lay two human bodies on their backs, feet entangled.

One wore armor, much blackened. About him clung a faint reek of burned flesh. The other wore robes and clutched the crumbling fragments of a stick of wood. A sword protruded from his rib cage, and a small shoulder bag lay crumpled beneath him.

Shandril clambered up the coins. Perhaps one carried water, or wine. . . .

The armored corpse was cooked black; Shandril avoided it. The other had a dagger, which she took, the bag, and boots—too large, but her feet had bled enough for her to take any boots over no boots. She thirstily drained a skin of water. What of the wand? She tugged the crumbling pieces free of the body and examined them curiously. The butt end of the thickest piece bore the word "Ilzazu," but nothing happened when Shandril cautiously said it aloud. She scrambled down the heap again.

The bag held hard, dark bread, a wheel of cheese sealed in wax, another half-eaten wheel speckled with mold (Shandril ate it anyway, saving the other for later), and a small book. Opening it cautiously, she saw crawling runes and glyphs, and slammed it again. There was also a hopelessly smashed hand lamp, a flint, and a metal vial of lamp oil.

Putting everything but the flint and oil back into the bag, Shandril slung it on her shoulder. Crawling back to the dead wizard, she tore off what she could of the man's robe and doused it in oil. Then she struck the flint against coin after coin in vain. Only when she dared to try it on the scorched armor of the other corpse did she manage to strike sparks. Thrice they rained onto the soaked cloth before at last it began to smolder.

Gingerly borrowing the blackened sword from the fallen warrior, Shandril lifted the bundle on its point. It flared up, and she clambered hastily down the heap of coins with her improvised torch, looking for a door or stairs or anything that might lead out.

Above her, a stone rack ran along the ceiling, supported by arches between the squat pillars. Upon the rack lay three huge barrels. From each hung a cobweb-shrouded chain.

With a shiver, Shandril realized that a fourth barrel had hung over the heap of coins. Its shattered wooden ribs lay at the base of the heap. A rusty end of chain trailed out of the coins . . . beside a pair of skeletal legs. Someone had been crushed by enough riches to bury him—riches that hung overhead right now.

Shandril backed away so rapidly that her torch almost fell from her sword. Those sprawled, helpless legs. . . .

Trembling, Shandril took deep, shuddering breaths. Soon the cloth would be burned up, and she'd be unable to see in the darkness. She hurried on, through a chamber as vast as the hall that stood above it. She knew there were no stairs nor door in that hall, save perhaps at the end she'd not investigated, where the stirges had come from. She turned in that direction. Daylight grew dim behind her.

Her feeble flame revealed a stone stair spiraling up from the floor, without railing or ornament. It looked impossibly thin and graceful to bear her weight.

The cloth burned through and fell from her blade in a small shower of glowing shreds. Larger scraps flickered on the floor, but proved too small to balance on her blade.

Shandril shrugged. In the last of the light, she slid the blade through her belt and grimly climbed the stairs on hands and knees.

When she reached the floor above, she was in complete darkness. This should be the ground floor, and if there were a door, it would probably be over in *that* direction, somewhere.

So, a short walk will find me the light . . . that is, if the floor doesn't give way and dump me into the basement again.

Holding the sword out crosswise before her to fend off unseen obstacles, Shandril advanced. She lifted and set down her feet with great care, as silent as possible. On into the dark she went, until her blade scraped on stone. She probed with the hilt, feeling the stone curve away: a pillar. Daring to draw breath, she went on.

One step made dry bones crackle underfoot. Another made her stub her toes on a large block of stone that had fallen from the ceiling.

Wrestling down terror—alone in the dark, underground with monsters that might even now be slithering closer, in a ruined city where devils ruled the daylight—Shandril went on.

It seemed a very long time before her blade found a wall. It ran off in both directions. Left, she decided arbitrarily, and walked in the wake of her probing sword tip until she found a corner.

Retracing her steps, Shandril scraped back along the wall until her blade found a wooden door, large and intricately carved. She felt for a pull ring but found none. Suddenly desperate to be out of the darkness, she ran full tilt at the door, driving her shoulder into the wood as she'd done before.

There was a dull thud, much pain, and Shandril found herself on the floor, the door unyielding.

"Tymora *damn* me!" she hissed, exasperated almost to tears. Would *nothing* go her way? Was this the gods' way of telling her she should have stayed dutifully at the Rising Moon?

Shandril got up and pushed and pulled at the door—as solid and unmoving as stone. She felt for catches, knobs, latches, and keyholes, high and low. Nothing.

To the right, she decided abruptly. Look for another door.

She found one right away. It opened on the first try, making no sound and swinging weightlessly. She blinked foolishly but happily in the sudden light. She peered out curiously, growled at herself for being a fool, and stepped into the sunlight.

Another mistake. Not two hundred paces away across the tilted stones and crumbling pillars of Myth Drannor, six warriors fought a losing battle against three winged she-devils.

Shandril stepped hastily back—changed her mind, and slipped out, sword drawn. She ran across tumbled stones to the nearest trees. Crawling under a thorny bush, she peered out across the courtyard where the well lay, deceptively placid, and watched the men fight for their lives.

No one shouted. Wings beat, warriors grunted as they took blows on their shields or swung heavy swords two-handed, feet scraped, and blades rang. Two more adventurers lay sprawled a short distance behind the fight. The men tried to keep moving and find cover. One ran a few steps, abandoning his protective crouch. A devil swooped.

Shandril caught her breath, but the run was a ruse.

The warrior turned and swung his silver blade with both hands, beheading the devil with a triumphant grunt. Black, smoking blood ran down the warrior's sword as he cut the body apart. The corpse smoldered. Greasy soot curled up in snaky wisps.

The man dared not take up the devil's fallen dagger. Two more swooped down with screams of anger, uncoiling ropes in their hands. The warrior looked from one to the other and suddenly turned to flee. The devils flew wide to strike at him from two sides.

Shandril swallowed and looked away.

The man must have been the leader, for as the devils tore him apart, his fellow adventurers ran, crying and cursing. The devils circled, teeth gleaming.

Shandril decided to flee before the slaughter was over and she might be seen. She crawled into the trees, hoping she was heading out of Myth Drannor. Judging by the sun, she was probably moving south, but she had no idea whether she was near the edge of the city or not.

After twenty minutes of clambering and skulking, she decided "not" was the correct answer. Tumbled stones and gaping, empty buildings were everywhere. Gnarled trees had broken through anything that got in their way, rending once-beautiful spires and high, curving bridges. Most of those bridges had cracked and fallen; a few were intact, though choked with creepers, trailing vines, and old nests.

Shandril stayed low and tried to avoid open spaces. Here and there in the ruins she saw devils: some black and glistening, some blood-red, barbed and scaled, and some mauve or yellow-green. They perched on crumbling spires or battlements or sprawled at ease on bridges or atop heaps of tilted stone. A few—winged devil women and horned, spine-tailed horrors—flew in lazy circles through the ruins.

If this was Myth Drannor, it was a wonder the dales still existed! What had brought the devils here, and what was stopping them from flying forth in all directions, murdering and wreaking havoc?

Well, it mattered not. What mattered was escaping.

Shandril lay huddled under the edge of a slab of stone carved with a very beautiful scene of mermaids and hippocampi, now forever shattered. Her large boots had rubbed her calves raw as they flapped with every step, and her borrowed blade was too heavy to lift quickly. Against these devils, she dared not fight. It was a long time before she dared leave the shelter of the stone slab.

The sun cast long shadows as day gave way to dusk. Shandril knew she had to move soon, or be trapped in the ruins after dark. She set off past more cracked and tumbled buildings, dreadfully afraid she might unwittingly be traveling in circles, touring her own death trap.

The ruins seemed endless, though she saw more trees among the stones than she had earlier. Perhaps I *am* nearer the edge.

It was then she saw them. In a place of tilted heaps of stone, where all the buildings had toppled, two figures confronted each other across a wasteland. A sharp-eyed man in robes of wine-red stood on the cracked base of a long-fallen pillar. He faced a tall, slim, cruel-looking woman in purple atop what was left of a wall.

"*Die*, then, Shadowsil," the man said coldly, and his hands moved like coiling snakes.

The thief from Highmoon crouched low and kept very still. The Shadowsil's hands also were moving. Shandril wondered briefly if everyone in Faerûn would arrive in Myth Drannor before she could get out of it.

From the man's hand burst sparkling frost—a white cone that spread, roaring, as it closed on the beautiful woman.

She stiffened, arms shining with frost. Four whirling balls of fire burst from her hands, trailing winking sparks as they flashed through the fading frost.

On hands and knees Shandril scrambled around a pile of rubble and behind the corner of a ruin. It was well she did. An instant later, there was a flash of flame and a roar, and a wave of intense heat passed over her.

When she peered cautiously back around the rubble, the man was gone. There was a large, blackened area on the rocks, and the woman in purple walked triumphantly across mountains of jagged stone to where her foe had stood.

The stone creaked as it cooled. The woman turned on her heel to stare levelly all around. She saw Shandril immediately. They stared into each other's eyes for an instant that seemed a frozen eternity.

Gasping, Shandril broke free of the thrall of that cold gaze. She ran. Scrambling down a ruined street in a few frantic, headlong moments, she ducked around a corner into a place of many vines and sagging walls. Her blood hammered in fear. Biting her lips to silence her panting, she stared wildly around, not daring to believe she'd escaped.

The air in front of Shandril shimmered. Suddenly the lady in purple stood before her. "Who are you, then, little one?" the wizardess asked softly. She was very beautiful.

Shandril stared at her, managing only to shiver.

The lady gave her a smile that held no mirth or welcome and added, "I am Symgharyl Maruel, called the Shadowsil."

Shandril held up her sword in silently menacing answer.

The lady mage laughed. Her hands wove swift, deft gestures.

Shandril rushed at the wizardess, knowing before she started that the woman was just too far away. Her limbs locked in midstride and she froze—straining, immobile, on the verge of toppling, and utterly helpless.

Purple robes swished nearer. The lady undid a rope from around her sleek hips as she approached.

Tymora, aid me, Shandril prayed desperately.

The lady mage put her rope gently around the thief's swordwrist. She looped it also about Shandril's neck, drawing it tight across her throat, and said crisply, "*Ulthae*—entangle."

Shandril's skin prickled in horror as the rope slithered of its own accord about her, tightening around arms and neck and knees, binding her securely. When it was done, Shandril was trussed as tightly as any Highmoon butcher's parcel. A short length of rope led from a great knot at her waist to the languid hand of the lady in purple.

Shandril caught her breath. At least this means she'll take me out of here . . . although with the favor Great Lady Tymora has shown me, devils will slay her and leave me a ready meal for anything that happens by.

She had a brief memory of the thing in the well, and in sinking horror found she could not even shudder. Her own body was her prison.

Symgharyl Maruel jerked on the rope that bound her, and

Shandril fell over helplessly to crash and bounce on broken stones that had long ago been a pleasant winding lane in the City of Beauty. The side of her face scraped painfully. Grit made her eye water, and her blade fell out of frozen fingers. It was left behind as the lady in purple dragged her away.

"I don't know who you are, yet," Symgharyl Maruel said with mocking malice, between tugs that bumped Shandril over heaved stones. "You remind me of someone. You may well be the one those stoneheads of Oversember let slip away. Are you, hmmm? The girl with the Company of the Bright Spear whose name isn't on their charter? You'll tell me, girl. Yes, you'll tell. Their lost one or not, the cult will value you highly for your blood, dear, if you are a virgin." Again the tinkling, mocking laughter. "But you shall be my present to Rauglothgor in any case. So pretty . . ."

Shandril could not even weep.

Narm took leave of the two Knights at the very spot where he and Marimmar had met the elf and his lady. Narm was surprised to see who waited there: the two ladies who'd been in the Deepingdale inn, who'd faced down the angry adventurers. Narm nodded to them as Torm made known to him (with many a verbal flourish, not all of them mocking) the names Sharantyr and Storm. To Narm's surprise, both smiled at him.

The younger woman clasped his arm and said, "Yes, we've met, at the Rising Moon in Deepingdale, though you were under the heavy eye of—your master of the Art? A strict man."

Narm nodded. Yes, Marimmar had been that.

The silver-haired bard nodded, remembering. Torm explained Mourngrym's decision to let Narm into the city. The two ladies acquired identical small frowns and shook their heads. They shouldered their bags and harp and took charge of the horses and mules.

As they settled into their saddles, Storm leaned down and said to Narm, "Until next we meet. I think our paths will cross again soon, good sir. Fare well in Myth Drannor!" With that, she and Sharantyr rode away.

"Will you go into the city after all?" Torm asked, after they'd watched the ladies disappear amid the trees.

"Yes," Narm said, grinning weakly.

"May Tymora smile upon thee, then," Rathan grunted. "Being such a fool and all, ye'll need the full favor of the Lady's luck to see even this day out. Don't forget how to run for thy life. The devils are the ones with wings."

"Most of them," Torm agreed with a smile, "though they can be hard to see with blood pouring into your eyes."

"Aye, that be *very* true," Rathan agreed gravely.

Narm grinned and waved farewell to them, shaking his head. A merry life the other Knights must lead, indeed, in the company of these two jacks! He set off down the path quickly before fear could slow him or turn him back.

The ruined city of Myth Drannor rose out of the trees before him. Alone, Narm drew in a deep breath and strode swiftly on. He was going to see devils. He was going to look his fill of them and somehow survive. By Mystra, he was going to do *something* on his own, now that Marimmar was gone!

Loose and broken stones shifted under his feet. Cautiously, Narm went on. Off to his right was a leaning stone tower, its needle spire still grand. Ahead lay heaved, tilted pavement choked with shrubs and clinging vines. Steps led down in a broad sweep from the street into unknown depths.

Motion caught his eye. Narm crouched and looked.

A slim woman in purple robes dragged someone thin and long-haired along the ground. Her hapless captive was completely entangled in a glowing rope. Mocking laughter rose as they descended from view down the stair.

Narm crept to the topmost step, but nothing was visible below. He hardly paused to think before he followed. The Art! Strong magic—just what Marimmar had sought here!

The stair became an underground way that led to a space lit only by a fitful glow. Narm walked quietly and cautiously toward it, until he could see that the passage had opened into a natural cavern.

Within it, the lady in purple and her captive stood before the source of the light. An oval of glowing radiance hung like a doorway in midair. Magic, indeed.

The woman in purple was stronger than her slim frame suggested. By main strength she held her captive upright—a girl who struggled violently. The rope that bound her moved by itself to fight her. She managed to tear its slithering, snakelike coils free of her face and throat.

Narm could scarcely believe it—he knew her! It was the girl from the inn. Her beautiful face had stared at him from the shadows. How came she to be here?

The woman in purple let go of the rope, laughing. The girl fell hard to the cavern floor. Her face was set as she battled the rope.

Anger burned in Narm. He raised his hands, pointed at the woman in purple, and spoke the word of the spell Marimmar had forbidden him to study, the spell he'd studied while his master slept. Its magical bolt burst from his finger like a racing arrow of light, and flashed at the lady.

She stiffened as it struck her and whirled in alarm. Seeing her foe, she laughed, her hands already moving.

Narm dodged aside, thinking how feeble the rest of his Art was. The mage completed her casting, gave him a cold, sneering smile, and locked her fingers in Shandril's hair. As Narm watched in dismay, she dragged the struggling girl through the oval of radiance and vanished.

Then, with a shattering roar, the fireball exploded all around him.

5

The Grotto of the Dracolich

There in the darkness many a wyrm sits and smiles. He grows rich and lazy and fat as the years pass, and there seems no shortage of fools to challenge him and make him richer and fatter. Well, why wait ye? Open the door and go in.

Irigoth Mmar, High Sage of Baldur's Gate
Lore of the Coast
Year of the Trembling Tree

The radiance faded and left her somewhere cold. She was lying on stone again. Shandril twisted against the ever-tightening, ever-slithering rope. "Where are we?"

The Shadowsil shrugged. "A ruined keep. Come."

The rope shifted to bind Shandril's arms to her torso; she found she could rise to her knees and, painfully, to her feet. The lady mage led her down a curving stone stair, but not before Shandril got a good look out the window.

Cold, jagged mountains jutted into an icy sky. They were many days' journey from Myth Drannor. A snow hawk glided across the scene.

Shandril could see no other life before she was forced down the dark stairway. It was narrow and steep, littered with old feathers and bird droppings. She was propelled down the stairs with a firm hand.

⊠ ⊠ ⊠

"I told you he'd poke his nose into something straight away and buy a swift grave before you'd even got to your next sausage!" said a familiar voice, swimming somewhere above Narm. "That's why I followed—not for treasure."

"Well, ye'd be the one to know about poking one's nose," said another. "By the gods, he caught it squarely! Do ye think he'll live?"

"Not if you don't use some healing magic quickly, leviathan belly! Don't wag your jaws—waggle your fingers! He grows weaker with each breath you waste. He smolders still. No, no, lie still, Narm. I can hear you."

Through excruciating pain, Narm struggled to tell them of the girl from the inn and the woman in purple. All that came out was a strangled sob.

"Lie down, Narm," Torm said gently. "We'll see to the pretty girl in the rope of entanglement, whom the purple witch—with our good fortune she's an archmage—just pushed through that gate. Lie still. Rest easy. You're lucky enough to have found the greatest reckless fools in all Faerûn, and we'll do it for you."

"Hush," said Rathan. "How can I work healing when ye're blaspheming Tymora?"

"I never!"

"Ye did! 'Our good fortune,' I heard ye say in a slighting tone. Now hold this healing quaff; he'll be able to drink it after this." There was much murmuring.

Through the watery red haze, Narm saw a flash of radiance. Sweet coolness spread through his limbs, banishing the shrieking pain. He fainted.

⊠ ⊠ ⊠

They descended the crumbling stairs for eight or more turns. The blocks gave way to natural stone scarred with tool marks.

"What is this place?" Shandril asked wearily.

The mage made no reply, and she dared not ask again.

The rough tunnel opened suddenly, joining other passageways in a small, slope-ceilinged cavern. Symgharyl Maruel pushed her firmly toward the largest passage, which led steeply down into darkness.

Shandril came to a stop. "I can't see!"

The Shadowsil chuckled softly behind her. "Do you do nothing in your life that you cannot first see where it leads?" She laughed again, gently. "Very well."

Four small globes of pearl-white radiance grew before Shandril's eyes and then drifted apart in midair. One moved to hang at her shoulder. Another drifted well ahead, revealing the rough stony descent. The other globes moved behind her for Symgharyl Maruel's benefit.

Shandril peered about. There was stone all around her, and cool air wafted to her from the depths.

Something struck her bottom, hard, driving her to her knees. The Shadowsil had kicked her.

"Up and on," came the cold voice. "My patience grows short."

Shandril struggled to her feet in the tight coils of the enchanted rope, biting her lip in angry silence.

Up and on. The uneven ramp became broad stairs cut out of solid rock. The air grew cooler, and many small points of light twinkled ahead, dim and scattered beyond the pale radiance of the floating globes.

Shandril turned to find the left wall and descend with it, but Symgharyl Maruel twitched the rope, and Shandril turned back.

The twinkling lights were farther away than they'd appeared—but when the stair ended, they hung on all sides.

A great open cavern lay before them. Its walls were studded with fist-sized, sea-green gems—the fabled stones known as beljurils. At odd intervals, one or more would give forth a silent burst of light. They were the many tiny, twinkling stars, and their light showed that the cavern stretched a long way to the right. It was vast.

Shandril shivered in the twinkling darkness. Would the mage slay her here or leave her in a cage to be tortured later, or killed or deformed by magical experiment? Or did something lair here? Shandril could hear only the soft sounds of the mage behind her and the noise of her own passage. Where in the Realms was she?

"Halt, little one, and kneel."

Shandril did as that quiet voice bade her. The rope tightened about her knees to reinforce the order. The pale globes winked out. Behind her, the Shadowsil chanted something softly—and sudden light filled the huge cavern.

Its floor fell away in front of her, its lowest reaches heaped with things that gleamed and sparkled in the light. There were gems and coins beyond number, and statuettes of ivory and jade. The gleam of massy gold caught her eye amid dazzling things Shandril had never seen before.

A great voice boomed and echoed around them, freezing Shandril in terror. It spoke deeply and slowly in the Common Tongue, a voice old, patient, amused—and dangerous.

"Who comes?" Deep in the cavern, beyond the mage's light, something moved.

Shandril saw it. Her throat tightened, and she would have fled if the coils had not held her firmly. Her struggles caused her to fall sideways onto the stone, where she lay facedown and did not have to see.

"Symgharyl Maruel Shadowsil stands before you, O mighty Rauglothgor, with a gift: a captive, gained among the ruins of Myth Drannor. Its blood may be valuable to you. But the followers of Sammaster would question it first. It may be one who escaped them at Oversember, and they'd very much like to know how that was accomplished." The lady faced the night dragon calmly, speaking in tones of respect but not fear.

Shandril peered sidelong at it. She dared not meet its eyes again, but the thief of Deepingdale saw its great skeletal bulk advance, vast and terrible, across shifting treasure. By its huge, arching wings and claws and tail, it was a dragon, but except for the chilling eyes, it was only bones. Its long, fanged skull leered down at her. Shandril sensed, with a stirring of defiant anger, that it was amused.

"Look at me, little maid," it rumbled, its voice echoing *inside* Shandril's head.

She shook in her bonds. She would *not* look at the creature!

The rope tightened again, pulling her to her knees, dragging at her brow and throat to turn her head up. Through a mist of furious tears, Shandril looked—and saw.

The cunning eyes held hers like cold reflections of the moon . . . like candles set at the head and foot of a shrouded corpse. Those eyes bored into her very soul. Shandril looked back as deeply herself and knew much.

When men first had come to the Sea of Fallen Stars and fought with the bugbears and kobolds of the Thunder Peaks, it had been old—this sly and gnarled giant among dragons. In mountains the elves called Airmbult or "Storm-fangs," Rauglothgor had been the fangs amid the storms. Rauglothgor the Proud, dragonkind had called the creature, for its presumption and quickness to take offense or pick quarrels.

In cunning and malice it had sought out weak, old dragons and slain them, often by trickery, to seize their lairs and treasure. Hoard upon hoard fell into its claws. It piled them up in deep and secret places beneath the Realms known only to it—for other creatures of all sizes who ventured therein were slain, from peryton to centipede, without mercy or patience.

Years passed, and Rauglothgor grew and devoured whole herds of rothé in Thar and buckar on the Shining Plains and more than one orc horde coming down the Desertsedge from the North. Rauglothgor became strong and terrible, most mighty among dragons. It thrust aside pretense and prudence and killed all other wyrms it met; in air, on land, and even in their lairs, slaying with savagery and skill, and adding hoards anew to its own.

Yet in its dark heart the old red dragon grew afraid that one day its strength would fail and some younger, greedier dragon would drag it down. All its striving would have been for naught. For years such worries ate at the creature's old heart, and when men came with offers of eternal strength and wealth, the dragon slew them not, and it listened.

By the Art of the Cult of the Dragon, the great and evil red dragon became, in time, a great and evil dracolich. Dead it was and yet not dead. The years touched not its vigor and might, for it had become only bones and magic. Its strength of Art could not be diminished by age.

The years passed, and Faerûn changed. The world was not as it had been. Rauglothgor flew less often. There was little left to match its memories. Few lived that it had known. Willing men of the cult brought it treasure to add to its dusty hoard. The dracolich grew moody and lonely as kingdoms fell and seas changed and only it endured. To live forever was a curse. A lonely curse.

Shandril could not look away from those lonely eyes.

"So young," said the deep voice.

Abruptly the bony neck arched up, the eyes closed, and she was alone in her head again—only Shandril and only human. Gods, what she'd give to be back in the kitchen of the Rising Moon. . . .

"Well met, Great One," Symgharyl Maruel said. "By your leave, I would question this one before I leave her with you."

"Given, Shadowsil," Rauglothgor replied. "Though she knows little of anything, I deem. She has the eyes of a kitten that's just learned to walk."

"Aye, elder wyrm," the Shadowsil replied, "and yet she may have seen much in the few days just past, or even be more than she seems." The lady in purple strode to stand before Shandril. At a gesture, the rope slithered slowly away, leaving her free.

Shandril gathered herself to flee, but Symgharyl Maruel merely smiled down in cold amusement and shook her head. "Tell me your name," she commanded.

Shandril obeyed without thinking.

"Your parents?" the mage pressed.

"I know not," Shandril replied truthfully.

"Where did you dwell when younger?"

"In Deepingdale, at the Rising Moon."

"How came you to the place where I found you?"

"I . . . by magic. There was a word on a bone, and I said it. . . ."

"Where's that bone now?"

"In a pool—a well, I think—in that ruined city. Please, lady, was that Myth Drannor?"

The dracolich chuckled harshly. The Shadowsil's eyes burned into Shandril's. "Tell me your brother's name!"

Shandril shook her head, confused. "I don't have a brother."

"Who was your tutor?" the Shadowsil snapped at her.

"Tutor? I've never had—Gorstag taught me my duties at the inn, and Korvan about cooking, and—"

"What part of the gardens did the windows of your chamber look upon?"

Shandril flinched. "Chambers, lady? I—I have no chambers. I sleep—slept—in the loft with Lureene most nights. . . ."

"Tell the *truth*, brat!" the mage in purple screamed, her face contorted in rage, eyes blazing.

Shandril stared at her helplessly.

Rauglothgor's deep chuckle cut through the lady mage's anger. "She speaks truth, Shadowsil. My Art never lies to me."

Symgharyl Maruel dropped her rage like a mask and regarded the disheveled, tearful Shandril calmly. "So she's not the missing Cormyrean princess, Alusair. Why then is she such a sheltered innocent? She's not simple, so far as I can tell."

The dracolich chuckled again. "Humans never are, I have found. Ask on; she interests me."

The Shadowsil nodded as her dark eyes caught and held Shandril's. The thief of Deepingdale prayed silently to any gods who might be listening.

Symgharyl Maruel regarded her almost sympathetically. "Were you a member of the Company of the Bright Spear?"

Shandril lifted her head proudly and said, "I am."

" 'Am' ?" The Shadowsil laughed shortly.

Shandril stared at her, heart sinking. She'd secretly hoped that Rymel, Burlane, and the others had somehow escaped the dragon in the mountain vale. In her memory it swept down again, huge and terrible. . . .

She knew the truth now. The mage's cold laughter forbade her to deny it any longer.

"You were taken by the cult and imprisoned in Oversember. How did you escape?" the Shadowsil pressed.

"I—I . . ." Shandril choked on her fear and grief. Anger rose red and warm within her. Who was this cruel wizardess to drag her here and bind and question her thus?

The dracolich's deep, hissing laughter rolled around the cavern. "She has a temper, Shadowsil; beware! Ah, this is good sport!"

"I found the bone and read what was on it," Shandril answered sullenly. "It took me to the place with the devils and the well . . . and you. I know no more."

Symgharyl Maruel angrily strode toward her. "Ah, but you do, Shandril! Who was that fool who attacked me before we took the gate here?"

Shandril shook her head helplessly.

"My *name*, witch," a new voice answered, "is Narm!"

The air flashed and crackled. A swarm of racing bolts struck the Shadowsil, sending tiny fingers of lightning over her body. She staggered and almost fell, face twisting in pain and astonishment.

Shandril scrambled up and looked back.

High above, at the mouth of the cavern, stood six humans. Two in robes stood in front. The one who'd spoken she recognized from those last moments before the magic gate. He was young and excited. The other, a woman whose hair was as long as the Shadowsil's, stood with one hand outstretched. Tiny wisps of sparkling smoke curled from it in the wake of the magic she'd just hurled.

The cavern rocked with Rauglothgor's roar of challenge. The dracolich reared up to face the newcomers, eyes terrible, bony wings arching.

Shandril hurled herself at the Shadowsil, who hissed a word of Art and vanished before Shandril could reach her.

Rauglothgor spat a word that shook the grotto. A fiery streak flashed high over Shandril's head, and bright, rending flame exploded in all directions.

The thief of Deepingdale dived flat and peered around wildly.

The newcomers leaped down toward her, apparently unharmed by the fireball. The purple-robed sorceress appeared on a ledge behind them.

"Look out!" Shandril screamed, pointing at the Shadowsil.

A man in plain robes glanced up and back. Red radiance

winked along the circlet he wore. From it burst a thin beam that struck the Shadowsil.

The lady mage stiffened, hands faltering in their spell-weaving, and slumped back against the rock wall. She clutched her side and screamed curses.

The dracolich roared again, and the long-haired woman lashed out with a bolt of lightning.

It crackled over Shandril's head, illuminating two figures leaping down to her: a mighty man with blue-gray armor and a sword in hand, and the young man named Narm.

Narm called out to her. "Lady! You from the Rising Moon! We come to aid you! We—"

His words were lost in the roar of the dracolich's second fire-ball, bursting just behind the two running figures.

Shandril turned in panic and ran downslope, slipping on coins. She caught her balance with a painful wrench and leaped, her boots finding rocks. The silent wink of the beljurils grew ahead; she was nearing a wall.

Behind her came a cry of pain. The hissing laughter of the dracolich rolled out, and all light abruptly faded in the cavern. Another flash came, and the clink of feet running fast on coins . . . feet that sounded like they were following her.

Shandril gasped. She climbed rocks with bruising speed.

Rauglothgor roared, and light flooded the cavern once more.

Shandril dived into a cleft between two boulders. *And I haven't even a blade!* she thought, rolling to her feet, banging knees and elbows. She peered back at the battle.

Symgharyl Maruel stood upon a high rock, hands moving—but she wasn't spellcasting. Rather, she slapped at something very small. Many somethings . . . insects!

The other lady mage cast a spell at Rauglothgor across the grotto. The man in armor stood knee-deep in coins at the draco-lich's feet, chopping and slicing at the skeletal form towering over him. Another warrior—an elf with a glowing blade—raced down to join him. The sword's radiance was briefly overwhelmed by a roaring blast of flames from the dracolich's bony maw.

Rauglothgor turned his head toward Shandril. Clenching her teeth, she scrambled up the cavern wall.

"Lady!" came that cry again. Narm pursued her, but Shandril dared not stop. She clambered over rocks and loose rubble, expecting the roar of the Art that would dash her life away . . . but one moment after another passed as she climbed, and no death came for her.

That slowed her climb not a whit. The dracolich, the Shadowsil, and these powerful newcomers all stood between her and escape . . . and the thief of Deepingdale doubted if the gods cared enough about Shandril Shessair to save her. Better to flee while they were busy slaying each other!

Another burst of flame reflected off the rocks before her. Shandril heard a man's roar of pain as the fire died away. Behind her, much closer than she expected, Narm chanted something rapidly. Was he trying to trap her with a spell? She scrambled on.

Suddenly, her fingers slipped on rocks. Shandril fought for balance, slipped again—and fell long and hard, back down the rough, curving cavern wall. She slammed to a stop, dashing the wind from her lungs.

The favored of Tymora, as usual, she thought grimly.

Someone landed hard on the stones beside her, jarring her.

Shandril rolled away and sprang to her feet, dizzy—

Hands grabbed her and pulled her back down. "Lady," Narm panted, "keep down! Yon witch-mage—" Abruptly, there was a flash and a deep, rolling explosion. Small stones clattered and fell about them. "She's free of the insects! Oh, *gods!*"

His curse made Shandril look up—into the dark and cruel eyes of Symgharyl Maruel.

Wearing a triumphant smile, she stood before them, her hands raised and glowing.

But the air behind her held a slim, dark, leaping figure. Somersaulting in the air, its boots struck the Shadowsil's shoulder and flank, knocking the smile from her face. The lady mage and her attacker fell out of view behind rocks.

"Well met, witch! I am Torm—and these are my feet!"

Rauglothgor hissed in fury, his great bony form rearing.

Crouching next to Shandril, Narm chanted, "By grasshopper leg and will gathered deep, let my Art make this one"—he touched her knee—"leap!" He thrust something small into her hand. "Lady," he hissed, pointing, "break this, turn, and leap up there! Swiftly, before the—"

Goaded by his fear, Shandril fumbled with the dried wisp in her hands, broke it, and jumped.

Narm's Art took her high and far in one mighty bound. She landed on a ledge high up near the cavern ceiling.

Behind and below the Shadowsil chanted shrilly, and there was another flash. She raised glittering, angry eyes to meet Shandril's, and her arms moved with angry, fluid grace.

Again, Torm sprang at her from the side.

The Shadowsil crouched at the last second, spun around with a laugh of triumph, and hurled the spell at him.

He met her laugh with one of his own, and it had fangs: two daggers flashed from his hands, silvery blades spinning end over end through the air.

Shandril turned and ran along the ledge without waiting to see who would die. A dull, rolling boom sounded behind her, and stones rattled under her feet. The cavern walls, rising still, were scattered with riches. Long-dead kings, carved from cold white ivory, stared as she clambered past. She felt her way past a curtain of strung amber, the toothed ceiling of the cavern low overhead. Another mighty blast came behind her. Dust swirled. Small pieces of rock rained down.

Behind Shandril came the hasty, sliding steps of someone running across coins. She hurried on, stumbling for the hundredth time, her hands already flung out to break her fall. The pursuer closed in.

"Damnation! I can't run anymore. When will this nightmare *end?*"

At last, it seemed, the gods heard. An earsplitting crash split the cavern behind Shandril. She was flung violently forward amid a helter-skelter of rocks, coins, gems, chains, coffers, and choking dust.

The anguished roar of the dracolich, mournful and enraged and sad, rose and fell thrice ere it died away in hollow echoes. The air erupted in three short, sharp explosions that struck Shandril's already-ringing head like hammers. The deep rolling did not die away this time, but went on and on. Small rocks struck her like stinging rain. Then came more booms and crashes as slabs and pillars of rock broke free and fell, unseen in the darkness.

Refusing to be entombed alive, Shandril crawled desperately on. Faint, despairing shouts far behind dissolved in never-ending echoes.

When chaos finally died to stillness, Shandril was alone in chill dark and drifting dust. Her ragged breathing was deafening in the sudden silence. She lay still, aching from bruises and scrapes, covered by sweat and dust and small stones.

Something glowed faintly in the rubble. Shandril stared at it. As her eyes adjusted to the gloom, she saw that the light—was it growing stronger? *yes*—came from a sphere of crystal. Its curves were glossy-smooth, and it was a little larger than a man's head. The radiance, steady and white, came from within. Perhaps it could serve as a lantern. . . .

Shandril picked her way to the sphere. When she nudged it cautiously with a toe, the glow did not flicker. She watched it for a time, alert for any change, peering closely to see if anything might be hidden within it.

Finally, she reached down and touched it, running her fingers over the cold smooth surface. Nothing flickered; nothing changed. Shandril gently lifted the sphere. It was light, and yet somehow unbalanced, as though something moved inside. But she couldn't feel, hear, or see anything in its opaque depths.

Raising the sphere like a lamp, Shandril looked around. The jagged cavern ceiling hung close overhead, stretching away perhaps twenty paces before it met the floor—a tumbled waste of broken stone rubble. She swung around slowly. Gold coins and other treasures winked as the radiance met them. She was at a dead end. The roof of the cavern had fallen in, and she was trapped underground!

Panicking, Shandril scrambled forward. There must be a way out! The whole high, wide cavern couldn't have been blocked, just like that!

"Oh, please, Tymora, whatever has gone before, smile on me now!" Those tremulous words were still falling from her lips when the light fell on an outflung arm.

Narm lay on his face—still and silent. A pile of stones half-buried his legs.

Shandril stared down for a moment. She knelt carefully amid the rubble and gently brushed the hair from his face.

His eyes were closed, his mouth slack—and still he was handsome, this man. He'd tried more than once to help her.

Under her hands, he stirred. Before she knew it, she'd set the globe down and was carefully lifting and cradling his head.

His jaw worked. Pain and concern raced across his face, his eyes stared sightlessly past her, and he gasped, "More devils! Is there no end? No—" His hands moved, and he caught at her.

Gods, but he was strong! Shandril found herself dragged down onto the rock beside him.

"Must . . . must. . ." Narm hissed weakly. His hands clawed at her, tightening with frantic force.

Shandril struggled against his grip, reaching for a weapon she no longer bore. Inches from her ear, she heard a surprised "oh."

Narm's grip became suddenly gentle. Shandril turned her head and stared into his eyes.

Now open and aware, they met hers in wonder and dawning hope, but also confusion and regret. "I—pray your pardon, Lady. I've hurt you." Narm's hands fell away, and he scrambled to rise. Rocks rolled, and he fell back weakly.

Shandril put out her hand. "Lie still! Stones must be moved first; your feet are covered. Do they hurt?" She clambered past him, wondering if it would be safest to leave him helpless—but no; she could trust this one. She must trust him. The stones lifted easily. They were many, but small.

"I feel," Narm said slowly, "a little bruised, but no worse, I hope." He smiled. "Lady, what's your name?"

"I—Shandril Shessair," she replied. "What do they call you?"

"Narm. Narm Tamaraith," he replied, moving one foot cautiously. He rolled over to help her free his other foot. "How came we here?"

Shandril shrugged. "I ran. The spell-fray went on, and . . . was that you, following me?"

"Yes," he replied, grinning.

After a moment she grinned back. "I see," she said. "Why?"

Narm looked down at his empty hands for a moment and then up into her eyes. "I would know you, Lady Shandril," he said carefully. "Since first I saw you at the inn, I've . . . wanted to know you."

Their gazes held for a long and silent time.

Shandril looked away first, cradling the glowing globe in her hands. She looked at him over it, long hair veiling her face.

Narm opened his mouth to tell her something, and then closed it again.

She look at him steadily. Her eyes were very large and dark. "The cavern fell in on the others. We're buried here—walled off."

Narm sat up, heart sinking. "Is there no way out?"

Shandril shrugged. "I was looking for one when I saw you, but found nothing. Can your Art open a way?"

Narm shook his head. "That's beyond me. But I can dig, gods willing." He stared at her again, saw that she noticed, and tore his gaze away to look at the tumbled stones. "Where did you leave off looking?"

Shandril went forward with the globe. "Here."

Slowly and carefully they moved together along the stones, shining the globe high and low, but found no gap. Reaching their starting point, they straightened wearily.

"What now?" Shandril sighed.

"I need to sit down," Narm replied. He selected a large, curving boulder and sat, patting the rock beside him.

Slowly, Shandril moved to join him.

Narm swung a battered sack from his shoulder. "Hungry?"

"Yes," Shandril replied, suddenly so ravenous her mouth ached.

Narm handed her a thick sausage wrapped in oilcloth, a half-eaten loaf of hard bread, and a leather waterskin.

Shandril lifted it, a query in her eyes.

Narm smiled. "Only water, I fear."

"Good enough for me," she said, taking a long swig.

They ate in silence until Narm looked up suddenly and asked, "Who was the mage in purple?"

"She called herself Symgharyl Maruel, or the Shadowsil," Shandril said. She suddenly found herself telling him of the

Company of the Bright Spear, of her imprisonment in the cavern, of how the bone had brought her to Myth Drannor, and the Shadowsil to this place. "Your turn."

Narm quickly swallowed a mouthful of bread. "There's little to tell. I'm an apprentice of the Art, come from Cormyr with my master Marimmar, to seek the lost magic of Myth Drannor. When we reached the ruins we met several Knights of Myth Drannor, who warned us away. My master distrusted their counsel, and tried to enter the city by another route."

Shaking his head, Narm drank from the waterskin. "Marimmar was slain. I would have died, too, if another pair of Knights hadn't rescued me. They took me to Shadowdale, where Lord Mourngrym respected my decision to face down a devil and my fear. He lent me an escort back to Myth Drannor. I came upon you and was nearly killed. The Knights healed me, and I persuaded them to come through the gate with me to—to rescue you!"

They looked at each other.

"I thank you, Narm," Shandril said slowly. "I'm sorry I ran from you and led you into this."

They searched each other's eyes in silence. Both knew this was their prison. They would die here, ere long.

Shandril felt sudden, raw regret that she'd found a man so friendly and attractive, too late. They'd met just in time to die together.

"I'm sorry I drove you here," Narm replied softly. "I'm not much of a rescuing hero, I fear!"

Wordlessly Shandril clasped his forearm as the company greeted their equals. "Perhaps not," she said after a time, finding herself wanting this shy, polite man, "and yet I live because of you."

Narm took her hand and raised it slowly to his lips, eyes on hers. She smiled, then, and kissed him.

It was a long time before they parted.

"More sausage?" Narm asked.

They laughed nervously, and then ate more sausage and bread, huddling together in the globe's gentle light.

"How came you by this?" Narm asked, touching the glassy sphere.

Shandril shrugged. "It was here, with the other treasure. I know not what it is, but it serves me as a lamp. Without it I'd not have found you."

"Yes," Narm said, "and my thanks."

The look in his eyes made Shandril blush. "What was that—that bone dragon?" she asked quickly.

"A dracolich," Narm said, sounding almost relieved. "I've never seen one before, but my master told me of them. They're undead creatures, created by their own evil and a foul potion, just as a fell mage becomes a lich. A depraved cult of men worship dracoliches. They believe 'dead dragons shall rule the world entire.' They serve all dragons so they'll be favored when this prophecy comes to pass."

"How does one serve a dragon, save as a meal?"

"By providing the potions and care it needs to achieve unlife," Narm replied. "After that, they provide the new dracolich with news, flattery, spells, and treasure. One bone dragon they really revere: Shargrailar the Dark. It has torn apart armies, rumor has it."

In silence, they ate again. After a time, Shandril asked quietly, "Narm, how great is your Art?"

"Feeble, Lady. Too weak to blast aside even a single rock—to say nothing of fallen heaps. My master was a blusterer but capable, though he never hurled magics such as Lady Jhessail of the Knights did, there." He waved a hand at where rocks had walled them in. "I know a few useful spells and a handful more that hone the will or make mind or fingers deft. My master's no more, and in Art I'm almost nothing without him."

"Something more than 'nothing' rescued me," Shandril countered. "You did, and your magic was strong and swift when I needed it. I—I'll stand with you and trust in your Art, if you'll have me."

Narm looked at her. Very slowly, he laid his hand on hers. "I thank you," he said. "I will, and 'tis enough, indeed."

They embraced, arms tightening fiercely around each other.

"We may die here," Narm murmured into her ear.

"Aye," Shandril replied with grim humor, tracing the line of his chin with her fingers. " 'Adventure,' they call it."

Abruptly, from the far end of the cavern, there came the click and clatter of a falling stone. They tensed, listening, but no more sound came. They exchanged wary looks.

Shandril picked up the globe and held it high. Its radiance fell across the rocks but revealed nothing.

Narm went carefully to the wall of rock, dagger in hand, and walked along it. He returned. "Nothing, my Lady, but I found this for you." He held out a pendant of electrum shaped into a falcon in flight, with garnets for eyes.

Shandril hesitated, and then accepted it with a smile and hooked it about her neck. "My thanks. I can give you only coins in return. I'm sitting on a heap of them, and one at least has fallen into my boot."

"Why not fill our boots?" he chuckled, bending to the coins. "If die we must, why not die rich?"

"Narm," Shandril asked softly, "could you gather coins later?"

Narm's head snapped up. Shandril was holding out her arms to him. When he embraced her, he found she was shaking.

"Lady?" he asked, trying to be of some comfort. "Shandril?"

"Please, Narm," she whispered, dragging him down atop her, her hands moving with sudden urgency. "If this is the end, I'd—I—"

Narm was surprised at her strength. Words failed them both. His discarded pack fell across the globe. Neither noticed as they twisted and arched fiercely in the darkness.

They lay face-to-face on their sides, Shandril's breath warm on Narm's throat. With such company, the young wizard decided, even cold coins made a comfortable bed.

"Lady," he said roughly. "I know it's been but a short time since we met, but . . . I love you."

"Oh, Narm," she replied, "I think I've loved you since we first saw each other at the Moon. That seems very long ago—a lifetime at least!" She laughed softly. "I'm not afraid to die now. It's not so terrible to greet the gods here, if we do so together."

Narm's arms tightened about her. "Die? Who knows but that a little digging might win our freedom? This cavern's too big to be completely filled with rock . . . I hope."

"We'll dig, then," Shandril said eagerly, "if you'll let me up!"

They rolled apart and uncovered the globe. Its radiance showed them each other, shadowed and bare.

Shandril snatched up her breeches.

"Lady," Narm asked gently, "may I not even see you?"

Shandril laughed in embarrassment, but her laughter became tears.

Narm held her until her sobs died away, murmuring gently, "We're not dead yet."

Shandril drew a deep, shuddering breath, nodded, and held him tight. They stood in silence, arms about each other, until the creeping cold drove them to dress and walk around for warmth. Gathering gold enough to fill both their pouches, Narm found another treasure for his lady.

He bestowed upon Shandril a ring and bracelet joined by fine chain. Curved plates and worked hoops of chased electrum covered her forearm from finger to elbow. Chain and all gleamed with many sapphires.

For himself, he found a dagger with a pommel worked into a snarling, ruby-eyed head of a lion. Passing over larger and more splendid treasures, he picked up a trade bar of gold. It was just settling into the bottom of his battered pack when he heard Shandril's hiss of surprise.

Something moved, approaching from the tumbled rockfall—something black and scaly, the length of a short sword. It darted and scuttled soundlessly over stones—a long-necked, worm-tailed lizard.

Narm stepped forward to blast it with his Art.

Without slowing, the lizard crested a rock five paces from Shandril, who raised the globe to see it more clearly.

In the light, it suddenly began to grow. It scuttled without pause down the rock, its sleek scaly body boiling, shifting, rising. Black scales melted into purple folds of cloth, rearing up with horrifying speed—.

Symgharyl Maruel stretched slim arms and smiled at them

triumphantly. "So we meet again. Cower there, dear," she told Shandril with a sneer, "while I deal in Art with this young lion of yours." Her hands moved like gliding snakes.

Narm's hands also moved, but he wore a look of brave despair.

The Shadowsil hissed a word of power and laughed triumphantly.

Red rage roar in Shandril, and she leaped forward. At least she would have the satisfaction of seeing the witch-mage surprised before she herself died.

6

DEATH IN THE DARK

On facing magic: Run, or pray, or throw stones; many a mage is a fraud, and you can win the day even while your heart trembles. Or you can stand calm and mumble nonsense and wiggle your fingers. Some few workers of the Art are such cowards that they may flee. As for others, at least when men speak of your death, they'll say, "I never knew he was a mage; all those years he kept it secret. He must have been a clever fellow." Of course, some who listen may disagree.

Guldoum Tchar of Mirabar
Sayings of a Wise and Fat Merchant
Year of the Crawling Clouds

The glowing globe was in Shandril's hands. Without thinking, she swept it up and smashed it with all her strength into the Shadowsil's face.

It shattered. Symgharyl Maruel shrieked. Darkness fell.

Shandril dropped the fragments of crystal and kicked out in fury, driving one foot deep into a purple-robed belly.

The scream ended in a strangled whistle, and Symgharyl Maruel sat down suddenly.

Narm ran toward Shandril. "My Lady! Are you all right?"

Through the blood running down her face, Symgharyl Maruel fixed one glaring eye on Shandril. The lady mage's hands began to move.

"Oh, *gods*," Narm moaned, running even faster.

As the Shadowsil snarled out an incantation, Shandril smashed a stone into the lady mage's face.

Cringing at the horrid wet thud, Shandril set her teeth and slammed it down again. The lady mage snarled. Each time the rock rose and fell, Shandril screamed in a howling rage: "Leave us alone, you *bitch!*"

Narm sprinted, stones flying under his boots.

The Shadowsil struggled to fend off Shandril's blows, clawing at the stone, trying to shape a spell with one blood-drenched hand. . . . until she sagged down to lie full-length on the rocks, bloody and unmoving.

Shuddering and trembling, Shandril threw her head back and moaned. She stared at the body beneath her. The rock fell from her bloody fingers—and she burst into tears.

Narm swept her into his arms, hardly daring to take his eyes off the sprawled form. Neither her spell nor his had taken effect. Perhaps Shandril's rock had spoiled the Shadowsil's magic . . . but nothing had spoiled his casting.

A twinkling cloud of light motes lit the darkness. Narm frowned. Where had they come from, the Shadowsil?

Symgharyl Maruel lay still and silent. Was it that easy to kill so strong a wielder of the Art?

Shandril mastered her sobs and held tightly to Narm. The twinkling mist surrounded them both. As they stood together, there came the distinct scrape and tumble of stones moving beyond the rockfall. Hope leaped in them both.

Shandril looked at Narm. "Do we shout to tell them we're here?"

The apprentice wizard frowned. "I think not. We may not want to meet the diggers. Let's shout only if they stop."

Shandril nodded. "That's well enough, if you stay with me."

Narm held her. "Think you, fair lady, I'm a vile rake?"

"A lady cannot be too careful."

He grinned. "Please make known to me, Lady, when this carefulness of yours begins."

Shandril wrinkled her nose, blushing. The cloud swirled about them both, and she frowned. "What is this?"

"I don't know!" The young man tried to brush the glowing mist away, but it clung close. "Strange . . ."

The rocks grated again, and this time the sounds of shifting stones went on and on. Someone was digging into their prison.

Shandril and Narm stood and watched warily. Soon there came a louder, rumbling clatter. A man's voice rose in a surprised oath. Yellow torchlight glimmered between two rocks—a flickering light that grew swiftly as more stones were lifted away.

"We should hide!" Shandril whispered, dragging Narm down into a crouch among the stones.

Torchlight blazed. "Narm?" a voice called from behind it. "Lady?"

"Florin?" Narm replied eagerly, rising and drawing Shandril up with him.

"Well met!" came the hearty reply. An armored man strode toward them over tumbled stones. It was the kingly warrior who'd walked with Elminster between the battling companies. "I heard screaming," Florin said, hefting his faintly glowing sword. "Is all well with you?"

"We're fine," Narm replied, "but she who screamed—the witch-mage—is not. She'll work her Art no more!"

"Aye? So be it." Florin's face was impassive. "Danger sought, danger found. You did well." He waved a hand back over his shoulder, and added, "The bone dragon lies buried, but may yet rise!" He took another step toward them, but froze, crouching to peer at Narm. "Hold, what's that?" He drew back in alarm. "A balhiir!"

He was too late. The swirling, sparkling cloud around Narm boiled up like a campfire drawn into fury by a rising wind. It struck the ranger's blade.

"A balhiir!" Florin shouted back over his shoulder in warning, swinging his sword wildly. The twinkling mist was already swirled around it. The weapon grew heavier in his grasp. The blue light of its enchantment flared once and then dwindled away. The twinkling mist encircled him, seeming a little brighter as it glided along in cold silence.

"Whence came this balhiir?" the ranger asked tersely, watching it spiral around him.

"I struck the wizardess with a crystal sphere," Shandril told him. "It shattered—and yon mist came out!"

The ranger gazed at his blade, shook his head ruefully, and then gave Shandril a sudden smile. It lit up his face like a flame. "Greetings, good lady. I am Florin Falconhand of Shadowdale and the Knights of Myth Drannor. Might I know you?"

Smiling back, she said, "Shandril Shessair, until recently of Deepingdale and the Company of the Bright Spear, though I fear that fellowship is no more."

"Your servant, Lady," Florin said with a bow. "You've unwittingly loosed an ill thing on the world. This creature feeds on magic, and only the one who loosed a balhiir can destroy it. Will you aid me in this task, Lady?"

"Will it be dangerous?" Narm snapped angrily.

"Your lives both bid fair to be filled with danger," Florin replied gently, "whether you slay this creature or not. Striving for something of worth ere—or even as—you die is better than drifting in cowardice to your graves, is it not?"

"Fair speech," Shandril replied. "I *will* aid you," she added firmly, putting a calming hand on Narm's arm. "But tell me more of this balhee . . . this mist-thing."

"In truth," the ranger told her calmly, "I know little more. Lore holds that the releaser of a balhiir is the only one who can destroy it. Elminster of Shadowdale knows how to deal with such creatures, but like all who use the Art, he dare not come near something that drains magic. Items of power fare poorly against the creature. It foils spells, too!"

Shandril frowned. "Why should it be destroyed? Doesn't it serve as a leash to dangerous Art?"

"Fair question," Florin replied. "Others might answer you differently, but I say we need Art. There're prices to be paid for it, but shrewd use of magic helps a great many people. The threat of Art rising, unlooked for, keeps many a tyrant sword sheathed."

Shandril met his level gray gaze and decided she could trust this tall, battered man.

Beside her, Narm asked in a rush, "The balhiir was about me

for some time—it drained my spells, and those of the witch-mage! Will I be able to work Art again?"

"So long as the balhiir is not present. It'll move to absorb unleashed magic if it can." Even as Florin spoke, the twinkling cloud stirred about his blade, spiraled up, and left him. In a long, snakelike mist of lights, the balhiir drifted back the way the ranger had come. Florin started after it. "Follow me, if you will. If not, I'll leave the torch."

The two hurried after him. Shandril glanced back once at the Shadowsil, but all she could see was one boot jutting from the rocks. As they clambered through the hole Florin had dug, that foot seemed to move in the dancing torchlight. Shandril shivered.

Rauglothgor's lair was much changed. The ceiling had broken away and fallen. The gleam of treasure was gone beneath rubble and drifting dust. There was a mighty rumble and clatter of stones to their right, as the eternal dracolich rose slowly from under a castle's worth of fallen rock. Far across the chamber, the longhaired lady mage of the Knights faced that tumbling tumult and prepared a spell.

Bright pulses of magic burst from her hands, streaked across the chamber, and struck the dracolich—outracing the winking, hungrily descending cloud of mist.

Rauglothgor roared anew in pain and fury, his deep bellows echoing about the cavern. "Death to you all! Drink *this!*"

There was a flicker of Art, but nothing more. The balhiir had reached Rauglothgor. The dracolich roared in surprise and rage. Its great claws raked huge boulders aside as effortlessly as a cat scrapes loose sand.

"What, by all the *gods*—?" it raged. Its hollow neck arched, its jaws parted, and flames gouted forth in a great arc.

Fire rolled out with terrifying speed and washed over the lady on the far slope. The air was filled with the stench of burning.

As the flames died the Knight mage stood seemingly untouched, her hands weaving another spell.

The sparkling mist danced about her—the balhiir had ridden the fire across the cavern.

"Jhessail," Florin called, "a balhiir—the Art is useless!"

"So I see," Jhessail replied calmly, ignoring Rauglothgor's roars. "Well fought, Narm. Come down here! How fares your companion? She looks worth our trouble."

Shandril found herself smiling. "Well met, Lady Jhessail."

Jhessail sprang to meet them, peering at Shandril. "You show a good eye, Narm." She smiled before glancing across the cavern at Rauglothgor. Florin and the elf, Merith, stood with drawn blades facing the dracolich. "Let's proceed elsewhere, lest none of us see another meal to get acquainted over." The mist swirled away from Jhessail, heading for the elf's steel.

"Your blade!" Florin warned.

"If drained it shall be, then drained 'twill be," Merith's merry voice floated back up to them. The two warrior Knights charged the bone dragon together.

"Gods be with them both," Narm said, shaking his head in admiration. The words had scarcely left his lips when there was a great crash and roar of moving rock. The world was falling on them again.

"Orders have changed, I tell you. Let us pass!"

The mage's dark eyes narrowed. "Orders from *whom*? And why came they not to *me?*" He waved his hand at the mountains around. "*Nothing* passes the Gates of Doom without my say-so. And my orders come from Naergoth Bladelord himself!"

"Stand aside, wizard—or Malark'll soon be hunting among his magelings for your replacement," the warrior at the head of the mule train said menacingly, his hand going to the hilt of his sword.

The mage gave him a brittle smile and lifted one hand almost idly. From the rocks all around, men in dark harness sprouted, javelins ready in their hands. The wizard said softly, "You're not passing the Gates of Doom."

The warrior looked back over his shoulder to the two men standing there. "Just as I told you, Ruld—so where's the 'telling argument' you promised?"

"Here," one of the men said. His arms shot up high into the air, darkening into glistening black, impossibly long tentacles that arced above them all to plunge down at the gaping wizard.

Javelins flew, but through their storm tentacles came down like rain—gods, there were *two* men sprouting tentacles!—and curled almost lovingly around the wizard. He had time to shout before he was plucked off his feet. A casual twist of rippling black tendrils tore his head from his body in a spray of gore.

Javelin hurlers screamed—those who weren't strangling on tendrils or falling silent among the snap and crunch of bones.

The warriors in the mule train stared open-mouthed at the slaughter. Not a few backed away from their tentacle-sprouting fellows.

Two javelin hurlers did not give ground. Instead, they sprouted tentacles of their own. Black serpentine arms streaked out, sent screaming mules bolting in all directions, and worked their own slaughter among tangled reins and scrambling men.

Soon, nothing lived in that narrow pass except four tentacled figures—two pairs of them, staring warily at each other.

One peered across the bloody, twitching bodies and asked, "Magusta?"

Tentacles stiffened. "You know me?" Magusta drew in a deep breath. "You're of the Blood of Malaug!"

"We are." The voice was as silky as it was cold. Dark tentacles wavered . . . a warning? A signal?

"And your names might be . . .?"

"Our own business."

There was a little silence. Magusta observed idly, "You know the decree of the Shadowmaster High forbids what we're doing."

"Dhalgrave's decrees don't apply to us." The reply was a sneer.

"You're not of House Malaugrym?"

Bright magic burst forth at her without warning—no muttered incantation, no powders or gestures, just flame and fury and searing, darting bolts.

Beside her, Stralane grunted in pain, and Magusta shuddered as the same agony clawed through her. Another spell flared, and she frantically reshaped herself, gaining wings and almost hurling herself into the sky while they were still forming. "Brother! To me!"

Stralane's wordless roar told her he was close behind. Magusta raced up the vale to the gate she'd found earlier—the reason that dead wizard had really been here, a ruined doorway that led to the other side of Faerûn—and plunged through it. If they were swift enough to reach the second gate before their attackers caught up to them . . .

Magusta raced as she'd never raced before.

⊠ ⊠ ⊠

"Who *were* they?" Magusta panted. "Their Art outstrips any of the House I know of!"

Stralane shrugged. "Elders covertly defying Great Dhalgrave . . . or exiles . . . or bastards reared here rather than in Shadowhome."

"But they know of his decrees," Magusta said, frowning.

Stralane laughed bitterly. "You think we're the only ones of the Blood to break the rules? The only Malaugrym to intrigue?"

Magusta gave him a scornful look. All-too-familiar sudden fury rose almost to choke her. "Brother, let me remind you *just* how far you'd have gotten without my schemes!"

A whirlwind of memories exploded into Stralane's mind and broke over his struggling will. He roared, overwhelmed in a sea of reveries and shouting mental voices. None of them was quite loud enough to drown out Magusta's cold laughter.

⊠ ⊠ ⊠

"We've lost them," he said bitterly. The last of his tentacles dwindled away to human arms again. "Now we'll have to watch behind us, every last living moment!"

"Haven't you been already, Brother?" his companion asked. "Surely Dhalgrave keeps watch over Faerûn as if it's his own personal garden. What one cannot have, one covets hard. Those two must be his spies!"

"Mother talked more to you than she ever did to me, Sintre. Does Shadowhome know of us?"

"This was not a topic Mother spoke of, or encouraged questions about . . . but I did learn some things. Mother so hated Dhalgrave—something personal between them left her fearing his attentions and feeling wronged—that she faked her own death and fled here. Most of House Malaugrym believe Amarune died childless . . . and so know nothing of us. When—posing as another—I mentioned the name 'Architrave' to some elders, they assumed I was speaking of Malaug's long-ago human servant; there was no hint that they suspected one of the Blood bore that name."

"So Dhalgrave must be our sire," her brother murmured.

Sintre sighed. "Perhaps, Architrave, perhaps. What does it matter? She's too dead now to tell us!"

In a high tower in Waterdeep, a scrying globe floated above a table. A voice hissed, "*Oh*, that I dared walk with you, children! How can you *be* so foolish, as to stand in the open talking of us and Shadowhome and the Shadowmaster High! Your recklessness will bring his regard down on you . . . so I must remain dead to you, too. Have my curses, ungrateful spawn. Amarune must bide lonely here for years—perhaps centuries—with no company but these idiot *humans!*"

Pale, shapely fingers closed around the edge of an iron-bound door and tightened in sudden fury. Eyes flashed like two golden flames. The hand clenched into a fist, scooping a piece out of the massive iron plates as if they were but crumbling mud.

" 'Too dead now,' indeed!"

"Do as you please, Brother," Magusta said coldly. "Go and get yourself killed. *I* shall hunt those two Malaugrym. I'd sent covert magic to pry at the mind of that wizard, but it yielded also a glimpse of the male's thoughts. They're up to something—something involving spellfire, and using it as a weapon against the Blood."

Stralane shrugged. "That only confirms that they're kin to us and love wild schemes, not that they've any real hope of smiting

House Malaugrym with some new spell . . . how many of *those* have you seen brandished about? 'Sure to sear the shadows,' every one of them—yet still Great Dhalgrave sits on his throne and sneers decrees that forbid us this playground."

"Forbid us, yes, but stop us, no," Magusta said. Her smile was part wolf and part snake. "Unless you think those two were his agents."

"Truly," Stralane replied, "I care not. Play with your schemes and speculations. Leave me to my hunting and slaying and wenching and devouring." Halfway into taking wyvern shape, he turned his long neck and looked back at her. "We have the power. Why not take the shape of every last lusty ruler and conquering warlord and sinister spellhound in the world? Who's to stop us?"

"The two we fled from," Magusta told him. "The Doom of the Shadowkin, this Elminster, other wizards, the gods—"

"Bah! Sister, you waste my life with your talk! Always, talk talk talk! Find your own amusements—this world sports more conspiracies than you can choke a wizard with; take part in some! Or find another Blood-she and scheme together—but *let me be!*"

A wyvern bounded into the sky and raced away northward like a brown bolt of lightning, snorting with its frenzied wingbeats.

"So be it," Magusta murmured, watching him go. "Yet I fear I'll be 'letting you be' *buried*, ere long. Stralane, you always were a willful fool."

⊠ ⊠ ⊠

Shandril hurt all over. Why did tales of adventure omit the constant pain and discomfort? Shandril rolled over, feeling aches and twinges. Stones must have fallen on her. Nothing seemed broken, thank the gods.

It was dark, but the cold flash of beljurils told her she was still in the dracolich's grotto.

"Narm?" She was alone again. "*Narm!*" she shouted. Her cry echoed back, her only reply. She drew a deep breath. Where to go? What to do?

The faintest of scraping sounds came to her left. Someone was moving quietly over the stones.

"Who's that?" Shandril demanded, feeling for her dagger. "What do you want?" Finding her blade, she stabbed out wildly.

"A less *pointed* greeting would do, for a start," a voice growled at her elbow.

Shandril jumped, startled.

The voice took on a gentler tone. "Well met. I'm Torm, of the Knights of Myth Drannor. No more noise now. It's best no one think you still live. I'll be your eyes and ears and hands; wait here."

Hope leaped in Shandril. She reached out—but her fingers brushed only rapidly receding cloth. "My thanks, Torm," she hissed quickly, "but why aid me, a stranger?"

The answer was faint as it moved away. "I've a weakness for fair ladies who reach for daggers and face the unknown unafraid. Now hush, and wait."

Shandril stared into the darkness, shrugged, smiled, sat down on the most comfortable stone she could find, and composed herself to wait.

After a long time there was a stirring in the darkness.

"Torm?"

"Rauglothgor's spells seek us," Torm whispered in her ear. "Your Narm lives and is unharmed. I'll take you to him as soon as the dracolich settles down. For now, we must abide here."

A hand patted her shoulder—how could he *see* in this?—and Torm settled himself on unseen stones nearby. His breathing quieted.

They sat in chilly darkness for a very long time.

Torchlight flared like a small, blinding star in the distance and bobbed nearer.

"Over here, most graceful of priests!" Torm called cheerfully.

A voice bawled out merrily, "Torm? Where by the Lady's winking eye have ye *been?*"

"Paying a visit to Elminster by means of a little magic I preferred not to lose to the balhiir," Torm called back. "I found Shandril and she found me. Have you spells left?"

"Aye, if the accursed balhiir stays elsewhere," Rathan rumbled, striding toward them.

Jhessail was at his back, with Florin and Merith and more torches. After them came the plain-robed man who had shot fire at the Shadowsil and—Narm!

Shandril sprang up and rushed to embrace him, passing Torm like the wind.

He chuckled and said, "Oh, yes, and there's one more little matter of immediate interest, gallants: Some seventy riders approach the keep above us; illustrious members of the Cult of the Dragon. Shall we rush to smite them with spells, or take them by surprise down here?"

"No magic remains that we can trust," Florin said grimly.

Torm grinned and spread his hands. "Ah, well, I never planned on dying of old age. . . ."

Shandril and Narm embraced, swaying in each other's arms. "As long as I have you," the thief of Deepingdale murmured into the apprentice wizard's ear, "I can face anything the gods hurl at us. Never leave me."

"Nor you me," Narm growled back, his arms tightening fiercely. "Lady most fair . . ."

Torm tapped him on the shoulder. "If ever, young Tamaraith, you find yourself tired or overly busy, and need someone to stand in for you in such an embrace—just call my name."

Narm's unappreciative look made Torm roar with laughter.

Jhessail cleared her throat briskly. "Not that I want to cut short Torm's merriment, but the only place we few can defend against so many is that dead end where Florin found Narm and Shandril. Shall we move?"

As if her suggestion had been a stern order, the Knights set forth, their torches flickering as they hastened through twisting tunnels.

No balhiir, bone dragon, or anything else rose to menace them. Soon they reached the space beyond the rockfall where Narm and Shandril had thought themselves entombed. Clambering through the gap Florin had made, the Knights turned and readied their weapons.

"I presume you returned to Shadowdale to stow your magic," Florin said to Torm. "Did you also ask Elminster to aid us?"

The thief grinned. "Aye, but the Old Mage suspects me of

youthful enthusiasm. I know not how serious he thinks our situation. I *did* mention the dracolich. That ought to intrigue him into putting in an appearance."

"Young and beauteous lady," rumbled the priest to Shandril, "let us speak of the chosen of the gods—priests. Myself, for instance." He grandly drew up his girth. "Rathan Thentraver, servant of Tymora." He bent ponderously to bring Shandril's hand to his lips. "With all this running and butchering, there's scarce been time to get to know each other, though I daresay ye two have managed." His chuckle was not—quite—a leer. "I know what it is to be young and in haste."

Shandril smiled and shook her head. "I must ask. You're a priest and yet seem so—forgive me—*normal*. Much like the men who came to the inn each night. Does the service of Lady Tymora not change one?"

Rathan nodded. "Aye, but we don't all live the stuff of rousing tales. For all the glory of victories and treasure won there are painful days of marching hurt, lying wounded, or swinging swords in weary practice. The Lady helps those who help themselves." He struck a heroic pose, and added grandly, "She doesn't ask for change—she merely asks for our best."

"Yes," Merith agreed, wiping his sword with an oily rag, "the gods are strange. Those who come against us now worship the monster that nearly slew us."

"The Cult of the Dragon," Shandril said slowly. "Why would anyone want to worship a dead dragon?"

"Don't worry about them," Torm said airily. "I keep around me a few magics that should . . . *hell's fire!*" A sparkling mist swirled around him. The balhiir was back. "Well . . . I *had* some magic."

"Why did it leave us?" Narm asked curiously, watching the mist rise above Torm to drift along the ceiling. It seemed larger and somehow *brighter*.

"I think it sought the greatest concentration of magic," Rathan replied, his eyes not leaving the balhiir, "either the dracolich's hoard, or Rauglothgor itself, hurling spells as it was." His head swung around to fix Torm with a glare. "*Seventy* cultists, ye said?"

"Aye, and a dracolich. Let us not forget the dracolich," Merith added dryly.

"Enough; something comes!" Florin warned sternly, hefting his great sword as if it were a thing of feathers. "Lanseril?"

The plain-robed man smiled and waved a hand. Every torch went out, leaving only drifting smoke. The balhiir plunged at the druid like a vengeful arrow but reached him too late to drain magic. Its sparkling stars swirled angrily around their heads.

It moved to where Merith crept catlike over rocks to join Florin at the gap. The druid meanwhile became a blur and then a small gray bird. The balhiir raced back—too late, again.

Torm turned to Narm and Shandril, indicating the hopping bird. "Be known to—Lanseril Snowmantle; our druid. His every feather quivers at thy service."

Narm and Shandril grinned at the thief's impudence. He waved at a heap of hand-sized stones. "And here's where your service can be, in the fray to come. A thrown stone can spoil spells and aimed arrows better than the strongest Art."

Shandril took one and hefted it, trying not to remember the Shadowsil's blood.

"Not too quick with those stones now," Torm added. "If they don't see us at first, we'll let them come ahead until there are some to slay. Strike when they notice us—not before."

Beyond the gap, a bobbing sphere of radiance floated nearer, dancing and playing like a curious firefly.

The balhiir gathered itself and raced along the roof of the cavern toward the light.

The radiant sphere shone on the robed shoulder of a lone, walking man. He wore a tall, large-brimmed, pointed hat. He was tall, too, and thin, with a long white beard, and bore a knobby staff of wood a head taller than himself. He strode in the air above the shifting rocks, and he hummed something soft and intricate.

When the balhiir reached the floating globe at the wizard's shoulder, radiance flared, flooded in a twinkling cloud, and died.

"Put away that overlong fang, Florin, and light me a torch," said a familiar voice disgustedly. "Ye have a balhiir indeed. Young Torm managed to cleave to the truth for once."

"Elminster," the ranger said in pleased greeting. "Well met."

"I know, I know . . . ye're all delighted to see me—or will be if ye ever manage to make a light to see *anything*."

Fire promptly flared on Florin's torch.

Elminster stood in its flickering light, his keen eyes fixed Shandril and Narm. "A fine dance ye've led me on," he said gruffly. "Gorstag was in tears when I left him, lass; nearly frantic. Ye might have told him a bit more about where ye were going. Young folk have *no* consideration, these days." His tone was severe—but his words ended in a wink.

Shandril felt suddenly very happy. She cast the throwing-stone in her hand so that it crashed at the Old Mage's feet.

"Well met, indeed," Elminster said dryly, "O releaser of balhiirs. We may as well get to know each other before the dying starts."

7

To Face The Bright Danger

Tell ye of the balhiir? Ah, a curious creature, indeed. I hear it was first—the short version, ye say. Very well, ye are paying. The short version is thus: a curious creature, indeed. Thank ye, goodsir, fair day to ye.

The sage Rasthiavar of Iraiebor
A Wayfarer's Belt-Book of Advice
Year of Many Mists

"I expected to greet cultists here long ago," Torm said, springing up onto a high, flat rock, "or at least entertain the dracolich. Why so quiet, so long?"

"Foes fear us," Rathan said with a grin, waving at Florin, who stood guard by the entrance.

"I'm so scared I can scarce stand still," Shandril burst out, "and you trade jests! How do you do it?"

"We always talk before a fight, Lady," Rathan answered. "Look ye: One's excited and among friends and may not live to see the dawn."

The fat priest shrugged. "Besides . . . how better to spend the waiting? Much of what bards call 'dashing adventure' is a little running and fighting and lots of waiting. We'd grow bored wasting all that time in silence!"

"Hmphh!" Elminster observed severely, "all this jaw-wagging's the mark of minds too feeble to ruminate."

As Torm chuckled, Jhessail rose from the rocks, the sparkling and glowing balhiir moving above her. She went to Shandril and took her hand. "Elminster, tell us of this balhiir. It's not approached you since destroying your globe, so you bear no enchanted items. It'll rob you of spells as it's done me if we don't deal with it. What say you?"

"Yes, yes," Elminster replied, "I'm not yet so addled as to forget the lass, or"—he pointed his staff at the shifting, twinkling mist—"that."

Settling the tall, knobbed length of shadowwood in the crook of his arm, he doffed his battered hat, with a flourish hung it atop the staff, leaned back against a boulder, and cleared his throat grandly. "The balhiir," the Old Mage began in measured tones, "is a most curious creature. Rare in the Realms and unknown in many—"

"Elminster!" Jhessail protested, "The short version! Please!"

The white-bearded wizard regarded her in stony silence. "Good lady, this *is* the short version. 'Twould do ye good to cultivate patience . . . 'tis a habit I've found useful on a few occasions these past several hundred winters!"

Pointedly he turned his head to speak solely to Shandril. "Listen most carefully, Shandril Shessair. In this place we lack all means for banishing or destroying this balhiir save one—and ye alone can master it. 'Tis a dangerous affair for all of us, but for ye most of all, but I fear there's no other way. Are ye willing to attempt it?"

Shandril looked around at the adventurers who'd so swiftly become her friends. Calmly they looked back at her. She stole a quick glance at Narm and as quickly looked away—up at the strange, twinkling, magic-eating mist above her. Letting out her breath in a long sigh, she met the Old Mage's eyes. "Yes. Guide me."

Elminster bowed formally, drawing looks of surprise from the watching Knights. "Lad," he asked, without turning his head, "ye retain a cantrip, don't ye?" His twinkling blue eyes, grave and gentle, never left Shandril's.

"Yes," Narm replied, unsurprised that the famous wizard knew such so much about his magic.

"Then cast it while touching thy lady," Elminster said, "and we shall stand clear. This will draw the balhiir to ye both. Shandril, thrust thy hands into the midst of its glow. Try not to breathe any of it, and keep thy face—eyes, in particular—away from it."

One long-fingered hand lifted in warning. "When Shandril touches the balhiir, Narm, ye must flee from her at once, as fast as ye can. All here, stand clear of Shandril from then on. Her touch may well be fatal."

The Old Mage stepped forward and clasped Shandril's shoulders. If he felt her trembling under his hands, he gave no sign of it. The balhiir coiled watchfully above them both.

"Lass," Elminster added, his voice gentle, "thy task is the hard one. The balhiir's touch will tingle and seem to burn. If ye'd live, ye must keep hands spread within it, and not withdraw. Ye'll find ye can take the pain—a cat of mine once did. Use thy will to draw the fire into thee, and 'twill flow down thy arms and enter ye. Succeed, and ye'll hold the balhiir's energy."

Shandril looked up involuntarily at the twinkling mist so close overhead. It descended a little menacingly.

"Ye must then slay its will," Elminster continued, "or perish in flames. Ye'll know when ye've destroyed it. Master it as quickly as ye can, for the fire within thee will burn more the longer ye hold it. Ye can let it out from thy mouth, thy fingers, even thy eyes—but beware of aiming the blasts carelessly. Ye can easily slay us all."

Shandril nodded. Her eyes were very dark.

"Ye must go out yon entrance," the Old Mage added gently, "if the dracolich or the cultists have not attacked us by then. Seek them out and blast them until ye've none of the balhiir's energy left in ye. Let go of it all, or it may slay thee."

Their gazes held a moment longer, and then he bent slowly to kiss her brow.

His beard tickled Shandril's cheeks, and his old lips were

warm. They left her forehead tingling, and she felt somehow . . . stronger. Shandril drew herself up and smiled.

"We shall tarry nearby," he said. "Narm will follow thee, and we'll guard ye both. Be ye ready?"

Shandril nodded. "Yes," she said, mouth suddenly dry. "Do it. Now." She hoped the effort of keeping her voice steady did not show on her face.

Elminster bowed and stepped back.

Shandril raised her hands over her head and cast a quick glance back at Narm. Reluctance and fear filled his face, and he slowly stepped toward her. She gave him a bright smile of reassurance. This, at last, was something she could do.

The balhiir winked and swirled closer overhead, as if waiting to be destroyed.

"Forgive me," Narm said, "but this cantrip will make you—uh, belch."

Her helpless laughter rang out across the cavern. Shandril was still laughing as the magic was cast. Her mirth became a loud eructation—and the balhiir descended and enveloped her.

She saw, heard, and knew nothing but curiously coiling sparks and a mist that smelled faintly of rain on leather. The pain began. Sparks, fire, energy somehow flowed *into* her, stirring her, awakening something. . . .

Shandril bent her head back to gasp for breath, arched and stared at the dark rock above for some time, heard herself sob, moan, cry out. . . . It hurt! By the gods, *it hurt!*

The tingle grew along with the searing pain until her whole body shook and twitched. She had to fight to hold her hands out. She wanted desperately to pull back and clutch herself as the fire spread down her shuddering arms and across her chest. Shandril sobbed. Blue-purple flames licked up her outflung arms.

Narm rushed forward, though the fire didn't touch her hair or clothes. "No!" He reached desperately for her.

Elminster extended a long, thin arm and caught hold of one robed shoulder. "Nay! Keep back, if ye love her!"

Narm scarcely heard the words, but the hand gripping his shoulder was like an iron claw; he could not break free.

Shandril's sobs rose into a raw, high shriek. "Gods have mercy!" Flames leaped from her mouth.

Elminster waved at the Knights to get down and seek cover.

Fire raged down Shandril's arms and flared up from her shoulders. She could not see; flames of blue and purple rose from her nostrils and mouth. Energy rolled restlessly around her arms and breast, coiling and flaring, drawing all of her in. Anger blazed in her, coiling behind her throat and snarling forth in roars like Rauglothgor's.

Flames rolled before her nose. Startled, she ceased her cries. She cast a burning gaze at Jhessail. The flames reflected from the mage's beautiful, anxious face as pain spread across it. Waving hasty apology, Shandril looked away. Her veins boiled; her body shook. Something writhed snakelike in her, awakening fear. She couldn't control it! She'd bring death to these new friends, to Jhessail, Florin, the great Elminster, Narm . . . *No!*

The flames rolled away, and she could see Narm's face. The reflected flames danced on it, his eyes meeting hers and darkening in pain.

Elminster stepped in front of her love. His eyes met hers gravely, wise and knowing, calmly urging her on. How like Gorstag's those eyes were—kind and jovial, roughly wise and knowing. . . .

Shandril closed her eyes and clenched her teeth to fight the coiling thing within her. Heat and pain rose sharply, squeezing her heart in a blazing grip. From somewhere a world away, came shouts and the clang and shriek of swords meeting in anger.

She fell onto rocks, and sharp pain exploded in her knees. White heat built within. She burned, shuddering, but she could master it. Exulting, Shandril rose.

Blades flashing, Florin and Merith fought many men in the narrow mouth of the cavern.

Shandril's heartbeat was deafening in her ears as she ran forward. The elf and the ranger drew aside, steel flashing. Florin raised his blade in solemn salute as she rushed past.

Shandril shouted. White lightning lanced from her hands, mouth, and eyes and crackled ahead of her. Wherever she looked, men burned and died. She heard screams and drowned them out with a long, triumphant shriek of her own, a howl that rose high and swept men away in flames.

When she let it die away, the cavern before her was blackened and empty, except for dead foes in sizzling armor, blades smoking in their crisped hands.

Oh gods, what have I done? Six, seven . . . twelve . . . how many? Is there no end to them?

Shandril recoiled, fighting the fire within her. As she stood there, hands spread and smoking, a skeletal neck swung down into the cave mouth. A chilling gaze stabbed at her. Rauglothgor the Undying opened his bony jaws, and the world exploded in flame.

Shandril moaned. Pain atop pain raged within her. Tears blurred the wall of flames; when she could see again, Rauglothgor's horned skull loomed over her.

His regard was a silent sneer, laughing down at her with all the arrogance and strength of cold centuries and dragon fire.

Her fear was suddenly swept away by anger. Aye, she was a mere lass, unskilled and unwise in battle and magic, but a rock—a mere rock!—had felled Symgharyl Maruel, in all her pride and magic. Yes, she faced a dracolich, but she had the means to strike back!

Burn, then, oh-so-mighty Rauglothgor. Burn and know how it feels, you who burn us like flies in torch fire . . . BURN!

Shandril flung her arms out as if she could stab the undead dragon with her fingertips. From them, with a vicious crackle and a cavern-shaking roar, streamed spellfire.

Rauglothgor burned. Hungry white flames raged around rearing bones. It howled. Stones raked from the cavern ceiling by its horns fell in a shower about it, its great claws convulsed. It tried to beat bony wings, seeking escape.

Bones scraped unyielding rock. Jaws that had forgotten how to scream shrieked high, girlish terror.

Shandril set her teeth and kept the fire flowing, her body shuddering with power.

The thing of bones writhed, clawing the air in trapped, unthinking agony. As fires raged on, the great undead dragon fell silent and sank down. Its bones blazed with white, blue, and purple flames as they blackened, split, and burst asunder. All that remained crumbled.

So passed Rauglothgor, Night Dragon of the Thunder Peaks.

Shandril stumbled into the darkness, spellfire raging in her.

The cavern beyond was large and dark but for a few torches flickering below. They glimmered on swords. More cultists! Blades raised, the new arrivals scrambled toward the easy prey.

Easy prey, indeed. Shandril opened her mouth and screamed. Flames gushed forth. She raised her hands and smote them with spellfire, hurling blasts, until none stood against her. Shandril stumbled on, exulting.

"Shandril!" Narm's anguished voice broke through the roar of her flames.

She shook her head and waved at him to stay back. Spellfire spilled from her fingers like bright rain, and she ran on. The fire coiled inside, and she dared not simply blast rock—she'd been buried alive once, and that was enough. She ran across the cavern and up its far slope, seeking daylight . . . and any cultists who might lie ahead.

She found them, laden with treasure, though they dropped it to snatch out blades. Her blasts reached the foremost of them. Some raised their hands to cast spells, but Elminster's bright bolts curled past Shandril's shoulders to strike them down before magic could be unleashed.

It was too late for the Dragon Cultists to run or fight. Under her spellfire, they had time only to die. They did that very well.

More cultists met her in the cavern above, and more died.

Shandril ascended the tunnels and climbed crumbling steps. Blue flames licked the stone wherever her boots touched. Shandril finally saw daylight, pouring through the door of the keep.

There were no cultists on the mountain slopes below, and the sky was clear and cloudless. She turned, flames blazing around her swirling hair, and screamed to the Knights, "Get back!"

They obeyed. Elminster's old hands dragged Narm back with surprising strength.

Shandril turned back to the sky and stones. She spread her hands, threw back her head, and screamed out her pain and exultation. Spellfire rolled forth. Stones cracked and fell around her, shards cutting her arms and face, and she laughed at them. Daylight grew as walls fell and stone crumbled. She backed down the stairs of the shattered keep as it fell around her.

"Back! Back!" she cried to the Knights again, smashing down stones with great sheets of spellfire. Pillars of broken wall stood like huge teeth against the sky for a few shuddering instants before they too toppled. The keep was gone, completely fallen, and still the fires raged.

Oh, Tymora, release me! Will this never end? Look, you gods—such power! *Nothing stands against me—not the dracolich, not his worshipers, not the stones themselves—not even this mountain!*

Shandril laughed. Her blazing fingers found the throat of her tunic and ripped it open. From her bared breast poured spellfire. She turned, backed down the steps, and blasted dark rock into the sky—here, and there, and over *there*. . . .

The fires diminished. Shandril shivered as the lessening flow poured out of her breast and mouth. Slowly she realized she was on her knees again, amid the scattered gold of the dracolich's treasure. The last shards of the great cavern's ceiling broke away and fell.

Exhausted, Shandril swayed, staring at her hands. The last rippling tongues of flame—blue and fitful, snarling into oblivion—faded. Her hands were—just hands. Empty.

Well, not quite. The ring and armlet of electrum and sapphires sparkled almost mockingly. Shandril managed to bring her arms up as she fell onto the cold stone.

The fire was gone. She was so cold, so numbingly cold.

"Shandril!" Narm shouted, snatching himself out of Elminster's grip at last. He crashed full tilt into an invisible barrier the Old Mage had raised before the Knights as a shield. He clawed his way along it in helpless frustration. "Let me *go* to her, gods curse you! Is she—is she dead?"

The wizard shook his head, pity in his eyes. "Nay, but she may not live. I'd no idea how much Art that balhiir had absorbed! Careful now!" The barrier was gone.

Narm raced forward, falling twice amid shifting stones.

"Gods," Florin murmured in awe.

Beyond where Shandril lay, the mountain had been blasted open into a vast crater, laying bare the dracolich's cavern.

" 'Rare in the Realms,' you said," Torm muttered to Elminster, shaking his head. "And a good thing, too!"

Narm knelt beside Shandril's sprawled body. The Knights reached him. The young apprentice raised his anguished face to Elminster. "Can I . . . will it hurt her if I touch her?"

Shandril lay on her face, motionless, her long hair spread over her back like a last lick of flame.

Elminster shook his head. "Nay, but Rathan, can ye heal yet?"

The cleric spread his hands doubtfully. "I've only a little favor of the Lady left to me."

Elminster nodded grimly. "Use what you can. Narm, after Rathan heals thy lady, carry her back to the cavern where ye waited for me. Haste matters more than gentleness. I go to Shadowdale now, for healing scrolls left hidden by Doust Sulwood when he was lord. We shall meet again shortly, at that cavern."

Rathan chanted softly, kneeling by the fallen girl.

Narm looked up from Shandril, eyes blazing. "You knew this would kill her! You *knew!*"

Elminster shook his head. "Nay, lad, I knew not. I feared it might, aye—but I saw no other way." He turned away. "Delay me not, now, or thy lady may die!"

Rathan touched Narm's shoulder. "I'm done, lad. Let's move her. If Elminster counsels haste, haste is the thing."

Narm tore his eyes from the Old Mage's back. "Yes. Sorry." He looked down at Shandril, lying so still and silent.

A brisk voice said, "Stop gaping and lift your lady by the shoulders. I'll take her feet. Jhessail, hold her head!"

Narm found himself looking at Torm, who waved his hand at Shandril. "Come on. *Haste*, the man said."

"Y-yes." Narm reached out a tentative hand and fumbled at the open front of her tunic.

"Leave it," Torm said firmly. "I promise you I won't look—much."

Narm shouted at him, a raw torrent of fury that made Torm

grin and roll his eyes in mock horror. Narm stopped in midword, realizing he had no idea what he was saying.

They clambered over broken rocks, Rathan at Narm's elbow and Jhessail hip-to-hip beside him, cradling Shandril's head.

Narm swallowed. Shandril's eyes were closed, her lips parted. She looked so beautiful. . . .

Ahead, Florin and the elf, Merith, hurled aside charred cultists, clearing the way to the small cavern where he and Shandril had been trapped. The smell of burned flesh was strong as they shuffled and clambered on. Narm looked down at his ladylove in disbelief and fought tears down to nothingness.

He'd seen it, yes—raging flames and falling walls, the dracolich burned to ash. How much force had it taken? How much had Shan held? How in the name of all the gods could she survive?

"The scrolls—is Elminster back yet?" he asked frantically. They stumbled forward into the small, now-familiar cavern. Torchlight greeted them. Lanseril, in his own form, sat against one of the smoother expanses of wall. On either side of him, lit torches stood upright amid piled stones.

"No, no overclever wizards here," the druid replied wryly. "I felt the mountain shake; Shandril?" Torm nodded. Lanseril shook his head in wonderment. "Bring her here. Not straight across—Elminster might teleport in there—around this way."

"A fair thought, but unnecessary, as it happens," came a familiar voice from the back of the cavern. "Rathan, behold: scrolls enough, and to spare. I only hope her fires did not damage her overmuch."

"Damage?" Narm asked, icy fear gripping him as they gently laid Shandril down.

"Spellfire burns inside," Elminster replied gently, advancing with a flourish of parchment rolls. "It can burn out lungs, heart, and even brain, if held overlong." He shook his head. "She seemed to be master of it to the last, but she held more than I've ever known anyone to bear without bursting into flames."

Narm gaped in horror at the Old Mage.

"Cheerful, isn't he?" Torm observed with a bright smile.

Jhessail gave Torm a dark look and knelt to put her arms

around Narm's shuddering shoulders. "Torm," she said in tones as sharp as a sword, "sometimes you're a right *bastard*."

The thief nodded—but broke off his florid bow to indicate Narm, and said gently, "He needed it."

Jhessail held his gaze for a moment and then said quietly, "You're right, Torm. I'm sorry I misjudged you." She enfolded Narm in her arms, and the apprentice mage burrowed against her like an inconsolable child.

"All Faerûn misjudges the bright and shining Torm," the thief announced mournfully, "almost all the time!"

"With no cause at all," Merith added innocently. "Now shut your clever lips—painfully unaccustomed though you are to such heroism—and help spread my cloak over her."

Rathan nodded to let the Knights know he was done with Shandril. He rose wearily to see to the wounded Lanseril.

"A hard day of healing?" the half-elven druid asked wryly as the priest approached.

Rathan grunted. "Hard on the knees, anyway." He knelt with a grunt of effort. "Now lie still, damn ye—'tis hard enough to convince the Lady to heal an unrepentant servant of Silvanus."

"True enough," Lanseril agreed. "How does the young lady fare?"

Rathan shrugged. "Her body is whole. She sleeps. But her mind? We shall see."

Across the cavern, Narm looked out of the comforting circle of Jhessail's arms to see Shandril, sprawled on the stones and breathing so softly. . . . "Why does she not awaken? She's healed, Rathan said—why does she sleep?"

"Her mind heals itself," Elminster replied. "Disturb her not, and calm thyself. A fine mage ye'll make, with all this weeping and shouting! Come away, rest, and eat something!"

"I'm not hungry," Narm muttered.

Jhessail rose and pulled him up, her slender arms surprisingly strong.

"Oh, aye," Elminster replied in obvious disbelief, handing him a sausage. He produced a knife from somewhere in his sleeve and sawed at the hard piece of bread on his lap.

Narm stared at what he held, thought of Shandril and himself and sausages, and burst into laughter. It proved wilder than he'd expected—beyond him to stop, in fact. Tears came again as he rocked helplessly back and forth.

"Stable fellow, isn't he?" Elminster inquired of the world at large. "Eat," he commanded, thrusting Narm's arm toward his mouth with a swiftly snapped spell.

Suddenly Narm ate ravenously.

Shaking his head, Elminster used magic to pluck a flask from where it lay beside Torm and loft it through the air to his own waiting hand. Torm snatched for it much too late.

Merith, who with Florin had been carefully examining the chamber, came to Narm in silence and touched his elbow.

Narm slowly surfaced from the sausage. "Umm? Oh, sorry!"

"No need for that, lad," Merith told him. "What we *do* need is to know where the Shadowsil lies."

Narm blinked at him. "There, among the rocks!" He pointed, but his hand moved uncertainly when he could not see Symgharyl Maruel's feet.

"Aye," Merith said soberly. "We thought so."

"She's gone?" Narm asked, astonished.

"She's nowhere in this chamber," Florin told him quietly. "Not even among the bodies at the entrance."

"Then—where is she?" Narm asked, his mind still full of Shandril, spellfire, and sausages.

"I'm afraid," the gleaming Knight told him, "we'll find out soon enough!"

Her jaw ached abominably. That little bitch had broken it, and her arm and probably her cheek, too. The cheek was so swollen her left eye was almost shut.

Symgharyl Maruel was still able to hiss spells and command words, though, and it would not be long before that wench would pay.

Pay dearly. Burn off her legs with a favorite wand's fire, and then her arms. Then set to work with a knife. Oh, she'd whimper and plead—until her tongue was cut out.

Symgharyl Maruel chuckled, wincing at the pain this brought to her jaw. Gods *spit* on the little whore!

The lady mage found her feet and unsteadily crossed her cave refuge. Too unsteadily. Gods, the *pain!* She leaned against the shelves that held her grimoires, arbatels, and librams. It was no use. She couldn't study Art in this pain. Where were those thrice-damned potions?

The silver-strapped chest! Of course. She clawed her way along the shelves, fell on her knees, and fumbled it open with her good arm. Careful, now; the right ones . . .

She searched among many vials for a certain rune. It would not do to make a mistake now.

She'd never thought to need these, carefully gathered here so long ago. If one plays with fire, one must expect to get burned. Her burns at least had come later rather than sooner . . . but from a mere nothing of a girl, and with a *rock!*

She snarled through the blood in her mouth—and winced. The *pain!* Would it never end?

Never, indeed, if she didn't drink the potions! Gather your wits, Symgharyl Maruel—who knows but one of them might follow here! Aye, the cave was spell-sealed, but not to anyone with a tracer spell.

There! This vial, and that one.

Carefully she drew the precious vials out and cradled them against her breast. She wormed her way across the floor to a heap of cushions where she was wont to lie and study. At last!

The liquid tasted clear and icy, with a tang of iron and an odd, faint scent. Symgharyl Maruel lay back. The balm spread in a delicious slow wave through her breast and shoulders and arms.

The stabbing, sickening pain in her arm sank to a dull throb. Ah, good. Now the second vial. Her long-ago mentor was a sentimental fool, but not devoid of cunning. He'd insisted she cache these potions, all those years ago. . . .

Well, even if he came to Rauglothgor's lair, he could save neither the little thief nor the powerless lack-lore who'd tried to protect her. They'd been gone when she'd come to her senses, with a stranger in the cavern—a druid, by his garb—and the stench of burned flesh from the cave mouth. Doubtless Rauglothgor had cooked some reckless adventurers. Perhaps the wench was among them, but not likely; she'd interested Rauglothgor.

Well, too bad, Symgharyl Maruel thought savagely. The dracolich can be interested in her corpse.

The pain was almost gone. She could think. She rolled from the cushions to her feet. Her robes were well and truly torn. Breeches and boots, yes, and a half-cloak; she'd be dragon riding, if all went well. Wands, rings, and potions, too; adventurers were always trouble if you lacked Art enough to overmaster their every crazed attack. They'd give her no second chance.

Symgharyl Maruel began the complicated ritual of passing the magical and monstrous guardians of her main cache of Art.

Oh, yes, pain had to be repaid, thrice over and more. Blood would spill, indeed.

Far away, in a high cavern within a mountain, a dracolich sat on much gold. Before it knelt three men in armor. Its voice was a vast hiss that held the echoes of hammers on metal and high winds through leathery wings. Its glowing eyes floated chilling-white in dark eye sockets. Otherwise, it seemed a gigantic blue dragon, vast and terrible rather than skeletal, its scales gleaming in the torchlight.

"Treasure, yesss, good treasure," it said. "As alwaysss. But I can play with treasure only ssso much. Pile it here, pile it there . . . asss with all, I grow bored. You never entertain me! What newsss in the world without?"

"A dracolich's lair is despoiled!" rang out a new voice. "The followers need your great strength, O Aghazstamn!"

The dragon reared its spike-crested head. "Who comesss?"

Swords flashed as the three cultists scrambled to their feet and turned to seek the intruder.

They had not far to look. Upon a coach of iron with chased gold and ivory panels, half-buried in a sea of coins, stood a woman in black and purple. She was beautiful, proud, and alone, appearing out of thin air.

The warriors of the Cult of the Dragon came at her to slay. Gold coins slithered underfoot.

She raised a hand. Before them flashed the image of the dracolich Rauglothgor, its huge skeletal wings spread from wall to wall.

Aghazstamn hissed involuntarily and spread its own wings. Wind scattered treasure like drops of rain and hurled one warrior to fall among high heaps of coins.

The skeletal dragon spoke in a deep, booming voice. "The Shadowsil, mage of the Cult of the Dragon, stands before you and would serve you. She seeks aid for one who is not used to asking for it; I, Rauglothgor of the Thunder Peaks. I am beset by thieves. They have loosed a balhiir that confounds my spells. Will you aid me? Half my hoard is yours, Aghazstamn, if you come speedily! Let the lady ride you. You can trust her." The bone dragon slowly faded away.

Symgharyl Maruel stood calmly silent, arms crossed on her breast. Her Art had shaped Rauglothgor's image; she knew not how the old bone dragon would take to losing half his treasure, nor did she care, so long as the wench died.

The cult warriors had halted in awe at Rauglothgor's speech. They looked to the real dracolich, their swords glittering with torchlight.

Aghazstamn's wings lowered slowly; its head sank, its gaze fixed snakelike on the lady mage. "That wasss not real," it said, "and yet I know you, sssmall and cruel one. You came to me before, not long ago, did you not?"

"Aye, great Aghazstamn. I brought you treasure fourteen winters past. One of my first duties in the cult."

Symgharyl Maruel's crossed hands rested on the ends of the wands sheathed on her hips. Her eyes darted from the warriors to the dracolich and back, but her voice and manner were relaxed and easy. The Shadowsil had come a long way to stand where she did in the cult; fear and timidity were luxuries she had no time for. She waited.

"Ssso!" The dracolich put its great head to one side and regarded her. It had been proud in life and very curious. It had thought much on the intricacies of the Art, and on death, and so had accepted the cult's offer to die and become undead.

Aghazstamn had accepted young. It had missed many years of high flying and dealing death on lesser creatures, of battling wyrms in clear air and mating in roaring silence. It regretted the losses.

Now here was a call to war. To leave its safe lair and its rich hoard, to face enemies . . . enemies, hah! Puny humans, even as these at its feet, waving tiny steel fangs and making much commotion. To ride the high winds again, to see the land spread out below, feel the cold bite of the air whistling past as lesser creatures fled in terror, far below . . .

"Kneel to me, Ssshadowsil, and pledge to turn not against me nor aid Rauglothgor in altering the ssstated bargain. Do that, and I will accept!"

Symgharyl Maruel knelt among the coins, on the ornate top of a coach that had once carried young princes of Cormyr to hunt in the high country. Hiding her smile in a low bow over the coins, she was rewarded by the great voice.

"Mount, then. Warriorsss of the cult! Attend! Guard well my hoard in my absssence, and let not one coin be missssing when I return, nor any of you gone, or all will answer for it. Bow and pledge your obedience!"

The cult warriors, with frightened looks at Symgharyl Maruel, did so.

She wasted a flight spell in bravado (she'd intended to have its protection about her when on Aghazstamn's back, in case of a fall in aerial battle or treachery from the great dracolich). The Shadowsil flew past the swordsmen, skimming low over heaped coins, gems, and splendidly inlaid armor to reach Aghazstamn.

She paused in the air before the dracolich's broad head and bowed again, eyes lowered. Even a great mage could not safely meet the eyes of a dragon, let alone a dracolich. She flew slowly up and around in a smooth arc to settle lightly between its wings.

"My thanks, Great One," Symgharyl Maruel said, as she drew gauntlets from her belt, settled the wands on her thighs for rapid drawing, and nestled herself behind a fin she could grasp once her gloves were on.

"Nay, little one," came the hissing reply. "The thanksss isss from me to *you*."

Great wings arched above them—and the dracolich leaped upward in a great bound.

The shaft from its lair twisted and bent back upon itself to entrap and discourage flying intruders, but Aghazstamn knew it well. The great wings beat twice, precisely where they had room to spread. Daylight burst over them, and they slid into a great roaring glide that curved up to become a steep climb. The dracolich let out a roar that echoed thunderously from the surrounding peaks. It wheeled out over the Desertsedge and back again through the Desertsmouth Mountains, where of old had been the realm of Anauria before the Great Sand Sea swept its greatness away, and gained the name Anauroch.

"Where is this lair we ssseek? In the Thunder Peaksss?" the great hiss came back to Symgharyl Maruel.

She did not shout into the wind, but used her cult ring to speak to Aghazstamn's mind: *Yes, Great One. On the eastern flanks of the range, above Lake Sember.*

"Ah, yesss! Fried Elf Water! I know it."

The Shadowsil managed to stifle her giggle. "Fried Elf Water"? No doubt. Hmm . . . there'd been an elf among the adventurers who attacked her. Well, well . . . who knows what the future holds and the gods see?

On the back of the mighty blue dracolich, she rode toward the lair of Rauglothgor, to deal death upon them all.

"Die, and let the Shadowsil rise on your bones!" She did not realize she'd shouted aloud until she heard Aghazstamn chuckle.

8

Much Mayhem

A woman, or a man, may come to hold many treasures in life. Gold, gems, a good name, lovers, good friends, influence, high rank—all are of value. All are coveted. But of them all the most valuable are friends good and true. Have these, and ye will scarce notice the lack if ye never win aught else.

The adventuress Sharanralee
Ballads and Lore of One Dusty Road
Year of the Wandering Maiden

"Treasure! Aye, treasure for all and to spare!" Rathan's voice rolled heartily out over the crater where the Knights stooped to gather treasure. "More than even ye can carry, Torm Greedyfingers!"

"Hah," came Torm's reply from beneath a pile of rubble. "Change your tone, faithful of Tymora?" The thief rose. In his hands was a gleaming disc of polished electrum, fully six handwidths across.

"For love of the Lady!" Rathan gasped delightedly. "Good Torm, may I—"

" 'Good Torm,' now, is it?" the thief answered mockingly. "Good Torm Greedyfingers, perhaps?"

"Shut your yapping maw, Good Torm Greedyfingers," Merith said close behind. "Or some good dale farmer may mistake thee for a nimble shrew and marry you!"

"Some nimble dale shrew *did* marry you," Torm told him in return, "and look whaaa—!" His words ended in the roar of a crockful of gold coins being dumped over his head.

Narm watched in amazement as the air filled with small pieces of treasure, pitched from Knight to Knight. "They're—they're like children!"

"Sir Mage," Jhessail said with a gentle smile, "they *are* children."

"The famous Knights of Myth Drannor, 'children'?" Narm protested, watching her smile widen.

"All of us Knights—nay, most adventurers—are children," she replied. "Who else happily rides into danger, swinging swords against fearsome foes, far from home and saner pursuits?"

"Hmm," Narm said thoughtfully. "Yet *you* are a Knight."

"Did I say I was not a child? Dear me!" Jhessail rose in a shifting of skirts, plucked up a set of knuckle-claws of wrought brass, admired them a moment—and threw them hard and accurately at Torm's back.

With swift grace, she sat down demurely and turned to check on Shandril, favoring Narm with an impish grin. Behind them, Elminster chuckled.

Torm roared and spun, seeking his foe.

Amid the tumult, Narm's lady lay motionless, eyes closed and breathing shallowly. She looked peaceful, young, and very beautiful.

Narm swallowed, finding his throat suddenly tight. "Will she—?"

Jhessail patted his arm. " 'Tis in the hands of the gods. We'll do all we can!"

Elminster took the pipe out of his mouth. Coils of greenish smoke and sparks drifted from its bowl. "She held and handled more power than I've seen come out of a balhiir," the Old Mage said. "More, I fear, than this one had in it."

Jhessail and Narm turned to stare at him in surprise.

"Well?" Jhessail asked, arching one shapely eyebrow.

Elminster shook his head. "Too soon. Too soon for aught but idle chatter. Such clack helps none, yet could upset our young friend."

Narm sighed. "With all respect, Lord Elminster, I'm upset already. What is it you fear?"

Elminster was lost in chuckles. "I fear being called 'Lord Elminster.' Now grip thy temper and grief together, and master them. There're good reasons not to talk on this. If it makes ye feel better, know I'm amazed and awed at what thy Shandril has done."

"Oh?" Narm tried to keep his voice calm. Shan lies dying, and this old goat wants to keep his precious secrets. . . .

"Aye. The most common way to destroy a balhiir involves at least three mages; at best, five or more. They must hold the creature between them by force of Art, adjusting their opposing telekinetic spells as net-hunters tug on lines, to offset its wild struggles. They then tear it apart, each absorbing what they can. A spectacular process to watch . . . and," he added dryly, "it kills a lot of mages!"

"Yet you sent Shandril *alone* up against the thing?" Narm snarled.

Elminster's gently sad gaze stilled his tongue. "I lacked five mages. We yet faced a dracolich and could not turn away, whate'er we desired, lest we all perish. If ye'd tried to stand as one of those five, Narm, ye'd be dead now." His pipe, which had floated patiently beside his mouth, slid back toward his lips. "Hold thy peace, I bid thee, for thy lady's sake. High words will not help her now."

"Are you *always* right?" Narm asked, more wearily than in fury. "Is the one true way always so clear to you?"

Jhessail shook her head in warning.

Elminster merely chuckled. "Slay me. Thy tongue is as sharp and as busy as Torm's!" The wizard sucked on his pipe once and turned within the smoky haze to regard Narm gravely. "In tavern tales, the hero's high and shining and his foes dark and dastardly. 'Twould be simpler if life were truly like that, each knowing if he be good or evil and what to do in the great play. But think how boring 'twould be for the gods—everyone a known force, events and deeds preordained or at the least predictable. Things are not so."

The Old Mage started to pace, his pipe trailing patiently in his wake. "We're here to entertain the gods, who walk among us. They watch and enjoy and sometimes even thrust a hand or word into daily life, just to see the result. From this come miracles, disasters, and much else we could do without."

Narm stepped into Elminster's path and met the old wizard's gaze. They locked eyes for a time before the young apprentice nodded and stepped back. "You do think and care, then," Narm said quietly. "I feared you swaggered about serenely blasting with your Art all who opposed you."

"That's just what he *does* do," Torm broke in heartily, arms full of gold. "Wizards! Wherever one sees battle, there's some attending dweomer crafter jabbering and waving his hands. Honest sword swingers fall doomed—slain by a man in a lady's gown too craven to stand against them. Less Art would please me. Then the brave and strong would rule, not sneaking old graybeards and reckless young fools who play for sport with the forces that give light and life to us all!"

"Aye," said Elminster with a smile. "But rule what? A battlefield shoulder-deep with rotting dead, the survivors dying of hunger and disease. No one would help the sick, or harvest, or sow seeds. 'Tis a grand king who rules a graveyard." He drew on his pipe. "Besides, 'tis no good complaining about what cannot be changed. Art we have; make the best of it."

"Oh, I intend to," Torm replied with a wolfish grin.

"Are you finished, Torm?" Jhessail asked sweetly. "Or does your tongue hold more that needs spewing forth?"

"Yes, as it happens," the thief replied. "Look you, old—"

"Enough talk!" Florin snapped. "A dragon comes!"

⊠ ⊠ ⊠

"They sssee usss, little one!" the great voice boomed back at her. "Why ssso amazed?"

Speechless and trembling, Symgharyl Maruel gazed down on the blasted mountaintop. She shook her head in disbelief, but the vast crater refused to fade away as the dracolich wheeled about it. The Tower Tranquil was gone.

The keep! She thought wildly to Aghazstamn. *Gone! The whole peak's been shattered and thrown down! We must turn away! We can't face power enough to do that!*

"Flee? Nay!" Aghazstamn roared at her. Its great neck arched around, nearly tumbling the Shadowsil off.

She clung grimly to the bony fin. "The entire top of the *mountain* is gone! We *cannot* prevail against—"

"Ssseee to your wandsss, little coward! I fly to fight and ssslay after all these yearsss! You want me to turn tail and abandon the gold and thisss challenge? Think again, weaver of weak Art!" Aghazstamn climbed and wheeled, moments from plunging into an air-splitting dive.

As the wind snarled past her ears, Maruel drew one of her wands and held it firmly across her breast. Peering down, she could see an armored man, an elf-warrior, and others below, swords in hand. There was no sign of Rauglothgor. Perhaps the old terror had destroyed himself and wrought this devastation. This handful of dare-alls looked incapable of such destruction. What did it matter? Slay, and wonder later.

Aghazstamn dived, racing down ever faster, wind whistling in his wake. The Shadowsil bent low, narrowing her eyes to slits. She aimed at the scattering foes and said, "*Maerzae!*"

Red fire blossomed from the wand. A tiny ball spun away, trailing sparks, to burst below in a thunderous, orange-red sphere.

One man flew, blazing, through the air and fell among rocks. Others whirled aside, but the Shadowsil missed their fates, intent on aiming her next blast.

Aghazstamn roared in triumph, wings drawn back over its vast scaled bulk. Lightning spat from its maw in a long, blue-white bolt. One foe jerked and staggered, outlined briefly in energy.

The Shadowsil coolly unleashed her second fireball at two robed figures. It blossomed into flames before reaching them, spreading against an invisible barrier. Symgharyl Maruel hissed. Swift, indeed, by Mystra! Still, they couldn't strike back at her without sacrificing that wall. . . .

With a mighty clap of wings, Aghazstamn leveled off just short of the tumbled rocks. It skimmed low, reaching with long, cruel claws for two warriors who stood with swords raised like tiny needles. The dracolich struck, then beat its wings to rise in haste from the sharp steel.

The lady mage looked back over her shoulder and locked eyes with the druid. His hands and lips moved as he glared at her, coolly calling a spell.

Aghazstamn turned away, rising steeply. The Shadowsil slid the wand back into its sheath. She turned to look back, tossing hair out of her eyes. *Steady, I pray you, Great One,* she thought through her ring. *I would cast a spell and need a stable flight from you.*

With a thunderous snort the dracolich spread vast wings, and the roaring winds abated.

This level glide wouldn't last for long. Symgharyl Maruel swiftly drew herself up as tall as she dared on dragonback, and turned to face the foes below.

The two swordsmen still stood, a tall one in armor and an elf. Bodies sprawled among the rocks, but the robed mages remained on their feet, a little distant. That might save them for a few breaths longer. They could watch their comrades perish. Carefully Symgharyl Maruel cast the mightiest fire spell she knew. Eight balls of flame rolled forth.

Done, she told the dracolich in satisfaction as she sat down. Aghazstamn hissed acknowledgment, and the great wings beat again.

Sudden heat and a rolling roar warned Symgharyl to reach for her wand. Armed, she whirled to see what was happening—just as the world around her exploded in angry flames.

Somehow those below had turned her greatest spell against her. She reeled, screaming seared agony, dimly recalling her old mentor's words: "Most mages survive not even one mistake. . . ."

"See to Rathan," said Elminster. "And Torm, too. Here! Hurry!" From under his robes he drew two metal vials and thrust them into Jhessail's hands.

"But master, the dragon! Wha—"

"I can yet speak spells," the Old Mage told her with some severity. "Now go." His eyes never left the blackened body of the wyrm as it fell, trailing flames. Odd, that a single such spell could slay so quickly. Dragons usually died slowly and noisily, with much . . . unless this was no dragon, but—

"Another dracolich!" Elminster growled.

Narm looked at him anxiously. "Aye? What now?"

Elminster sighed. "Go help Jhessail. There's nothing ye can safely do here."

Large and dark, the dracolich loomed as it fell. Sagging wings rolled it over and over. On its back clung the Shadowsil, struggling weakly.

Elminster almost lifted his hands to pluck her magically away, but she bore a ready wand. Even as he saw it, he knew it was too late to save her. The white-bearded wizard watched expressionlessly as Aghazstamn crashed to earth.

The dracolich struck head and neck first, toppling forward onto one shoulder with a horrible splintering sound. It tumbled until its great back smashed into the ground. The Shadowsil spilled. The dracolich came to a halt in a smoking heap, broken bones against jagged rocks.

"Get her!" Lanseril shouted.

Florin and Merith leaped past, blades flashing. The elf's armor was twisted crazily at one shoulder where a dragon claw had caught it. Had Merith not jumped into its closing grip to stab with his sword, his body would have been torn apart too.

Elminster hissed hasty words, exerted his will—and vanished.

The Shadowsil struggled feebly on one elbow and rolled herself over, the wand still in her hand. She half-snarled and half-sobbed through a tangled veil of long hair.

Florin raised his sword and sprinted in desperate haste. He didn't hold with slaying women, but this foe could be the death of them all, were he not fast enough. Merith crashed along behind him, slipping and staggering among scattered rocks and treasure.

Suddenly, out of empty air, Elminster barred their path. "Stay back!" he commanded. "No more butchery!"

Waving swords wildly, they skidded to a halt before the Old Mage, glancing about to ensure the stern figure wasn't some enemy illusion.

"Put steel away," Elminster growled wearily. He went to his knees beside Symgharyl Maruel. "The time for that is past."

With a groan, the wyrm-riding witch collapsed on her face. Her wand clattered on the rocks.

Gently Elminster took that broken body under the shoulders and turned her until the Shadowsil lay faceup in his lap.

Florin and Merith watched warily, the elf's blade wavering uneasily in his hand. Florin drew off his gauntlets and squatted, facing the Old Mage across the body of the foe who'd sought to slay them. "Elminster, what are you doing?"

Symgharyl Maruel opened her eyes and stared dully up at them. She had the look of one who had traveled a very long way. She spat blood weakly ere her gaze found Elminster.

"Master," she hissed, blood bubbling horribly in her throat. "I—hurt!" The last word was almost a sob.

"Little flower," Elminster whispered gently, "I am here."

She coughed blood and tears ran down her cheeks.

The Knights gathered in astonished silence.

"If ye lie quiet," the mage murmured, "I'll see if I can find Art enough in my tower to heal thee." He clasped her hand gently and slid it out from beneath her.

She feebly plucked at his sleeve, and the witch-mage mastered her tears. "No," she gasped fiercely, eyes burning into his. "Promise me you'll not bring me back. . . . I'm too set to change now. I cannot learn this 'good' you stand for." The Shadowsil's eyes closed, and her head fell back wearily. Her eyes flickered. "*Promise*," she hissed, hands trembling.

"Aye, Symgharyl Maruel, I promise thee," Elminster said gravely, stroking her shoulder.

Symgharyl Maruel smiled. "Good, then. 'Ware my belt . . . it has a poisoned buckle." Her voice was a faint, hissing ruin. "One more thing."

Elminster leaned close to her bloody lips to hear.

The failing hands that gripped his robes were white. Her body shook. Dark eyes shone defiantly as she struggled to raise herself.

When her head reached Elminster's shoulder, she clung there, shaking like a leaf in a gale, and then rolled over to kiss his cheek, softly and yet fiercely. "I love you. I—always have. I wish I could have had you."

The Shadowsil turned her head against his chest, smiled, and died.

Silence stretched for many breaths. The Old Mage sat motionless, cradling a still body in his arms. Slim hands slowly loosened their hold on him, but Elminster held the lady mage close. No one moved or spoke; all stood waiting.

After a time, the wizard looked up, laid his burden gently down on the stones, and slowly rose to his feet. Symgharyl Maruel's bone-white, unseeing face was still smiling, but it was wet with the old man's tears.

Elminster stepped away from her, waving at Narm and the Knights to draw away. When he judged them distant enough, he nodded and started to sing. The Old Mage's voice, scratchy and hollow from disuse, gained in strength as he sang the leave-taking, until the last lines rolled out deep and clear.

The sun comes up, and the sun goes down.
Winters pass swiftly, and leaves turn brown.
Watching each day and at last it has found
Another dream to lay under the ground.

Another name lost to the wind,
Wailing away north past ears of flind,
And all she has been crumbles away.
Of all that great spirit, can nothing stay?

Mystra, Mother, take your own.
Skill and power now dust on bone.
Good or bad, what matters now?
Her song is done, her last bow.

Mother of Art, I pray now to thee,
Take back her true name in mercy,
And as her body is lost to flame,
Greet your own Lansharra again.

As his song ended, Elminster's hands moved, he murmured a few quiet words, and fire burst forth to strike the Shadowsil. Though no wood or fire-oil lay around her, flames roared fiercely from her limbs, howling skyward in a many-hued pillar.

Silently, the old wizard stared into the greedy flames.

Narm watched, and then hesitantly approached. When he stood behind Elminster's shoulder, he said, "She called you Master."

The flames roared and crackled. "Aye," Elminster muttered, not turning to look at him.

Narm shifted around to where he could see Elminster's face.

The Old Mage was smiling faintly, and there were tears in his eyes again. He looked out over the waters of the Sember, far below, but his gaze was on things long ago.

"I once trained her and rode with her." The words seemed reluctant, and the lips that spoke them crooked into a mocking smile. "I was much younger then."

Narm turned to look at Shandril, lying so still upon his cloak. Struggling to keep his voice under control, he asked, "Does a mage of power often see friends die?"

"Aye," Elminster whispered. He roused himself and caught Narm's eye with a familiar wry look. "So 'tis that even one's enemies are to be honored. If it falls in thy power, let no creature die alone."

Narm stared at him, lips white, swallowed a large lump in his throat, and managed to nod.

A moment later, a long arm was around him. Elminster said gruffly, "Bear up, lad, and stand steady. It's not so bad as all that. Thy Shandril lives."

Narm drew a trembling breath and stared into a stunningly blue sky. "Lansharra," he began, before he thought whether such speech might be prudent. "Did you love her very much?"

"Yes," the old wizard said simply. "Sometimes she was like a daughter, and other times, like a lady avidly hunting a man. Had I been several centuries younger and she not quite so quick to cruelty . . ."

Abruptly, he whirled to face the pyre. His voice rolled out, rich and imperious. "Look, all of ye!"

He raised his hands and gestured. Above the thinning smoke, a form came slowly into being: a young, slender woman with long glossy hair and chalk-white skin. She wore a simple robe of white and gold bound with a blue sash. She looked around at the Knights and the wizards young and old. Joy and wonder filled her face. She was very beautiful.

The Knights watched in silence, hardened veterans all. Guttering flames flickered ruddy reflections across their armor.

In utter silence, the image of a youthful Symgharyl Maruel worked a simple cantrip. Blue radiance sparkled into being at her fingertips. She laughed in sheer delight and held up one hand to show them. Tossing her hair back merrily, she waved—and was gone.

In unison the Knights turned their heads toward the man who had spun the illusion. Elminster stood looking into the last of the flames, his old face expressionless.

"You did that, did you not?" Torm asked, awe in his voice. "That wasn't . . . her doing . . . ?"

"Aye, I did it, though not alone; she helped. You saw her as she was one summer before any of ye but Merith was born. Her spirit lingered. I shaped an illusion, and she came into it to bid me—all of you—farewell." The mage turned to Rathan. "Thy holy water, good brother?"

Rathan nodded, stepped forward, and reverently unclasped a flask from his belt. A scorched smell from the Shadowsil's fireball hung about him, and he moved with the careful stiffness of the newly healed.

At Elminster's gesture, the flames of the pyre sank and died. Rathan doused the charred bones from head to foot. Gray smoke rose and slowly drifted away.

With a sudden swift movement, Elminster doffed his cloak. Florin and Lanseril stepped forward to lay the bones on it. Jhessail joined her voice with the Old Mage's in a prayer to Mystra.

When it was done, Elminster bundled his cloak. "All well, friends? Rathan? Torm? Ye took the worst, if memory serves."

"Well enough," the cleric replied.

Torm agreed with a terse, "Yes."

Elminster nodded. "Well, get thy treasure and let us see to Shandril. I would be gone from here as soon as she can travel—wyrms who are not as dead as they should be seem to have a distressing habit of showing up for a visit!"

The Old Mage rose with his bundle and went to where Shandril lay. "I wonder who shall call on us next?" He looked down at the bundle he bore and shook his head, looking both angry and older.

Outside, the afternoon sun blazed on the towers and parapets of Zhentil Keep. Within the Tower High, all was dark save for a circle of glass-globed candles in one corner of the high-paneled feasting hall. No grand company had eaten there for twenty winters. Beneath the flickering candles stood a small circular table where the high lords of the Keep sat in council.

Lord Kalthas, Battlemaster of the armies of Zhentil Keep north of the Moonsea, spoke almost lazily, words purring from beneath his sandy mustache. "Defending the empty wastes of Thar is not the problem, now that the lich Arkhigoul is no more. The Citadel's strong, and I see no need to weaken our forces by placing small garrisons here and there. If something comes over the mountains, let it come. We can move in strength when any invader is committed to a long journey and a particular target—and crush them at our leisure. Why defend a week's ride of barren rocks and snow? Any fool—"

The deep boom of a bell echoed in the darkness above them.

There was a sudden squeal of wood. The dark-robed figure of Manshoon, first lord of the Keep, rose with a sudden, violent movement—almost a leap. Table, papers, ink and quills, crystal decanters, and ornate metal flagons all crashed to the floor. More than one noble lord, chair and all, went to the flagstones, too.

"My lord!" protested Lord Kalthas from the floor, wiping wine from his fur-trimmed doublet. His words died to an uncertain whisper as he realized his peril. "What means this?"

Manshoon was not even looking at him. White-faced, he stared into empty air.

"Symgharyl Maruel," he whispered, his voice quavering. His eyes were bright with tears.

Lord Chess gasped aloud. More prudent nobles gaped in silence. None had ever before seen Manshoon cry or show any sign of weakness (or as one lord had once put it, "humanity").

The moment passed.

Coldly furious, Manshoon snapped, "Zellathorass!"

A glowing crystal globe swooped into view above the stairs, danced sideways like a questing bat, and darted to spin before him. Manshoon seized it and peered into its depths, where a light kindled and grew.

He was silent for a moment. His handsome face grew as hard as drawn steel. He released the globe, said "Alvathair," and watched it vanish back the way it had come. His mouth tightened.

"Sirs," he said curtly, "this meeting is at an end. For your safety, leave at once." He crooked a finger. Horribly grinning gargoyles, hitherto motionless on stone buttresses overhead, flexed their slate-gray wings.

The High Lords of Zhentil Keep found their feet and cloaks and swords and plumed hats, stammered their thanks, and exited with comical speed. A patient golem closed the door they left standing open.

Manshoon spoke to the gargoyles in a hissing and croaking tongue. On leathery wings, they began to glide about the tower, watching in terrible silence for intruders.

Their lord stood in the dark hall and uttered more words. The candles sank and died. He spoke in the gloom, and a stone golem as tall as six men strode ponderously toward him from a corner of the hall. It waited there to greet anyone foolish enough to enter unannounced.

Manshoon looked about the hall once—and then raced up the stairs like an angry wind, his robes billowing. His ragged shout of rage and loss echoed down the stairs behind him. "*Shadowsil!*"

As he stepped out into the chill air atop the Tower High, the First Lord of Zhentil Keep spoke a certain word.

Part of the tower beneath him moved. A great bulge of stone shifted and humped. Vast wings opened out over the courtyard.

A great neck arched up, and glimmering eyes regarded Manshoon with eagerness . . . and fear. Huge claws caught and pulled, and the massive bulk rose up the tower wall. A stone broke loose to clatter far below. Great wings beat in a single lazy clap that echoed from the rooftops of the city.

Frightened faces appeared in the windows of temple spires and noblemen's towers, and vanished again hastily.

Manshoon smiled without mirth and fearlessly locked eyes with the huge black dragon he had freed. Cold eyes looked back at him, ice gazing into dark ice.

Few men could retain sanity and will before the gaze of a dragon. The wyrm regarded him with vast age, knowledge, and amusement. Manshoon merely smiled and held its eyes. The fear in the dragon's eyes grew.

Manshoon hissed in the tongue of elder dragons: "Up, Orlgaun. I have need of you."

The great neck arched over the parapet for him to mount. With a bound and flurry of beating wings the black dragon soared aloft.

Manshoon was coming, racing across the sky with fire and fury to destroy the slayer of his beloved.

9

The Battle Ne'er Done

The worst trouble with most mages is that they think they can change the world. The worst mistake the gods make is to let a few of them get away with it.

Nelve Harssad of Tsurlagol
My Journeys Around the Sea of Fallen Stars
Year of the Sword and Stars

"I wonder," Torm said slowly, silver and gold coins streaming through his fingers, "how long the bone dragon had been gathering this!" He looked across a glittering sea of metal and shook his head in wonder.

"Ask Elminster," Rathan growled. "He probably recalls the day Rauglothgor arrived, what—or whom—it ate at the time, and all." The priest scrutinized a handful of coins, plucking out only platinum pieces, and adding them to an already bulging purse.

Torm made a face. "I'll not ask. I've felt enough cold disapproval backed by the weight of oh-so-ancient cares—"

"Ah, Torm," came the Old Mage's voice from startlingly close behind the thief's shoulder. Elminster could move with disconcerting stealth. "Thy respect for my feelings never fails to astonish me—in one so young and foolish."

The thief sighed disgustedly. "Whereas the length and reach of thy flapping ears, Oldbeard, fascinates me."

"Everything does," Rathan commented dryly. " 'Tis one way to keep life interesting. Offering casual rudeness to mighty archmages is another."

Torm made a certain gesture.

Elminster raised his eyebrows slowly, one after another, in a way that turned mild reproof into crushing insult.

Torm's face flamed. With sudden interest, he plunged his hands into the nearest treasure.

Nearby, Merith shifted heaps of coins with his feet, looking for more unusual treasure.

"Is this why we go through all the blood and battle?" Jhessail asked, coming up to him with her hands full of sparkling gems.

"Yes, depressing, isn't it?" Lanseril replied from where he knelt at Narm's side. The young mage watched over Shandril, who still lay white and motionless, for all the world as if dead.

Elminster joined them. He puffed on his pipe thoughtfully as he stood looking down at the thief of Deepingdale, but said nothing at all.

Lanseril gave Narm a gentle shove. "Enough brooding. Get up and find some gems and platinum coins while it's still lying about for the taking." At Narm's dark look, he added more gently, "Go on. We'll watch her, never fear. You'll need the gold, if you plan to learn enough Art to see you both past all the enemies you've made these past few days!"

Narm's doubt slowly gave way to thoughtfulness. "You may be right, but—but Shandril . . ." He looked helplessly at her.

Lanseril laid a hand on his arm. "I know it's hard. You do the best for her and yourself if you get up and go on with what must be done. The schemes of gods and men unfold even while you sleep. You can do nothing for Shandril sitting here." Lanseril pushed Narm again. "Go, lad, and play among the coins. You'll see few enough of them before you die! I'll keep your spot warm and will call you if she should awaken and want to kiss someone." He grinned at the expression those words brought to Narm's face. "*Go*, idiot!"

Narm rose slowly, looked down at Shandril again, traded

quick glances with Lanseril and Elminster, glanced again at Shandril—and hurried away.

Lanseril sighed. "These younglings . . . their love *burns* so!"

"Aye, indeed, 'Old One,' " the mage replied gravely, leaning on his staff. The two friends looked at each other for a moment in silence and then spoke as one, the druid who'd not yet seen thirty winters and the mage who had seen many hundred. " 'Well, when you get to be *my* age—' " They broke into chuckles.

All around them the Knights strode back and forth with small, clinking bundles, gathering Rauglothgor's hoard. In the distance, Narm peered curiously at a ruby in his palm. Gold coins crept forth from between the fingers of his other hand.

"Not much magic. Damnation on that balhiir," Torm said to Jhessail. He spilled a dozen brass rings from his hand to bring them in range of her awakened spell. They failed to glow with the radiance that betokened magic.

Jhessail spread her hands. " 'Tis the way of balhiirs. Poor Torm," she added in mock sorrow and commiseration. "You'll have to settle for mere gold, gems, and platinum . . . and so *little*, too!"

Torm grinned. "Scant compensation, good lady, for the discomfort and danger attendant on my every breath. What good are coins to a dead man?"

"*Precisely* the thought that prevents most sane beings from taking up thievery," Jhessail replied mildly.

Torm bowed in acknowledgment of a point well made.

Lanseril looked beyond them to the broken ridge of the crater. Florin stood there, blade in hand, bearing a special shield Elminster had brought back with the healing potions. The ranger was silent and alert, his eyes flicking over the cold gray peaks above and the tree-cloaked land below.

Elminster, too, was silent and intent, but his eyes were on Shandril. She moved slightly and frowned, murmuring something so faint they could not hear it.

Lanseril leaned forward to reach for her, and the long, knobby end of Elminster's staff came down before him warningly. The druid looked up its length. "Do we tell Narm?"

Elminster smiled. "No need."

Crashing sounds, growing swiftly louder, heralded Narm's progress through the coins toward them. "Shandril!" he cried, and then met their gently silent gazes. "Is she—?"

"She stirs," said the wizard. "If ye must shake her, do it gently, and only once or twice."

Narm threw him a frightened look and flung himself to his knees, scattering coins. "Shandril!" he pleaded, laying a timid hand on her shoulder. "Shan, can you hear me?" He shook her gently. She moaned and moved one hand. "*Shandril!*" he cried with sudden urgency, and shook her. "Sh—"

Elminster's staff tapped him firmly on the shoulder. "How is she to heal if ye awaken her with such violence?" the Old Mage asked gently. "Leave be for a time, and see how she does."

Narm stared at Elminster, throat tight and eyes very full.

Florin shouted a warning. " 'Ware, all!"

The Old Mage's head snapped up, his eyes lighting like lamps as he looked to where the ranger's blade pointed.

Far off in the sky to the north, a dark, winged shape approached—large and serpentine.

"Dragon!" several Knights snarled unnecessarily, as they scattered to the cover of large boulders.

"Gods' laughter," Torm muttered as he ran past, jingling and bulging with loot, "will this *never* end?"

Merith and Florin suddenly stood with Narm, Lanseril, and Elminster.

The white-bearded wizard looked unconcerned as he watched the approaching dragon. Setting his staff into the crook of his elbow, he quietly began to work a spell.

"We must move your lady," Florin told Narm and nodded at a spur of rock far off to the right. "Yonder place is best for protection. Stay with her there." His tone, for all its gentleness, was a command.

Narm made no protest as they gently lifted Shandril and bore her in stumbling haste across the scattered rock and treasure.

Jhessail and Elminster both cast spells. Rathan, his mace ready in his hand, quaffed hastily from a wineskin Torm held.

"This is not a good time for us to fight a dragon," Narm snapped as they laid Shandril in the lee of the rocks.

"Lad, it's *never* a good time to fight a dragon." Florin turned swiftly away from the young wizard.

Lanseril squeezed Narm's shoulder in passing, and the Knights headed across the open rubble pit, weapons flashing. A faint belch echoed in their wake. Torm darted back out to wave and grin at their approaching foe.

Elminster spoke in grim recognition. " 'Tis the ancient black wyrm Orlgaun, mount of Manshoon."

The dragon roared down upon them.

⊠ ⊠ ⊠

Orlgaun descended in a long glide out of the chilly heights, great black wings spread stiffly. On its back, Lord Manshoon spoke loud, grim words of magic. Eight balls of fire sprang from his fingertips, flashing past Orlgaun's black neck like shafts streaking from a bow. Down they sizzled, trailing flame. Orlgaun arched its wings like sails to slow its dive.

With a flash and a ground-shaking roar, the whirling spheres of flame exploded. In the inferno, figures staggered, yet stood. Manshoon drew a wand from his belt.

Orlgaun eagerly lowered its neck and spat blue-green acid. Spray struck dying flames and still-hot rocks; amid writhing smoke, one of the foes fell. Orlgaun hissed triumphantly, tossing its head, ere hastily turning to climb back into the air. The cold gray Thunder Peaks rushed up to meet it.

Great wings beat once, twice. A sudden, sickening shudder shook the beast. Orlgaun's vast body faltered and twisted.

Manshoon grabbed at a razor-sharp bone fin on the wyrm's neck and shouted in alarm, juggling the wand.

Orlgaun convulsed and sheered off sideways with breath-robbing speed, revealing their foe.

In the air behind them flew a human in full coat-of-plate, shield up before him, long sword reaching again toward Orlgaun.

Manshoon snarled and blasted the fool with his wand. Enchanted bolts pelted man like a sudden rain, and he fell away, writhing and tumbling.

Manshoon hissed a curse into the wind. Orlgaun's wingbeats

came more slowly, and the dragon's battle roars ceased. The wyrm was hurt already, and these ragtag adventurers looked to be tougher than he'd thought.

He readied a lightning bolt as Orlgaun swept around once more. Then he saw the old, bearded man standing on the rocks below. Beyond him was a longhaired maid in robes. Manshoon dismissed her as nothing. He bent his gaze on the bearded one and cast his bolt.

Lightning seared the air in its crackling descent. It turned aside mere feet in front of the old man and crawled harmlessly away, as if it had struck something unseen.

His target looked up calmly, casting a spell of his own. Manshoon recognized him with shock: Elminster of Shadowdale. The Old Mage wasn't off meddling on some other plane or fussing scatterbrained among dusty scrolls—but here and alert and completely unafraid!

Manshoon snarled, a little unsettled, and reached for a more powerful wand. Orlgaun would not stoop as low as last time; the great wings were lifting them already.

A great hand loomed in the air before Manshoon. Before he could even groan, Orlgaun's flight swept them into it with stunning speed.

The clap of their meeting was thunderous.

A broken wand and a dagger spun down out of the air as the dragon screamed shrilly and thundered past above them.

Almost laughing, Merith turned in the wind of its passing. "Now!" He dispelled the protective barriers about the mage.

Jhessail lifted a wand of her own and breathed its word of command. Streaking bolts of magic hissed forth, twisting to follow the slumped mage clinging to the back of the dragon.

The huge disembodied fist hung in the air by the dragon rider's shoulder, and moved with him. Elminster watched its flight. He frowned in concentration, but hints of a smile played about one corner of his mouth.

Orlgaun swept around again. Manshoon rose in his saddle,

roaring his rage and pain. He spat a word, and his wand spewed lightning. The fist struck at him again, and Manshoon was hurled against Orlgaun's rough scales.

Florin flew up at him, long sword swinging . . .

The dragon's wing smashed into the ranger. Florin's blade skittered harmlessly across scales, and Orlgaun rolled swiftly away, wings flapping wildly.

Far below, Jhessail said the last words of a spell of flight and touched her husband's forehead. Merith kissed her and sprang aloft, blade flashing, to join the fray.

Kneeling by the moaning forms of Torm and Rathan, the druid Lanseril calmly summoned insects to attack the enemy mage.

The great dragon slashed at Florin with its claws, cartwheeling across the sky. Merith Strongbow flew after it as fast as he could. The uncanny fist struck again in midair, and Manshoon cast down lightning once more.

Lanseril finished his spell, pointed at Manshoon carefully, and then turned again to healing his companions.

Jhessail raised her wand and staggered as the lightning struck, crackling across the smoking rocks.

Narm clenched his teeth and winced as the ground shook. Something the dragon rider had hurled had exploded in front of Elminster. Stones flew. Narm shielded Shandril desperately with his own body. A stone struck his shoulder, and then his back. He hadn't even time to sag before something else hit him on the temple.

All he could see was red everywhere, deepening steadily into darkness. . . .

The ground heaved, jolting Shandril into confused awareness. Where was she? Wearily she wriggled into the light, scarcely aware she was pushing away a body, and unaware it was Narm.

Dust and smoke swirled everywhere in the crater of rocks and coins. Elminster stood in its center, calmly looking upward.

Shandril peered in the same direction, and through scudding

smoke saw a dark form approach rapidly. It was Merith, blade in hand, and he was flying!

He seeks Jhessail, Shandril thought dully, as she saw his dark, anxious face and where he headed: the rock Jhessail had sagged down onto, pain twisting her face.

Something loomed in the air beyond the hurrying elf—a nightmare right out of bard's tales. A gigantic black dragon cleft the air, darting as sharply as any chimney swift hunting at eventide. Someone rode it—and Florin was somehow flying too, hanging from a shield in midair and hacking with his sword at the dragon rider!

Whoever it was twisted under Florin's blows, and then straightened with a roar of triumph. There was a flash. Florin was hurled end over end through the air like a husk doll.

Shandril tried desperately to scream and found her throat too dry to utter a sound.

The dragon turned ponderously and thundered down out of the sky at Elminster. The Old Mage stood alone.

No, not alone, thought Shandril. Fire roiled deep within her, where there should have been none. It glinted briefly in her eyes. Not while I live.

She struggled to her knees, set her teeth, and pointed her arms at the mage riding the dragon. She felt sick and as weak as a newborn kitten. Her head throbbed, but fire flowed within her.

Let it be as it was before, she thought. "Whoever you are, evil one, burn! Burn! How *dare* you harm my friends!" she screamed aloud, and spellfire roared up out of her. The crackling bolt drained Shandril utterly. Her knees gave way, and she could not even see if she'd struck true. She fell on her face on the rocks.

Manshoon stared in astonishment at the rushing white fire. Then, in the teeth of its blinding, searing roar, all he could do was scream.

Orlgaun fell away weakly, hearing its master cry out. The dragon drew back, uncertain. It dared not attack anything that had slain Manshoon—and if Manshoon was dead, there was no reason to tarry. It had hurts of its own—deep, raw pain that stabbed its lungs with each wing beat. . . .

Manshoon yet lived, clinging to wits and saddle grimly, barely able to hold himself upright. He could not survive another blast like that—and it had not even come from Elminster. The Old Mage stood calmly waiting. . . .

Manshoon could not continue this battle and live.

Beyond Elminster lay the young maiden who'd come crawling out from the gods only knew where to smite him with raw magical fire . . . fabled spellfire!

Manshoon shuddered, glanced around quickly to be sure neither of the flying foes was near, and urged Orlgaun northward. With a snarled command, he bade the dragon tilt its body to shield him from any spells the Old Mage might unleash. Just now, a good battle spell would finish him.

The air crackled, and there was a flash as one last lightning bolt struck. Orlgaun convulsed, great wings shuddering. For long moments they fell through the air before the dragon caught itself and raggedly flew again.

Manshoon drew a deep breath. He'd escaped alive. Not quite the achievement he'd expected.

"Shandril!" was all Narm said. It was all he needed to say as they hugged each other fiercely.

Around them, the Knights of Myth Drannor used Art to heal each other. They packed more treasure, saw to their weapons, and laughed.

In their midst, Elminster had cast another spell and now stared north with a frown of concentration.

At last, when the Knights were as whole as could be managed and heavily laden with coins and jewels, Jhessail went to the embracing couple and touched Narm on the shoulder.

"Are you well?" she asked softly. The other Knights gathered around, Rathan and Torm grinning openly.

"Yes," Narm said thickly, into Shandril's hair. "Right well." He anxiously disengaged himself and asked, "How fare you, my lady?"

Shandril smiled. "I live. I love you. I'm most well!"

Narm smiled back, and then asked very softly, "May I take you to wife, Shandril Shessair?"

Jhessail turned to seek Merith's eyes and found his gaze already on her. They shared a smile of their own.

The Knights waited. Shandril's face was hidden in her hair, her head bent. Florin looked away in sudden dismay. Silence fell.

Shandril's shoulders shook. She was crying. Her slim hands reached out, found Narm's shoulders, and pulled herself into his embrace. "Oh yes. *Yes*. Please the gods, *yes!*"

The Knights let out a roar of pleasure and congratulation. Hands pounded the young couple's shoulders. Jhessail and Merith embraced, Rathan raised a wineskin, and Torm laughed and tossed a dagger high. It fell twinkling.

The thief raced over to Elminster, who stood motionless, his back to them all. Torm caught at his sleeve, tugged the startled mage around, and shook him in glee.

Elminster spoke mildly, but there was a glint in his eyes. "Ye've ruined the spell, and I've lost him. Ye'd better have a good reason for this, Torm, son of Dathguld!"

Torm stopped in midlaugh, astonished. "Y-you know who my father was?"

Elminster waved one hand in dismissal. "Of course. Now, I asked thee thy reason for all this hooting and slapping me about and dancing even now on my very *toes!*"

"Oh." For once in his life, Torm could think of little more to say. He backed his feet clear of the Old Mage's and his hands free of Elminster's clothing. Then his joy and purpose returned to him in a rush. "Narm and Shandril are to be wed! What say you? *Wed*, I say!"

The wizard looked bewildered, and then cross. "Is *that* all? Oh, aye—any fool could see it coming. Ye spoiled my spell and lost me my hook on Manshoon for *that*? Garrrgh!" He stamped his foot and turned in a swirl of dusty robes, leaving Torm to stare after him, mouth agape.

The thief recovered his customary grin when he saw that Elminster headed straight for the laughing, embracing couple.

"Dolt," said Rathan affectionately, and pressed his wineskin into Torm's hands. "Come, sit, and have drink."

Torm shuddered. "I hate this swill! Can't we just play pranks on each other, instead?"

"I have wondered, friend Torm," came Florin's grave voice, "just what you do when really happy . . . and now I know. Wonders anew unfold before my eyes every day. But the message I presently bear is to your damp companion. Rathan, Narm and Shandril would speak with you and myself as soon as the gods will and our pleasure is met."

Rathan looked at him, surprised at the ranger's smooth formality, and nodded in understanding. "Aye. Of course!"

He thrust the skin into Torm's hands, and said, "Mind this for me, Torm? Thankee." Two strides away, he stopped, whirled, and added sternly, "And no pranks, mind!"

Torm shrugged and spread his hands in mock innocence. "Is it my open, honest face? My kind, forgiving manner? My gentle disposition?"

"Nay," said Elminster dryly. " 'Tis thy long, crooked tongue." The Old Mage put his hand under the thief's elbow as he passed and drew him along. "Come. Thy presence is required."

Narm looked up at Rathan, his arm about Shandril and an eager light about his face. Yet he spoke gently and hesitantly. "I—I've no gift to give you, good guide of Tymora. But I—we—could you wed us two, and soon?"

Rathan grinned back. "Of course, but a gift indeed ye have!" He gestured about them where coins gleamed amid the dust. "One of those, perhaps," he said gruffly. "Mind 'tis a gold one."

Stammering his thanks, Narm plucked up a gold piece in fumbling haste and pressed it into the priest's palm.

Rathan held it high, looked around at the Knights, and announced, "Tymora looks down on us and finds this good, and shines the bright face of good fortune upon this union."

As he spoke, the coin suddenly shone with a glow of its own. Rathan cradled it as if he held something precious. "By this sign of her favor, I declare ye two handfast, to be wed at the nearest convenience. All ye who are here, cry: 'Aye.' "

The chorus of "ayes" rang out. The sun shone with sudden

brightness through clouds and drifting smoke. A beam of golden light touched the coin in Rathan's fingers. There was a flash, and it was gone.

Narm, who'd secretly doubted the stout priest's piety, gasped in awe. Rathan spread his empty hands in benediction, and took Narm's hand. He clasped it with Shandril's under his own, and then stepped back, bowed, and became the stout and sodden Rathan again.

"Our thanks, Rathan," Shandril said huskily.

The priest bowed again. "Tymora's will, but my pleasure."

"My lord Florin," Narm said to the tall ranger in the scorched and claw-scraped armor, "may we come to Shadowdale for a time? We've no home, and my lady . . . no, we are *both* weary of running and fighting and never knowing rest, or a home. This is much to ask, I know, but—"

"No more drivel," said Torm unexpectedly. "Of *course* you'll come to the dale . . . where else would you go?"

Florin looked at him sternly, and then grinned. "In truth, Torm, I could have put it in no better words. You're both welcome as long as you desire. I daresay you can study Art better in Shadowdale's peace and quiet—relative though that may prove—than out here, as mage after mage hurls it at you."

"Study?" asked Narm faintly, staring at Elminster, who puffed his pipe expressionlessly.

"Yes, with Illistyl and I," Jhessail told him. "*He*," she added, nodding at Elminster, "will be studying your bride. It's been a long time since someone mastered spellfire so ably—and survived its use so well."

In a vaulted stone hall, flames flickered red and orange in two braziers. Between them stood an altar of black stone, polished smooth and shaped like a gigantic throne, forty feet high. At the foot of the Seat of Bane was a much smaller throne, and on it sat a cold-eyed man with pale brown hair and wan features. His high-cowled black robe was of simple cut, and his hands gleamed with many rings. None living knew his true name, save himself;

few knew his common name. He was the High Imperceptor of Bane, and he was very angry.

"Give me good reason," he said coldly to those who knelt before him, "why I should not put you to death. You've failed me. We cannot move against the traitor Fzoul with Manshoon in the city, or we shall know certain defeat. You had the message to Manshoon but delivered it not. Why?"

"M-my lord," said one of those kneeling, "the message was about to be passed to Manshoon, in a believable manner—for that, we needed the lords to be on the topic, or he might have smelled out our ruse. The meeting was scarce begun, the fool Kalthas telling all grandly that garrisons across the North were needless, when Manshoon rose, upsetting table and all. He—he wept, Dread Lord. He whispered a word, 'Maruel' or some such, and summoned a scrying crystal. He peered into it . . ."

"The word of summoning!" the High Imperceptor interrupted. "What was it?"

"Ah . . . a moment, Dread Lord. It began 'Zell'. . . ah . . . ah, 'twas 'Zellathorass'!" the kneeling man said triumphantly.

The High Imperceptor nodded. "Rise, and continue."

Bowing, the man did. "The—the word he banished the globe with, Dread Lord, was 'Alvathair,' I do recall. He seemed furious, and dismissed us, saying, 'Sirs, this meeting is at an end. For your safety, leave at once.' And he called down gargoyles on us, and—we fled."

"Did you see where Manshoon went?" asked the High Imperceptor eagerly.

"N-no, Dread Lord. He was not seen in the city all the rest of that day." The speaker spread his hands. "We came straight to you, for fear of delivering our message wrongly once the chance you'd directed us to take was lost."

The High Imperceptor nodded shortly. "Well spoken, well recalled. Rise, all of you." When the shuffling and rustling had died away, he looked down at the line of men. "Do any of you have aught else to report?"

One named Theln spoke. "Aye, Dread Lord!" He was gestured to continue. "I met with a merchant loyal to the Black Lord"—he bowed to the great throne—"who told me of a young girl on her way to Shadowdale with those who call themselves the Knights of Myth Drannor. This maid can by some means produce spellfire. He said this fire can strike through magical barriers and empty air and is very powerful."

The High Imperceptor leaned forward on his throne, interested. At his subtle gesture, an unseen upperpriest behind black tapestries cast a spell to detect lies. "They take her to Elminster, no doubt. Very powerful, indeed. If we held this power, we could strike down those who oppose our Great Lord"—all save the High Imperceptor bowed again—"and those traitors who were once our brothers. We must try for this spellfire, if this tale be true. This faithful—who is he, and how old his news?"

"One Raunel, a dealer in sausages from the Vilhon Reach. He spoke to me on the road very close. He said he'd spoken with a forester who'd seen the girl near the Thunder Peaks late yestermorn. He shared a roadside fire with this forester, one Hylgaun, yestereve."

The High Imperceptor almost smiled. "You've done well, Theln. You'll be rewarded. Go call on the priest Laelar to attend us at once. All of you, leave us!"

The last to leave stepped from behind tapestries, bowed, and said merely, "No lies, Dread Lord." He left.

Good, thought the High Imperceptor. That leaves only two possible liars: Raunel and Hylgaun. It *felt* true.

When he was alone, the cold-eyed man looked thoughtfully across the empty chamber. "Maruel . . . Maruel. I know that name." He caught up the great black mace and hefted its dark, cruel length. Why could he never remember such things? Why? It could well bring death one day . . . the wrong detail forgotten, the wrong precaution taken. The High Imperceptor sighed. It had not been a good day.

The black dragon's flight was heavy and ragged. Often its wings faltered, and it sank to one side or the other. Orlgaun was sorely hurt, and might never bear Manshoon again.

That thought burned Manshoon, atop his defeat. He almost

turned back in anger to slay with the Art he held ready. Nay, such a foray was impossible. Orlgaun was flying on the last of its lagging strength, lower than Manshoon would have preferred. The endless green of the Elven Court stretched beneath them. The dragon flew north and east.

Manshoon thought back over the fray and concluded bitterly he'd not slain a single foe. Elminster had shielded them at first, aye, but few could survive Manshoon of Zhentil Keep and Orlgaun both. That cursed elf, and the ranger with his flying shield! He could feel their blades. . . .

They'd not live long, once he had that girl in his hands, even if they hadn't slain Symgharyl Maruel.

The thought of the Shadowsil's passing made him feel dark and weak inside. He rose out of that momentary sadness feeling savage. Manshoon clutched a wand, wanting very badly to strike down something.

Then he frowned. The girl. Yes. It *had* been spellfire that had scorched him. He still smarted despite all the healing potions he'd drunk, emptying the belt across his stomach.

Gods, but it hurt! It was fortunate she was so untutored in battle, or Manshoon might well have fallen. Her power must be his own, and soon, before Elminster mastered it! Not such an old fool, that one. Not aggressive, but even stronger in Art than most thought. His killing would take considerable whelmed Art, something best prepared forthwith, back at—

Bane preserve us! We're flying among the trees!

Orlgaun had sunk as Manshoon pondered, the great wings moving more feebly—and suddenly its claws and belly were crashing through the uppermost branches of the tallest trees.

Manshoon shouted, hauling on the fin before him. Shadowtops and duskwoods loomed ahead. The dragon did not respond, and trees stretched on as far as the eye could see, with only a few gaps, just ahead.

Manshoon cursed feelingly. The dragon descended through snapping, whipping branches, buffeting its rider. The blows grew steadily harder as Orlgaun sank full into the trees. The fierceness of its fall smashed larger trunks aside and crushed saplings outright.

Slowing, they struck the next tree, and the next. Manshoon crouched, grimly fending off branches, as the great wyrm came down to earth.

Orlgaun did not even grunt; perhaps its spirit had already fled its torn and battered body. Certainly this would be its last flight. One wing struck a gigantic phandar that broke into man-length splinters. The wing shattered, too. Head-on, the dragon hit a stand of shadowtops, and the world itself seemed to shake and split asunder.

Manshoon found himself hanging head-down in a tangled ruin of shadowtop boughs and leaves. Orlgaun lay belly-up, twisted and impaled on smashed and splintered wood. The mage crawled and slipped until he fell out of the branches to the leaf-strewn ground.

Gasping, he scrambled out from under the vast carcass. He'd lost the wand, though he still carried items of power aplenty. Ahead, in the direction the dragon had been flying, the trees thinned into a clearing. In all other directions stretched vast green dimness, still echoing with Orlgaun's fall.

Manshoon took a step forward, and another, and then stared in shock at a bat-winged, horned, tusked, grinning creature. A malebranche! It had sprung out of the trees in front of him.

Beyond it, another flashed fangs in an eager smile. Quick glances showed others, approaching swiftly. The devils of Myth Drannor!

Backing away, the High Lord of Zhentil Keep cast a spell in grim haste. As his lightning struck down the nearest devil, he cursed loudly and fled as fast as his legs would go. The trees here grew too thickly even to fly!

Devils laughed. Manshoon snatched a wand of paralyzing rays from his belt and thought about how best to use the paltry magic. It had not been a good day.

10

Full Flagons

I have known high honor, proud fame, and great riches, and have drunk deep of good wine at feasts where my mouth watered and my belly was filled with delightful viands amid good fellowship and conversation . . . and I tell you that all these pale and drift away as idle dreams before the gentle touch of my Lady.

Mirt "the Moneylender" of Waterdeep
in a letter to Khelben Blackstaff Arunsun
proclaiming his lover Asper his lawful heir
Year of the Harp

The Knights had left Rauglothgor's shattered lair behind and traveled north into the woods. The Thunder Peaks marched on their left as they went, walking until night. They rose with the dawn and continued again until nightfall.

In Mistledale, they purchased mules. Elminster let lapse the last of a succession of floating discs he'd conjured to carry Shandril, despite her protests.

A footsore Narm clambered onto his mule, which gave him an unfriendly look. Narm's thighs ached. He glanced enviously at the Knights, who vaulted into their saddles and traded jests with unflagging enthusiasm. They were obviously used to walking miles at a stretch, from aged Elminster to graceful Lady Jhessail.

As they plunged back into the woods, along a narrow, gloomy path, Rathan began a ballad of Tymora's favor. Torm parodied line after line until Rathan ceased with a sigh. Though they were barely out of sight of Mistledale, deep green dimness surrounded them now.

Shandril leaned close to Narm. "How far is Myth Drannor?"

Before Narm could say he knew not, Jhessail turned in her saddle. "Due east, several days distant. The river Ashaba lies between us and Myth Drannor at all times. The gate the Shadowsil forced you through took you across half the dales to the dracolich's lair."

The couple's shared sigh of relief was cut short by Torm's dry, sharp voice: "We can head that way if you'd like. I hear one can have a *devil* of a time there, heh-heh. . . ."

He smiled benignly at the chorus of dirty looks flung his way. Someone had to provide entertainment, after all.

⊠ ⊠ ⊠

The golden light of approaching sunset glinted on leaves ahead, yet the Knights pressed on. Biding beside each other except where trees forced them into single file, Narm and Shandril clasped hands. Whatever happened, they were together.

When dusk came, Merith and Jhessail conjured glowing motes of light that drifted along with the Knights, bobbing and darting to illuminate this or that tangle of brush. They rode on slowly through gathering darkness. The soft singing of crickets died away in front of them only to begin again behind. In the forest gloom to the right, the travelers saw occasional glows of eerie gray-green and blue.

"What's that?" Narm asked, pointing at one. "Witchfire?"

Merith nodded. "Glow moss, witchfire, and other fungi that shine at night. Elves call them all, in Common, 'nightshine.' " The elf lounged in his saddle, helm hung on its horn, very much at ease.

Of course, Shandril thought, feeling less awed and much safer.

To Merith, this endless wood is home. She relaxed and soon sank low in her saddle.

Jhessail quietly worked a spell of sleep on Shandril and Narm, who rode nodding along on slumber's edge. Merith took charge of the mules as his lady cast a floating disc.

Torm chuckled softly, boosting the sleepers from saddles to disc—and then yawned himself.

"Oh, no, you don't!" Jhessail warned. "Get back on your mule!"

Torm spread his hands in injured and feigned innocence. "Why you think these terrible things of me I don't know—let Faerûn know I'm grievously wronged, and—" He staggered under a solid nudge in the back from his mule.

His friends burst into laughter.

"Be an adventurer," he grumbled as he settled himself in his saddle. "Become rich and famous, they said. Hmph!"

"Famous, anyway," Merith assured him. "I've seen notices with your picture posted here and there—parchments that mention large sums of coin. Then there're all these men with knives who keep calling on you. . . ."

Torm made a rude noise. It was returned with spirit from Elminster, who rode in stately dignity ahead, startling everyone into silence. It all made no difference to the mules.

The sun was bright and high when Narm and Shandril slowly awoke. Their arms had crept about each other in slumber, and they were drowsy and deeply rested.

Narm saw sun-dappled leaves overhead, heard the familiar creak of leather and soft thud of mule-hooves, and relaxed. Shandril lay warm against his left side. His hand tingled. He wiggled his fingers to bring feeling back, and felt her stir. Then he realized he was flat on his back, with no mule bumping and shifting beneath him. He sat up in alarm.

He and Shandril floated serenely along on a disc of firm nothingness. Jhessail rode just behind them and Merith just ahead. Beyond Elminster's shoulder, Lanseril led them along a brightening way.

Jhessail smiled reassuringly. "Well met, this morn. We're almost in Shadowdale."

Shandril sleepily pulled herself up Narm's shoulder to see. They emerged from the trees into a passage between two redoubts of heaped stones. Silver and blue banners, emblazoned with the spiral tower and crescent moon of Shadowdale, stirred in the faint morning breeze. Men wearing the same emblem on their surcoats stood watching warily, pikes and crossbows ready in their hands.

" 'Ware!" called one guard formally, barring the way to the bridge. The sudden recognition of the lords and lady of the dale had them bowing and standing aside. The sight of Elminster made the guards fall completely silent. Without a word of query or challenge, Narm and Shandril passed over Mill Bridge into the dale.

No escort rode with them as they passed lush green meadows. The dale opened before them, framed by forest on either side. Trees stood in great green walls.

Shandril looked about happily.

Narm, who'd seen it before, asked Jhessail, "Lady, may we ride? I would feel . . . less the fool. My thanks for the traveling bed—'tis a trick I must learn one day. It moves where you will it?"

"It does, though if you mind it not, it follows twenty paces behind—and if you proceed where it can't follow, it passes away, dumping what it carries!" Jhessail grinned. "Of course you shall ride—'twould not do for you to look different fools than the rest of us."

So they rode to the Twisted Tower. Mourngrym came striding out, his cloak flapping, and looked at Narm.

"So here you are back, and not only do you stick your neck into clear danger, but you drag all my protectors and companions with you, even Elminster, and leave the dale undefended." His eyes twinkled. "And do I look upon the reason for your return to peril? Lady, I am Mourngrym, the lord left behind to sit the dale seat whilst his elders take the air, see sights, and enjoy journeys. Welcome! How may I call you?"

"Lord Mourngrym, I am Shandril Shessair," Shandril said,

blushing faintly in shyness. "I am handfast to Narm." Her voice lowered in curiosity. "These Knights are your comrades? You've ridden to battle together?"

Mourngrym laughed. "Indeed," he said, handing her down onto a stool. "What you know of them hints at how wild the saga of our adventures is, thus far." Merith clapped him on the shoulder, and Mourngrym's grin widened. "I'm afraid you'll have to wait until too much drink has flowed before I start telling such tales, though others here"—he looked meaningfully at Torm—"are weaker."

They went into the tower. "How was your journey?" Mourngrym asked Narm as they entered a feasting hall. The mingled smell of cooking bacon and a great spiced stew made mouths water.

"Oh," Narm replied mildly, steadying Shandril as they came to the table, "eventful."

"You are called to feast, Lady," said the serving maid. Through the open door Shandril could hear soft harping. "One waits to take you down. Shall I send him in?"

"Oh—yes. Please," Shandril replied, rising from the round, canopied bed.

She gazed around at the beautiful bedchamber, with its hangings of elven warriors riding stags through the forest—the High Hunt of the Elven Court, a unicorn glowing in the far-off trees ahead. Shandril's gown, too, was a beautiful thing, Calishite silk overlaid with a fine tabard for warmth in the stone halls of the North. The tabard's beading interwove crescent moons, silver horns, and unicorns. On her arm, she proudly wore her joined ring and bracelet of electrum and sapphires. It awed Shandril to see herself in the great burnished metal mirror.

In came Narm, in a great-sleeved tunic of wine-purple velvet, matching silk hose, and boots trimmed with fur. The lion-headed dagger hung from his belt. His hair had been washed and trimmed and doused with perfume-water, and his eyes outshone the rings on his fingers.

Eyes shining, he took a hesitant step. "My lady?" She turned wordlessly. "Shandril? You're beautiful." His voice was very quiet. "As graceful as any high lady I've ever seen."

"And how many such ladies have you seen?" Shandril teased. "It's still the same me, if I'm in plain gray robes or a man's tunic and breeches!"

"Yes," Narm said. "But I fear even to touch you, when you're clad thus. I could only mar perfect beauty." Torm would have made that sentence a lilting mockery, but Narm's voice was husky and serious.

"Shameless flatterer," Shandril reproved. "If that's so, I'll have this all off and go down in thieves' leathers. I'd rather be on your arm in rags than grandly clad but walking alone."

"No, no," Narm said, taking her arm. "I can conquer my fears—see?—only promise you'll talk with me after all the hurly-burly. I would not soon forget how you look now."

"Let us go down to table, my lord. Your hunger is weakening your wits." Shandril led him to the door.

In the passage, under the politely averted eyes of a guard, the young mage turned Shandril about and kissed her. The soft fanfare summoning all to first table sounded twice ere they parted and went downstairs. The guard kept his face carefully expressionless.

⊠ ⊠ ⊠

"Thank you, but no, Lord. Truly, I can eat no more," Shandril protested, holding up a hand in front of a platter of steaming boar in gravy.

Mourngrym laughed. "Well enough, but the more you eat, the longer you can drink. When these here can't eat a crumb more, they can yet find room to drink. It's a mystery why some who come to my table say they are come to a 'feast,' when they eat a few bites and then hoist flagons all night through."

"I—I should be sick if I tried, Lord," Shandril said simply.

Mourngrym smiled again. "I'm similarly affected. If you two can spare us a few words before retiring, my Lady Shaerl and I would be happy to have your company in the bower upstairs. I believe you've met Storm Silverhand and Sharantyr. We'll have other guests, Jhessail and Elminster among them. Go up when you can't hear each other anymore—it grows much noisier. If you'll forgive me, I must walk among my people. When their tongues are wet and loose, I learn their true grievances and concerns." He nodded to them and rose.

Narm and Shandril exchanged glances. All around them was tumult. Softly glowing glass globes lit the hall. At one end, a gigantic fire blazed beneath spits of boar and ox, filling the room with aromatic smoke. The long board was crammed with platters and decanters. A harpist and a glaurist played almost unheard in the din of laughing and talking.

Most of the Knights were there. Torm was nearly unrecognizable in dazzling, almost foppish finery—fur-trimmed silks with winking gems. Fine chains of gold studded with large rubies and emeralds looped across his stomach. His doublet flared into slit and puffed sleeves. A single giant king's tear hung in silky clarity on his bared breast, cupped in a webwork of polished electrum. The thief outshone Mourngrym and all the bejeweled ladies in the room. He strode grandly about, drinking from a massive chased silver tankard as tall as his forearm.

He caught Shandril's eye, winked, and from one sleeve plucked a silver-hilted dagger whose blade was needle-thin and dull black. Tossing it casually into the air, he caught it, winked again, and put it away in one casual, smooth motion.

Rathan rolled his eyes at the feat. Ruddy-faced and amiable, the priest looked resplendent in green velvet, a disc of Tymora gleaming in mirror-bright silver on his breast.

Many diners stood now, and a few danced. Far across the room, Narm caught sight of the commanding height and broad shoulders of Florin. The ranger looked every inch a king. Beside him stood a lady Narm had last seen on a forest trail near Myth Drannor, and before that in the taproom of the Rising Moon in Deepingdale—Storm Silverhand. She wore a simple gown of gray silk, with only a broad black cummerbund and a silver-hilted dagger for ornament.

"Look," Shandril breathed, pointing. Storm looked so regal that the maid of Highmoon forgot what her own fine gown did for her.

"Yes," Narm murmured and swallowed audibly. "I see." Swiftly, he turned to Lanseril, who stood nearby, talking to a burly, bearded man in amber and russet. The druid wore a simple brown woolen robe. Narm said, "Pray excuse my interruption, friend Lanseril."

"No excuse needed, Narm," Lanseril replied with a warm smile. "My life is a series of interruptions." He bent his head near. "What is it?"

"Lord Florin—is Lady Storm his—ah, handfast to him, or—?"

Lanseril chuckled. "Florin's married to Storm's sister, the ranger Dove, who's soon to bear his child, and is for her safety presently elsewhere. Storm's man, Maxam, was killed this past summer. She does not speak of that, mind. Florin and Storm are friends who keep each other from being lonely at dance and table. Despite what Torm may hint, they're no more than that."

The druid turned and touched the sleeve of the man he had been speaking with. "May I introduce Thurbal, Captain-of-Arms and Warden of Shadowdale?"

Thurbal, a man of weather-beaten and plain features, whose eyes were both shrewd and kind, bowed. "Lady Shandril and Lord Narm, I bid you my own welcome. Have you enjoyed the feast thus far?"

"I—I, yes, greatly," Narm, replied, eyes falling to the plain-scabbarded broadsword Thurbal wore at his side.

"It's the first feast I've ever been invited to, Lord," Shandril replied. "I—I'm no high lady, I fear."

Thurbal frowned slightly. "My pardon. I assumed—ah, but no harm done if you'll forgive me. I'm no lord, either. Lord Lanseril told me something of your importance. I hope you'll not take offense if I seem to always be watching you closely. My brawn is on the block, so to speak, if you're endangered when I might have prevented it."

"Endangered?" Narm asked, as Shandril paled. "Here?"

Thurbal spread broad, heavy hands. "We live in a world of magic, Lord. There are no sure defenses. All the steel I can muster to your lady's guard can't stop magic. I sometimes wonder what Faerûn would be like if all men had to stand or fall by their actions at the end of a sword, and there was no magic.

Then again, such a world might be a worse mess than this one!"

"But we have enemies?" Narm asked soberly.

Lanseril shrugged. "Shandril, or the two of you together, can create and hurl spellfire, something infamous in the histories of Art—a weapon very powerful indeed. Many would like to have sole control over it. Watch the shadows, expecting trouble, even here."

"And get used to being 'lord' and 'lady'," Thurbal added with a grin. "All the Knights hold that title, and you stand with them until you declare and choose otherwise. My men will obey and aid you the better if they think you are lord and lady of the dale." He added a trifle hesitantly, "Lady Shandril, I've been told of how you put Manshoon of Zhentil Keep to flight. I bow to you. Even using Art the rest of us lack, that's no light thing to have done."

"Have you enemies, indeed?" Lanseril put in. "Manshoon is no little one—I don't doubt he yet lives!" Shandril shuddered. He patted her shoulder hastily. "Think no more of this. Enjoy this night, and let the morrow look to its own problems."

"Easy enough to say," Narm told him. "Not so easy to *not* think of something!"

Lanseril nodded. "True, and I'm sorry I brought your thoughts to this now. On the other hand, 'tis the most important training you can have for magecraft. You must be able to control your thoughts as an acrobat controls his hands if you're to survive spell against spell." He waved northeast, in the direction of distant Zhentil Keep. "If ever you speak with Manshoon, you'll find him cold and controlled. Elminster might seem whimsical, but he is not underneath. Those who lack control never live to reach such power, unless their Art's never challenged." He smiled. "But enough. I must watch over these fools while you speak with the more sober upstairs."

"You?" Shandril asked in surprise.

Lanseril looked at her. "Of course. Are these"—he spread his hands to indicate the revelers all around—"not creatures under my care here in the dale, even as the chipmunks and the farmwives' cats?"

He left Shandril staring thoughtfully after him and strode to where Torm stood laughing, each arm around a local beauty.

Narm shook his head. "I don't know these folk, really, yet," he said in her ear, "but they're good folk—as good as any I've ever known."

"I know," Shandril whispered back. "That's why I'm so afraid we'll bring death down upon them by coming here."

Narm looked at her somberly. In a low voice, he said, "We have to, Shan. We'll die without their protection."

Shandril nodded. "Yes. So I am here." She saw Mourngrym walking slowly with Storm and Florin toward the doors. "We should follow. They're going up now, I think."

Narm nodded and led her through the tumult of dancing and talk and laughter. Thurbal quietly followed, staying distant, eyes moving constantly.

Torchlight filled the passage, reflecting off flagons and goblets in plenty. Richly clad men and women leaned against the walls, laughing and talking, drinks in hand. Shandril heard a snatch of one story that was considered old even in the Rising Moon. On Narm's arm, she ascended the stairs. They followed a regal lady in shimmering blue-green who wore a twinkling diadem. At the top, when she turned, they saw that it was Jhessail.

She smiled. "Such long faces. Do you like feasts so little?"

"No, it's not that," Shandril whispered. "We fear to bring danger on you all."

Jhessail shook her head as they walked together. "We stand in danger at all times. Zhentil Keep attacks every summer, at the least. The Cult of the Dragon and the dark elves constantly menace. Myth Drannor's devils, the lawlessness in Daggerdale . . . adventurers may move on, but we cannot move the dale. Once we accepted Shadowdale, we became targets, and remain so. Why else live so high as we do tonight? I could be slain tomorrow. Should I therefore be miserable today? Why not make the best of every moment?" She took Narm's free hand, and drew them both into the bower. "Come, let us talk of other things!"

Behind them, Thurbal watchfully topped the stairs.

Within, it was much quieter than below. Florin greeted them with a firm arm clasp, warrior to warrior.

Storm smiled and kissed them, saying, "Seldom do I see two who've entered Myth Drannor return again alive!"

Beyond her stood another lovely lady with long, silky hair. She wore a gown of rich blue that left flanks and back bare. It had been a long road from the taproom of the Rising Moon, and some moments passed before Shandril recognized her.

"Sharantyr!" Shandril burst out and found herself in a warm embrace.

Illistyl meanwhile introduced Narm to Mourngrym's wife, Lady Shaerl.

A sudden silence fell. Atop a table that had been empty a moment before, someone appeared. Thurbal came in the door, sword half-drawn, and then halted, shaking his head.

"Elminster!" Jhessail greeted him. "Well met!"

"Aye . . . aye," Elminster told her. "I've seen all of ye before. 'Tis Narm and Shandril I'd speak with tonight." He looked to where the young couple stood in astonishment. "I fear I lack the patience for courtly graces, glib flattery, and suchlike. So I'll just ask ye straight, Narm and Shandril—will ye agree to a test of thy powers this next night?"

Shandril nodded, her throat suddenly dry.

Narm asked quietly, "Will it be dangerous?"

Elminster looked at him. "Breathing is dangerous, lad. Walking is dangerous. Sleeping can even be dangerous. Will it be more dangerous than these? A little. More dangerous than entering Myth Drannor alone? Nay, not by a long road!"

Narm flushed. "It would be a terrible thing, Old Mage, to fight you tongue to tongue."

A roar of delighted laughter rose around him.

Elminster chuckled. "So, ye agree?"

Narm nodded. "Yes. Where and when?"

"Ye'll know that only at the last. 'Tis safer." Around them, talk began again. The wizard leaned close. "Do ye enjoy this company?"

Narm and Shandril nodded together.

"Good. Most of these folk will be at the testing!" He patted Narm's shoulder in farewell, turned to the table, and then whirled back around. "I do grow forgetful. Shandril, what know ye of thy parents?"

Shandril reeled in surprise and sadness. "I . . . I—nothing."

Narm and Elminster looked at each other, and the Old Mage clapped Narm on the shoulder again. "Forgive, if ye will. I'd no wish to upset. Comfort her, will ye? You can do it best of all living in Faerûn!" The wizard turned away, muttering to himself, "That explains much." Stepping onto the table by way of the chair beside it, he was gone.

⊠ ⊠ ⊠

A guard touched Torm's shoulder. "Lord," he said, voice carefully neutral, " 'tis the hour."

Torm looked up from the wench he'd been kissing and sighed. "My thanks, Rold." A sudden thought made him grin impishly. "Take my place, will you?" He rolled off the bed to his feet, adroitly twisting to avoid the girl's angry slap.

Rold solemnly held out his sword and belt. "Me, Lord? 'Twould be more than my life's worth."

"Aye," Torm said as they hurried out together. "I think you have the right of it." He halted midstride, lifted a fine chain off his neck, and handed it to the mustachioed veteran. "Give her this, as a gift from me. My apologies, also, and say I'll try to see her as soon as I can. My duty to Shadowdale comes first."

"Of course, Lord," Rold replied, and turned back to calm Torm's angry companion. He found her sitting morosely amid the disarray of the bed and dropped the chain into her hand.

"It's no fault of yours," he said, "that Lord Torm's so young and ill-reared he cannot give you a night when he's not called to guard duty. He gives you this by way of clumsy apology and sends me to pour soothing words in your ear. I doubt he even knows we're kin."

"I could tell," Naera said, taking her gown as he held it out to her. "Are you angry with him, Uncle?"

Rold shook his head. "Nay, lass, not for long. I've seen something of the road he walks. Are you?" He buttoned and adjusted with much skill and patted her behind fondly when he was done.

"Not after a breath or two. Where did he have to go in such haste?" She looked at the chain dangling in her hands.

"He patrols with Lord Rathan. Elminster expects trouble . . . someone trying to get at our guests."

Naera lifted an eyebrow in astonishment. "The young lad and lass? What danger could they be to anyone?"

Rold chuckled. " 'Young,' says Naera, who dallies with a man younger than herself, a—Oh? Did you not know? Yes, the lord's seen a winter less than you. Don't look like that, now. Was he any greater the monster for that?" He grew serious. "The young lass, as you rightly call her, defeated the High Lord of Zhentil Keep himself, the fell mage Manshoon. Scared him into flight, and him riding a dragon, too! She holds some great power."

Naera stared at him. "Torm's needed to guard *that?*"

Rold nodded. "Why else d'you think I've never spoken ill to you of pursuing him? 'Tis a rare one you chase, for all his rashness and rudeness and dishonest ways. I'd not want to stand against him in a fight." He paused at the door and looked back. "You'd do well to remember that, little one, when next you're sending slaps his way. Come down now, and we'll see what's left at table. You must be hungry after all you've been up to!"

Naera made a face at him, but rose to follow. She wore the chain proudly around her neck as they swept downstairs.

In his chambers, Torm tore off his fine clothing and jewelry like so many rags and pebbles, leaped around finding his gray leathers and blades, and burst back out the door, almost colliding with Rathan.

The priest stood waiting, arms crossed patiently, leaning against the wall.

"Remembered, did ye?" Rathan greeted him jovially. "I warrant ye had help. 'Tis short stature, I tell ye . . . that small head on thy shoulders has no room for a brain that can think, once ye've filled it with mischief until it runs out thy ears and mouth—"

His words were cut short by a shrewd elbow in the belly. They hurried downstairs. Puffing for breath, the cleric leaned on a pillar by the door, furiously thought a prayer to Tymora, and bustled out into the night.

"Remembered, did you?" a mocking voice asked out of darkness.

"Tymora forgive me," Rathan Thentraver said aloud. He swept a pike from the hands of a door guard and rammed its butt into the shadows. He was rewarded by a grunt.

Satisfied, he returned the pike with a nod of thanks. "If ye're *quite* finished playing the bobbing fool, perhaps we can proceed. It might interest ye to know, that the guard ye gave the chain to is the uncle of the maid ye dallied with."

"Oh, gods," came the softly despairing cry. "Why me?"

"I've often wondered that. Truly, the gods must have grander senses of humor than we," Rathan replied. They clapped hands on each other's shoulders and drew weapons. "Now, let's get on with this, shall we?"

They had much wine and talked until late. At the last, Illistyl—she who'd rescued Narm from devils not long ago—and Sharantyr were left in the bower, the ranger a head and more taller than Illistyl as they stood together.

"We should say good night, if we're to be fit for testing on the morrow," Illistyl said wearily, putting down an empty goblet. "You've seen them in battle, have you not? What manner of spell weavers will I be training?"

Sharantyr shook her head. "I never saw them fight. Perhaps you should come to the task, if it falls to you, knowing nothing of them and alert for all. What say you?"

Illistyl nodded and sighed. "You have the right of it." She turned for the door. "Good even, sister-at-arms. I must seek my bed before I fall on my face."

"Good even," Sharantyr replied, hugging her. Kissing cheeks, they parted.

The ranger wandered down the stairs a little dizzily, nodding to the guards. Setting her goblet on a table, she sought cool air to clear her head, and went out by the front doors.

One of the guards asked, "Would you have an escort, Lady?" He eyed her gown. " 'Tis cold."

"Aye? Oh, no, thank you," Sharantyr told him. " 'Tis the cold I seek," she added, putting the back of her hand to her forehead in mock faintness.

Both guards chuckled and saluted her. "The Lady of the Forest and Tymora both watch over thee, Lady."

Sharantyr nodded and smiled. Past other guards, flaring torches, and the last fading sounds of revelry, she went out into the cool, dark night.

Overhead, Selûne rode high in the starlit night sky, trailing her Tears. Sharantyr stood looking at the bright moon, and then set off for the river at a brisk walk. It'd not do to catch a chill by remaining still too long—and in the cold, her bladder wanted to be free of much wine.

The tall ranger smiled at the dark trees ahead. This was her true home, for all that she'd come to it late. The dizziness was leaving her as she came out into the road, the dew of the meadow on her boots. She let fall the hem of her gown and strode soft-footed toward the bridge.

"Most will be drunk by now," Laelar, the Hammer of Bane, grunted in the dappled moonlight. "Dalefolk are all alike. Too much to eat and too much to drink, and they'll be as sluggish as worms in winter until tomorrow eve, when they do it all over again. The ones we want will be inside and well guarded, but if we're swift enough that they can't wake any mages, there'll be few others to aid them!" The High Imperceptor's henchman spat thoughtfully onto the unseen ground. "You two cast a spell of silence on that stone and bear it as we swim across. Remain by the bank until we have the rope up the tower, and then guard its end and deal with anyone who happens by. We'll up and do the grab. If we pull on the rope thrice, come up to us. Otherwise, stay where you are."

There were nods all around. The curly-haired priest of Bane jerked his chin at the tower across the murmuring, silver-shot river. "Right, onward! Cast your spell!"

The guards on the bridge greeted Sharantyr with polite curiosity and let her pass. In the trees, she glanced back, saw them shrug at each other, and smiled ruefully. No doubt they considered all the Knights truly crazed. She walked on swiftly and quietly, past the temple of Tymora into the deep woods, until she found a stump where she could sit and relax.

After a time, she heard unmistakable noises, and looked up with a frown. There were men moving off to her right. Best to be quiet until she knew who they were and why they were here.

Utter silence fell.

Puzzled, Sharantyr rose and peered through the trees. Eight men crept soundlessly down to the river Ashaba.

⊠ ⊠ ⊠

"Time to stop shivering and make another round of the tower," Torm said. "Even fools know that everything and everyone of value is within. If said dastards aren't creeping through these trees, they'll be over there on the other side of the river, in *those* trees!"

"Think ye so?" Rathan grunted. "If they're as foolish as ye say, why don't they ride right up to the gates pretending friendship and then do their fighting? It'd save a lot of time and creeping around."

Torm chuckled. "Not all bladesmen are as bold—nay, reckless—as certain faithful of Tymora!"

"Of that, ye can be sure. I may be reckless enough to please Tymora, but I'm not reckless enough to creep around as ye do!" He peered ahead. "Look ye, down by the old dock . . . was that not a man moving?"

"I see nothing," Torm muttered. "Get down, will you? They'll be well warned if some great giant with a mace, all aglow with the sanctity of Tymora, sails into their midst. Down!"

Rathan grunted reluctantly to his knees and then chest in the dewy grass.

"Now," Torm continued, "look along the ground and see if Selûne lights them from behind!" His tone changed. "There! Was that the place you saw before?"

"Aye, and there's another." The priest rose to his knee. Holding the disc of Tymora out by its chain, he chanted softly. The silver disc sparkled. Rathan turned his head. "Evil. Aye."

"The prudent thing to do would be to summon guards and create a big fray. Look, they've one of those magical ropes that climbs by itself! By the time we roused all, yon rogues could have done much damage."

Rathan clambered to his feet. "Ye want to have fun? Right. Let's go." His mace gleamed in Selûne's pale light as he raised it. "Don't fall. 'Twould not do for a priest of Tymora to rush like raging lion upon them but arrive alone."

"Keep up, if you can," Torm replied, breaking into a run of frightening speed.

Rathan shook his head, set his shoulders, and followed.

⊠ ⊠ ⊠

Laelar was third of four men on the rope. The adept at its top looked cautiously in a window. If the alarm were raised now, before they could get proper footing, things could go ill indeed. He belched to ease his taut stomach, knowing the magical silence would cover the sound. Overhead, the moon shone uncaring.

There was a violent tug on the rope, and the warrior immediately above Laelar lost hold and crashed down on the Hammer of Bane.

⊠ ⊠ ⊠

Torm rushed right at the two warriors. Blades swept out to impale him, but he dived at the turf in front of them, rolled, and straightened his legs to catch those blades and bring their points down.

Rathan leaned over him, mace glinting, and struck a weighty blow. His target crumpled, neck shattered, and fell to the side, forcing his comrade to leap away or be struck and encumbered.

Torm, on the ground, scissored the second man's legs between his own and twisted. The warrior toppled, arms and blade flailing, and Rathan dealt another heavy blow with his mace.

He spun to see if any of the other rogues were close enough to attack, but the velvet silence had prevented warning. Only the man at the bottom of the rope was turning, startled.

Torm slammed into him like a dark wind and swept him away from the rope into the wall beyond, knife flashing repeatedly as they fell. Only Torm got up.

Rathan hurried to the rope, wrapped his hand around it, hauled mightily, let go, and stepped back—not a breath too soon. Two mailed bodies crashed into the space he'd just left. Rathan struck again with his mace.

Tymora smiles, surely, or it could never be this easy.

It wasn't. One of the two still moved.

Torm sprang catlike, dagger raised—and was struck by a black rod out of nowhere. The impact shook him from teeth to fingertips. He staggered back soundlessly.

Rathan moved in. Rod struck mace. Rathan felt the jolt up his arm, shuddered—*magic! Gods laugh, wouldn't you know it!*—and struck again.

His blow was countered with a force that drove him back.

A warrior slid down the rope and drew a long blade.

Rathan and Torm advanced together cautiously. A flurry of blows, much shoving and twisting, and the men reeled apart again.

Torm threw daggers at the curly-haired priest with the rod, more to spoil any magic than to injure. The knives were struck aside harmlessly.

The warrior plucked something from his throat and threw it over Torm's shoulder. The world burst into flames.

Torm and Rathan were thrown forward in that terrible silence. Blistering flames raged over and past them. Their foes reeled against the tower wall in the searing heat. The rope, still standing, was blackened in an instant but not burned.

Torm sank to his knees, face twisting in a soundless scream.

Laelar staggered grimly forward, his rod of smiting raised to strike.

Out of the night came something long and slim, feetfirst.

The Hammer of Bane was struck in the neck and throat and flipped over backward like a child's toy. The black rod bounced free of his weakening grasp as he hit the ground.

After her devastating kick, Sharantyr, wet gown plastered to her, landed on her shoulders. She rolled over and up in time to face the warrior. Panting, hands spread but weaponless, she fixed her eyes on his advancing blade.

Suddenly she could hear wet grass slithering under her foe's boots and Torm groaning on the ground nearby—the spell of silence had lifted.

Light sprang into being all around, and Rathan struggled to his feet. Someone—she'd not time to see who—plunged out of the darkness above, smashing to earth with a horrible wet thud.

The warrior rushed her. "Die, bitch!" he hissed, and slashed at her crosswise, a blow she couldn't avoid.

Sharantyr flung herself back. The tip of his blade burned along her ribs. She cursed weakly and struck the ground, rolling straight into Torm.

Oh, gods, she thought, this is it.

She twisted, trying to raise her feet to kick away the killing blade.

It never came. There was a solid, meaty thwack to her right, grunts and the ringing clang of hard-driven metal, and a crash in the wet grass.

A weak whisper by her elbow said, "Good lady, I fear you're lying on my arm. It's almost worth the pain, for the view."

Sharantyr grinned in spite of herself. "Sorry, Torm." She fell onto her side and rolled clear.

Across the beaten grass, a blackened Rathan thoughtfully picked up the black rod. Hefting it, he brought it down on the back of the warrior's neck and then smartly rapped the helm of the priest of Bane. He looked up.

Mourngrym leaned out the window above, Jhessail beside him, wand in hand. "All well?" he called.

Mutely shaken heads answered.

Guards and hastily roused acolytes rushed up, waving weapons.

"Don't kill that one," Rathan said faintly, pointing the rod at the cleric of Bane. "Mourngrym will want to question someone about this, and I'd rather it wasn't me." Then, laying aside his mace and his cares, he quietly fainted.

11

To Make a Cat Laugh

There comes a time in the dance of man and maid when truths must be told. Wise folk see to it that such times come early and often. Most of us leave such uncomfortable moments until far too late, when words are apt to burn—or worse.

Dauthin Maer
master merchant of Baldur's Gate
My Battered Tankard Filled
Year of the Bridle

Dawn came clear and chillingly cold, though the sun shone on the Thunder Peaks above. The small party of Dragon Cultists climbed the last reaches of a familiar trail and stopped to stare at the destruction.

Where a stone keep had stood above the cavernous lair of Rauglothgor the Undying Wyrm, there was now a vast, round basin of tumbled rock. Coins glimmered in the early light.

"May the dead dragons wake," a shocked Arkuel muttered.

Malark ignored the blasphemy in his own amazement and gathering rage. It was as those cowards had said. The girl had blown the entire mountaintop asunder. The hallowed Rauglothgor, his treasure, and the armory of the Followers were gone.

This was magic such as the gods must have hurled when the world was young! Oh, aye, a dozen archmages could wreak such a result on undefended, unmagical walls, given time—but *one* girl-child, untutored and alone, in the midst of battle?

Malark drew off his gloves. A formidable foe, if she could do this to great Rauglothgor. She must die. The honor of the cult, of Sammaster First-Speaker, now dust in a ruined city, and of Rauglothgor, now destroyed, demanded it.

The safety of us all, he thought wryly, also demands it.

Malark, Archmage of the Purple, sat slim and cruel in his saddle and stared with cold black eyes. He gestured to the coins. "Pick those up—all of them. Let the treasure of Rauglothgor be recovered."

He dismounted, cloak swirling, and strode to stare at the shattered stone. Gods above, he thought, shaken anew. The entire mountain has been smashed. He looked at the fist-sized rubble, recalled the tower on its bare ridge of rock, and shook his head. He was this but could scarcely believe it. Even the great Shargrailar could not work such shattering.

He, Malark Himbruel, must stand against—and defeat—the power that had done this.

If not he, who? There were the liches, yes, but liches were chancy. They served only themselves and, like the wine of Eversult, did not travel well. There were lesser mages among the Followers, but he dared not let one prevail against an important foe, lest his own standing in the Purple be threatened.

He was not loved. Most of the Followers hated and feared magic they couldn't control. They'd not be slow to replace him if more biddable mages came to hand. Of course, they'd merely exchange one dangerous blade for another—but by then it would be too late for Malark.

What would it be—poison? A knife while he slept? A spell duel? The Purple would run red then.

There were ten nonmages in the Purple: Salvarad, a dangerous renegade priest of Talos; Naergoth Bladelord; seven warrior-merchants—vicious clods, every one; and the soft-spoken, slimy little master thief, Zilvreen. They'd all watch Malark Himbruel to see if he put a foot wrong in this affair.

Malark thought silent curses on the head of this mysterious girl and resolved to find a witness to the fray. He *had* to know just what this power was!

Malark let none of this show on his hawkish face as the men-at-arms scrabbled on the rocks. "Enough, Arkuel," he called. "You and Suld, to me. You others, find all treasure, the remains of Rauglothgor, and any other recently dead creatures, and bear them to Oversember." He turned his back and began casting a Tulrun's tracer.

The girl who destroyed this place, Malark ordered firmly in his incantation. The air about him began to glow. The radiance streamed north down the trail, into the trees. Well enough.

"Arkuel, Suld!" he snapped, and led his horse down the trail without looking back. Looking back was a thing the Purple could seldom afford to do.

⊠ ⊠ ⊠

The Seat of Bane stood as empty as ever. The wan-faced High Imperceptor regarded it in awe, as always, in case one day the Black Lord himself should be sitting there.

Empty. The head of the church of Bane sighed and took his own seat. Beside his throne stood a little gong, which he rang with the Black Mace, wielding the great weapon with a strength and skill surprising in one so thin and sallow.

An upperpriest hurried in and knelt before the throne.

"Up, Kuldus. The reports should be in by now. Tell me."

The priest nodded. "There's no report from Laelar yet, Dread Lord, or any with him. Eilius has just come from Zhentil Keep, and he says Manshoon has been absent from the city since the meeting he dismissed! The other lords seek him, and the rebel Fzoul seeks to contact Manxam and the other beholders. The Zhentarim plot and whisper like Calishites!"

The High Imperceptor's smile lit his face as if a flame had kindled within. He rose. "Call the upperpriests! If Laelar reports with the girl, well and good. If he reports and has not taken her, have him return here at once. To Limbo with this maid and her spellfire while we have a chance at Zhentil

Keep and the traitor Fzoul! Go, speedily!"

He whirled the great mace overhead as if it weighed nothing and brought it down on the stone altar with a crash that shook the Seat of Bane.

Kuldus scurried out, the wild laughter of the High Imperceptor ringing in his ears.

⊠ ⊠ ⊠

Dawn's light laid a network of diamonds on the bed as it came through the leaded windows. Narm woke as it touched his face, reaching vaguely for a dagger. Abruptly he recalled where he was: in Shandril's bedchamber. But—where was she?

He sat up, which made his head throb, and looked around. The tapestries were beautiful, as were the vaulted corners of the ceiling, but they were not Shandril. He looked the other way, past an arched wardrobe and a burnished mirror, to the door—which obligingly opened.

A robed but barefoot and damp-tressed Shandril looked in and grinned. "Ah, awake at last. Not feeling ill, I hope?"

Narm held his aching head. "Not really, my lady. Is there morningfeast? And—and a chamber pot?"

Shandril laughed. "How romantic. Morningfeast is an ask-in-the-great-hall affair that lasts until highsun. The pot's under there, if you must, but behind yon door is a jakes with a waterfall-seat—you flush with the jug or hand-pump. All the ladies here have one. Was there not one in your room?"

"No," Narm said, vanishing through the little door to investigate. "Nothing like. It has only a bed, clothes chest, wardrobe, and window."

"That," said Jhessail from the doorway, "is because Mourngrym and Shaeryl figured you'd spend more time here."

"Oh?" Shandril asked with lifted brows. "How came they by that idea?"

"I suspect," Jhessail said innocently, "someone must have told them." She chuckled at Narm's hasty reappearance to find the door handle and pull it closed.

A muffled complaint came from within. "It's *dark* enough!"

"Just like a cavern," Jhessail said encouragingly. "You'll get used to it . . . or you could light the lamp by the door. Just mind you quench it when you leave, or the place'll be a smoke hole." She turned to Shandril. "Have you two plans for the day?"

Shandril shook her head. "No. Why do you ask?"

Jhessail strolled thoughtfully to the mirror. "Well, 'tis usual to see the dale, and hunt or ride the countryside after highsun, with gaming and talk in the evening . . . but I'd like to advise a far less interesting alternative, if I may—Narm, the lamp—at least until after the testing."

"Say on." Shandril opened the jakes door and thrust Narm's robe within.

"If you don't mind," Jhessail suggested, "Illistyl and I will bring your meals. Stay in this room until nightfall. Any of the Knights you desire will come to call, or you could spend the day together, just the two of you. . . ."

The jakes door swung open, and Narm emerged, grinning. "No words against that from this mouth."

"Nor from mine," Shandril agreed. "But why?"

Jhessail studied the rich rugs beneath her feet, and then raised solemn eyes. "Eight men tried to get into the tower last night, using magic. They were sent by the High Imperceptor of Bane, and they were after you, Shan, to capture you for your spellfire. All are dead now. They might well have succeeded but for Torm and Rathan, who were out on an extra patrol, and Sharantyr, who went for a walk to clear her head."

Shandril's face had gone slowly white.

Narm's had grown more and more angry. "You mean that folk we don't even *know* are going to be hunting Shandril the rest of her *life?* I *won't* have it! I'll—"

"How'll you stop them?" Jhessail asked quietly.

Narm stared at her. "I . . . I'll master Art enough to destroy them or drive them away!"

Jhessail nodded. "Good. 'Tis about all you can do. Once they get the idea you're powerful, as all know Elminster or the Simbul of Aglarond is, they'll leave you alone—unless they've business with you or your tombstone. All who look upon you as weak and easy targets will fall away once you show Faerûn you're not to be trifled with. But that time hasn't come, so stay in this room today, will you?"

Shandril smiled weakly, but gave a swift nod. After a long moment Narm nodded, too.

"Good!" Jhessail said, and clapped once.

The door opened wide, and a smiling Illistyl came in, bearing a dome-covered silver tray that steamed around its edges. With practiced ease, she hooked a toe under a certain carving on the side of the bed, pulling it out to reveal an unfolding pair of legs, and set the tray on the table thus created.

Shandril peered in open pleasure at the craft and construction of the bedside table, but Narm fixed Jhessail with a hard stare. "You had this planned. You'd given us no choice!"

Jhessail shook her head. "No . . . if you'd refused, Illistyl and I would have shared this morningfeast—I swear, by holy Mystra!" She grinned. "Elminster will tell you never to force by magic what you can trick a man to do. But know, please, we'll *not* force you to act as we desire—ever. You can still change your minds; only tell us so we can best guard you."

She kissed them both fondly on their foreheads. "Still, a whole day together in bed . . . not something I'd pass up." She went to the door, where Illistyl had already gone. "Fare you well until eventide. We'll call for you. Worry not about the testing; the whole affair is simply to know what you are, not change you. Illistyl and I have both been tested by Elminster—when I came to the dale, and when she came to her powers. There's a guard outside; call if you need me—or anything." She went out slowly.

(Between her feet, a smoky gray cat slipped in before the door closed, winked with Illistyl's eyes, and darted unseen under the bed.)

The door closed, and they were alone. "Well, my lord?" Shandril teased challengingly.

He grinned and reached for the tray. "Morningfeast first." He uncovered spiced eggs fluffed with chopped tomatoes and onions, fried bread, slices of black sausage as large across as his hand, and steaming bowls of onion soup. "Holy Mystra. We had less than this for evenfeast at some inns!"

"Mourngrym told me yestereve," Shandril replied, reaching for the soup, "that in a prosperous dale, there's no better rule for a happy life than, 'Before all, eat well.' "

"No disagreement here," Narm mumbled around his fork. "This is a fair place—at least, what we've seen."

"Yes, it is," Shandril replied, suddenly ravenous.

They ate in companionable silence.

(Unseen, a long, slim centipede crawled through a tiny gap in the window frame and cautiously descended to the floor. Once there, it shifted, blurred, and was suddenly a rat. The rodent darted sleekly under the bed—and froze as it saw the cat watching from a paw's reach away. The two stared at each other for a moment. The rat shifted and became a crouched cat, lightly larger than Illistyl. They stared at each other again.)

Above, Narm pushed away his plate with a contented sigh and looked at Shandril lovingly. "Well, my lady, we still know little of each other. Will you trade life tales with me?"

Shandril regarded him thoughtfully. "Yes, so long as you believe me when I say I know little about my lineage."

"Is that why you were upset when Elminster asked?"

"Yes. I . . . I've never known who my parents were. As far back as I can recall, I've lived at the Rising Moon. Gorstag, keeper there, was like a father to me. I never knew a time before the inn was his, nor seen the world beyond its gate. I—I wanted to know adventure, so I ran away with the Company of the Bright Spear—and that's truly all there is to tell."

"How came you to Myth Drannor?"

(Under the bed, both cats cocked an ear, but kept their eyes firmly on each other.)

"I know not. Some magic or other. I read a word written on a bone, and was trans—tel—what do you call it?"

"Teleported," Narm said eagerly, "as Elminster did, to fetch the healing potions for Lanseril."

Shandril nodded. "I was snatched to the heart of Myth Drannor. I wandered its ruins until I was caught by that lady mage, Symgharyl Maruel, and you saw me."

(More interest beneath the bed.)

"How, if you grew up only in the Moon, do you know so much of life and Faerûn?" Narm asked curiously.

"In truth, I know little," Shandril replied with an embarrassed little laugh. "My tutors have been tales told in the taproom by far travelers and old Deepingdale veterans. You heard one such. Splendid tales they were, too. . . ."

"Could Gorstag be your father?"

(Tense interest, beneath the bed.)

Shandril stared at Narm, her face frozen on the edge of a laugh. "No. No, I think not, though I'm not as sure as I was before you asked. We're not at all alike in face or speech, and he always seemed too old . . . but he could be." She sat in silence. "I'd like Gorstag to be my father . . . but I doubt he is."

"Did you never see Deepingdale? Did Gorstag keep you locked up?"

"No! It was just . . . there was always work. The cook forbade me some things, and the older girls would forbid me others. Gorstag said outside the inn and woods, the wide world—even Highmoon—was no place for a young girl, alone. I was no one's special friend except his, and I wasn't big or strong enough to fetch and carry, so I was never taken along on errands." She shrugged. "So the days passed."

"What did you, in the inn?" Narm asked quietly.

"Oh, most anything. Chopping, washing in the kitchen, and fetching water, cleaning taproom tables and floors." She waved a hand, remembering. "Emptying chamber pots, and lighting hall candles and lamps, cleaning, washing bedding. There're many little tasks in running an inn, things seldom done, like repainting the signboard or daubing the chimneys, and I helped with those. It was mainly the kitchen, though."

"They worked you like a slave all those years?" Narm burst out. "For what? You took no coin when you joined the company! Were you not even paid?"

Shandril looked at him in shock. "I—no, not a single coin."

Narm got up, furious, and paced. "You were treated little better than a slave!"

"*No*. I was fed, and given clothes, and—"

"So is a jester; so's a mule, if you count its livery! Before the gods, you were done ill!"

Shandril suddenly snapped, "Enough! You were not there and

cannot know the right of it! Oh, yes, I got sick of the drudgery, and ran . . . and left my only friends—Gorstag, and Lureene—and I sometimes wish I had not, and I hated Korvan, but . . . but—" Her face twisted, and she turned away.

In astonished silence, Narm stared at her back. He opened his mouth to speak, not knowing what to say. Shandril whirled around to face him, eyes large and dark.

"I was happy at the Rising Moon," she said coldly and clearly, "and I do not think Gorstag did me any ill. Nor should you judge him." She drew a deep, unhappy breath, and put away her furious glare. "But before all else, let me not quarrel with you!"

"Let *me* not quarrel with *you*, my lady. Ever." He looked away, white-faced, his hands trembling.

Shandril felt her face grow hot, and hastily turned away, striding to the door.

(Beneath the bed, two cats, looked at each other and did not—quite—smile.)

When she turned back to face him, the look in Narm's eyes made the last of Shandril's anger melt into regret. She hurried back to him. "Oh, Narm," she said despairingly as they embraced.

"I'm sorry, Lady," he whispered, his arms tightening around her. "I never meant to upset you, nor darken Gorstag's good name. I . . . I lost my temper."

"No, forgive me," Shandril replied. "I should have let you yell, and not rebuked you, and there could be no quarrel."

"Nay, the fault is mine. Forgive—"

"Disgusting," Torm's cheerful voice said loudly from behind them. "All this sobbing and forgiving—and not even wed yet!"

The Knight gave them no time to reply. He strode forward to pluck the food tray from the table. "Terrible stuff, isn't it? And such small portions, too! So, have you heard each other's life stories yet? Picked out any juicy bits to pass on to old, bored Torm? Pledged undying love?" He crooked an eyebrow and raised the tray to his shoulder with the deft skill of a tavern wench. "Changed your minds? Decided what to do next? Yes?"

"Ah, fair morning to you, Torm," Narm replied cautiously. "Are you well?"

"Never better! And you two?"

"Don't leer, it makes you look ill," said Shandril crisply. "I hear you prevented my capture last night. My thanks."

"Ah, 'twas nothing!" Torm replied, waving tray, bowls, and all perilously. "I—"

"Nothing, was it?" Jhessail challenged him severely from the doorway. "Three healing spells you took, with much moaning and complaining, and 'twas 'nothing.' Next time we'll save ourselves the Art so you'll appreciate your folly the more." She took him briskly by the arm. "Now come away . . . how'd you like someone to burst into your bedroom, when you are alone with your love?"

"That would depend very much on who the someone was."

Jhessail propelled him firmly out the door. "My apologies, you two. He's just come from his bride-to-be, Naera, and is in high spirits."

Torm gaped at her. "Bride-to-be?" he gasped. "B-b-but . . ." His voice faded as he was marched away down the passage.

"Well met, Torm," Narm said dryly as the door closed again. He and Shandril looked at each other and burst into laughter.

(Beneath the bed, both cats looked pained by Shandril's giggles.)

When they subsided, the two embraced and sat in comfortable silence.

"What do you think this test will be, love?" Shandril asked, her head cradled on his shoulder.

Narm shook his head. "I know not. Your spellfire, surely, will be put to the test, but how I cannot guess!" He frowned. "But another thing occurs to me . . . this Gorstag must know who your parents are . . . and by the way he put it to you, Elminster may know, too."

Shandril nodded. "Yes. I want to know, but have lived a fair tally of winters without. I'd rather know *you* better, Narm . . . I know not even your family name, let alone anything of your parents."

"Oh, have I not—Tamaraith, 'tis, my lady. Sorry. I never thought I'd told you so little as that."

Shandril laughed. "We haven't had overmuch time for talk. You may have said, and I've forgotten in all this tumult. . . . If this is adventure, it's a wonder any soul survives it long!"

(Two cats exchanged amused glances. The one that was Illistyl pointed at the other, spread its paws in question, and put its head to one side suspiciously. The other nodded, traced a sigil in the dust, saw Illistyl's knowing nod—and hurriedly brushed it out. The cats settled at ease together.)

"Well said," Narm agreed. "I've not the love of constant whirl and danger that Torm does! Will we ever be able to relax and do just as we please?"

"I'd like to try." Shandril's eyes were very steady on his.

Narm took her in his arms, face set and serious. "I would like that, too. . . ."

(Under the bed, the strange cat shook its head, rolled its eyes, and yawned.)

When their lips parted, Shandril pushed Narm away a little, and said, "Tell me of your life. Who's this man I'm to marry? A would-be mighty wizard, yes, but why? And why do you love me?"

(Four eyes rolled.)

Narm looked at his lady, opened his mouth, shut it, and burst out, "Gods, I know not why I love you! I can tell of things about you that I love, and how I feel, but as to why—the gods will it, perhaps. Will you accept that answer? 'Tis honest, and no base flattery." He paced, agitated, and turned by the window. "I promise you this, I *will* love you, and as I learn the whys, I'll tell them to you."

"My lord," Shandril answered, eyes shining, "I'm honored you're so honest with me. Pray we both remain so with each other, always. I approve, yes—now get on with your tale! I would *know!*"

(Two cats burst into soundless laughter.)

Narm chuckled. "I was born some twenty-two winters ago, in the far city of Silverymoon in the North. I was not a winter old when my parents journeyed to Triboar, and thence to Waterdeep, and—"

"You've seen great Waterdeep? Is it as they say, bustle and gold and beautiful things from all Faerûn in the streets?"

Narm shrugged. "It may well be, but I cannot say. I was there but a week when my parents moved on. We traveled the Sword

Coast North often, with the trade. My father was Hargun Tamaraith, called 'the Tall,' a seller of weapons and smith work. I think he'd been a ranger before he fell ill; he had the shaking-fever. My mother was Fythuera—Fyth to myself and my sire—and her last name I never knew. They'd been wed long before I was born. She played the harp and traded as my father's equal. I know not if ever she'd been an adventurer. They were good people."

He stared into nothingness, and Shandril laid her hand upon his. His face was sad and wistful. "They're both dead, of course. Burned to ashes in a sorcerous duel in Baldur's Gate when I was eleven. The ferryboat they were on was struck by a fireball flung at the wizard Algarzel Halfcloak by a Calishite archmage, Kluennh Tzarr. Algarzel flew aside. All others aboard—who had no part in the dispute—perished. Algarzel was slain later, or escaped into another plane, some said. He's not been seen since."

The young mageling started to pace. His arms swung easily, his eyes remote. "Kluennh Tzarr left for his citadel in triumph. 'Tis said dragons serve him and he has many slaves. One day, if another does not get there first, I will be his death."

Something in his soft tone chilled Shandril.

(Under the bed, the cats nodded approvingly.)

"To defeat an archmage I needed magic—so I tried to become an apprentice." He laughed, a little bitterly, at the memory. "Imagine it—a ragged, barely lettered boy, alone and with no wealth to buy a mage's time or trouble, in Baldur's Gate where there are a dozen homeless boys on every street. I pestered every mage that passed. Only by Mystra's grace did I escape being turned into a toad or burned to nothing. . . ."

His smile changed, rising spirits making it more real. "One day, two years after I started, a mage said yes. A pompous, sour mage—Marimmar, my master. His pride weakened him. He never worked to strengthen his Art where he lacked spells or technique. He couldn't—or wouldn't—see where he was weak. But I learned much from him, perhaps more than I might from a masterful spell weaver. He had a temper and little patience—and was perhaps the laziest man I've ever met, so he needed an apprentice to do all the drudgery. You know about drudgery."

Shandril gave a rueful grin.

"Marimmar disliked strife, so he never fought mages to gain spells—and he was so loud and proud that no wizard challenged him. Those of real power saw him as a posturing know-nothing, with no spells worth seizing. Those of lesser power feared he had something up his sleeve. His overconfidence killed him, in the end. He nearly took me with him.

"He saw Myth Drannor as his chance to become a great mage by seizing the magic lying around in the ruins. I doubt there's much to be easily found. It's been seized already by the priests of Bane, or whoever summoned all the devils."

Shandril nodded. She could well believe that magic raged or lurked in many a crumbling corner of Myth Drannor—but not scrolls or tomes of magic just waiting for a wandering wizard to stroll up and take them.

"The devils slew Marimmar," Narm continued, "and almost killed me, too. Lanseril and Illistyl of the Knights rescued me—they're so kind. I went back to Myth Drannor because . . . because I knew not where to go, really. Also I felt I owed it to the crusty old windbag—and I couldn't sleep for fear of devils until I'd faced them again. By some miracle of Mystra, or the whim of Tymora, I was not slain . . . and saw you."

Narm turned thoughtful eyes on her. "Forgive me if I've talked too long, my lady, or spoken bluntly about the dead. It was not my intent to upset you."

Shandril shook her head. "I am not upset, but much relieved. I had to *know*, you see."

She drew back the bed furs. "And now, my lord, if you'll be so good as to drag that chest over in front of the door, we'll to bed." She smiled slyly. "The test is to be late. I must sleep first. Will you see me to sleep?"

Narm nodded. "Aye, willingly."

(One cat rolled its eyes again, became a rat, and flashed over to the wall before Illistyl could even stretch. It dwindled and twisted and was a centipede again. It gained the sill while Narm heaved the chest door-ward and Shandril hung her robe on a bedpost. Illistyl saw a raven appear outside the window and swoop away. She nodded and curled up for a nap. Eavesdropping was one thing, but there were limits. . . .)

Narm finished with the chest, straightened slowly, and caught sight of Shandril in the mirror. In two bounds, he was on the bed. Few delights come, 'tis said, to he who tarries.

12

Spells To Dust

High magic is strange and savage and splendid for its own sake, whether one's spells change the Realms or no. A crafter who by dint of luck, work, skill, and the Great Lady Mystra comes to some strength in Art is like a thirsty drunk in a wine cellar—he or she can never leave it alone. Who can blame such a one? It is not given to all to feel the kiss of such power.

Alustriel, High Lady of Silverymoon
A Harper's Song
Year of the Dying Stars

Jhessail slipped softly into the bedchamber. Illistyl straightened from dragging the chest aside, and they shared a smile. "Worth hearing?" Jhessail asked softly.

Illistyl nodded. "I'll tell you later." They crept to the bed.

Among the twisted covers, Narm and Shandril lay asleep in each other's arms. The lady mages gently laid a fur coverlet over the sleeping couple before Jhessail leaned close to Shandril and said, " 'Tis time. Rise, hurler of spellfire. Elminster awaits."

Shandril shivered in her sleep and clutched Narm more tightly. "Oh, Narm, how it burns."

The lady mages exchanged glances. Carefully Jhessail laid

a hand on Shandril's shoulder. Heat tingled under her fingertips.

"She holds yet more power," Jhessail whispered, "and this cannot be of the balhiir. Things are as Elminster suspected." She bent again to Shandril's ear. "Awaken, Shan. We await."

Eyelashes flickered. "Narm . . . Narm, we're called t—ohh. Where—?" Shandril lifted her head. In the leaping glow of the lamp Illistyl lit, she saw the two ladies of Art standing over her. She involuntarily tensed to hurl spellfire, and then relaxed. "My pardon, Lady Jhessail, Lady Illistyl. For a moment, I knew you not." She shook her head ruefully. "Up, love. Arise."

"Eh? Oh, gods, 'tis time already?"

"It is," Jhessail said gently. "Elminster awaits!"

"Gods *belch!*" Narm growled, rubbing his eyes and flinging back the fur. Just as hastily he pulled it up again. "Ah—my clothes?"

Shandril laughed helplessly and handed him his robe.

Illistyl smiled. "We'll await outside the door. Come when you're ready."

In the passage, she turned and whispered, "Tell no one yet, Jhess, but the Simbul came in by the window and listened, even as I did."

Eyebrows lifted. "What did you hear, aside from lovemaking?"

"The life tale of Narm Tamaraith—full, open, and unadorned. His mother may well have been a Harper," Illistyl replied. They both had cause to thank that mysterious group of bards and others who served the Realms.

Jhessail nodded. "He thinks so?"

Illistyl shook her head. "The thought hasn't crossed his mind; 'twas his description."

The door opened, and the two hastily dressed guests stepped out. Narm looked at the ladies curiously. "I mean no disrespect, but is there a secret way into this room? That chest . . ."

"We workers of Art have our secrets," Illistyl replied crisply. "I dragged it."

"Oh," Narm said, "I see. Uh, sorry."

They descended the stairs, nodded to the guards, and went out into the night. It was very warm and still, Selûne shone overhead, and Merith and Lanseril waited with mules. "Well met," the elf said softly.

"Where're we bound?" Shandril asked as he knelt to help her into the saddle.

"Harpers' Hill," Merith replied—a name that meant nothing to either Narm or Shandril—and they set off.

Save for its heights, cloaked in silver moonlight, Shadowdale lay dark around them. Narm spotted guard posts atop the tower, on the Old Skull tor, by the bridge, and at the crossroads ahead. Silently the guards watched as the small party rode through the dale, east into the trees.

It was very dark, and the mules slowed to a walk on the narrow forest trail. Someone by the path saluted Merith. As they passed, Shandril saw a grim man in dark leather, a sword ready in his hand.

"A Harper," Jhessail explained. "There will be others."

The forest changed as they went. The trees became larger, older, and closer together. The dark stillness deepened.

Thrice more they passed guards, and at last came up a steep slope onto a bare hilltop. On the smooth earth, moonlight lay like a sheet of silver.

Torm and Rathan waited at the edge of the light. More leather-clad Harpers—men and women, bareheaded with swords drawn—stood beyond.

The thief and priest greeted Narm and Shandril with quiet smiles and encouraging pats. They took their mules.

Merith drew Narm to one side, proffering a cloak. "Remove your clothes and leave them here," he said. "Cover yourself with this." A little way along the hillside, Jhessail did the same with Shandril. "Boots, too—the ground's soft."

"Will this be . . . dangerous?" Narm asked Merith.

The elf shrugged. "Aye, but no more than spending your night any other way. Come, off with it all, lad."

The newly robed couple were brought together again. Narm saw Shandril shiver. He doubted it was from cold, and reached for her—but the two Knights stepped smoothly between. Taking their hands, they strode at a brisk pace to the top of Harpers' Hill.

Elminster stood in the moonlight at the center of the hill, flanked by Florin and Storm. As Shandril and Narm were brought to them, Elminster scratched his nose and said, "Sorry to get ye from bed for all this mystery and ceremony, but 'tis necessary. I need to know thy powers. Shall we begin, the earlier to be done?"

The Knights embraced Narm and Shandril, and then left them alone with the Old Mage.

He drew from his robes a small, battered book and handed it to Shandril. "First, can ye read this?"

The book was old, but on its brown and crinkled pages, runes sparkled clear and bright. Shandril stared at them, but she recognized nothing. Even as she looked, the runes writhed and crawled, moving as if alive. She shook her head and handed the book back. "No," she said, rubbing her eyes.

Elminster nodded, opened the book to a certain page, and extended it to Narm.

"And ye? Only this page, mind, and at the top *only*. Tell me the words aloud as fast as ye can make them out."

Narm nodded, peered, and said, "Being a Means Both Efficient and Correct for the Creation of—"

Elminster waved him to silence, took the book back, and selected another page.

Narm looked longer this time, forehead furrowed. "I—I . . . 'A Means to Confound,' I think it says here," Narm said at last, "but I can't be sure, nor is a word more clear to me anywhere on this page."

Elminster nodded. "Enough, and well enough!" He turned to Shandril. "How do ye feel?"

Shandril looked at him with a little frown. "Well in head and body, or at least nothing amiss, but there is a . . . stirring . . . a tingling. . . ."

Elminster nodded as if unsurprised and looked to Narm. "Have ye any spells or cantrips in thy head?"

Narm shook his head. "No. I've scarce had time to study, since . . ." His voice trailed off under Elminster's grin.

"Aye, and good!" the wizard told him. From somewhere else in his robes, he drew forth a scroll and handed it to Narm. "Read this and cast it at thy lady. 'Tis but a light spell; have no fears of harming her." He stepped back to watch.

Narm glanced around the bare, moonlit hilltop, feeling the watching eyes amid the trees. He took a deep breath, and then carefully cast the spell. He centered the Art on Shandril, who stood waiting.

Light flared around her—but instantly died away.

Elminster strode close to peer at Shandril. Nodding at the fire in her eyes, he handed another scroll to Narm. "As before."

Narm cast another light spell. Again it was absorbed.

Shandril's eyes glowed brighter. A third scroll, a third casting, and Shandril's body took it in.

The Old Mage waved at Narm to back away and went to Shandril. She reached out in welcome, but he stepped back so as not to touch her. "Lady, see yon boulder? Shatter it with spellfire, if ye will."

Shandril looked at him, trembling. Fire leapt in her eyes. "Yes!"

Fire coiled and raced within her, roiling in her veins. She bore down on it with her will and thrust it into one arm. It built to a soundless thunder.

Spellfire burst from her hand in a long, rolling gout. The boulder was enveloped in orange flame that built to a blinding white inferno. Watchers felt heat on their faces. An instant later, the rock shattered with a sharp crack, spraying shards across the hillside.

Shandril let her flames die away, and silence fell. It stretched for a long time.

Elminster turned to Narm and growled warningly, "Stand back—over beneath that tree."

The young mage hastened to obey. Beside him, Merith gave a tight smile, but his eyes scarcely left the hilltop. Narm stared back into the moonlight, too—in time to see the white-bearded old wizard cast a light spell of his own at Shandril.

It, too, was absorbed.

Elminster cast two more light spells, using no scrolls, and Shandril's body drank them. Her eyes flamed like burning coals.

The Old Mage wove a more complex spell, creating a shimmering, translucent wall in the air—what mages called a wall of force. Elminster nodded to it.

Shandril obligingly raised her hands and hurled spellfire.

The flames clawed at the wall and raged, becoming blinding as Shandril bent her full will upon the barrier. At last she gave up and let her flame die, shrugging. The wall still stood.

Elminster asked, "How do ye feel?"

Shandril shrugged. "A little scared, but not hurt." She pushed with her will, letting flames leap from her palms and then wink out in a little spurt. "I hold more yet."

The old wizard's response was swift. "I'll raise a wall of fire there, before thee. When I nod, kneel before it and hurl spellfire through it, angling into the sky so as not to harm the forest. Only a little, mind. Cast it for the length of a long breath, then cease."

Shandril smiled, flames dancing in her eyes. "As you will . . . a short but steady burst."

No sooner had Elminster raised the wall of flames than Shandril knelt and sent spellfire roaring through it. Fire snarled into the night air, drawing the mage's flames with it.

When the burst ended, curling away with a rippling and tearing of air, the wall was gone. Tendrils dimmed and vanished in the starlit sky.

Shandril rose from her knees and sighed.

"Are ye well?" Elminster asked, his voice alert. Shandril nodded, and the Old Mage added, "Right, then," raised his hands, and without warning hurled a bolt of lightning at her.

It crackled and struck, and Shandril reeled.

Narm cried out involuntarily, but already his lady was standing upright again, and the lightning was gone. The sharp smell of the bolt hung in the air. She turned, bleeding a little where she'd bitten her lip, and smiled reassuringly at Narm.

Elminster took a step closer. "How fare ye now?"

"Well enough." She wore the ghost of a smile. "I feel weary, but not sick or strange."

"Good," the Old Mage said gently. "I shall cast more lightning at thee. Gather and hold it as long as ye can. If it starts to hurt thee or ye feel it trying to burst out and cannot stop it, let it flow into yon boulder. Release it not until then, so that I may learn thy capacity. We have healing means near at hand. Be not afraid."

Shandril nodded and stood waiting, hands at her sides. She flinched when the next lightning struck her, but then stood quiet. Elminster hurled bolt after bolt at—no, *into*—her. The very air crackled.

Narm twisted his hands but could not look away.

The Old Mage poured more bolts into Shandril. She stood silent and unmoving. Lightning arced over Harpers' Hill. At last she bent at the waist with a sob, threw her arms wide, and burst into a pillar of coiling flame.

"Mother Mystra!" Narm gasped in horror.

Merith laid hands on him quickly, to prevent his running to a fiery death. Narm screamed his beloved's name, wrenching and twisting in vain. Through sheer fury he dragged the silent elf forward until Florin set his strength against the young mage's. Narm struggled in their combined grip.

On the hilltop, a pillar of living flame writhed where Shandril had stood.

Abruptly, flames shot from it, lancing to strike the boulder. There was a flash, and everyone who stood watching ducked. Small, red-hot shards of stone showered down through the leaves around them.

Jhessail hastily worked a wall of force from a scroll she held ready. Lanseril used muttered magic to quench many little fires.

A smoking scar was all that remained of the boulder. On the summit, a pillar of flame roared, higher than the Twisted Tower, as if to touch the glimmering stars.

Elminster watched it calmly, a fragment of stone cooling in his hands.

Slowly the roaring flames died, faded to an angry red, and winked out. Shandril stood nude in the moonlight, sniffing at the stench of her own scorched hair. Its ends were burned, but she was otherwise untouched; her cloak had burned to nothing, but the flames hadn't marked her.

Narm burst free of Merith and Florin and ran across the hot stone, heedless of the pain in his bare feet.

Elminster moved to intercept him, and Shandril backed away. "Keep back, love!" she warned, sharply. "My touch may slay just now." Narm came to a halt barely a pace away. "I'm well," she added gently. Her long hair rippled and stirred in the calm air as if with a life of its own.

Narm stared at her, terror and worry warring on his face. When she smiled again, he whirled to face Elminster, "And what *now?*"

"I'll touch thy lady myself, to end the test," the Old Mage replied firmly. "I'm protected by potent spells, where ye are not. A moment longer, lad, if ye can contain yourself. If ye cannot, expect not to live long or rise far in the Art." He strode forward and took Shandril's hand in his own.

"Well met, sir," Shandril said, greeting him with grave courtesy.

"At thy service, fair lady," Elminster replied, bowing. His face was expressionless, but his eyes twinkled.

Narm shook his fists in impatience. "Is she *safe?*"

The Old Mage nodded—and was fairly bowled over by Narm's rush to embrace his lady.

Elminster stepped back with a wry smile and waved at the trees. Harpers, Knights, and guardsmen of the dale appeared from all sides at a swift trot.

Elminster looked almost fondly at Narm and Shandril, then smote his forehead. "Gods, I *must* be getting old!" He swept his cloak about Shandril's shoulders.

As he did, the stone he held twisted from his grasp, landing with a thump rather than a clatter. In an instant, it grew into a strange-eyed woman in tattered robes. Her long silvery hair strayed wildly about her shoulders.

Approaching Harpers reached for their blades.

"Well met," Elminster greeted her calmly. "Shandril Shessair, I present to thee the Simbul, Queen of Aglarond!"

A murmur broke over Harpers' Hill, followed by silence. Everyone waited for the infamous archmage to speak.

Shandril gently freed herself from Narm and bowed solemnly.

The Simbul almost smiled. "Impressive, young lady, but dangerous—perhaps too dangerous. Elminster . . . all of you . . .

have you thought on this? Here stands a power you might need to silence. She may have to be destroyed."

There was another brief babble, and another hush.

Shandril stared white-faced at the archmage, but Elminster stepped between her and the Witch-Queen.

"No," he said simply. He swept everyone on the hilltop with eyes that were sad and wise and very, very old. "Ye," he said to the Simbul, "I, and all gathered here are 'dangerous.' Should we then be destroyed out of hand, forthwith, because of what we *might* do? Nay! 'Tis the right and the doom of all creatures who walk Faerûn to do as they will; this is why we of the Art frown at those who cast charms."

Elminster drew himself up and seemed to gather brightness until he glowed. "Not even the gods took unto themselves the power to control ye or me so tightly that we cannot walk or speak or breathe save at another's bidding! 'Tis their will that we be free to do as we may. Slay a foe, sure, or defend thyself against a raider—but to strike down one who may someday menace thee? That's as monstrous as the act of the usurper who slays all babies in a land for fear of a rightful heir!"

"Aye, well said," Florin agreed in grim, deliberate challenge to the woman in black.

No other of the gathering spoke, but waited in breathless silence.

The Witch-Queen stood in their midst, alone and terrible. They'd all heard of the awesome Art she commanded that held Red Wizards at bay and hurled back their armies time and again. They knew the tales of her temper and cruel humor. The hilltop smelled of fear. Not a sword moved.

The Simbul nodded, slowly. "Aye, Great One, you truly have the wisdom lore grants you. I agree. If others had not thought likewise, many winters gone, I would not have lived to stand here on Harpers' Hill now." She stepped around Elminster, and he did not bar her way.

Narm moved protectively in front of Shandril. The Simbul came to a halt facing him.

"I have trusted," she whispered, her eyes very proud. "Will you not also trust me?"

Narm stared back at her for a long, tense breath, and stepped aside.

The Simbul bowed her head and glided up to Shandril. "My forgiveness, if you'll take it. I wish you well."

Shandril nodded, swallowing, and managed a tentative smile. "I—I hold nothing against you, great lady."

The Simbul smiled back. Her hand went to the broad black belt about her waist and drew from it a plain brass ring. "A gift for you!" She leaned close until Shandril could smell a faint, strange perfume at her throat. Shandril had never seen eyes so steel gray, stern, and sad.

"Use this only when all else is lost," the Simbul whispered. "It will take you, and anyone whose flesh touches yours, to a refuge of mine. It works only once, for the going, and not a return journey. Its word of command is on the inside of the band, invisible save when you heat the ring. Reveal it as often as you like—but speak it not aloud until you intend to use it. Your spellfire will not harm this." Cold fingers touched Shandril's, pressing the ring—strangely warm—into her palm.

"One last thing," the Simbul added. "Walk your own way, Shandril; let no one control you. Beware those who stand in shadows." She smiled again and kissed the wondering girl gently on the cheek. Her lips were like both fire and ice.

As Shandril stared at her, lips trembling into another smile, the queen of Aglarond winked, patted Elminster's arm, and whirled away in writhing black cloth that seemed smoke. The brief tumult sprang up in the moonlight and became a black falcon; it soared among the stars and was gone.

Everyone spoke at once.

Amid the hubbub, Elminster said firmly, "The test is at an end. Narm, take thy lady home, and sleep. My thanks, Shandril. Keep thy spellfire quiet, within, until ye've need of it. I know now 'twill not harm thee to carry it. Guard well that ring—a gift from the Simbul is rare indeed!"

Behind them, Florin quietly arranged a ring of guards to escort the couple back to the Tower.

"Think on this, and let us know what ye decide," Elminster added, as they went down into the trees. "Jhessail and Illistyl will train thee, Narm, if ye wish, and I'll show thee what I can of working together spellfire and spells. The cloak is thine to keep. It will protect thee in battle—I'll say more on the morrow. 'Tis old, its Art no longer strong, so take care not to drain its magic without intention." The wizard coughed. "Go now and get to bed—where these old bones would be if I'd any sense. After all, ye could be needed to save Faerûn tomorrow."

Shandril nodded, suddenly exhausted. "Thank you, Lord," she replied—Elminster winced at the title. "I fear I must sleep soon or fall where I stand."

"Thanks, Elminster," Narm added briskly, "and good fortune this night and hereafter. After I get our clothes back from the Knights, we'll think on your words as we fall asleep!"

They chuckled together, and then the young couple went down the wooded hillside. The guards closed in around them. Florin and Merith flew watchfully above, leaving the Old Mage behind with Jhessail and Illistyl.

"Satisfied?" Illistyl asked her sometime master.

Elminster looked at the scorch marks on the rocks. "The power to unleash spellfire. Her mother had it." Both lady Knights looked at him, startled, but Elminster merely smiled a distant smile that warned he'd say no more. "So what did ye hear of interest, Illistyl? Ye may edit such things as ye feel mine aged ears should not hear, out of consideration for my vulnerable heart."

"Well, then," Illistyl impishly, "there's precious little to tell."

Mist streamed through the trees as Korvan of the Rising Moon reached the butcher's shop.

"Fair morn," said a stooped stranger. The man leaned on the stockyard fence, the mud of travel on his boots and breeches.

"Morn," Korvan replied sourly. He had come for meat not talk. Since that little brat Shandril had run off, he'd had to get his meat earlier, when he'd rather be abed.

"Buying lamb? I've thirty good tails in the pen there, just down from Battledale." The herder jerked his head at the muddy paddock behind him.

"Lamb? Well, I'll look . . . if I can find two good hand counts among them, I might do business," Korvan begrudged.

The herder stared at him. "Two hand counts? You must have a monstrous large family!"

"No, no. I buy for the inn down the road, the Rising Moon."

"Do you? Why, I've a tale for you, then . . . about that young lass who left your inn."

"Oh?" Korvan said, turning his head sharply. "Shandril?"

"That's her name? Pretty, that," the herder replied. "I saw her in the mountains a few nights back, while I chased strays."

"The Thunder Peaks?" Korvan asked, nodding toward a gray and purple wall of mountains above the trees.

"Aye, near the Sember. I came on a great crowd of folk asking this girl if she was all right, after she'd unleashed something they called 'spellfire.' "

"Spellfire?" Korvan snapped in astonishment.

"Aye, I heard it plain. I hid, mind you—there were gold coins all over the place, and they had swords out; I wasn't sure an uninvited guest would be left alive."

Korvan nodded. "Aye, but who were these people?"

"Folk of Shadowdale, they were. That old wizard, and the ranger who rides about the dales speaking Shadowdale's will—Falconhand, is he?—and the elf-warrior who lives there, and a priest, I think. They were all excited over the lass . . . seems she burned up a dragon or suchlike with this spellfire. There was something about someone called Shadowsil, too, but I couldn't rightly hear that bit. Never found my sheep, either, but I got their price and better in gold by keeping hid and coming out for coins after they'd gone."

"Thence to—?"

The herder grinned. "North, friend, down into the forest. To Mistledale, I suppose . . . and Shadowdale, beyond."

Korvan sighed, feigning sorrow. "Too far to follow. If she'd wanted to come back, she'd have headed our way by now." He shook his head. "Well, my thanks for your tale. She's alive, at least; that's good to know. Now, you'd some sheep? The faster I buy, the faster I can be smoking and hanging."

The herder threw open the gate and waved him on.

Korvan's mind was busy on how best to pass this news to certain ears. He never noticed the herder's unlovely smile, or how the man's arm reached a few inches farther than any human hand could as he drew the gate closed, or how his fingers—just for an instant—seemed like black tentacles.

Shandril must die, decided Malark. Not yet, but after these altruistic fools of Shadowdale have trained her to her full powers. Somehow she'd destroyed Rauglothgor and the dracolich's lair, slain or escaped the Shadowsil, and driven away Manshoon of Zhentil Keep. She'd been lucky. It would be simply impossible for a slip of a girl to defeat the gathered mages of the Cult of the Dragon.

The wagon rocked through a particularly deep pothole. Malark cursed. Through the wagon's open front door, Arkuel grinned apologetically.

Malark snarled a wordless, mirthless reply, rubbed his aching shoulder, and considered how best to separate this Shandril from her protectors in the Tower of Ashaba. The cult had a loyal agent in its guard—Culthar. He could strike at Shandril when the time was right.

Malark snorted. He did not trust his underlings to saddle a horse unsupervised, let alone make such a capture and escape, given the Art and the swords that would come against them.

On the other hand, the longer the cult waited, the more likely someone else would try to snatch the source of spellfire—the Zhentarim or the priesthood of Bane. Perhaps that would be for the best. In the ensuing confusion, Malark could storm in and prevail for the greater glory of the Followers.

The archmage was jolted out of that pleasant daydream by a pothole. One wheel struck, bounced, and sank—and then another wheel pitched sharply down into an even larger hole. The rattling wagon surged upright just as its rear wheels skidded alarmingly sideways on loose stones.

Claws of Shargrailar! The gods alone knew how fat little merchants managed this, day in and day out—and this was one of the better roads in the North!

Malark questioned the wisdom of his own plan for the forty-third time, as the wagon—blessedly—slowed for the guard post that would admit him, a traveling merchant who dealt in love philters and medicinal remedies, into Shadowdale.

Well, it was under way now, for good or ill. Let the killing begin.

13

Gods Help Us All

Look to your priests and prayers and altars, for salvation comes from the gods. All aid, all beauty, all fortune and reward and plenty. It almost makes up for the beasts and bloodshed and heart-ravages they also send.

When red war sweeps the land and swords rise, is it not curious that every third warrior calls on this god or that, and swears divine favor is with him?

Yet the blood runs, and whenever one war falters, another bursts forth. Truly, the gods must starve for entertainment.

Hammeth Ilcarth of Telflamm
A Somewhat Honest Merchant's Say
Year of the Weeping Moon

Morning light made the bare, fissured rock of the Old Skull a warm and pleasant place, despite the whispering wind. When it howled, the knoll-top was the coldest, bleakest guard post in Shadowdale. Three leather-clad figures stood there now, looking down over the green meadows and farms to the south and the grim, defiant Twisted Tower.

"Gods help us if the Red Wizards hear of Shandril before she and Narm are grown wise at battle and Art," Storm said.

"Without my sister, the defense of this little dale falls on a few Knights and Elminster. And for all his Art and holy Mystra's favor, he is but *one* old, busy man."

"Things will get bad enough with just the Zhentarim, if Manshoon sends them," Sharantyr replied. "You all miss Syluné very much. She must have been special indeed. They still speak of her often—and wistfully—in yonder inn!"

Florin smiled. "She fell defending the dale against dragons, a danger we may soon face again with Shandril here. Cultists must be searching for her now—and with the testing's bright fires in the night, it won't take them long to find her."

Storm smiled ruefully. "Elminster plays a deeper game than we do. He did that in front of everyone quite deliberately, though why . . . ?"

Florin's smile was every bit as rueful. "You think the public display was unwise. I, too—yet Elminster seemed an actor in the streets of Suzail, playing to a larger audience than those standing around him, hoping to attract other eyes. Our Old Mage is no fool, and not feeble in wits—unless the gods have given him some feebleness that affects judgment but not power of Art!"

"There *is* such a thing," Sharantyr teased. "It strikes the young, too. It makes us adventurers when we could stay safe at home, doing dull, honest work to earn local respect slowly as we grow gray and bent."

Storm nodded. "Well said, yet I agree with Florin: Elminster has some purpose in displaying Shandril's power so dramatically." Storm shook her head. "I've not spoken formally with others who harp, but I can say that most who saw the testing were of like mind: 'twas the act of a rash youngster."

Florin nodded, turning his gaze thoughtfully to Elminster's small fieldstone tower below. "Shandril's a danger to him, more than any other in all the Realms. With one hand she can smash spells to dust. If ever she moves against Elminster or is duped into foiling him, the Old Mage can be destroyed—and our defense against Zhentil Keep will be gone. Those who'd work such a deed are far too many for my comfort."

"Aye," Storm said, her silver hair stirring in the breeze. She looked to the tower where Shandril was, and her eyes were very dark. "So that must not be allowed to happen."

⊠ ⊠ ⊠

"A lot of folk have died here, it seems," Shandril said, her voice too soft to hide the fear in it.

Illistyl sat down on a cushion, waving Shandril to the next seat. "Many have died, yes. Zhentil Keep has attacked the dale twice since the Knights came; almost half the farmers I grew up with are dead now. So are more adventurers than you could cram breast-to-breast in this room." She shrugged. "Real life is not all tavern tales and fond memories. In the crypts ten levels beneath us, three Knights sleep forever. It's a price they never intended to pay—but pay it they did, most without choice." Illistyl leaned forward, took Shandril's arms, and looked her full in the face. "The adventurer's life may well take Narm from you, or cripple one of you beyond putting right. Once folk know you've power, though, you've little choice. You become a foe and a target for many, and must become an adventurer or a corpse."

"So I fear. Yet I chose to leave the inn. All else has followed on that. I suppose there's no other choice left." Shandril smiled. "Yet I regret none of it, for it's brought me Narm."

"Hold to that," Illistyl said almost fiercely. "Never forget you've felt so. Hard times lie ahead; your power, wielded with deliberate intent, is a menace to all weavers of Art. Many folk will try to destroy you or wield you as a weapon." On the verge of shaking Shandril, she let go and sat back. "You'll see wizards enough to sicken you, and no matter how mighty you become, there's always someone more powerful. Learn that quickly; the lesson's fatal if ignored. It can happen to you, too, Shandril—something of Art may well counter spellfire, perhaps something as simple as a cantrip."

Shandril nodded. "Sometimes I think I can't go on with this . . . and yet hurling spellfire feels so *good*, even with the pain. I see how happy Jhessail is with Merith, too—and both of them are adventurers. As an elf Merith must know his lady will die hundreds of winters before he does. Yet they wed, and seem happy. It *can* happen."

Illistyl nodded. "It's good you see that. It takes work and patience, mind. How does Jhessail seem to you, in manner—her character?"

"Warm, kind, yet strict and proper . . . understanding. I can say little more; I barely know any of you!"

"Indeed, yet I'd say you've seen Jhessail well enough. But there's more. Her control's so great that one doesn't notice she's passionate—not just romantically, mind, but strong-willed. She and the priest Jelde were lovers when I first came to the tower. There was a great fight between Jelde and Merith over Jhessail. Jhessail decided she loved Merith more, so she set out to win him, before all the Elven Court and mindful of her brief span of years. She seeks longevity by her Art, but she's never thought to outlive even his youth."

Illistyl rose and started to pace. "That sort of self-discipline is required to master Art. You'll need control to stand at Narm's side through all that will come against you both. Hear and heed, Shandril, for I would be your friend for more than a few years." The mage grinned suddenly. "I seem to be one for long speeches this day."

Shandril shook her head. "No, no, I thank you! I've never had someone my age—or close—that I could talk of things to, and not have to curb my words. Even Narm . . . especially Narm!"

"Yes. Especially Narm." Illistyl glanced around. "Remember the places I'm going to show you now. One day you and he may be glad of a place to hide away in, together." As Shandril rose to join her, the lady mage turned and gave her a grim look. "One day soon."

Shandril could only nod.

Night had fallen, deep and dark, before Rozsarran Dathan rose from his table in the Old Skull's taproom, waved a wordless goodnight to Jhaele, and staggered to the door.

The plump innkeeper shook her head ruefully as she went to mop up the table where two of Rozsarran's fellow guards slumped snoring in their chairs, dice and coppers fallen from their hands.

They're like children betimes, she thought, lifting one leather-clad sleeve out of a pool of spilled ale and adroitly avoiding the instinctive yank and punch its sleeping owner launched. Good lads, but not drinkers.

Outside in the cool night air, Rozsarran reached the same conclusion, albeit slowly and less clearly. Hitching up his sword belt, he set off hastily toward the tower. An overcast sky made the night very dark, and a brisk walk might make him feel less rock-witted before he reached his bed. Late duty tomorrow, praise Helm. He could use the sleep. . . .

A silent shadow rose out of the night, clutching a horse-leather knotted about a fistful of coins. The figure tipped Rozsarran's helmet sharply forward to expose the back of his head and gave sleep to him.

The guard slumped without a sound. Suld caught him under the arms and heaved him upright. Arkuel caught his boots, and together they hurried him into the trees.

There, Malark worked magical darkness and commanded Arkuel to unhood the lamp. In its faint light the cult archmage cast a spell of sleep on the guard.

"Strip him," he ordered. When it was done, he studied the man's face and hair intently and had his underlings turn the body, seeking birthmarks. None. Right, then.

Slowly and carefully Malark cast yet another spell. His form twisted, dwindled, and grew again. . . . A double of Rozsarran stood where Malark had been moments before. The disguised wizard donned the real guard's clothes, ensured that his magic-warding amulets were still secure under them, and ordered coldly, "Wait here. If I return not by dawn, withdraw a little way into the woods and hide. Report in Essembra if I come not back in four days. Understood?"

"Aye, Lord Mage!"

"Understood, Lord Malark."

"Well enough. No pilfering, no wenching, and no *noise!* I don't plan to be long!" And Malark was gone, adjusting his sword belt.

Urkhh. How did guards even *lift* such blades, let alone swing them as if they were wands? This one was as heavy as a cold corpse. The false guard felt his way back out of his enchanted ring of darkness and reached the road.

There he found two guardsmen weaving slowly toward the tower. They were half asleep, irritable, and smelled of drink.

"Aghh, it's Roz!" one greeted him, nearly falling. "Bladder the better for it, old sword? Fall over any trees?"

"Arrghh," Malark answered, loudly and sourly, thinking it the safest reply. He deftly ducked and rose up between their linked hands, putting an arm about the shoulder of each. One of the guardsmen gave at the knees and almost fell. Malark winced at his weight.

" 'Tis good y-you came," the collapsing guard rumbled. He hauled himself up Malark's arm and rocked on his heels before catching his balance. "I need your shoulder, I fear. Gods, my *head!*"

"Arrghh," Malark said again, stifling a grin.

"Urrghh," the guard on his other arm agreed sagely.

They stumbled on. Ahead, the torchlight at the tower gates grew brighter and closer, step by bobbing step. Elsewhere, Malark might have crept or flown in the shape of a bird or vermin to a window and dispensed with all this dangerous foolishness, but not here. Not with Elminster about, and all these Knights.

"Best I ever drank," one of his companions said dreamily, "was at the Lonesome Tankard, where the roads meet in Eveningstar . . . 'at's in Cormyr, old sword!"

"Ummhuh," Malark noted.

Somehow he got the three of them through the guards and inside. He let them stumble slightly ahead to guide him, down a long, high hallway to the guardroom.

Luck was with Malark. His spy Culthar was one of the two guards standing duty. The other was just rising, with an oath, to answer a bell three floors up. On his way to the back stairs, he growled to no one in particular, "Why can't Rold relieve himself *before* he takes his post?"

Malark's companions stumbled across the guardroom, catching at the table for balance, heading for the bunkroom door. One began to sing under his breath: "Oh, I once knew a lady of far Uttersea . . . she'll never come back, now, no, never come back to me. . . ." The door banged, and there came a fainter crash from the other side of it.

Culthar rolled his eyes. "He's *always* falling over that chair. It'll be broken now, sure, and we'll have to fix it again because"—Culthar's voice rose in vicious mimicry of the vanished guard—"I'm not too good with my hands!"

At that moment, Malark's other companion heaved, shuddered, and made a sickening gulping sound.

"Oh, *gods!*" Culthar cursed. "Quick, get his face into that bucket! *Hurry!* I should have known Crimmon would drink himself sick!"

Malark scooped a leather bucket from its peg, just in time.

When the retching was done, Crimmon roused himself blearily and walked toward the bunkroom. "No more for me, I think. I'd best be getting back, Jhaele."

"Yes, dearie," Culthar said in disgusted mockery.

Crimmon passed into the bunkroom and another splintering crash came. Malark chuckled despite himself. After a moment, Culthar joined in. Crimmon's curses trailed away.

Shaking his head, Malark put down the bucket, closed the bunkroom door, and turned to face Culthar, who frowned at him.

"And how much have *you* had to drink?"

Malark let his face shift back to his own features for two slow, deliberate breaths before he said, "Nothing, Culthar. Sorry to disappoint you." When he grinned, an instant later, it was Rozsarran's own lopsided grin.

Culthar stared at him in astonishment. "Lord, why are you here?" he whispered. "Is Roz . . . ?"

"Sleeping. I've little time for talk. Take this!" He pressed a ring into Culthar's palm. "Hide it well, on your person, and do *not* part with it. Magics on it serve to hide it from normal scrutiny by one of the Art, but wear it openly only when you intend to use it. Its command word is the name of the first dracolich you served. Speaking that while wearing this will instantly take you and one other creature you're touching flesh-to-flesh to Thunderstone—specifically, a hill above that town where one of us lives as a hermit, Brossan by name. If he's not there, go to . . ." Several more instructions followed, then: "One thing more. I may appear to you and give the sign of the hammer, or a redcrest may fly into this guardroom—an illusion, mind. These both are signals that you're to swiftly take Shandril Shessair and escape with her by means of the ring. Otherwise, you're to take her when you think best—you guessed the task before I said it. Good. You'll do this?"

Culthar swallowed. "Aye, for the glory of the Followers."

Malark nodded, smiled grimly, and picked up the reeking bucket. "Before your fellow watchmen return, I believe I'll go be sick outside."

Holding the bucket before him, he staggered out and down the hall, every inch the drunken Rozsarran.

It was a white-faced and thoughtful Culthar who drew off his boot and slid the brass ring onto his little toe where he'd feel its reassuring presence at every step.

A loudly and realistically sick Rozsarran staggered between the guards at the gate, out into the night—but a coolly efficient night cat loped from where bucket and clothes had fallen, heading for a certain spot in the trees. The night cat became a rat, crept close to the waiting cultists, and listened.

"Do you hear anything?" Suld asked suspiciously.

"Probably the master, coming back," Arkuel said. "Just sit quiet, now, or we'll both catch it."

"Sit quiet, yourself, cleverjaws. It wasn't me who bought a wagon whose seat was as full of splinters as a carpenter's beard!"

"Pierced your wits, did they? You shouldn't carry them so low down," Arkuel said smugly.

"Well met," said Malark dryly, stepping from the darkness in a spot neither of them faced. "I'm glad to hear you both so happy and good-natured." He pointed at the sleeping Rozsarran. "Take up our sleeper and come. Hood the lantern, and I'll carry it."

When the light was hidden, the mage dispelled his darkness and set off back toward the tower. There he raised darkness again, and within its ring, they dressed Rozsarran and left him with the bucket in his hands, for the other guards to find.

"Back to the inn," Malark commanded simply, banishing the darkness. He raised his arms, and his fingers flowed and grew, and then branched and branched anew. In moments, Malark's upper body looked like a large bush. A mouth opened high on one of the branches. "Come! Stay behind me!" Together they crept through the night to behind the inn stables.

"The dogs sleep," Arkuel whispered.

"Yes, but the stable master does *not*," Malark hissed back. Withdrawing a few paces, he became himself again and murmured a spell. Arkuel and Suld stood guard, swords drawn. Rejoining them, Malark eyed their blades with contempt. "Put those away. We'll not be carving roasts."

"The stable master, then?" Arkuel asked hopefully, but his blade slid back into its sheath.

In the hills to the north, a wolf howled. Axe in hand, the stable master stood and glimpsed a faint, bobbing glow.

"He's watching something of my making, by the well," Malark replied. "Come, now—quick and quiet!"

He crept across the inn yard, his underlings at his heels. At the base of the wall, the archmage's body shifted shape again. He rose into a long pole with broad rungs—a ladder that gripped the windowsill of their rented room with very human hands. The ladder sprouted two eyestalks that peered across the inn yard.

"Hurry," commanded a mouth that appeared on the crossbrace Arkuel was reaching for.

He flinched back and almost fell from the ladder. "Don't *do* that."

"Move!" the ladder responded coldly. "You, too, Suld. Our luck can't hold all night."

They all reached the chamber and closed the shutters without incident.

As he cast a wall of force between himself and his underlings, Malark wondered what would go wrong when the time came. Everything had gone smoothly, yet he could feel in his bones that spellfire was not fated to come within the grasp of the Followers.

Such hunches had given him sleepless nights before, but this time he fell asleep before he could fret. Soon he was falling endlessly through gray and purple shifting mists, plunging toward something he could not quite see that glowed red and fiery below.

"Horse cobbles," he said to it severely, but the scene did not go away. He went on falling until he reached morning.

❖ ❖ ❖

"I would speak with the cook," the traveler said. "I eat only certain meats and must know how they are prepared. If you've no objection—?"

"None," Gorstag rumbled. "Through there, on the left. Korvan's the name!"

"My thanks," the dusky-skinned merchant said. " 'Tis good to find a house where food's deemed important." He strode off, leaving Gorstag staring after him in bemusement.

After a moment, the innkeeper caught Lureene's eye and nodded at the kitchens.

She straightened from a table where a fat Sembian merchant was staring into her low-laced bodice. Turning with her hand on her hip in a way that made the eyes of every man at the table involuntarily follow her, she glided toward the kitchen.

Within, a silky voice asked in Korvan's ear, "What news have you for the Followers?" A dusky hand helpfully took up a bowl of chopped onions and conveyed them to the board beside a pan of mushrooms sizzling in bacon fat.

Korvan shuddered, looked up, and nodded briefly. "Well met," he muttered, as he added the onions to the pan. "Little news, but important. A herder saw a girl who used to work for me here, a little nothing named Shandril who ran off a few tendays back. She was in the Thunder Peaks with the Knights of Myth Drannor and Elminster of Shadowdale. She'd just wielded spellfire, and with it burned 'a dragon or suchlike;' Rauglothgor the Undying, I fear. The man heard the Shadowsil's name and said there were gold pieces all around—"

"There will be, indeed, Sir Cook, if you do the boar just so," the merchant replied smoothly.

Korvan, looked up with knife in hand and saw Lureene gliding into the kitchen. He glared at her. "What keeps you, girl? Can't seduce patrons as fast as you used to? I'll be needing butter and parsley for those carrots, and I need the fowl-spit turned *now*, not on the morrow!"

"Turn it yourself," Lureene replied crisply, "with whatever part of you first comes to hand." She swept rolls from the warming shelf into a basket and was gone with an angry twitch of her behind.

The merchant chuckled. "Well, I'll not keep you. Domestic bliss, indeed. My thanks, Korvan. Is there anything more?"

"They all went off north, from near the Sember. Nothing more!" The onions sizzled with sudden enthusiasm. Korvan stirred them energetically to keep them from sticking.

"Well done, and well met, until next time."

When Korvan turned to reply, the merchant was gone. On the counter beside Korvan were three gleaming red gems, laid in a neat triangle. The cook's eyes bulged. Spinels! A hundred pieces of gold each, easily—and *three!* Gods above!

Korvan snatched them up in one meaty fist, and then his eyes narrowed in suspicion. What if this were some trick? He'd best not be caught with them about the kitchen.

The outside door banged. Korvan glared all around until he was satisfied no one watched. With a grunt, he put his shoulder to the water barrel beside the back door. Ignoring the water slopping down its far side, he tipped it so that he could lay the gems, and a dead leaf to cover them, in a hollow beneath the barrel's base. Carefully he lowered the barrel again and straightened to look about for spying eyes. Finding none, he rushed back into the kitchen—where the smell of burning onions greeted him.

"Gods *blast* us!" he spat as he raced across the kitchen.

Lureene stuck her head in at the door and grinned at him. "Something burning?" she inquired sweetly, and withdrew her face just before the knife he hurled flashed through the doorway and clattered off the passage wall.

Korvan was still snarling when Gorstag found the knife, minutes later. "*How* many times have I told you not to throw things? And a *knife*, man! You could've killed someone! If you must carve something to work off your furies, let it be the roast! The taproom is filling up right quickly, and they'll all want to eat!" Gorstag tossed the knife into the stone sink and left.

Seeing his face as he went behind the bar to draw ale, Lureene sighed. Gorstag smiled all too seldom now, since Shandril had run off. Perhaps the tales whispered in Highmoon had been true—the ones that insisted Shandril was Gorstag's daughter.

He'd brought her with him as a babe when he bought the inn. Lureene shrugged. Perhaps someday he'd say.

Lureene remembered the hard-working, dreamy little girl snuggling down on the straw the other side of the clothes-chest, and wondered where she was now. Not so little, anymore, either . . .

"Ho, my pretty statue!" the carpenter Ulsinar called across the taproom. "Wine! Wine for a man whose throat's raw with thirst and calling after you! The gods gave us drink—will you defy them by denying me my poor share of it?"

Lureene chuckled and reached for the decanter she knew Ulsinar favored. "The gods also gave us patience, to cope when drink is not at hand. Would you neglect the one in your haste to overindulge in the other?"

Other regulars in the taproom roared their approval. "A little patience! A good motto for an overworked inn, eh?"

"I like it!" another laughed. "I'll wait with goodwill—and a full glass, if one's to be had—for Korvan's stuffed deer or his roast boar!"

"Oh, aye! He makes even the *greens* taste worth the eating! Wh—"

The man fell silent as his wife turned a cold face to him. "And I do *not?*"

Ulsinar—and not a few other men—laughed. "Let's see you wriggle, Pardus! You're truly in the wallow this time!"

"Wallow! Wallow!" others called enthusiastically.

The wife turned an even stonier face on them all. "Do you ridicule my man, who's worth more than all of you, twice over?" she inquired icily. "Would you like to lose the few teeth you collectively own?"

The roars died away.

Gorstag strode over. "Now, Yantra," he said with a perfectly straight face, "I can't have this sort of trouble in the Rising Moon. Before I serve all these rude men who've insulted you and your lord, will you have the deer or the boar?"

"The boar," Yantra replied, mollified. "A half-portion for my husband." Gorstag stared quickly around to quell the roars of mirth. The innkeeper winked as he met the eye of Pardus, who, seated behind his wife, was silently but frantically trying to indicate by gesture and exaggerated mouthing of words that he wanted deer, not boar, and most certainly not a half-portion.

"Why, Pardus," Gorstag said, as if suddenly recalling something. "A man left word here for a saddle maker—that he'd like a single piece, but a good one, for his favorite steed. I took the liberty of recommending you, but did not presume to promise times or prices. He's from Selgaunt and will call by again in a few days, on his way out from Ordulin to Cormyr. Will you talk with me, in the back, over what I should tell him?" He winked again, lightning-swift.

"Oh, aye," Pardus replied, understanding. There was no Sembian saddle-coveter, but he'd get his half-portion of boar out here, in the taproom, and as much deer as he wanted in the back, with Gorstag standing watchful guard, a little later. He smiled.

Good old Gorstag, Pardus thought, raising his flagon to the innkeeper. Long may he run the Rising Moon. Aye, let it be long, indeed.

Late that night, when all at last were abed and the taproom was red and dim in the dying firelight, Gorstag sat alone. He raised his heavy tankard and took another fiery swallow of dark, smoky-flavored wildroot stout. What had become of Shandril?

He was sick at heart at the thought of her lying dead somewhere, or raped and robbed and left to starve by the roadside . . . or sweltering in her own sweat and muck in slave-chains, in the creaking, rat-infested hold of some southern slave-trader wallowing across the Inner Sea. How much longer could he bear to stay, without at least going to look?

His glance went to the axe over the bar. In an instant, the burly innkeeper was up from his seat and vaulting a table. Another quick whirl, and he soon stood behind the bar, the axe in his hands.

There was a little scream from behind him—a girl's cry! Gorstag whirled, snake-quick and expecting trouble. Slowly, he relaxed.

"Lureene?" he asked quietly. He couldn't go. They needed him here, all these folk . . . oh, gods, bring her safe back!

His waitress saw the anguished set of his face and came up to him quietly, her blanket about her shoulders. "Master? You miss her, don't you?"

The axe trembled. Abruptly it swept into the crook of the innkeeper's arm. With whetstone, oil-flask, and rags, he came around the bar in almost angry haste. "Aye, lass, I do!" He sat.

Lureene came on silent bare feet to sit beside him.

He worked, turning the axe in his fingers as if it weighed no more than an empty mug. After a long silence, Gorstag pushed the tankard toward her. "Drink, Lureene. 'Tis good . . . you'll be the better for it."

Lureene sampled it, made a face, and then took another swallow. She set the tankard down, two-handed, and pushed it back. "Perhaps if I live to be your age, I'll learn a taste for it."

Gorstag chuckled. The axe blade flashed in his hands. Firelight glimmered down its edge.

Lureene watched him work. "Where do you think she is?"

The strong hands faltered and then stopped. "I know not." Gorstag reached for the brass oil-flask and stoppered it. "I know not," he said again. "That's the worst of it." Abruptly he clenched his hand; the flask in his grasp was crushed out of shape.

"I want to be out there looking for her, *doing* something!" he said fiercely, and Lureene put her arm about him impulsively. She could tell Gorstag was on the edge of tears. She'd never heard his voice like this before. "Why did she go? What did I do wrong that she hated it here so much?"

Lureene had no answer, so she kissed his rough cheek. When he turned his head, startled, she stilled his sobs with her lips.

When at last she withdrew to breathe, he protested weakly, "Lureene! What—?"

"You can be scandalized in the morning," she said softly, and kissed him again.

14

Shadows Creep

The hawk circles and circles and waits. Against most prey, he will have but one strike. He waits for the best chance. Be as the hawk.

Watch and wait and strike true. The People cannot afford foolish deaths in battle. War to slay, not to fight long and glorious.

Aermhar of the Tangletrees
advice before the council
in the Elven Court
Year of the Hooded Falcon

"I—I'm too *tired*, Lady," Narm apologized. "I can't concentrate!"

Jhessail nodded. "I know. That's why you must. How else will you build your will to something sharper and harder than a warrior's steel?" Her smile was wry. "You'll find, even if you never again go adventuring, that you'll almost never have quiet, comfort, good light, or space enough to study. You'll always struggle to fix spells in mind whilst overtired, or sick, or wounded and in pain, or in the midst of the snoring, groaning, talking, or crying of others. Learn now, and you'll be glad of it then."

"My thanks in advance, good lady."

Jhessail grinned. "You learn, you learn. Well, why stare you not at the pages before you? The spells won't remember themselves."

"Aarghh!" Narm struck the table with his fist. "I can't *think* with you talking to me! Always talking! Marimmar never did this! He—"

"Died in an instant because his foolishness far outstripped his Art," Jhessail replied. "I expect more of you than that, Narm. Moreover, *you* must expect different ways of mastering Art with each tutor. Question neither their methods nor the opinions freely given, even if they make you flame within, or they'll shut off as a turned tap, and you'll get no more for all your pleading and coins. You'd be a mage, and know not what sort of pride you'll have to deal with? *I* know. I'm dealing with *your* pride right now!"

"I—my apologies, Jhess—Lady Jhessail. I've no wish to offend. I—"

"—can avoid such offense by looking to your pages and trying to study through my jabber, and not wasting my *time!* I'm older than you by a good start, lad; I've less left to me than you do, if you've wits enough to live to full growth—an increasingly doubtful prospect, 'tis true—"

Narm flung up his hands in wordless despair and bent his head to the open spellbook.

Jhessail grinned again. "Well enough. Remember—no, don't look up at me. You already know I'm beautiful, and I know it, too, but the Art of Mystra is far more beautiful. Its beauty lasts where mine will wither with the years. Remember that I've learned Art from Elminster himself—" Narm looked up in surprise, but Jhessail scowled and pointed severely down at his book again. "—and I'm fast running out of severe things that he said to me, to parrot back at you. So for the love of Mystra, Narm, look down at your spells and *try*. That way I can lecture you on the kings of Cormyr, or the court etiquette of Aglarond, or recite the love songs of Solshuss the Bard, and not have to tax my wits so!"

Narm looked up at her. "Aye, I—I'll try. One question of you if I may, Lady." Jhessail smiled and nodded. "Elminster spoke so to you? Why?"

"Because it is necessary at this stage in the training of one who wields the Art. Your Marimmar never knew such discipline. Illistyl, who wields far less powerful spells, has known it, and is the better for it. Elminster thinks his tutoring remiss if a mage knows not such frustration."

Narm's opinion must have shown in his face, because Jhessail leaned forward, silver-gray robes shimmering. "The Art is a thing of beauty in itself. It can also be helpful and creative. Too many mages neglect such facets in their haste to gain wealth, influence—and enemies—by mastering fire and lightning. *Remember* that, Narm. If you forget everything else, remember that. You saw the Shadowsil die. Elminster trained her for a long time. You saw what a fascination with power, and power only, can do!"

"Aye . . . but why else become a mage?"

"Why? Why become anything other than a farmer, a hunter, or a warrior? The world forces those three professions on any who try to scratch out a living in the wilderness. All else—carpentry, painting, weaving, smithing—one does because one has the aptitude and the desire. If power is all you want, become a warrior—but mind you always strike at the weak and unprotected. Your arm may grow weary with all the slaying, but power you'll have and power you'll use over others—until you fall before the greater power of another. Keep up questions of this ilk, Narm, and you'll find I can keep up the testy temper of Elminster! *Why* aren't you looking at your books?"

"I—aye. Sorry, Lady Jhessail."

This time, Jhessail flung up her hands in despair. "Gods above. To think I once behaved as this one does! 'Tis a wonder Elminster didn't deem the form of a slug or a toad more apt for the end of my days! Patience, above all, *patience!* Pity the poor student of Art; this lesson still waits ahead of him!"

Narm looked up, alarmed.

Jhessail winked—and then screamed, "*Again* you allow meaningless noise to distract you! Call yourself a wizard?" She rose in a rustling of robes and strode at Narm, snarling, "Have you ever seen a rat? Oh, they'll crouch back to avoid a stick—but if you run about yelling and they're eating in the grain sack, they'll bite and chew as long as they can. If they must run, 'tis with mouth full, intending to return! Have you no more brains than a *rat?* Study, boy, *study!* Kings are born to their station; rats are born to theirs, too. All the rest of us must work for ours! *Study*, I say!"

The door opened and Illistyl peered in. "Quite a performance," she remarked. "Now, if you could only imitate Elminster's *voice. . . .*" She closed the door again hastily as Jhessail hurled a quill stand in her direction. After its crash, Illistyl looked in again rather anxiously. "You haven't any more of those, do you?"

"Unfortunately not. He's using it."

"Using it? Whatever for? He hasn't written a line all this time! He seems to have been otherwise occupied," Illistyl declared with exaggerated innocence. Her eyes found Narm, staring up at them both in astonishment, and she grew a head taller upon the instant. Her hair rose, and her eyes flashed. "What's *this?* We exchange a few words and this student breaks off studying? Is he weak-minded? A prankster? Or is he just *wasting* his teacher's *time?*"

Illistyl rushed at a frightened and dumbfounded Narm and halted only a hand-span away—whereupon she smiled sweetly. "Narm, how're you *ever* going to advance your Art if you can't concentrate as well as any three-year-old playing in the mud?"

Narm looked as if he were about to cry, and then burst into helpless laughter. "I've never learned Art like this before!"

"You must be used to a lot of ponderous dignity and mystical mumbling," Illistyl said. "Now look down at your book again . . . you can't read runes while you're looking at *me*."

Narm sighed loudly and feelingly. "Mystra aid me."

"She'll have to. But give her a little help, too, eh?" Illistyl turned to Jhessail. "Well, it's nice to know I'm not the only one to climb stone walls in frustration at this stage of your teaching!"

Jhessail raised an eyebrow. "You think I didn't, in my turn? Elminster continually threatened to spank me with an unseen servant spell while I studied. *Then* he threatened to force me to battle him with the spells I'd managed to memorize through all of that!"

Illistyl chuckled. "You never told me that! Did he make it any more than a threat?"

"No. I learned to study through nearly anything, with astonishing speed."

"Think he'll do as well?" Illistyl asked quietly, nodding at Narm's bent head. Jhessail shrugged.

"For himself, aye. But as protector and mate to one who'll be attacked day after day because she has spellfire—that's less certain. Are you listening again, Narm?"

Narm looked up. "Sorry?"

"*Much* better," Jhessail replied. "See that you apply yourself in this, Narm. Your life—and your lady's life—depend on it."

Shandril looked around the cavern in awe. It was vast and dark and littered with rubble.

"An accident, long ago," Elminster said gruffly. "Be ye ready, little one?"

"Aye," Shandril answered in mimicry. "What now?"

Elminster looked grave. "A few more tests. Things better learned before thy life depends on it." He walked a few paces from her. "My Art shields this chamber against prying magic," he added. "First—hold thy hand up, so . . . now the other."

Shandril looked at him, a little afraid. "Do you want me to turn my spellfire upon myself?"

Elminster nodded slowly. "We must know," he said, "but mind ye proceed very gently. Stop at once if it affects thee."

Shandril nodded back, and bent her will to the task. The thought of burning herself made her feel sick. She set her teeth, glanced at the Old Mage, and then stared at the hand she was to scorch. Spellfire blossomed from her other hand in a small, delicate flame to lick at her unprotected hand.

No pain came but a tingling that grew in intensity as she wreathed her hand in fire. She withdrew it from the raging, blistering heat, found it unmarked, and plunged it in once more. The flames roared; her uncontrollable shuddering grew.

Elminster grasped her arm, drawing her hand from the flames. His hand took its place. He grunted in pain and drew back. With his good hand, he touched her shoulder, and then, slowly and deliberately, her bare cheek. No flame erupted. "Enough."

The flames died.

Elminster faced her, working the fingers of one blackened hand. His frown mingled interest and pain. "Well, then. It does not burn thee, but the force may harm thine innards, circling back in. It does burn another, regardless of defenses of Art. When ye're not so full of energy that it burns in thine eyes, it harms only where ye intend it, and not at any touch. Narm should last longer than I'd feared."

Shandril giggled at his tone. "You'll want to watch the two of us abed to further your investigations?"

Elminster looked disapprovingly up past his brows at her. "It may not surprise ye to learn that over many hundred winters, I've seen such things a time or two before." He grinned. "I'd have seen far more, too, if I'd had the courage to keep my eyes open at a younger age. But 'tis an unsuitable topic for an old man to discuss with a young lady alone in the dark. Turn thy spellfire on this wall—nowhere else, mind; this cavern may not be entirely stable! Let us see what befalls."

Again Shandril set her will, and spellfire flamed out. It struck the wall with a hollow roar and burst in all directions. Sparks and tendrils of flame leapt among the rocks. The wall held, despite Shandril's fierce efforts to hurl all she could at it. When Elminster patted her on the shoulder to desist, the cavern wall was red-hot.

"How does it feel to hold such power?" Elminster asked softly.

"Eerie," Shandril answered truthfully. "Exciting. Fearsome. I—I never seem able to relax anymore!"

"Could ye at the inn?"

"Well, yes. Short moments by myself, now and then. But it's not just the adventure . . . nor the spellfire. . . . "

"It's Narm," Elminster said dryly. "Would ye try something else for me?"

"Yes. What's your will?"

"See if ye can hurl spellfire from thy knee, or forehead, or foot, or behind . . . or eyes. See if ye can hurl it in a spray, or curve the flames around sharp bends, or hurl small balls or streamers of flame. Knowing the accuracy of thy aim would also be useful."

"How long d'you—never mind. Guide me." Shandril mopped her sweating forehead; her fire had made the cave hot.

Elminster held out his pipe wordlessly.

She pointed one finger and pushed, just a little, with her will. A tiny spurt of flame shot out.

The old wizard turned the pipe bowl adroitly to catch the flame and puffed contentedly. "Aye, we'll start so. . . ."

That night, the hall was quiet despite the gathered Knights. They sat at the great trestle table that stretched thirty paces down the center of the warm, smoky chamber.

The remains of a good feast still lay upon the table. The guards who usually lined the walls and the servants scurrying between table and kitchen were absent, barred by Mourngrym.

The lord and lady of Shadowdale sat at the head of the table and Elminster at its foot. On one side sat Storm Silverhand, Shandril, and Narm, facing the Knights on the other. The rest of the seats stood empty.

Jhessail rose. "My lords and ladies, Narm Tamaraith has advanced his Art considerably since his arrival. He lacked not aptitude or dedication, but merely suffered from poor and insufficient training." She smiled, and to Narm's intense surprise added, "He was a joy to train. Illistyl and I have no hesitation in presenting Narm before this company as an accomplished mage. It is my understanding Elminster wishes to examine and train Narm yet, to further him for the special task of Art required in supporting the unique power of his betrothed. I yield to my master."

As Jhessail sat smoothly, Elminster rose. "Aye. I'll talk to Narm of that before long. But I'm here this night in answer to Mourngrym's request." His subtle emphasis on the last word made the lord of Shadowdale suppress a smile. "I'll report on what I've learned of the powers of Shandril Shessair, specifically that unique ability we call 'spellfire.' The power to wield spellfire has been known in the Realms in the past—"

" 'Tis my duty this time, I fear," Florin interrupted, standing with a polite bow to Mourngrym and to the Old Mage. "Elminster—the short version, please. No disrespect intended, but we lack both your lore interest and patience."

Elminster eyed him sourly. "Patience certainly seems in short supply these days. 'Tis a lamentable state of affairs when things happen at such a pace that folk can scarce grumble before the land changes again. Woeful days, indeed—" He forestalled several Knights who'd opened their mouths by saying, "But I *digress*. To the matter directly at hand: Lady Shandril, betrothed to Lord Narm Tamaraith, both of whom sit among us."

He nodded at the small figure sitting between Storm and Narm. "Shandril can now, without benefit of the balhiir that apparently awakened her spellfire, draw in spells without much personal harm—though some occurs, with certain magic—and store it for an unknown length of time and without apparent ill effects. She can subsequently send it forth, upon command and with some precision, as a fire that burns through most magical defenses and affects all things and beings I've observed it against thus far. Shandril has a finite capacity for absorbed magic, but we're presently uncertain what that is. We know neither the precise effects of the spellfire upon Shandril, nor the limitations of the spellfire she wields."

The Old Mage felt for his pipe, forgetting that it floated serenely by his ear. "I can tell you what spellfire is: the raw energy that all workings of Art are composed of, broken down by Shandril's body in some unknown manner. As the Simbul, distinguished ruler of Aglarond, pointed out at the test, such a power is dangerous—to Shandril personally and to those nearby. When her body holds so much energy that her eyes flash, her very touch can harm through unintentional discharge. She's also a threat to those who work magic everywhere in this world. Those who see this threat will act to destroy or possess her."

Elminster discovered and took hold of his errant pipe. "Certain fell powers undoubtedly already know of her abilities and will act soon. There's much more to be said, but—hem—ye asked for the short version." The Old Mage sat down.

"So you're saying war will come to the dale again because the source of spellfire is here?" Lady Shaerl asked.

"Aye," Elminster replied, "and we must be ready. To arms and alert! We must defend Shandril's person with our swords, and whelm the Art at our command to defend against the many mages who'll come for her spellfire. She cannot be everywhere to battle all of them, were she the most willing slayer in the world. Our spells we must also cast at Shandril, to feed her spellfire—'tis this her man Narm does best. Days of blood, I fear, are upon us."

Mourngrym rose and looked down the table. " 'Tis hardly fair, you powerful and experienced adventurers, to drag these young folk into a battle that will almost certainly mean their deaths, just to use them as weapons against those who come!"

"They are in such a battle as we breathe now," Elminster said sharply. "We delivered them out of it once, as a knight drags a weary fellow out of the fray for a time to catch his breath, quell his pain, and set to again. 'Tis the price of adventuring, such strife—and don't tell me they're not adventurers. One ran off with a chartered company, while the other willingly returned to Myth Drannor, alone and unarmed, to 'seek his fortune' after the death of his master at the hand of devils. We do not intend to 'use them as weapons,' but to see they know their powers fully."

The Old Mage glanced around at the Knights. "Why invite such peril? Why see a young maid become a threat to one's own powers? Why build her strength, and that of her consort, to make them an even greater menace? Because . . . because, after all these years, it still feels good to have helped someone, and accomplished something. This first fight is part of that, and we cannot avoid it. When 'tis done, our duty will be to let them go whither they will, and not compel them or make their choices for them."

As the last words left Elminster's mouth, a large green glass bottle on the table, full of wine and unopened, began to grow and change shape.

As all watched in astonishment, it became the Simbul, kneeling atop the table with proud and lonely eyes. The Witch-Queen nodded to Narm and Shandril, and then looked to Elminster.

"You'll let these two walk freely?" she asked. "Truly?"

The archmage nodded. "Aye. I will. We all here will."

"Then you have my blessing," she said softly. Her tall, slender body shifted, blurred, and shrank again. Suddenly it was a black bird. With a whir of wings, she darted up the chimney and was gone.

The Knights relaxed visibly.

"One day I suppose I'll be used to that," Torm remarked. "Old Mage, can't you tell by Art when she's near?"

Elminster shook his head. "Unless she actively uses Art of her own, nay. Her cloak-of-Art is as good as any great archmage's—which is to say, well nigh perfect."

"Such as yours, perhaps?" Torm pressed him.

Elminster smiled broadly, and suddenly wasn't there. His chair was empty, without flash or sound. Only the faint smell of pipe smoke hung in the air.

Jhessail sighed, cast a spell, looked about keenly, and shook her head. "Faint magic, all about, and those things I know to be enchanted, but no Old Mage."

"You see?" Elminster said, appearing and kissing her cheek. " 'Tis not as easy as it might seem, but it works."

"Now *that's* a trick I'd give much to learn," Torm said.

"Much it will cost ye," Elminster replied. "But enough. Be thankful, all of ye, that the Simbul favors our desires in this matter. If she did not, all of my time would be spent thwarting her; my Art would be lost to you. Who knows what foes we yet face? Ye may have need of me!"

"We *always* need you, Old Mage," Mourngrym answered, a twinkle in his eye. "Is there anyone else who'd now speak? Narm and Shandril, you needn't say a word you don't desire to—nor answer any queries put to you."

"I would speak, Lord of the Dale," said Storm Silverhand softly. She rose, silver hair swirling about the leather that sheathed her shoulders, and looked at Narm and Shandril. "We Who Harp are interested in you. Think on whether you might want to walk our way."

Eyebrows lifted in silence all around the table. Rathan looked about and asked noisily, "Is all the formal tongue work done?

Can we enjoy ourselves and let all the others back in?"

Mourngrym grinned. "I think you've cut to the heart of the boar, Mighty of Tymora. Open the doors! Let us feast! Elminster, don't go, I pray you!"

The Old Mage had already risen. "I'm a mite old for all the babbling and flirting of your feasts. I look at all the comely lasses and see only the faces of those I met at feasts long ago, in cities now dust—truly, Mourngrym, I enjoy it not. Besides, I've work to do. My Art stands not still, and more things unfold under the eyes of Selûne than just spellfire. Fare ye well, all." He strode forward, crouched before the fire—and was suddenly a great, gray-feathered eagle. He soared up the chimney just as the Simbul had.

"Show-off," Jhessail said affectionately.

Rathan saluted the departing wizard with a rude noise, waving a bottle in either hand. Torm meanwhile dragged Narm up out of his seat and led him in the direction of a sideboard that sported gleaming decanters.

Shandril leaned to speak to Jhessail. "Lady, wh—"

"Call me Jhess!" Jhessail responded fiercely. She bent her head conspiratorially, hair almost falling into a dish of cheese-filled mushroom caps. "This 'lady' business keeps me thinking a noble matron stands behind me, disapproving of my every move!"

"Jhess, then; forgive me. Why does Rathan drink so much? He never seems to get drunk, but . . ."

"But he drinks a goodly lot?" Jhessail agreed. "Yes, you should know. 'Twas what our companion Doust Sulwood gave up lordship of this dale for."

"Rathan's drinking?"

"No, no. I meant they faced the same problem: A good priest of Tymora must continually take risks—reckless ones, most would say. Worshiping Tymora truly and trusting in the Lady's Luck is a problem if you're sensitive to what your recklessness does to others, or are by nature cautious or considerate. The life of trusting to luck sits not well with contemplating consequences or desiring security and comfort. You see that?"

"Yes." Shandril nodded. "But how—?"

"Well, Doust as lord had to make decisions that affected the lives of the dalefolk. Concern for their safety was his duty. He couldn't do well by them *and* serve the Lady of Luck. In the end, his calling proved the stronger, and he gave up the dale rather than rule poorly. I wish more who fought such battles within themselves between office and belief reached the right choices."

Jhessail looked fondly across the room at Merith. "As my lord, too, has done." She looked at Rathan. "As for yon buffoon, his jesting's but an act. He's sensitive and romantic, easily moved to tears. He hides it and overcomes the barbs of Torm with his drunken sot act."

Rathan gave them a merry wave; both women returned it.

"He drinks because he's sensitive and prudent," Jhessail continued, "and must favor luck and live in danger. He steels himself with drink. As he doesn't want to become falling-down drunk, he eats like a starving wolf. This makes him fat, and able to take in more drink without staggering and slurring. Do not think him a drunkard, Shandril; he's not. Nor is he a lecher or fraud, but a true servant of Tymora. I'm proud to ride with him."

Rathan roared with laughter at a jest of Storm's.

"You've given me different eyes to see him by, Lady."

"Jhess, remember?" Jhessail said softly. "The most valuable thing I've learned from Elminster is to look at all things and folk, however strange they seem, from all sides."

Shandril nodded, and it seemed tiny flames leaped in her eyes.

"Act as you must," Jhessail added, "but think as you act. You'll see things as others do, as well as the way you're used to. If you walk with the Harpers," she nodded toward Storm, "they'll tell you the same thing, dressed up in grander words."

The room was filling up as the good folk of Shadowdale and the staff and guards of the tower crowded into the large, high-vaulted hall. There was much laughter and chatter.

Narm joined Shandril in the tumult, kissing her.

"They party with a right good will here," Shandril said in greeting.

"We drink, love, laugh, and eat as if we may be dead tomorrow," Jhessail replied, "for death hangs over us."

"What?" asked Narm, taken aback.

"Zhentil Keep could sweep down on us any morn. Hillsfar's new ruler has intentions unknown. Devils walk in Myth Drannor to one side and Daggerdale to the other. Now you're here, and powerful foes may attack anytime to slay or capture you. Some know a duty to defend you; some merely fear they'll be caught in the way. They fear you, too, Shandril, no little bit. Your spellfire on the hilltop is a scene told often, and vividly, in the Old Skull. You're 'Lady Spellfire' now."

Narm and Shandril stared at her, stricken. "We should leave," Shandril whispered.

Jhessail caught at her sleeve and smiled. "No! Stay; the dalefolk accept you, and will fight for you as they would for any guest before their hearth. You're welcome, truly. Besides, you'll upset Elminster terribly if you run off now; he's not finished with you. Come, let us dance, you two and Merith and I!"

"But, I—"

"We've never learned—"

"No matter. Merith shall teach us all a dance of the Elven Court—we'll all be new to it. Come!" The lady mage pulled them out into an open space, her long hair swirling about her shoulders, and let out a birdlike call.

Merith looked up, excused himself from two fat farmwives, and joined them. "Storm! Will you harp for us?"

The bard smiled and took down the harp of the hall from the wall where it hung among rusting shields of long-dead lords. It was of black wood inlaid with silver, and it sang like a mournful lover as Storm ran her fingers over its strings.

"A gift from Myth Drannor," Jhessail murmured.

"You'll be wanting to dance, my love?" Merith asked.

"Of course. One of the gentler tunes, my lord, one that human feet can follow. Narm and Shandril, and you and I?"

Merith bowed. "Of course. What say you to the frolic that of old we danced on the banks of the Ashaba? Storm, you know the tune. . . !"

⊠ ⊠ ⊠

It was late, or rather very early. Stars glittered coldly in the clear dark sky as revelers climbed the stairs, footsore and happily sleepy.

"Elves must be stronger than I'd thought," Narm grunted as he and Shandril mounted the last flight to the bedchamber. The Twisted Tower was quiet around them. Far below, revelry continued unabated, but no sound carried this far. The guards stood silent at their posts.

At the head of the stairs, Shandril stripped off her shoes and set her aching feet on cold stone. The chill on her bare flesh roused her somewhat. She slipped out of Narm's grasp and, laughing, ran ahead.

He grinned, shook his head, and made haste to follow.

They were both running when the blow fell.

Shandril heard a dull thud behind her, followed by a thumping and scrabbling sound. "Narm?" she called, turning as she reached the door. "Narm? Did—"

A grim-faced guard ran hard for her, the mace that had felled Narm raised in a mailed fist. Shandril had no time to dodge or fight. She ran. Lady Spellfire fled on bare feet down the long, dim hall.

The guard Rold stood far ahead under a flickering torch. He turned to look at her.

A wild rage grew in Shandril out of shrieking fear for Narm's life. She looked back through streaming hair. A mailed hand reached for her. Without thought, she dived to the rugs of the hall and rolled.

Armored boots struck sharp, numbing blows on her back and flank. A startled curse rang out as her assailant tripped, landing in a crash of metal.

Shandril rolled free and to her knees.

The guard, fast and well trained, spun about, his legs kicking the air, and drew back his mace to hurl at her. Their eyes met across too little space.

Fire exploded from Shandril's raging glare.

The guard yelled in fear as his mace whirled from his hand. Large, dark, like a bolt from the gods, it smashed aside hastily raised fingers and struck her hard on one side of the face.

Shandril slid into a yellow haze of confusion . . . and down into darkness.

Without mercy, Rold struck Culthar from behind, war hammer crashing down his helm. "Are you *mad*? You're sworn to *protect* her!"

Culthar slumped limply aside, blood running from nose and mouth. He crumpled against the wall and was forgotten as the man who'd felled him scrambled to reach Shandril.

Rold recalled that her touch was said to be death when she hurled spellfire, but he drew off a gauntlet and gently felt her temple.

He wiped away the blood, cursed, and flung his gauntlet at the nearest alarm-gong. Wrapping her shoulders in his half-cloak, he held her close and drew a silver disc on a fine chain from his belt.

"Lady Tymora," he prayed hoarsely as the hollow singing of the gong rolled around him, "if you favor those cursed to be different from most folk, aid this poor lass now. She's done no wrong and needs your blessing dearly. Hear me, Bright Lady, I beseech you! Turn your bright face upon this Shandril!"

The old soldier held Shandril in his arms, waiting for the sound of running feet, and prayed on.

A turret on the inner wall of Zhentil Keep held a small, circular room with no window, and in that room, Ilthond waited with scant patience. The time was come; still Manshoon came not back to the city of the Zhentilar. If Ilthond held spellfire and knew how to wield it, such a return would not have to be feared overmuch.

The young mage paced before his crystal. The eagle that had to be Elminster even now came to earth by the door of the old, slightly leaning tower where he dwelt. The eagle became Elminster—pipe, battered old hat, and all—and went into the tower.

Ilthond watched an instant more, and then drew forth a scroll tube fashioned from the hollow wing bone of a great dragon. He opened the scroll—a teleport spell, set down by the wizard Haklisstyr of Selgaunt. Since his bony back had met with a dagger, thoughtfully poisoned by the ambitious Ilthond, Haklisstyr wouldn't need it anymore.

That same ambitious mage rolled out the scroll on the table beside the crystal. He set coins, a dagger, a candlestick, and a skull at the corners to hold it open. Fixing in his mind a clear picture of a certain blanket-room on the third floor of the Tower of Ashaba, he began to cast the spell.

From below him, from another room of the turret, came the faint piping of a glaurist blowing the mournful melody of an old ballad:

Good fortune comes fleeting, and then it is gone,
But the heart heavy with weeping must carry on.
Ill luck comes and stays like winter's cold snow.
Always you must weather more than one blow. . . .

Ilthond spread his hands in a grand flourish to finish the casting—and vanished.

The floating, disembodied wizard eye that had been watching him from beneath the table winked out an instant later, leaving the little room once more as dark and uninhabited as it was supposed to be.

15

Hawks Weep, Fools Plan

Afterward, the greatest victories always look like the work of brilliant warcaptains. In the midst of the fray, they're just as much cursing and slipping and tangles of death and disaster as the greatest defeats. The trick is to wind up among those who survive such battles relatively unmaimed.

The gods reward those who die gloriously in their service. The rest of us have to reward ourselves.

Raulavan Emmertide of Suzail
Swordlord and Survivor:
Forty Summers Under the Purple Dragon
Year of the Bright Blade

"Of *course* she'll live, if ye get out of my way for a breath or two!" Rathan roared. "Lanseril, stay and heal! Rold, ye saved her; ye stay too. Florin, bring Narm over here . . . be he awake yet? All others, get hence! Downstairs, the lot of ye! Mourngrym, ye and Shaerl may stay, of course. The rest—clear out! Get gone!"

"Narm stirs," Jhessail reported tersely. "We'll take this guardsman, if Rold hasn't quite slain him, and learn the whys of this. All others—back to your posts. Our thanks for your haste in coming." The guards saluted her and left.

Florin laid Narm gently on a sleeping fur, letting his bruised head down with care. "How is she?" Florin asked, looking at Shandril's still face.

"Well enough," Rathan replied, "considering the blow she took. I only hope it hasn't somehow harmed her ability to wield spellfire, now that half Faerûn will attack her to gain it."

"Why would just one guard attack?" Mourngrym muttered, frowning.

"One seemed to do well enough," Shaerl remarked, gesturing at the two still forms.

"No, love—I meant I'd expect to find other attackers near at hand. Rold, I want this tower searched forthwith, this floor first. Jhessail, will you rouse Illistyl and stand guard over our two guests? I'll remain also." Mourngrym drew his slim, jeweled sword, set it point-down before him, and leaned on it.

Shaerl nodded and knelt by Narm, who had begun to moan faintly.

Florin was ready with strong, sure arms when the young mage suddenly surged up, arms flailing. "Where's—? Shandril! Danger! Beware! Danger!"

"Aye . . . aye," Florin agreed gently, holding him. "Danger 'twas, indeed. Stay still now, and we can see to your lady."

"Shan—how *is* she? Sh—"

"Quiet and still, please. She lies behind you. Rathan and Lanseril tend her."

"I—yes." Narm sank back, as pale as snow, wincing as his head came to rest on the furs.

"Narm, lie quiet and still, as you were bid," Lady Shaerl said.

Narm grimaced, and then he heard Shandril say softly, "I thank you. Narm was hurt; have you seen to him?" His heart knew peace, and he sank into the warm, waiting darkness . . . and was asleep, not even hearing Rathan's reply.

It was dark and close in the blanket room. The smells of pomander and moth mix were strong. Ilthond stifled a sneeze, nodded in satisfaction at his accurate journeying, and listened.

He could hear nothing. Well enough. To work, then.

The mage worked invisibility on himself and eased the door open. The passage beyond seemed empty. He stole forth and looked about.

Better and better, he thought. Muttering a spell of flight, Ilthond rose to drift unseen along the corridor. No guards . . . why? Was Shadowdale truly so lax? No, there must be some strife or alarm. . . .

Around the corner came a dozen guards with drawn swords and forbidding glares.

Ilthond floated over and past them in careful silence. Where might the young maid be? The tower's mortar was mixed with substances to prevent scrying, but all he needed to do was find enough grim guards gathered before a closed door, and she'd be beyond.

She might be above, in the plainer but more secure rooms, or below, as befitted a guest of importance. The greater risk lay downward—but so, too, did all chance of learning who was where. Ah well—a short, risky road leads fastest to the top, they say. . . .

Ilthond reached a stair and headed down, keeping near the sloping stone ceiling. Carefully and quietly he went, nosing through rooms and along halls like a silent shadow, flitting swiftly, yet taking care not to be brushed against.

After a time, his search brought him to a long hall where torches burned every twenty paces. At its far end, humans in rich garb stood or knelt near two more who lay on the floor. Ilthond drifted slowly and silently closer, straining to hear.

"How d'ye feel?" Rathan growled. "Better, I trust?"

Shandril nodded slowly. "My head still aches. My thanks indeed, good Rathan. Again I'm in your debt for healing me."

"Not in my debt," Rathan corrected. "The Lady 'tis whom ye

owe!" With the middle finger of his right hand, he traced a circle about the disc on his breast.

"Yes. I'll not forget the Lady's favor," Shandril replied. "How fares Narm?"

Rathan looked over at Narm. "He sleeps. Best to let him sleep on. But ye must try thy spellfire."

Shandril had risen onto her elbows. Drawing her legs under her, she extended an unsteady hand. From her spread fingers spellfire spat down the hall in a long tongue of flame. It died away, curling into air. "As before, I can still—"

A pain-racked groan came out of empty air down the hall.

Florin and Mourngrym drew steel and stepped in front of Shandril. Shaerl drew her dagger and rapped the nearest gong with its pommel.

A robed man with hawkish features and glossy black hair faded into view in midair. His face was twisted in pain, his robe smoldered, and his shoulder and breast were burned bare. Glaring, he hissed a word that unleashed the power of the wand in his hand.

Forked lightning crackled down the hall, striking both Florin and Mourngrym. The lord of Shadowdale staggered and fell heavily, blade clattering. Shaerl cried out and ran to him. Florin was driven to his knees by the bolt, but struggled up into a slow, weak charge, face black with pain.

Shandril stood, furious and heartsick, and lashed out with spellfire. "Wherever I go! Always beset, always friends and companions hurt! You seek spellfire? Well, then—*have it!*"

Spellfire roared out of her in a tumbling inferno that lasted for but a breath—but raged down the hall. It swept over the flying mage like a wave over rocks.

The lightning had shaken Narm into dazed wakefulness. Gasping in pain, he struggled to his knees to work Art and protect his lady from this new menace. His hands froze as he saw the blackened, crippled thing that the spellfire left on the scorched rugs of the hall.

The man moved weakly and twisted cooked lips in words of Art. Shandril raised a hand again but did not unleash her flames. His head sank down between smoking shoulders that shook with pain—and the mage vanished, gone as if he had never been.

"Wherever we go," Shandril said wearily, turning to Rathan, "your healing services are needed. I hope you'll not grow tired of it all before this comes to an end!"

"Lady," Rathan replied, as he hastened to where Mourngrym lay. "This never ends, I fear. Worry not about my patience—'tis what I walk these Realms for." He knelt by the lord of Shadowdale and looked back at her over one shoulder. "Ye do impressive work, I must say."

Jhessail arrived, robes held high as she sprinted along in the forefront of a large group of guards. "Shandril? Florin? Mourngrym?" Merith was at her side, blade out.

"We need healing," Rathan called. "The time for blasting and all that is past! Send four guardsmen for Eressea at the temple. . . . I've no more power to heal, and Mourngrym needs it."

Jhessail relayed his orders and then asked, "What happened?"

"Another mage," Rathan snapped, "flying about and invisible. Shandril touched him with spellfire purely by chance when I asked her to test her powers. He struck Florin and Mourngrym with lightning from a wand. Shandril burned but did not slay him. He teleported away."

Jhessail looked at Shandril. "You slew him not?"

Shandril nodded. "I could not. 'Twas . . . horrible."

"I can't fault you," Jhessail said slowly. "Yet when you fight, Art to Art, seek to slay—and finish the job. A foe who escapes will return for revenge!"

"Aye," said Shaerl, eyes hot. "A man who struck down my lord lives! I blame you not, Shandril. It must be terrible to hold such death within you, always knowing you can slay. Yet, if that man were within my grasp right now, I'd not hesitate to strike and slay. One who'd harm my Mourngrym does not deserve to live."

Sounds of running feet came. A guardsman reached the head of the stairs, shouting, "Lord Mourngrym! Lady Shaerl!"

Shaerl turned. "Say on."

"My lady, the prisoner is gone! We had him in the cell, and his hands were bound—yet he vanished before our eyes."

"The man Culthar?" Shaerl asked. "How could this happen?"

She turned to Jhessail. The lady mage nodded calmly, and Shaerl sighed and turned back to the guard. "I hold you and all the guard blameless. Bid a search be mounted for Culthar, and return to your post with our thanks."

The guard nodded, bowed, and hurried off.

Jhessail shrugged. "A teleport ring, perhaps, a rogue stone, or another way of Art I don't know. All would require outside aid. The Zhentarim, perhaps, or the priests of Bane. Culthar was someone's eyes here in the tower." She spread her hands in futility with a ghost of a smile. "The ravens are gathering."

Shaerl sighed. "Aye, and I'm growing tired of it."

Rathan looked up. "*Ye* grow tired of it! What of we who heal?"

"Ah, but you enjoy divine aid," said Mourngrym weakly from beneath the priest's hands. "Mind you see to Florin, too. I need him healthy and alert."

The man who'd once declined the lordship of Shadowdale, and led the Knights from their early days, was leaning against a wall in pain-racked silence.

"Florin?" Jhessail asked hesitantly. "Are you badly hurt?"

"As usual." Florin's voice was rueful, and he lowered it so only she could hear. "I'm growing too old for constant battle, Jhess. 'Tis not the thrill it used to be!"

"Oh, no, you don't," Jhessail said briskly, putting a slim arm about his great shoulders. "Not now. We need you." She drew him down until he sat against the wall. "You'll feel much better once you've been healed."

Merith joined them.

Florin nodded gratefully to them both and quietly fainted.

Jhessail let his head rest on her shoulder and said to her husband, "My lord, please run to our strongbox for a potion. He's hurt worse than I thought!"

Shandril turned her face to the wall and leaned her forehead on her arm. "I—I—we must leave you. Again and again you're hurt for our sake, one attack after another. You're my friends! I must not do this to you, day after day!" She burst into tears.

"Must we have all this weeping?" Rathan complained. " 'Tis as bad as the fighting. Nay, worse—ye can stop the fighting by slaying thy foe!"

Narm rose to defend his lady, but Rathan pushed him down again with but two stout fingers. “Don't start! Ye're not fully healed. I'm not having ye rush around getting hurt and crying all about the place. D'ye hear? Just lie down and wait. We'll see if there's time to listen to such foolishness.”

Merith went to Shandril and tickled her gently under the ribs until she turned from the wall. He swept her into his arms and kissed away her tears. “Nay, nay, little one, you needn't be ashamed or upset on our account. 'Tis a hard road you walk, an adventurer's road. Would you not walk it with us? 'Tis not so lonely or hard, with friends!”

“Oh, Merith,” Shandril said, and sobbed into his shoulder.

Merith carried her to Florin and Jhessail and sat her down on his own lap.

“Cry not so,” Jhessail bade. “Does the hawk weep because it has wings? Does the wolf howl because it has teeth? We do what we can with our Art or skill-at-arms. Is your spellfire so different? Use it, and hold yourself not to blame for the attacks others make on you or this place. We do not blame you.” She patted Shandril's knee. “Let's all go to the great hall as soon as Eressea has done her healing and see if there's aught to eat or drink. Violence always makes me hungry!”

In a turret on the inner walls of Zhentil Keep, in a small, circular chamber, Ilthond sprawled on a familiar floor. He lay on the painted circle he'd practiced teleporting to, and he groaned in pain.

None were there to see or hear; he was alone behind three locked and hidden doors. Pain crashed over him in waves of red agony, as if he struggled seaward through the breakers on a beach. Ilthond crawled forward between waves, seeking the cabinet where he kept his potions.

He wondered dully if he'd reach it.

"That's quite enough foolishness," Elminster said peevishly. "I leave ye, and within half a dozen breaths ye're scorching *another* mage! Well then, I'll not leave ye. . . . Ye'll stay in my tower, ye two, with my scribe Lhaeo and myself. To draw off all who're hunting spellfire, Illistyl and Torm will impersonate ye, in a tent with Rathan upon Harpers' Hill. Merith, ye and Lanseril will keep watch on them. Now pass that wine ye're curled so lovingly about, Rathan, and let's have no argument; the matter's settled."

"I'm glad of that," Florin said dryly. "Have you no task for Jhessail or me?"

"Eh? Gods look *down*, man! Someone has to watch over the dale and shatter the armies of Zhentil Keep if they come calling. Ye two ought to be able to manage that!"

There were dry chuckles, and then a yawn. Shandril's eyes were nearly closed.

"Love," Narm said gently, shaking her. "Are you sleepy?"

"Of course," she replied faintly. "We were going to bed when this uproar started, remember?"

"To bed, then!" Elminster said gruffly. "We'll all prance yonder to my tower together—and then mind the lot of ye return here, except our two innocents. I don't want to be falling over a lot of snoring Knights in the morning!"

"At this rate," Lanseril replied, "you're safe on that score. You'll be falling over snoring Knights at highsun, instead."

Amid chuckles, they went out into the night.

⊠ ⊠ ⊠

"Keeping you awake, Rold?" one of his fellows grunted jovially at dawnfry that morning. The guardroom was strewn with gloves, helms, and scabbarded blades, as their owners lingered over the last fried bread, tomatoes, and bacon.

The old veteran yawned again. "Glad I am, indeed, that the young lord and lady are out of the tower. No offense to them. It's just that I'll be more likely to sleep when I'm off duty."

"Fewer sinister mages and night slayers skulking in every hall and peeking through every window," agreed another, sharp-voiced guard, buckling on his sword.

"Aye, Kelan. Less Art we can't fight and less treachery within." A little silence fell at Rold's words.

Kelan said softly, "Who d'you think got to Culthar? What did they offer him to chance such a reckless grab at one who could cook him to the bones?"

"Who can know another man's price?" Rold replied. Several guards nodded. "I doubt he needed much persuading. Belike he was already loyal to someone outside the dale, someone who told him to do this thing."

"What 'someone'?"

Rold shrugged. "That, I know not, or I'd be at Lord Mourngrym to let me go after him. Don't laugh! 'Tis easier on one's temper to be moving and attacking instead of growing cold and weary at a guard post, never knowing when attack will come."

"Where did they go?" asked a young guard, a late riser, still heavy about the eyes, dawnfry on a plate in his hand.

Rold chuckled. "Mind you aren't late for your own funeral some morn, Raeth. The young lord and lady'll be camping out by Harpers' Hill with Rathan Thentraver. Practicing hurling this spellfire where Lord Mourngrym's fine rugs won't be scorched. Most of the Knights will be off about the dales at Elminster's bidding!"

"Ah, things'll get a mite quieter for a few days," Raeth said with satisfaction. The older guards chuckled.

"Think you so?" Kelan asked. " 'Tis a long run through the forest, in full armor, to Harpers' Hill!"

Rold was still chuckling as the bell rang and they hastened to their posts. Raeth, his mouth full of bacon, wasn't.

"This is a fool's plan," Rathan grunted. "One only Elminster could have come up with." The Mighty of Tymora surveyed the tents sourly. "Lady, aid me. I'm surely going to need thy help."

"Cheerful, aren't you?" Torm answered. "I'm enjoying this."

"Ye have weird enthusiasms," Rathan grunted. "Ye can't even enjoy thy lady when she must wear the shape of Shandril every instant."

Torm grinned. "Oh? That's going to hamper me? How so?" He raised dark eyebrows. "Besides, *I* look like Narm for the present."

"Shameless philanderer," Rathan growled. He looked at the trees around. "I wonder when the first attack will come?"

"While you're standing there," Torm replied, "if you keep yapping about Elminster's wisdom and the danger you've so foolishly plunged headlong into. Go in and pray to the Lady for healing Art. No doubt we'll need it soon enough."

"Aye, there ye speak truth," Rathan replied darkly. "Is there no wine about?" He peered into the tents. Illistyl smiled back at him out of one, looking like Shandril. She moved with smooth innocence, abandoning her own defiant strut.

"No," Torm answered brightly. "We've left it behind at the tower. A tragedy, I agree."

"Indeed . . . well, one of the guards will just have to go back for it," Rathan concluded, squinting at the sun. "My thirst grows."

"Here, then." Torm passed him a flask.

Rathan unstopped it and sniffed suspiciously. "What is it? I smell naught—"

"Water of the gods," Torm replied. "Pale ale. Tymora's Tipple!"

"Eh?" The priest frowned. "Ye blaspheme?"

"No, I offer you a drink, sot. Your thirst, remember?"

"Aye," Rathan agreed, mollified, and took a swig. "Aaagh!" he said, spitting most of it out. "It *is* water!"

"Aye, as I told you," Torm replied smoothly, leaping nimbly out of the way as the priest reached for him.

The Mighty of Tymora pursued his sly tormentor across the rocky hilltop, while Illistyl watched from the tent, shaking her head.

"Playing already, I see," she remarked, just loudly enough for Torm to hear. He turned and waved at her, grinning—and promptly fell over a stone, with Rathan on top of him. Illistyl burst into laughter before she realized she couldn't recall what Shandril's laugh sounded like.

The leaning stone tower rose out of a grassy meadow beside a small pond. It was built of old, massive stones, without gate or fence or outbuildings. Flagstones led up to a plain wooden door. It looked small and drab in comparison with the Twisted Tower, rising against the sky across the meadow. But it seemed somehow a place of power, too—and more welcoming.

Inside, it was very dark. Dust lay thick on books and papers stacked untidily everywhere. The smell of aging parchment filled the air. Out of the colonnade of paper pillars rose a rickety curving stair, ascending to unseen heights. A bag of onions hung over the doorway. Beyond an arch, faint footfalls sounded.

"Lhaeo," Elminster called. "Guests!"

An expressionless face appeared in the doorway.

"There's no need for thy simpering act," the Old Mage added.

The face smiled and nodded—a pleasant, green-eyed face with pale brown hair and delicate features. Its owner was about as tall as Merith, very slim, and wore an old, patched leather apron over plain tunic and hose.

"Welcome," Lhaeo greeted them, in a soft, clear voice. "If you're hungry, there's stew warm over the fire. Highsunfeast will be herbed hare cooked in red wine . . . that Sembian red Mourngrym gave us. I deem it good for little else. I fear I've no dawnfry ready."

Elminster chuckled. "Ye'd have been wasted on a throne, Lhaeo. I've eaten no better fare since Myth Drannor fell than what ye cook. But I forget my manners, such as they are . . . Lhaeo, these be Narm Tamaraith, a mage who flourishes these passing days under the tutelage of Jhessail and Illistyl, and his betrothed, Shandril Shessair, who can wield spellfire!"

Lhaeo's eyes opened wide. "After all these years? You were right to bring them here. Many will rise against her."

"Many already have," the white-bearded wizard replied dryly. "Narm, Shandril—I make known to thee Lhaeo, my scribe and cartographer. Outside these walls he's counted a lisping manlover from Baldur's Gate. He's not, but that's his tale. Come up, now, and I'll show ye thy bed—I hope ye don't mind there's only one—and some old clothes to keep ye warm. We don't feel the cold, but I know others find it chill."

"Keep him to one speech," Lhaeo added as they started up the stairs, which creaked alarmingly, "and I'll have tea ready when you come down again!"

They went up through a thick stone floor into a circular room. Shandril cast an eye over the maps and scrolls cluttering a large table—but looked away quickly as runes crawled on the parchment.

Over the table, a globe hung in midair, a pale sphere of radiance like a small moon. Its light showed a narrower stair curving up into the darkness. Books and scrolls littered the chests and lay piled atop a tall black wardrobe. The old wooden bed, with a curved rail at head and foot, looked solid and cozy. Shandril felt tired after the battles and conferences. She swayed on her feet.

Narm and Elminster both put out a hand to her. Shandril waved them away. "Thank you both. I've been a burden to many since I left Deepingdale!"

"Second thoughts?" the Old Mage asked quietly, no censure in his tone.

"No. No, not when I can think clearly. I just couldn't have lived through it alone!" She turned to the wizard. "There's only one bed. Where will you sleep?"

"In the kitchen. Lhaeo and I are rarely asleep at the same time; someone has to watch the stew."

Narm laughed. "The greatest archmage in all Faerûn, and you spend nights watching a pot of stew!"

"Is there a higher calling?" Elminster replied. "Oh, speaking of pots, the chamber pot's by the foot of the bed, yon. Aye, I know it looks odd—'tis an upturned wyvern skull, sealed with paste. I stole it from the bedchamber of a Tharchioness in Thay, in my wilder days."

He made a quick gesture. Various pipes and tobacco pouches rose and darted away down the stairs like hurrying wasps.

"Come and have thy tea, and then ye can sleep. Ye'll be safe here, if anywhere in the Realms. Do as ye always do together, so long as it does not involve a lot of screaming. A little noise will not bother us. If ye pry about, be warned: the Art here can kill in an instant!"

"Elminster," Narm said, as the wizard started downstairs, "our thanks. You've gone to much trouble!"

"And if I did not, what sort of greatest archmage in all Faerûn would I be?" came the gruff reply over the Old Mage's shoulder. "I'm stepping out for a pipe. Mind ye come in haste—Gond alone knows what Lhaeo'll put in thy tea if you're not there. He thinks every cup should be a new experience." Below, the door banged.

"By the gods, I'm tired," Narm said.

"Aye, too tired," Shandril agreed, "I hope we can sleep." Her hands, as she reached to him, were shaking. They wearily went down to tea.

When Elminster finished his pipe, he knocked its ashes out on the doorstep and came back in. "All well?"

Lhaeo came to the door, Narm leaning limply on his shoulder. The scribe held him up with casual strength. "All well. They'll sleep until morn. I mixed the dose carefully, and they drank it all down."

"Good. I'll take his feet. A sound sleep'll do them good. When he's rested and not worried sick about his ladylove, I'll get a look at the lad's castings."

"How about her?"

"No training needed. She's already learned much precision. When we fought Manshoon, she was still a child hurling a snowball. Now, she can do more with it—mind this bit; the lad's heavy!—than most mages ever do with fire magics."

They laid Narm on the bed and went back for Shandril. Lhaeo frowned as they carefully ascended the stair. "We've much that will fit the lad, but what of this little lady?"

Elminster looked wise. "I've already thought on that," he replied. "Some of the gowns Shoulree Talaeth wore when Myth Drannor was bright. They're in the chest near the stairs. She, too, could wield spellfire. She won't mind."

"Walks she yet?" Lhaeo asked, as they laid Shandril gently beside Narm and drew off her boots.

Elminster looked thoughtful. "I doubt she does . . . but perhaps some who joined the Long Sleep years ago stir now. That'd explain why the devils in Myth Drannor have not troubled us more. Something to look into." His face grew a wry grin. "In my copious free time. . . ."

⊠ ⊠ ⊠

"I know this is wisest and safest," Shandril said, "but I grow so *bored*, Lhaeo! Is there nothing I can do? I can't pry into spellbooks—I'd only get hurt or changed into some beast. I can't tidy for the same reason!"

"Do you cook?" Lhaeo asked expressionlessly.

"Of course! Why, at the Rising Moon—" She stopped, eyes alight. "May I cook with you?"

Lhaeo bowed and smiled. "Please. 'Tis seldom I can converse with another who spends time in a kitchen. Who wants to talk to someone who speaks thus?" he asked with a mincing lisp.

"Why do you pretend to be . . . Elminster's companion?"

Lhaeo looked at her soberly. "My lady, I'm in hiding. I'll tell you who I am only if you never tell anyone, beyond Narm."

"I promise, by whatever oaths you wish."

Lhaeo shook his head. "Your word is enough. Come into the kitchen."

Warmed by a small hearth fire, Lhaeo's lair smelled deliciously of herbs, simmering stew, and onion soup.

"Are you a lost prince?" Shandril prompted jokingly.

He waved her to a stool and went to inspect the huge stewpot. "I suppose you could say that," Lhaeo said, stirring with a long-handled ladle. "I'm the last of the royal house of Tethyr."

Shandril's mouth fell open.

Lhaeo smiled and waved his ladle. "In happier times I was so far from the throne that I never thought of myself as a prince. But there've been so many deaths that I am, so far as Elminster and I can tell, the last alive of royal blood."

"Why do you hide?"

Lhaeo shrugged. "All who seize power expect others to do as they would. Anyone of royal blood must want to wear the crown, they think. I live because they don't know I live. That's all there is to tell. Not so impressive, is it? But 'tis a secret that must be kept, for my life hangs upon it."

"I'll not tell it," Shandril said firmly. "What can I help with, here?"

Lhaeo looked at her. "Cook what you like and teach me as you go, please?" They smiled at each other across a bag of onions. "And, my thanks."

"For keeping your secret?"

"Aye. Each secret has a weight all its own. They add up, secrets, to a burden you carry all your days!"

Shandril looked up from selecting onions. "You carry many?"

"Aye. But my load is nothing to Elminster's."

Shandril looked down. "Whose gown is it that I wear?"

"That's a secret. I'd tell, but 'tis his to unfold, not mine."

"Well enough. Have you an old apron I can wear?"

"Aye, hanging behind you. Tell me of the Rising Moon."

She did. They serve others most who ask the right question, and then listen. The day passed, and they marked not the time.

The day passed, and Narm grew weary. He was used to the clear and careful teaching of Jhessail and Illistyl. Elminster's methods were a rude shock.

The Old Mage badgered and derided and made testy comments. The simplest query on a small detail of casting brought a scholarly flood of information—a voluminous barrage that never included a direct answer. Elminster had worked over Narm's newest spell, the Sphere of Flame, until Narm could have screamed.

Weary hours of study to impress the difficult runes on Narm's mind, and then a sharp lecture on precisely how to cast the spell in view of his obvious shortcomings became grinding irritants. Then came a moment of casting, a ball of scorching flame, and a thrill the first few times. Now, though, Narm saw each as a failure even before Elminster spoke in scathing critique. Clumsy, slow, lazy, inattentive, imprecise, off-target . . .

"Have ye not seen your lady hurl spellfire?" Elminster demanded in acid tones. "She can shape the flame—a broad fan or a thin, dexterous tongue—bend it around comers, or pulse short spurts to avoid setting her surroundings ablaze. I suppose ye couldn't tell me the hue of her *eyes*, either!"

"Hey! They're . . ." Narm angrily replied—but Shandril's face wouldn't come to mind. Confused and badgered, he hurled fire angrily, tossing the ball of flames twenty feet before it landed and rolled.

"Temper, boy," Elminster admonished, watching it. "Too easily it can be thy death. Mages cannot afford it—not if it affects the precision of their casting. Here ye are, furious with me, and we've spent merely a morning together. Not good! Oh, I'll grant ye that's good enough for lesser talents, who swagger about throwing fireballs and bullying honest farm folk. I'd hoped ye'd look for something more in the service of Mystra."

Their gazes met—the one sorrowful, the other glowering.

"Ye can be a great mage, Narm, if ye develop just two things: precision in spell effects and imagination in Art. The latter ye'll need later, when ye reach past most mages. The precision ye must master now, else thy every spell will have some waste about it. Thy Art will lack that edge of shrewd phrasing and maximum effect that may mean the difference between defeat and victory."

Narm opened his mouth to speak, but Elminster continued, "As ye advance, ye'll become a target for those who gain spells by preying on other mages. If ye lack precision in a duel of Art, ye'll be utterly destroyed—then 'twill be too late for my lessons. Such a waste of my time that would be."

"But I can't *hope* to win a duel now! How will spending all day throwing balls of flame about make any difference to that? If I win a duel, surely it will be because I have stronger spells and more of them!"

"Perhaps. Yet, know ye, a mage can do more with a few simple spells he knows back-to-front, and can use shrewdly, than with an arsenal hastily memorized and poorly understood. D'ye follow?"

Narm nodded.

"Good," the Old Mage said briskly. "I'll leave ye to thyself, if ye promise to study and cast your flaming sphere at least four times more, here in this field, before ye rest for the day. Move the sphere just where ye want it and form it precisely in the place ye choose. Think on how ye can use such a weapon against, say, a group of goblins who scatter in all directions when they see it coming—but try to get past it toward ye." He started to trudge away. "Only foolish, arrogant mages stand still after they've cast. *Move*, or a simple arrow will make ye a dead wizard, no matter how impressive ye were in life. Oh, and worry not about the stubble; ye're doing the farmer a favor by burning it off. Try not to take the fencing with it—'tis harder to term that 'friendly help.' Have I thy promise?"

"Yes, and my thanks."

"Thanks? 'Tis impatient ye are again, Narm! The task's not done. Save thy thanks till ye master this spell. Then thank thyself first. I can talk all day and only waste breath if ye fail to heed, work, and master the Art."

Narm grinned. "You do."

Elminster's grin lit his face only an instant, but the twinkle in his eye remained as he became a falcon and flew away.

Narm stood in the field and watched him go, sighed, and reached for his spellbook. The sun was bright on the Old Skull. He bent his head to the book.

Much later, when he stood to cast his first flaming sphere, Narm drew a deep breath of satisfaction. At least he was alone and could work Art without watching eyes and sharp comments. He turned to look at the stubble, choosing what he could burn.

A small boy had appeared from somewhere and hung on the fence rails, watching.

"Go away!" Narm said crossly.

"This your field?" the boy asked laconically.

"You could get hurt! I'm casting spells."

"Aye. I've been watching. But I won't be hurt unless you cast spells at me. You won't; there're no evil wizards in Shadowdale. Ma says Elminster won't allow it."

"I see," Narm snapped, his jaw set. He turned and hurled fire.

The boy watched fire roll away and stayed glued to the fence. All day long he stayed, as Narm hurled fire, sat down to study, got up and threw fire, and went back to his books. Narm was weary and thirsty when he went to the gate at evening.

The boy climbed down from the fence and fell into step beside him. "I wish I could be a great mage, like you."

Narm laughed. "I wish *I* could be a great mage. I know so little. I feel so useless."

"You?" The boy shook his head. "I saw you cast balls of fire. You point them where to go, and they move at your bidding! You *must* be mighty!"

"Being a mage is a lot more than hurling fireballs."

The boy nodded thoughtfully, waved a sudden farewell, ducked through a gap in the hedge, and was gone.

Narm shrugged and walked on. Ahead he could see a patrol of guards on horseback, trotting with lances raised. It must be nice to call a place like this home.

When Narm came up the path, Elminster sat smoking on a boulder near his front step. "Well? Can ye put a sphere where ye want to?"

Narm nodded.

"So are ye a mage?"

Narm shrugged. "I've a long road to go before I'm strong in Art. But I can stand in most company, now, and know my Art will serve me." He added proudly, "There'll always be others more powerful, but I've truly mastered what I do know."

"Oh?" Elminster asked. "Think ye so?" His features blurred and shifted beneath the battered hat, flowing and changing. Narm suddenly faced the young boy who had watched his spell practice from the fence. The little face grinned; its mouth opened, and in a perfect imitation of Narm's own voice, said solemnly, "Being a mage is a lot more than hurling fireballs."

Narm stared in anger, then resignation, and then sheepish amusement. "Elminster won't allow it, indeed. I'll have to rise early in the day to get ahead of you!"

"I've several hundred years' start on ye. Come. Evenfeast's ready. Ye've chosen wisely; thy lady's a cook of rare skill. See that ye serve her as well, boy." He knocked his pipe out on the doorstep and went in.

Narm looked once at the stars beginning to sparkle in the darkening sky, and followed him inside.

16

To Walk Unseen

Bards soon forget a warrior falling without a great feat of arms. Would you be forgotten? Face each battle, each foe, as though it is your last. One day it will be.

Dathlance of Selgaunt
An Old Warrior's Way
Year of the Blade

Morning sun laid bright fingers across the table in the audience chamber of the Twisted Tower. Shandril watched stray dust motes sparkle above the table as she and Narm waited for Elminster. Narm's hand found hers. They sat together in contented silence, alone with the fading tapestries of Shadowdale's past and the empty throne.

"Before we two met, I was brought here by Illistyl," Narm said quietly, "and spoke with Mourngrym. It seems an age ago."

Shandril nodded. "I'd swear I left Deepingdale very long ago, yet 'tis tendays, not months!" She looked at the great painted map of the Dragonreach. "I wonder where we'll be in a year?"

The doors opened, and Elminster came in. The wizard was alone. He walked slowly and truly looked *old*. He sat in a chair beside them and fixed them with a bright gaze. "So quiet? Have ye both stopped thinking, then?"

"No," Narm replied boldly. "Why say you so?"

The Old Mage shrugged. "The young are said to be always talking or laughing or fighting; ye two surprised me." He took out his pipe, looked at it, and then put it away again.

"I asked ye here to tell thee I've watched and seen and judge ye two as well trained with Art and spellfire as we can make thee. 'Tis up to thee, now, if ye'd grow more powerful. More—'tis time for ye to decide what to do with thy lives!"

"Do?" Narm asked.

Elminster nodded. " 'Tis not good to drift along under the influence of the Knights and myself. Ye'd be swept into our councils and struggles . . . and grow embittered as ye lost the will to walk thine own roads and think for thyselves."

"But we've found friends here, and happy times," Shandril protested, "and—"

"And danger," Elminster interrupted smoothly. "I want to keep ye with me; one can't have too many friends, and I grow weary of losing them one after another with the years. But if I let ye stay, I draw doom to ye, just as will settling down together in the dale."

"What? Living together will bring danger?" Narm asked.

"Nay—staying in one place will. With thy talent," Elminster said, pointing a long finger at Shandril, "one mage after another will seek to slay thee. Mulmaster, Thay, and the Zhentarim all would destroy anything that threatens magecraft. So walk ye out into the wide Realms—and disappear. I can alter thy outward selves, though to each other ye'll look the same. Pass from sight, and thy menace will be forgotten in the struggles these tyrants of Art have with one another."

"Just 'disappear'?" Shandril said. "Doing what, exactly?"

"My advice is to wander and hide. Ye'll need friends to raise sword or Art to aid thee, so walk with Storm Silverhand and her fellow Harpers, to find thine own ways and adventures. Mistake me not—I'd not be rid of ye." The wizard put his pipe in his mouth. "If ye stay, ye'll soon be slain or stunted in Art and spirit. Come back and visit, though." A flame sprouted from Elminster's forefinger, and he puffed his pipe furiously into life, his eyes misty.

Shandril and Narm looked at each other. "I—we both think you're right," Shandril replied. "Yet we'd speak with the Knights before deciding."

Elminster looked to Narm, who nodded silently.

"We don't want to leave this place—our friends," Shandril added. "If we must, we'd know where in the Realms 'tis best to go."

"Well said," Elminster agreed gravely. "If ye like, I'll tell Mourngrym."

Shandril nodded. "Please." She did not burst into tears until after he'd gone.

"He's right," Narm said gently, his arms about her.

"Oh, I know," Shandril sniffled. "It's leaving *friends*. First Gorstag and Lureene at the inn, then Delg, Burlane, Rymel . . . and now the Knights. I'll even miss Elminster, the crusty old bastard."

"Well, *that's* as polite and honest a calling as I've had in a long time," the wizard's unmistakable voice said dryly, from just behind them.

Narm and Shandril whirled around. "You must have been waiting outside the door!" Shandril said hotly to Mourngrym.

The lord of Shadowdale raised calming hands. "Everyone must stand somewhere. I lost five gold pieces at dice with the guards, if 'tis any consolation. The others'll be here in a breath or two."

He strode to a tall cabinet. "In the meantime, a flagon of wineapple? I strained it myself. 'Tis not fermented; you can't get drunk."

"Well, seeing as you've yon cabinet *open* . . ." Rathan growled from the door.

Mourngrym sighed. "Is Torm with you? I thought as much. Leave something drinkable that I can give to visiting gentles, will you?" He sat on his throne, flagon in hand. "Well met, Jhess . . . Illistyl. Where's Merith?"

"Along in a minute," Jhessail told him. "He was in the bath when Shaerl called!"

"Ah, that's why she isn't back yet!" Torm said innocently, addressing the glass he raised to his lips. An instant later, Mourngrym's empty flagon bounced off his head.

"My lord, if I may borrow your boot?" said a voice from the door, sweet and low.

"Of course, Lady," replied Merith beside her, drawing it off and proffering it politely.

Shaerl threw hard and accurately.

Torm groaned and dropped Mourngrym's flagon with a clatter, amid general mirth.

"All here?" the lord of Shadowdale asked. At the door, Lanseril nodded as he settled an ornate lock bar into place. "Good. Narm and Shandril have something to ask you!"

Silence fell. Shandril gazed around, suddenly shy, and nudged Narm.

He looked at her uncomfortably, cleared his throat, and—lapsed into silence.

"Ye need no speech, lad," Elminster said. "Just say thy piece straight out, before someone *else* attacks the tower to seize thee."

Amid chuckles, Narm swallowed and got to his feet. "Well, then, Shan and I think we should leave, to live our own lives. We don't want to insult or upset anyone. You've been good friends and protectors; my lady and I will be ever grateful. Yet as long as we stay, Shadowdale will be an armed camp. We must go . . . but where, we know not." He looked at Shandril, read something in her eyes, and added, "We would talk it over with you and then decide, the two of us, afterward. We alone must live with our decision—and with each other." He sat down suddenly, feeling foolish.

"Good speech," Illistyl said. "Well then, what would you know?"

Shandril spoke. "What are the Harpers? Not who, but what?"

Florin answered, "My wife is one, yet even to me they remain mysterious. They're secretive about their ranks and precise aims, as a defense against foes, but do work for good. When you see a silver moon and harp, you face a Harper. Storm Silverhand is openly a Harper, as is the High Lady of Silverymoon. Many bards, rangers, and half-elves are Harpers. They oppose the

Zhentarim and those who plunder wilderlands, thoughtless mining and felling of timber—the merchants of Amn, for instance. In Shadowdale, we respect and aid Harpers."

"Well enough, " Narm said, nodding. "Where should we wander, Harpers or no?"

"Somewhere you can get filthy rich," Torm said with a grin, "and hide among masses of people, finding any living you fancy—Waterdeep, for instance!"

Mourngrym, whose family was of noble Waterdhavian stock, shook his head ruefully.

"Have you *no* honor?" Jhessail inquired wearily of Torm.

"Aye, indeed. I keep it at the bottom of my pack and take it out to polish and admire on windy nights in the wilderness. It shines grandly, but 'tis poor company, and keeps one not warm."

"Ignore him," Rathan said. "His ratlike city breeding leads his lips astray. Waterdeep is a good place to hide, aye, but more dangerous by far than Shadowdale. 'Tis full of prying eyes, and not a few folk who'll take all they can and leave what remains in a gutter."

Lanseril nodded. "Better to travel the wilds of the Sword Coast North, High Forest, and fair Silverymoon. The Unicorn Run's breathtaking in its beauty—great trees gowned in moss that have stood since the world was young . . . worth the trip, I tell you!"

"Aye, go where few tread and see what few see and ye'll always remember," Rathan agreed. "I envy thee thy journey, bring what perils it may—"

Elminster rolled his eyes. "Is every lord and lady here going to philosophize pompously the whole tenday through?"

"Why not? 'Tis *our* turn, after years of listening to your fulminations," Torm returned wickedly. A hush fell as the curious waited to see if he would forthwith become a frog.

Elminster merely chuckled. "True enough. My turn to listen and be entertained."

Visibly disappointed that Torm had escaped frogdom, Florin and Lanseril refilled their flagons and strolled about the chamber.

Shandril frowned. "Is this converse not the way to do things?"

"Well," Lanseril told a decanter, "Few have sense enough to talk beforehand. Most are in too much hurry to rush into battle—or trust secrets only with themselves."

"Never think jaw-wagging's bad or necessary," Rathan agreed. " 'Tis one of the most important things priests do."

"Well said," Torm put in. "Such talk's as needed as the sword in an ordered life—and the deeds of kings. 'Twas the sage Mroon who defined the famous Circle of Diplomacy: 'Why talk but to end the fighting? Why fight but to end the talking?' 'Tis as true today as a thousand years ago. . . . Well, Old Mage? Did I remember, or did I not?"

"Ye did . . . perhaps the first thing I've told thee ye have managed to recall rightly," Elminster said severely. "But enough banter. It helps not these good people to decide, and grants them but weariness and lost time!"

"Aye," Florin agreed. "We should unfold the Realms to you so you can choose your best route."

"Danger, ye'll find," Elminster out in dryly, "lies on every hand. We'll tongue-tour now, but also make thee a map on soft hide. Were I ye, I'd seek Silverymoon or Neverwinter or the Moonshaes. Ye must, I think, leave these lands about the Sea of Fallen Stars, at least for a time. The South is no hiding place for thee. Go west, and find fortune."

Jhessail nodded. "Whatever you choose, do so quickly and quietly. Those who'd slay you are looking for you."

"Lord Marsh." The voice was cold. Its red-haired owner turned from a many-paned window inset with rubies. Fzoul Chembryl, High Darkpriest of Bane and Master of the Black Altar, laid even colder eyes on his visitor, extending a hand that bore a black, burning banestone.

Lord Marsh Belwintle knelt, kissed it, and rose, keeping his face impassive. The slave trade was too profitable to jeopardize it with a quarrel. Marsh did not love this priest. One day there would come a reckoning between them—and if Tymora smiled, Fzoul would serve Bane more eternally than he did now.

"I've called you here to discuss the matter of spellfire, in light of the continued absence of Lord Manshoon," Fzoul said, striding away. "The others are here already."

"Too often, matters of state devour time," Marsh replied, following Fzoul across a drafty bridge—a rail-less span of stone where one misstep meant a killing fall to a stone floor twenty fathoms below. They went to a high chamber Marsh had not seen before, wherein assembled senior Zhentarim. They nodded coldly to him as he entered. He half-bowed to them and took the sole empty seat.

The chairs of Sashen, Kadorr, and Ilthond had been removed. So had Fzoul's own, for he now sat in Manshoon's high-curved seat. Marsh wondered what had happened to the others, but decided it would be safer not to inquire. He little liked the Black Altar, with its priests and traps and guardian creatures, and liked this chamber less, with its air of a prepared trap. The last seat, indeed!

"I'll waste no time on pleasantries," Fzoul began. "Manshoon is yet absent. Our strongest magic can't find him, nor has he been seen. He can, of course, block or lead astray most spells, but we've no reason to believe he does now. I fear, fellow lords, that Manshoon is dead."

He received no answer but silence; this conclusion was no surprise.

"This may not be so," Fzoul continued, "but we've waited for his reappearance too long. We must act on one matter, at least, without further delay. If Manshoon likes not our actions upon his return, I shall bear responsibility. The pressing matter is spellfire. Legendary, very rare, and one who can wield it has emerged. I wish to know your minds about spellfire."

For a moment, no one spoke. Then the wizard Sememmon leaned forward. "The last wielder of spellfire before this Shandril was the incantatrix Dammasae, who spent her youth in Thunderstone. Is it mere coincidence that two bearers of spellfire have arisen in the southern Dragonreach near the Thunder Peaks, or are they related by blood?"

Fzoul leaned forward. "A most intriguing question! Has anyone knowledge on this matter?"

Sarhthor shrugged. "They could be mother and daughter; the years allow of it. But, with respect, what does it matter? Dammasae is long dead, as is her husband. This offers us no hilt with which to wield Shandril."

"Aye," Casildar agreed. "Her lover Narm is the means to move Shandril to our bidding. What I want to know is the strength of his Art. How easy a hilt to grasp is he?"

Sememmon shrugged. "He's been in Shadowdale long enough for Elminster to teach him much. If that's befallen, I can't say. Yet I doubt his Art can be overly terrifying: Marimmar the Mage Most Magnificent was his tutor until recently!" The mages chuckled dryly.

The priest Zhessae frowned. "Is mastery of Art needed to wield spellfire?"

There were shrugs.

"I doubt it," Fzoul said. "This maid had no known skill at Art before using spellfire against the dracolich Rauglothgor. Interestingly, the keep she destroyed was the Tower Tranquil—once home of the archmage Garthond, husband of the incantatrix Dammasae."

"Does that mean," the mage Yarkul asked, excited, "spellfire may be contained in an item or process left in the tower by Dammasae? Which, in turn, argues that other wielders of spellfire could be created!"

"There have been several wielders of spellfire active at the same time before; it's not an ability the gods give to only one being at a time. An item or ritual is possible. Against that, one must place the strong likelihood that Dammasae never visited the Tower Tranquil," Fzoul replied.

Casildar said carefully, "That still leaves open the question of what actions, if any, we should now take."

"We *must* control the maid, or destroy her. Her spellfire threatens us all!" Ashemmi burst out. The curly-bearded mage's earring chimed as he snapped his head around to glare at Fzoul. "We can't afford to sit idle. What if Mulmaster or Maalthiir of Hillsfar gains spellfire? Even if Shadowdale uses it only to aid their friends in Daggerdale, it will set our plans back. If someone sets out to destroy us with it, we could fare far worse!"

"Aye, well said," Casildar agreed. "We must move. But how? Our armies?"

"I prefer not to whelm our hosts in Manshoon's absence," Fzoul said. "Shadowdale need merely spread the rumor that we've mastered spellfire—and Cormyr, Sembia, Hillsfar, and all will strike together against us. No, we must move more quietly, my lords. Yet as Casildar says, we must move. What say you?"

"Our assassins?" Yarkul suggested.

Zhessae sighed. "The replacements are poorly trained, yet," the priest murmured. "Even strengthened by our lesser brothers of Bane and the magelings, I fear they'd anger Shadowdale more than harm it."

"Aye," Sarhthor agreed disgustedly, in his deep voice. "I recall the disasters of our going that way before."

"Yes," Scemmmon put in. "We've all seen what happens when we send the magelings. Everyone wants to be the hero, to make his name among us. Reckless and foolish, they over-reach themselves and fall. Elminster is no foe to be mastered by a mageling."

"Are you suggesting we go in force, ourselves?" Ashemmi asked. "Leaving aside our personal peril, does that not leave Zhentil Keep undefended? Surely the High Imperceptor has heard of Manshoon's absence. Will he not strike against you, Fzoul, and all of us?" His words fell into a deepening silence.

"No doubt," Fzoul agreed coldly, "he will try. But the Black Altar, and Zhentil Keep about it, are not undefended." He waved a hand.

From behind a curtain far down the chamber floated Manxam. The beholder was old and vast and terrible. Lichen grew on its nether plates, and its eyestalks were scarred and wrinkled with age. Its central eye turned to survey them all as it drifted closer. In the depths of that dark-pupiled, bloodshot orb, each man saw his own death and worse. A deep, burbling hiss came from its toothy maw; its ten smaller eyestalks moved restlessly as Manxam the Merciless came to the table. The eye tyrant hovered above its center, rolling over in slow, awful majesty until its ten small eyes hung just above them. At least one looked at each man there.

"I feel we can all be persuaded," Fzoul said without a trace of a smile, "to reach consensus now."

The beholder did not blink.

Nervously Sememmon cleared his throat. "What do you propose?"

Fzoul said steadily, "The most powerful mages here should go forthwith to Shadowdale and do whatever's necessary to capture or destroy Shandril—Elminster or no Elminster. As we're not sending weak or incompetent magelings, as you've so correctly advised against, I've every confidence you shall return with spellfire . . . if you return at all."

Sememmon, Ashemmi, and Yarkul went white and silent. Only Sarhthor looked unsurprised. He merely nodded. Sememmon glanced up to find that Manxam had silently rolled over again so that its central eye, the one that foiled magic, gazed at them all.

The reason for seating the mages together around one end of the table was now all too apparent. Manxam and Fzoul were too far away for both to be caught in a time-stop spell, and no other magic would allow Sememmon to ready a wand. Certainly he couldn't smite both—nor was there a great chance of besting Fzoul here, in his temple. Against Manxam, the mage stood almost no chance. Sememmon doubted he could even escape if he tried to flee. Perhaps if he, Ashemmi, Yarkul, and Sarhthor worked together, with spells planned beforehand, they might have a chance. If Casildar and Zhessae, and any number of priests hiding behind the tapestries, were ready to aid Fzoul, that slim chance was . . . none.

"It certainly seems the right thing to do, Brother Fzoul," Sememmon said slowly. "However, I feel uneasy in undertaking such a mission without even a single priest of Bane to pray for our success and aid us with the god's will. What say you, Lord Marsh, as one who neither serves Bane nor works Art?"

Weaken them by one priest, Sememmon thought, and cut that one down as a warning to Fzoul. And if we win spellfire, we'll come back and try it on one of the beholders.

Had Fzoul done something to Manshoon? Or perhaps Manshoon was behind this, to rid himself of all his most powerful rivals. If not, and he did return, would Fzoul tell him all the mages had denounced him and gone off to act as they pleased?

Lord Marsh rubbed his jaw and frowned at the tabletop, avoiding both the calm scrutiny of the beholder and the icy stares of Fzoul, Casildar, and Zhessae. It was a long time before he looked up. "I must concur with you, Brother Sememmon. We've always won our greatest gains by careful use of all three of our strengths: the favor of great Bane; the versatile Art of mages; and the might of Zhentilar swords. It might go ill were we to neglect more than one of those strengths." He spread his hands as if apologizing for pointing out the obvious. "Without magical aid, our warriors can't reach Shadowdale in time to capture the spellfire maid, certainly not in numbers enough without alarming our foes. We must, therefore, forego force-of-arms. It would be foolish to abandon also the strength of Bane in this matter. Moreover, the warriors under me, and probably many underpriests and magelings, would think the same—and seriously question our collective wisdom!" Marsh sat back, looked directly at Fzoul, and toyed with a bauble at his throat, which most at the table knew to be an enchanted explosive globe.

Sememmon almost smiled. The hard-faced warrior lord, it seemed, bore no love for the Master of the Black Altar.

The eye tyrant hung over them, silent and terrible.

Ignoring it, Sarhthor rubbed his hands. "Well, I'm for such a strike, and the sooner the better. Spellfire must be ours."

Sememmon nodded in calm agreement even as he raged inwardly. Was the fool actually that simple and enthusiastic? Or was he working with Fzoul? Nay, listen to the way his words were spoken—the little soft twists at the end of each, flashing like daggers turning over! Sarhthor was telling Fzoul, openly and cuttingly, that he knew Fzoul's game and thought little of it.

"I'm *so* glad we were able to come to an understanding so quickly," Fzoul said, his voice like an assassin's dagger being wiped clean on velvet.

The deep voice of the beholder rolled out from overhead, "Consider well the nature of your understanding."

As Sememmon looked up to meet Manxam's many gazes, he took sudden satisfaction in the fact that Fzoul had to be more upset at the eye tyrant's comment than any of the rest of them; its disapproval was aimed directly at him. Sememmon nodded again, and saw all of the other mages nodding, too.

He left that chamber feeling almost satisfied, despite the danger ahead.

⊠ ⊠ ⊠

The moon scudded through tattered gray clouds. Amid the spires of the city, the air was cold and still. Fzoul stood on a high balcony of the Black Altar and smiled up at Selûne. Strong magic protected him from attack by Art, and none but servants of Bane could enter the courtyard below.

The mages would have no choice. No doubt they'd slaughter Casildar, but he was too ambitious anyway, and his death was a small price to pay for the destruction of Manshoon's spell hurlers. The Zhentarim would serve Fzoul at last.

Even if Manshoon did return, he'd find himself isolated, with only upstart magelings—all too eager to betray him for their own advancement—to stand with him against the loyal of Bane who served Fzoul. The beholders cared not which humans they dealt with, so long as their wants were met. Zhentil Keep would be his.

Until someone took it from him.

Fzoul never noticed the wizard eye floating above and behind him, keeping carefully out of sight among the spires. No eye could have seen its invisible owner, regarding him from the dark window of a tower nearby.

A commotion rose in the courtyard below as warrior-priests of the High Imperceptor crept over the wall—and were met by alert and waiting underpriests. Fzoul leaned forward and cast a spell that unleashed a whirl-storm of deadly black blades down into the growing fray below, caring nothing for the fate of his own acolytes. Let them see Bane the sooner.

⊠ ⊠ ⊠

Sememmon heard the screams and clash and clatter of many razor-sharp blades below. One of the attackers boiling over the temple wall cast magical light on the scene. Bloody slaughter filled the yard.

Sememmon leaned out swiftly before Fzoul could leave the balcony and struck with the most brutish of his magical rings, snarling as he forced more Art out of it than ever before. He did not aim directly at the Master of the Black Altar—Fzoul would be well protected—but struck instead at the balcony.

It shivered, cracked as if struck by a battering ram, crumbled, and fell, into the shrieking and death below, seeming to descend with awful slowness. Sememmon intently watched Fzoul's plunge. The priest had no time to employ snatch-to-safety magic—unless he managed to do so after the first blade had sliced crimson across his red mane of hair. A falling chunk of stone blocked Sememmon's view moments before the shattered balcony reached the crowded courtyard.

Sememmon turned in satisfaction, resolving that the attack on Shadowdale would begin and end with the destruction of Casildar—at least until the spellfire maid was out from under the eye of Elminster.

He never noticed another wizard eye floating just above the dark window.

That eye was gone, however, some six breaths later, when a great, round shadow drifted out of the Black Altar's depths, its many eyestalks coiling and writhing like a nest of serpents. Then the slaughter *really* began.

Two priests rushed at each other along a narrow alley. Green flames flickered around the wrists of one, brightening with fearful speed. The other cursed softly and shot out a hand that became a black tentacle. The stabbing tendril was countered, inches from the other priest's throat, by a tendril of his own.

"Is that you, Brother?" The priest with green fire hissed.

"Yes, Sintre," the other murmured, withdrawing his tentacles. "A-hunting spellfire—as you are."

"We need it, Architrave—our spells couldn't slay those two Blood-kin we met. We need something more!"

"Yes—a sword to slice Dhalgrave! I've no desire to end my days in torment, on my knees before the Shadowmaster High."

Sintre gasped. "Brother, take care! He rules the shadows not because he's loved—his Doomstars can slay any of us!"

Architrave laughed, and a tentacle held forth something dead and dull under her nose. It seemed a gem with no sparkle. Dull and dark, it drank the light. "Recognize this?"

"No," Sintre told him honestly.

Architrave whisked it back into hiding. and laughed again—a cold, cruel sound that reminded Sintre of the Great Dhalgrave. "Malaug the Founder made the Doomstars, and he came from Faerûn. I found one of his lairs."

"No!" Sintre gasped, excitement leaping cold inside her.

"*Yes*," her brother exulted. "And this gem was once a Doomstar, no doubt left behind by the Founder because it's drained. What if spellfire could set it aflame once more? A Doomstar Dhalgrave doesn't know about, used against him . . . and there'll be a new Lord of the Shadows!"

He was still laughing as he turned and raced away down the alley, leaving Sintre to stare after him and shiver in foreboding.

The night was cold. Overhead, Selûne sliced the clouds. Shandril shut the windows against the chill and sat on the bed, facing Narm, her eyes dark and beautiful. "Well, my lord?"

Narm shrugged and spread his hands. "What do *you* want, my lady?"

"To be happy. With you. Free of fear. Free to walk as we will, neither cold nor hungry. To have friends. I care little about all the rest."

"Simple enough," Narm agreed wryly, and they both laughed. "Right, then, we go west, as they all say. But advice be damned, let us go by way of the Rising Moon and Thunder Gap, so you may see Gorstag once more. What say?"

"*Yes!* But what of the Harpers?"

"Well . . ."

Outside in the night, Torm strained to hear, but slipped. He breathed a curse upon fickle Tymora as his splayed, iron-strong fingers slid slowly down the wet slates. He soon ran out of roof and fell over the edge.

Desperately, with his last instant of grip, he swung himself inward—and then he was falling, mind racing coolly. *Now!*

His fingers closed on a window ledge. With a jerk that nearly wrenched his arms from their sockets he brought himself to a halt, to hang grimly. It was then that he noticed his left hand had come down hard on a nesting dove and crushed its frail body.

"Ugghh," he said, suppressing an urge to snatch his hand away.

"I'd put it even more strongly than that!" said the crumpled bird, opening one eye to glare at him.

At that, Torm did fall.

The bird sighed, became Elminster, and murmured a word. Strands of sticky web raced from his fingertips, stabbing like lances at the grounds below—and enveloping Torm on the way.

The thief came to a slow, rubbery halt mere feet from the ground and hung helplessly. He began to struggle.

"Serves ye right," Elminster muttered darkly, and became a bird again.

Above the two eavesdroppers, Shandril and Narm had decided to join the Harpers. "After all," as Narm put it, "if we don't like it, we can back out!"

"Shall we tell them now?"

"No. Sleep on it, Elminster said."

Outside, Elminster smiled quietly, though one couldn't see it for the beak.

"And so to bed again, you and I," Narm said, "and *this* time I'll neither hear nor proffer any life story."

Shandril's answering laugh was low and delighted.

Outside, on the window ledge, the bird that was Elminster rolled its eyes and looked at the stars glimmering above Selûne. The Silent Sword had ascended above the trees; the night was half done.

The dove's beak dwindled and became a human mouth—which softly sang a snatch of a ballad that had been old when Myth Drannor fell:

. . . and in the wind and the water
the storm-king's fire-eyed daughter
came a-rolling home across the sea
leaving none on the wreck alive but me. . . .

17

Harps and Bright Hope

'Tis the greatest happiness of all to find a worthy, steadfast partner to share life with. The gods grant a rare few a consort loyal, skilled, and loving who becomes our closest friend. But thus the gods entertain themselves, by granting rather less—someone suitable during the good times, but whom we could cheerfully murder on some mornings.

Jerenneth Ghaluin of Neverwinter
Tavern Dancing My Way to Wizardly Might
Year of the Bridle

The morning sun rose hot over Shadowdale, glinting on helms and spear points atop the Old Skull. Mist rolled down the Ashaba in a swift, silent storm.

Narm and Shandril rose early and set out for a brisk morning walk, accompanied by six watchful guards. The constant flash and gleam of bright armor reminded the two lovers of danger lurking near—and of the spellfire that lured it.

Despite a good dawnfry of fried bread and goose eggs at the tower, they still felt hungry, and stopped at the Old Skull Inn for bowls of hot stew. Jhaele Silvermane bid them fair morning as she served them, waved away their coins, and asked when the wedding would be.

Shandril blushed, but Narm said proudly, "As soon as can be arranged—or sooner."

The guards chuckled, and developed sudden thirsts for ale, which made Shandril shudder at the early hour. All soon set forth up the road toward Storm Silverhand's farm.

The dale was quiet despite the morning vigor of workers in the fields. All Faerûn seemed at peace, under a cloudless sky. Striding happily, his arm linked through Shandril's, Narm realized they had only a vague idea where Storm Silverhand's farm was. He turned to the nearest guard, a scarred, mustachioed veteran who bore a spear lightly in his hairy hand. "Good sir," Narm asked, "could you guide us to the dwelling of Storm Silverhand?"

"It lies before you, Lord—from this cedar stump here up to the line of bluewood yonder."

Narm nodded and said his thanks. Shandril had already hurried ahead. The others trotted to catch up to her.

The farm lay hidden behind a high, crown-hedged bank. Over the hedge appeared the upper leaves of growing things. All was lush and green. Bees danced among the blossoms of a creeper that coiled along the hedge. The guards walked watchfully, weapons ready, but Shandril couldn't believe any swift danger could lurk in such a place, on such a morning.

They turned off the road where a broad track cut through the hedge, following it along twisted oaks to a large, rambling fieldstone house. Its thatched roof was thick with velvety moss and alive with birds. Vines on tripods and pole-frames stretched away in rows, like hallways amid the green, rustling walls of a great castle. Far down one they saw Storm Silverhand at work, her long silver hair tied back with a ragged scrap of cloth.

The bard wore torn leather breeches and a halter, both shiny with age. Swinging a hoe with strength and care, Storm was covered with a glistening sheen of sweat. Stray leaves stuck to her here and there. She waved. Laying down the hoe, she hastened toward them, wiping her hands on her thighs. "Well met!"

"I'm going to *hate* leaving here," Shandril said in a small, husky voice.

Narm squeezed her hand. "I am, too, but we can come back when we are stronger. We *will* come back."

Surprised at the iron in his tone, Shandril smiled in agreement.

Storm reached them. The pleasant smell of the bard's sweat—like warm bread, sprinkled with spices—hung around her. Narm and Shandril both stared. Storm smiled. "Am I purple, perhaps? Grotesque?"

Narm said hastily, "Pray pardon, Lady! We did not mean to stare!"

"None needed, Narm, and no 'Lady,' please . . . we're friends. Come in and share sweetwater, then let us talk. Few enough come to see me." Leading them toward the house, she asked, "So what's so strange about me?"

Shandril giggled. "Such brawn." She pointed at the bard's flat, tanned midriff. Corded muscles rippled on Storm's flanks and arms as she walked.

The bard shook her head. "It's just me." She led them through a stout wooden door that swung open by itself into cool dimness. "Sit here by the east window and tell me what brings you here on such a fine morn. Most seek Storm in fouler weather."

"Urrhh," Narm winced. "Jests as bad as Elminster."

Storm grinned and handed him a long, curving drinking-horn of blown glass, shaped like a bird.

He held it in awe. "It's really glass!"

"Aye," the bard replied, filling another. "From Theymarsh in the south, where such things are common. It breaks easily."

Shandril held hers apprehensively, too.

A guard backed away when offered one. "Ah, no, Lady. Just a cup, if you have one. I'd feel dark the rest of my days if I broke such as that."

Shandril murmured agreement.

The bard smiled, hands on hips, and spoke softly to the guardsmen. "We must be alone, these two and I, to talk. Bide here, if you will. The beer is in that cask; 'tis not good to drink more sweetwater so soon. Bread, garlic butter, and sausage is in the cold-pantry—eat hearty, but come with speed if you hear my horn." She took down a silver horn from a beam near her head, and turned to Narm and Shandril. "Drink up. There's much to talk about." She went to the back of her kitchen and swung open a little arched door, letting in the sunlight. "Follow this path into the trees, and you'll find me," she said, and vanished down it.

The visitors looked around the low-ceilinged kitchen. Herbs hung from its dark wooden beams, and all was cozy and friendly—but not the wild showplace of Art and lore one might expect of a bard's home. A small harp stood half-hidden in the shadows near the pantry door. Narm almost dropped his glass when suddenly, and all alone, it began to play.

They all stared as the strings plucked themselves.

One guard rose, clapping hand to blade, but a veteran turned on him. "*Peace*, Berost! 'Tis Art, aye, but no Art to harm us!"

The harp played an unfamiliar tune that rose and fell gently ere it climbed and died away on a high, chiming cluster of notes.

"Sounds elven," Narm said quietly.

"Let's ask," Shandril said, standing her empty glass carefully on the table. "I'm done."

Narm drained his with a last tilting swallow and set it beside hers.

They nodded to the guards and went out the little door. The path twisted down a little ravine, beneath overhanging trees. They followed it through dappled sunlight and deepening shade, to emerge by a small pool where a stream widened.

Storm stood beside it in a robe, her hair a wet silver cascade. She sat on a rock at the pool's edge and beckoned them to adjacent rocks. Near her head, the silver horn hung from a branch.

"Come and bathe, or sit and dabble your toes; 'tis soothing." Storm's eyes were dark and serious. "And tell me what hangs on your hearts."

"The harp that played by itself," Narm asked, "was that an elven tune?"

"Aye, an air of the Elven Court that Merith taught me. Is that all that troubles you?" she teased, shaking water from her hair.

"Lady," Shandril said hesitantly, "we think we'd like to join the Harpers. We've heard only good of Those Who Harp—yet we've heard only little. Before we set foot on a new road we may follow most of our lives—and that may lead us to life's end sooner than not—we would know more from you of what it is to be a Harper, if your offer still stands. Lady, does—"

Storm held up her hand. "Hold! No more queries until we've seen these clear between us. I'll try to be brief." She drew her bare feet up beneath her, glanced at the woods, and nodded, as if reaching a decision.

"A Harper is one of a vast, scattered company who share similar interests—a fellowship of men, elves, and half-elves, more women than men. Most bards and many rangers in the North are Harpers. We've no ranks, only varying degrees of personal influence. Our badge is a silver moon and a silver harp, upon a black or royal blue field. Many lady mages and most druids are our allies, and we are generally accounted 'good.' A Harper tolerates many faiths and deeds, but works against warfare, slavery, and wanton destruction of the plants and creatures of the land. We oppose those who'd build empires by the sword or spilled blood, or work Art heedless of consequences."

Silver hair stirred around Storm's shoulders as she spoke, flowing and coiling with a life of its own. "We see the arts and lore of Myth Drannor as a high point in the history of all races. We work to preserve history, crafts, and knowledge, and seek to regain what made Myth Drannor great: the happy sharing of life's good things among all races. We work against and often fight the Zhentarim, the Cult of the Dragon, the slavers of Thay, those who plunder or destroy tombs and libraries—and all who'd overturn peace and unleash war to raise their own thrones."

She raised one empty hand, cupped as if she held something precious. "We guard folk against such perils. We also guard books and lore, precious instruments and music, and Art and its good works. All these things serve hands and hearts yet unborn, who'll come after us."

Storm's hair was quite dry now; it still curled and wavered about her shoulders. "We seek to keep kingdoms small and busy with trade and the problems of their people. Any ruler who grows too strong and seeks to wrest knowledge and power from others is a threat. More precious knowledge is risked when his empire falls, as fall it must."

She smiled a little sadly. "Only in tavern-tales are humans

wholly evil or shiningly good. We do what we can for everyone, and stand in the way of all who threaten knowledge. Who are we to decide who shall know or not know lore? The gods have given us the freedom and the power to strive among ourselves. They've not laid down a strict order that compels us to do thus and so. Who knows better than the gods what knowledge is good or bad, and who shall have it?"

Narm regarded her thoughtfully. "Does that mean, good lady, intending no disrespect, that there should be no secrets, and wild-willed six-year-olds should be tutored in destroying spells, because knowledge should be denied to none?"

Shandril looked at him fearfully. Would Narm's tongue lose any chance of aid—or welcome—from the Harpers?

Storm laughed merrily. "You've chosen well, Shandril. Unafraid, and yet polite. Inquiring, not hostile and opinionated. Well said, archmage-to-be!" She got up, drew on her soft, battered old boots, and rose to pace thoughtfully.

"My answer is 'no.' All in the Realms hold and guard knowledge as they see fit. That, too, we've no right to change. Much should be secret, revealed only to those who've the right or ability to handle it. Harpers seek not to reveal the truth to all, but to preserve writings, Art, and music for later years and beings. We work against things that threaten the survival of such culture or erode its quality by tainting it with unchallenged falsehood."

A soft radiance grew about Storm as her voice rose. "Harper bards always sing true tales of kings, so far as truth is known. They do not sing falsely of the grand deeds of a usurper, or falsely portray as bad the nature and deeds of his predecessor. Even if such would make good tales and songs, a Harper cleaves to the truth. The truth—though slightly different for everyone—must be the rock the castle of knowledge is built on." Her smile flashed brightly. "Strong words, eh? I feel strongly. If you come to do so, too, you'll truly be Harpers. If one falls out of such belief, he or she should leave our ranks before doing all of us, and our cause, ill.

"I hope only that whether you walk with us or no, or join and then leave, you walk together and take joy in each other's company. 'Tis through such love—and longing—that much learning and celebration comes, adding to the lore we nurture and save.

More than that, whether you be Harpers or not, I would be your friend!"

Shandril and Narm looked at each other, and then at the bard. "We would be Harpers!" Shandril added awkwardly, "If you'll have us."

Storm gathered them both into her arms. "If *you* will have *us*, we'll be proud and pleased to have you. *You*, Shandril and Narm, not your spellfire or your Art. Walk far and see much, and grow in your own counsel and powers. If you work against evil, you'll be Harpers whether you bear our badge or no. Fight not always with blade or spell. The slower ways are the surer: aid freely given and friendships and trust built. These, evil cannot abide. It shrinks from what it cannot destroy."

In the warm strength of the bard's embrace, evil seemed a long way off. Narm leaned into the comfort of Storm's arms and asked, "Where then should we go?"

Storm's reply was soft and low, her words almost lost in the gentle chuckle of the water. "Go by way of Thunder Gap. Watch for Dragon Cult agents. They're thick in Sembia, and there's one in Highmoon. His name is Korvan."

Shandril stiffened.

"Go to Silverymoon. Seek out Alustriel, High Lady of that city, and say you come from her sister Storm, and would be Harpers. With Alustriel is a good place to be if you intend to have a child." The bard looked meaningfully at Shandril, who blushed. "Well, you're not quite the first couple to make *that* mistake." She looked at Narm. "If your lady feels too sick to eat, feed her lots of stew. In the evenings, she'll feel more like dining."

Narm looked at her, dazed. "Pray, lady, let me get used to discovering I'm going to be a *father*, first."

Storm chuckled. "Think well on the names your offspring must carry through life. I was born in a storm and won the name because of it—an ear-catching name, I'm told, but when I was small I fought many larger lads and lasses because of it." Freeing herself from the shared embrace, she undid her robe.

After a startled look, Narm politely turned his back. Unconcerned, the bard drew on her clothes. Shandril saw that her arms, back, and flanks were covered with faint white sword scars.

The bard winked. "I've walked many roads. Some leave little maps behind." She traced one long scar with a finger and tied her halter. "You can turn around now, Narm. I grow tired of talking to your shoulders!"

Narm obediently turned.

"Now, a few things about the journey ahead of you. First, trail marks. You'll see a few runes scratched or burned on rocks, trees, or in the dirt." She picked up a stick—and then shrugged. "Nay . . . I'll draw them in the house. 'Tis Elminster's way to expect one to remember half a hundred things in a morning. I'll not do that. I *will* tell you the names of Harper agents along your way; look to them for aid if you need it. These, too, I'll write on a bandage. I'll need you to prick your finger and bleed on it. It must look stained and disgusting if you don't want it to be looked at too closely, if someone searches or robs you. But I'll tell you the roster, in case you get separated or lose the list. If you lose your list of runes, stay clear of all that you see!"

The Bard of Shadowdale held up her fingers to count, as a small child does. "Now first, in Cormyr . . ."

After a long time, Storm rose, belted her horn at her waist, and led them back up the path to her back door.

"What if someone—by Art, I mean—heard all this?" Narm asked, looking at the trees.

Storm shook her head. "I've Art of my own to cloak this little hidden place. Manshoon himself could not hear us unless he sat with us."

She went in and set the guards to cutting cheese and apples for all, while she prepared the bandage. Soon she took Shandril's hand, and they vanished up a stair half-hidden in the shadows of the old stone kitchen. When they reappeared, there was no sign of the bandage, but Shandril's eyes told Narm it was hidden on her somewhere.

The guards looked at Storm with interest; the bard now wore black fighting leathers and a sword.

"To the temple," Storm said briskly, "for we've much to talk about with Rathan and Eressea. Weddings can all too easily become overblown things."

"The young lord and lady to be wed? Gods' good wishes to 'em! I tell you, Baerth, I saw flames come from her very *hand!* 'Spellfire' they're calling it—but 'twas no spell like I ever saw cast! No dancing about or chanting; she just frowned a little, like Delmath does when hefting a full barrel, and there 'twas! Aye, you wouldn't want to be marryin' that, now would you?"

Malark, in the shape of an owl on a branch overhead, grinned sourly at the guards' coarse laughter, and thought again how to slay Shandril.

All this skulking infuriated him. At every moment, the girl and her mageling were together—and flanked by at least one mage or a Knight armed with powerful wands or rings, with reinforcements close at hand.

The desolation of Rauglothgor's lair was not easily forgotten. A mistake in this matter could be his last. Malark turned tired eyes toward the Twisted Tower. She was guarded even now. Especially now.

The wedding ceremony would be one chance to get at Shandril, but not a good one. Shadowdale's most powerful protectors would be gathered. Perhaps later . . . these two had to leave the dale *sometime*. Malark had the uncomfortable feeling others were watching and waiting for just that to happen, and when Lady Spellfire finally set her dainty feet out into the wider world, he might find himself in the heart of a furious battle. He might even have to fight Oumrath.

Malark inwardly growled and took flight, heading restlessly south. Soon, Shandril of Highmoon, he thought. You'll feel my Art soon. . . .

The day dawned cool and misty. Shandril and Narm had slept apart as custom demanded, Shandril in the Temple of Tymora with the priestess Eressea, and Narm in the Twisted Tower with the priest Rathan. Both were up before dawn, bathed in holy water, and blessed. By then, folk had begun to gather by the banks of the Ashaba; word spread swiftly in Shadowdale.

Rathan filled a glass from a crystal decanter and held it high. "To the Lady," he said, and emptied it into the bath. He looked at Narm. "That's all the wine I'll touch this day."

Narm rose, dripping. "You'll miss all the festive tippling?"

Rathan shrugged. "How else can I mark this a special occasion? Eressea and I will go off together somewhere when 'tis done and share a glass of holy water." He stared in reverie for a moment and then blinked and said gruffly, "Come on, then—out and dry thyself! If ye're so heedless as to get the chills, Shandril will be wedding a walking corpse!"

"Cheery, aren't you?" Narm observed.

Rathan unwrapped linens from around fire-heated rocks, grunted, licked his fingers, and held them out to the young mage. "If 'tis a clown ye want, I'll send for Torm," Rathan replied. "But don't blame me if he gets ye so drunk and distracted ye forget to come to thy wedding—or locks ye in a chest so he can marry Shandril himself."

"Torm?"

"Aye. And if he's busy misbehaving elsewhere, I may take his place myself!"

Eressea kissed Shandril's forehead formally, and then hugged her fondly. "We must make haste now. Your lord-to-be awaits you. Shadowdale awaits you, too. So, in the words of Elminster, let us 'scoot.' "

Shandril rolled her eyes, Eressea laughed, and together they hurried down the stairs.

From the fire-scorched stones where Syluné's hut had been, a lone horn blew, the sound echoing down the dale. It was answered immediately from the battlements of the Tower of Ashaba. The bride-to-be and the Preceptress Eressea set forth on the long walk south.

Behind them as guard of honor paced Storm Silverhand, blade drawn, bareheaded but in full and shining battle-armor. Any hostile eyes could not help noticing the bright glows of Art that hung about her. Storm's eyes flicked this way and that; she was armed with power and expecting trouble.

The dalefolk muttered at the display.

Well ahead of the three women strode Mourngrym, Lord of Shadowdale, also bareheaded but fully armored. The arms of the dale shone bright on his breast, and a great sword hung at his side.

The guards standing to attention along the way bowed to him but did not sound their horns until Shandril reached them. One by one their calls rang out as the bride drew nearer.

Two men waited where Syluné's hut had stood. When he reached them, Mourngrym saluted Narm and stepped aside.

When Syluné lived and was lady of the dale, no temples had stood in Shadowdale; all desiring to be wed had come here to plight troth before her. Now the bare stones would see one more marriage.

Rathan stood square upon those stones, watching Shandril. On his breast, the disc of Tymora began to glow. He unclipped it from its chain and cupped it in his hands.

Nearer they came, Shandril and Eressea, and the last trumpeter blew two high notes. A fanfare of all the horns joined him, loud and long and glorious. When its last, thrilling echoes died away, Shandril stood before Rathan.

The priest smiled and cast the disc of Tymora into the air. It hung a man's height above their heads, spinning gently, and its glow grew brighter.

"We're gathered beneath the bright face of Tymora to join Narm Tamaraith, this man, and Shandril Shessair, this woman, as companions in life. Let their ways run together, say I, a friend. What saith Tymora?"

Eressea stepped forward and spoke. "I speak for Tymora, and I say, 'Let their ways run together!' "

Rathan bowed his head. "We stand in Shadowdale. What saith a good woman of the dale?"

Storm Silverhand took a step forward. "I say, let their ways run together."

"We stand in Shadowdale and hear you. What saith a good man of the dale?"

The mountainous smith Bronn Selgard stood forth from the gathered dalefolk, his great, grim face solemn, his mighty limbs clad in old, carefully patched finery. His deep voice rolled over them all. "I say, let their ways run together."

"We stand in Shadowdale and hear you," Rathan responded. "What saith the lord of the Dale?"

Mourngrym stood forth. "I say: Let their ways run together."

"We stand in Shadowdale and hear you." Rathan's voice suddenly rose, loud and deep, in a cry of challenge: "What say the people of the dale? Shall the ways of these two, Narm and Shandril, run together?"

"Aye!" came the cry from a hundred throats.

"Aye, we hear ye. We have heard all, save Narm and Shandril. What say ye two? Will ye bleed for each other?"

"Aye," said Shandril, speaking first as was the custom.

"Aye," Narm said, as quietly.

"Then let ye be so joined," Rathan said solemnly, and took their left hands in each of his.

Mourngrym stepped forward with his dagger drawn.

In the throng nearby, Jhessail and Elminster tensed. Their protective spells on Mourngrym might be tested by someone seeking magically to compel him to strike the young couple. Rathan's watching face, too, was tense.

Gravely the lord of Shadowdale reached out his dagger and pricked the upturned backs of the two hands, Shandril's first. He wiped the blade on the turf before them, kissed it, put it away, and stepped back in silence.

Jhessail breathed out, long and silently; Elminster did not.

Rathan murmured to the couple, "Now, as we told thee," and stepped back.

Narm and Shandril brought their bloodied hands to each other's mouths, and then stepped into each other's arms and kissed, embracing fiercely. A cheer arose from those watching.

"Of one blood, joined, are Narm and Shandril," Rathan pronounced grandly. "Let no being tear asunder this holy union, or face the dark face of Tymora forevermore!"

Above their heads, the spinning disc flashed with intense light. There were cries of surprise and wonder.

"See the sign of the goddess!" Rathan shouted, delighted. "Her blessing is upon this union!"

The disc rose, shining brightly. Narm and Shandril stepped back, hands clasped, to watch. From it sprang two shafts of white radiance, with a noise like high, jangling harping. The beams reached down, one to touch Narm and the other Shandril.

Narm stood motionless, smiling, eyes wide in astonishment. Power rushed through him, cleansing and strengthening him. At the touch of the light, Shandril burst into flames, and she embraced Narm in wild joy. Her spellfire rose above them both in a great teardrop of fire. Their clothes blazed away, but their hair and bodies were unharmed.

Elminster clucked disapprovingly and wove a spell.

For a moment, it seemed another lady—a smiling woman with silver hair and a robe of the same hue—stood with Rathan and the bridal couple on the fire-scarred flagstones. The wraithlike figure raised a hand in benediction, and then faded silently away.

"Syluné!" Jhessail whispered, tears rising.

As the flames died, robes spun by Elminster's illusion spell clothed Narm and Shandril.

Rathan bellowed, " 'Tis done! Go forth in joy! A feast awaits at the Tower of Ashaba! Dance, all!"

Harpers in dark leathers stepped from trees, startling the guards. They held harps in their hands, and played *The Ride of the Lion.* As the ballad rose, the bright light of Tymora leaped to each instrument. The harps shone and glittered.

Amid the happy tumult that followed, Elminster and Jhessail came forward to join Storm, Mourngrym, and the clerics standing guard about the happy couple.

"So, 'tis done," Jhessail said softly, and kissed both Narm and Shandril. " 'Tis time to give you what was given Merith and me on our wedding day. Foes gather in the woods, and there'll be battle—mind you fly high, and take no part."

Elminster gravely cast a spell of flight upon Shandril, and Jhessail did the same to Narm.

When they were done, Elminster said gruffly, "Remain aloft no more than ye must—this magic lasts not forever. Go now!" He guided them into another embrace, and patted Shandril's bare back. "Rise, before the fighting reaches us!"

"Think 'up,' " Storm and Jhessail murmured in unplanned unison, "and so you'll go!"

Thanking everyone a little dazedly, Narm and Shandril ascended slowly, in a tight embrace. Awe kept them silent as they rose through a clearing sky. The bright disc of Tymora rose with them and followed.

"I do hope Tymora sends back her holy symbol," Rathan muttered, watching its radiance moving east, over the forest.

"And I hope," Storm said as gently, "our two innocents have the sense to steer clear of Myth Drannor."

"I'll see to that, Sister," came a soft voice from above. A black falcon swooped out of the mists and climbed away, heading east.

Elminster growled, "The Simbul! Now I suppose I'll have to keep eyes alight for whatever *she* might do to seize spellfire!" In a flashing instant, an eagle sprang from where he'd stood, soaring arrow-swift into the sky.

Those who still stood where Syluné's hut had been looked at each other, and then at the dalefolk hastening back toward the tower.

The skirl and clang of battle broke out in the forest. Swords flashed and sang amid the trees. Harpers and guards of the dale clashed with warriors in a motley of leather and rusting, mismatched armor—mercenaries, a lot of them, breathless as if they'd hurried a long way.

Jhessail sighed. "Well, back to the battle."

"Aye," Storm agreed with a mirthless smile. "As always."

The four standing on the stones drew blades, a wand, and two maces, and charged into the fray.

As always.

18

Talk Turneth Not Danger Aside

Open the door, little fools: We wait outside.

The green dragon Naurglaur
Sayings of a Wyrm
Year of the Spitting Cat

"We should go down," Shandril whispered into the wind.

Narm's arms tightened about her, and they flew for a time in silence, the green expanse of the elven woods unfolding below. "Aye. I'll not soon forget this!"

"Nor I. As I should hope not!"

Narm chuckled at her mild indignation. Bending his will, he turned them northwest over the seemingly endless trees, back toward Shadowdale. "I can't help feeling we're being watched."

"I'm sure we are—and have been since first we rode with the Knights," his lady replied. "How else could they protect us?"

"Well, yes, but I mean *now*."

"I'm sure they've seen such things before," she said serenely. "Elminster's hundreds of winters old, remember?"

"Yes," Narm sighed, peering all around again. "Would that

none of this were necessary, and we could walk unafraid!"

Shandril fixed him with very serious eyes. "I feel so, too, but without spellfire, we'd both be bones by now!" They passed over the bare top of Harpers' Hill and swiftly left it behind. "Besides, this fire in me is a gift of the gods. Rage as we might, 'tis their will I have it."

Narm nodded. "Aye, and it can be handy enough, but does using it harm you?"

Shandril shrugged. "I know not. I don't feel amiss or in pain, most times. But I can't stop it or give it up, even if I wanted to. 'Tis part of me now."

She turned in his grasp to look back, and something circular and silver drifted out of the empty sky into her hands. It was smooth, cold and solid, and it tingled in her fingertips.

"Rathan's holy symbol!" Narm gasped. "How comes it here?"

"By the will of Tymora, to answer your doubts!"

Narm nodded almost sternly, and the fine hairs on his arms stood stiff with fear. Yet he held her as gently and firmly as before.

"Whither now?" he asked, as they passed over the Old Skull Inn. "The Twisted Tower?"

"No," Shandril replied, pointing at chain mail flashing on the backs of men below. "In all the alarm, the archers might shoot us down before they knew us!"

"Or even," Narm muttered, "because they knew us."

Shandril slapped him lightly. "Think no such darkness! Have any truly of the dale shown us aught but kindness and aid? We must be suspicious, yes, or perish—but ungrateful? Yet, truly, I've little wish to greet the folk of the tower clad as we are!"

Narm chuckled. "Ah, the *real* reason," he said, halting their flight over Elminster's tower. "My apologies for such black thoughts. Still, 'tis better to look often over one's shoulder than to die swift and surprised!"

"Aye, but let not the looking make you sour. You would come down here?"

"Have we anyplace else?" Narm asked. "I doubt the Art protecting Storm's home would be kind to us if we came calling when she wasn't there."

"True," Shandril agreed and took one last look around, glancing north over the Old Skull's stony bulk to the rolling wilderlands beyond. The wind slid gently past their bare shoulders. "Learn this spell as soon as you can," she urged, clinging to her husband. " 'Tis so beautiful."

"Aye." Narm replied huskily. " 'Tis the least of the beauty I have known this day."

Shandril's arms tightened about him . . . and she and Narm sank gently to the earth in front of Elminster's tower.

Overhead, a falcon waggled its wings to an eagle and veered away to the south. The eagle bobbed in slow salute and wheeled about, sighed audibly, and dived to earth.

"Must ye stand about naked, kissing and cuddling and inflaming an old man's passions?" Elminster demanded, inches behind Narm.

The wedded couple jumped, but barely had time to unclasp and turn before the wizard pushed them toward his front door.

"In! In, and try your hands at peeling potatoes. Lhaeo can't feed two extra guts on naught but air, ye know!" Shandril's fending hands encountered a deep and silky beard. Elminster came to a dead halt and glared at her. "Pull my beard, will ye? Ridicule a man old enough to be thy great-great-great-great-great-great-and-probably-great-again-grandsire? Are ye mad? Are ye passion-mazed? Or are ye just tired of life?" Shandril shrank back. The Old Mage seemed to loom larger and larger over her as he thrust his bristling beard forward—and followed it, step by menacing step. "How'd ye like to enjoy the rest of thy life in the mud—as a toad? Or a slug? Or mute, creeping, dung-moss? Aye? *Aye*? AYE?"

He pushed them back, step by step, to the door. Narm had begun to chuckle uncertainly, but Shandril was still white and openmouthed as her bare shoulders brushed old, silver-weathered wood—and the door swung open.

Without pausing for breath, Elminster added in calm tones, "Two guests, Lhaeo. They'll be needing clothes."

"Indeed," came the dry reply. " 'Tis cold in the corners. How are they at peeling potatoes?"

Elminster's chuckle ushered the dumbfounded couple in, and he closed the door with a brief, "I'll follow, anon . . . some tasks remain!"

Narm and Shandril found themselves in the flickering, dusty dimness with Lhaeo, who was already moving to a certain closet. "We've gone through more clothes since you've come to the dale," he murmured. "You were a head shorter than I, were you not, Shandril?"

"Yes," Shandril agreed, and began to laugh uncontrollably.

After a moment, Narm joined her.

Lhaeo shook his head as he handed clothes backward. Truly they serve most who know when to laugh . . . and when to listen.

Stew warm inside her and heart full, Shandril happily leaned her stool against the wall and smiled at Narm. He was resplendent in the silken robes of some grand, long-dead mage of Myth Drannor. The hearth glowed as Lhaeo moved softly back and forth before it, stirring, tasting, and adding pinches of spice. Pheasant hung from the rafters above, and a plump gorscraw lay waiting to be plucked and dressed.

Narm sipped herbsimmer tea and regarded Lhaeo's deft movements over his stewpots. "Is there aught we can do to help?"

Lhaeo looked up with a quick smile. "Aye, but 'tis not cooking. Talk, if you would. I've heard little enough speech that's not Elminster's. Tell me how 'tis with you."

"*Wonderful*," Narm told him. "I'm as happy now as I've ever been in my life. We're wed this day—and henceforth!"

Shandril nodded, eyes shining.

Lhaeo smiled. "Both of you: Remember how you feel now, when times are darker. Turn not on each other, but stand together to face the world's teeth. But enough; I'll not lecture you—you hear enough of that from other lips hereabouts!"

They all laughed.

Shandril asked, "Lhaeo . . . the battle at our wedding? Who was trying to reach us?"

"I was not there. Forgive me; I abide here to guard . . . certain things, but Lord Florin has told me of the men who struck with swords from the woods."

"Yes?" Narm asked quickly.

The scribe looked up, and the two men held each other's eyes. "There were over forty, we believe. Thirty-seven—perhaps more, now—lie dead. One talked ere his life fled. They were mercenaries, hired for ten pieces of gold each and meals, to snatch you both—Shandril alone, if they could take but one of you."

Shandril swallowed. "Take me . . .where?"

The scribe spread his hands helplessly. "They were hired in Selgaunt only a few days back and flown here in a ship that sails the skies. Oh, yes, such things exist, though they be rare triumphs of Art. They were hired in a tavern by a large, balding fat man with a wispy beard, who gave his name as Karsagh. Their orders were to take you to a hill north of here to be picked up by the sky ship."

Lhaeo idly tasted a ladle of stew as if they'd been discussing the weather. "They would then be paid in full. Each had received only two coins; many died still carrying them. Who this Karsagh is and why he wants you, we know not. Have you any favorite thoughts as to who he might be?"

Narm and Shandril shook their heads.

"Half the world is looking for us with swords and spells," Shandril said bitterly. "Have they nothing better to do?"

"Evidently not," Lhaeo replied, " 'Tis not all bad, this seeking. Look who did find you, Shandril: this mageling called Narm, and the Knights who brought you here!"

"Aye," she replied, her voice shaking, "and 'tis here we must leave—friends and all—because of this accursed spellfire." She stared down at her hands, and angry spellfire leaped and spat in tiny, crackling threads from one palm to another.

"Not within these walls, good lady," Lhaeo murmured. "Some things sleep herein that should not be awakened."

Shandril sighed, shamefaced, and let the fires subside. "Sorry, Lhaeo. I've no wish to burn down your house!"

"I know," said Lhaeo gently, turning to his cutting board. "Nor do I fear its coming to pass. You must not hate your gift, Lady, for the gods gave it to you in no such fury. And did not Tymora bless your union?" The scribe indicated the consecrated silver disc that Shandril had carefully set on a high table. It seemed to glow for a moment as they looked at it.

"Aye," Narm said, getting up. "So we're helpless in the hands of the gods?" He began to pace.

Lhaeo looked up, a knife flashing in his hand. "No, for where then would be your luck—the very essence of holy Tymora? What 'luck' can there be if the gods control your every breath? And how dull for them, too! Would *you* take any interest in a world if all the creatures in it had no freedom to do anything you'd not determined beforehand? The gods don't fate men to act thus-and-so, despite the many tales—even those told by the great bards."

"So we walk freely, and do as we will, and live or die by that," Shandril agreed. "So where should we walk? You know maps, Lhaeo. Where in Faerûn should we go?"

Lhaeo shrugged. "Where your hearts lead is the easy answer, and the best. But you really ask me where you should run to, just now, with half Faerûn at your heels." He paced alongside Narm for a few strides, and added, "I'd go south, quick and quiet, then through the Thunder Gap into Cormyr. There, keep to smaller places and try to join a caravan or pilgrims of Tempus seeking the great battlefields of the Sword Coast. Go where there are elves, for they know what 'tis to be hounded, and may well defend you with fierce anger."

Narm and Shandril traded glances

"We've heard such directions before, yes," Narm said, "almost word for word. If the best way's so obvious as all that, will those who hunt us be waiting?"

"Aye, most probably," Lhaeo agreed, with the ghost of a smile. "So you must take care not to get caught."

Shandril surprised herself by laughing. "Well enough," she said, saluting him with a flourish. "We'll try to follow your advice, good Lhaeo. Know you ways of avoiding Shandril-hunters?"

Lhaeo lifted his eyebrows. "You both work with Art and walk with those mighty in Art, and you ask *me*? If you'd learn the ways of stealth and disguise without Art, ask Torm. I've escaped my hunters thus far, true, but I was truly cloaked in the Lady's Luck."

He turned to Narm. "If you must pace like a great cat in a cage, could you slice potatoes while doing it?"

Elsewhere, things were not so peaceful. In Zhentil Keep, two men faced each other across a table.

"Lord Marsh," asked the mage Sememmon carefully, "does it seem to you that the priests of the Black Altar have fallen into confusion and disarray too great for us to leave the city? All reports agree that the beholder Manxam holds sway in the temple . . . where the sprawled corpses of many hundred clergy have begun to stink!"

"I've heard those same reports," Lord Marsh Belwintle agreed smoothly, "and am forced to the same conclusions. This matter of one girl who can create fire will simply have to wait. If she shows up at our gates, I'm confident the power and skill of the gathered mages would defeat her—so long as they've not all been destroyed or weakened in the fulfillment of missions commanded by one who had transparent reasons for wishing them out of the city."

"Exactly. I'd thought to discuss with you the advisability of setting just one of our mages of power—Sarhthor, perhaps—to observing this maiden's doings, so her seizure by any foes could be noted or countered. Prudence seems to indicate some such vigilance."

"An excellent thought," Lord Marsh agreed, reaching for his glass of bloodwine. "An eye must serve where a claw might be cut off, if we're not to be taken unawares. Yet you will send some magelings forth to impress their fellows and my warriors with our alacrity and attention to this matter?"

"Of course," Sememmon replied, not quite allowing a smile to reach his lips. "The ambition of our younger spell weavers remains legendary. I was planning to send four rivals forth."

"Excellent." Marsh rose. "My own younger blades seem so busy just now, disposing of priests regrettably driven mad by this latest outrage of the eye tyrants. Untrustworthy allies, as I've said before. Order must be maintained; duty presses—so, for now, oloré to you."

"Oloré to you." Sememmon walked away.

An eye that neither of them saw under the table watched Sememmon go, and then winked out.

"The Wearers of the Purple are met. For the glory of the dead dragons!" Naergoth Bladelord intoned. The leader of the Cult of the Dragon was, as always, coldly calm.

"For their dominion," came the ritual reply in unison.

Naergoth surveyed the large, plain underground chamber. Everyone of the ruling council of the Cult was present save the mage Malark. To work, then—all the sooner to feast in some fine festhall of Ordulin, far above.

"Brothers, we're gathered to hear of a matter that's set all mages into eager uproar: spellfire. Brother Zilvreen, what say you?"

"Brothers," the master thief Zilvreen said with his soft, sinister grace, "I've learned little of the fates of the dracolich Rauglothgor and the mage Maruel. It seems likely, though, that Rauglothgor, its treasure, the she-mage, and even the sacred night dragon Aghazstamn have all been destroyed."

There was a rumble of surprise and dismay, but Zilvreen's next words cut it off like a sword stroke. "Destroyed by the accursed archmage of Shadowdale, Elminster, his pet brigands the Knights of Myth Drannor, and by this Shandril Shessair . . . with her spellfire!"

"All?" rumbled Dargoth, of the Perlar merchant fleet. "I can scarce believe they *all* have been destroyed. Such slaughter would require an army large enough that we'd all see its whelming over many days!"

"No such swords've been raised," added Commarth, the bearded general of the Sembian border forces.

"Men sent back by Malark describe the site of Rauglothgor's lair as a pit of fresh-strewn rubble," Zilvreen replied. "Draw your own conclusions."

Dargoth shook his head in disbelief. "So just what is this spellfire, that it can destroy mighty mages and great wyrms alike?"

Naergoth shrugged. "A fire that can be hurled as a mage casts lightning," he said, "to burn spells and enchanted things as readily as wood and flesh. More than that, we know not—wherefore we sent Malark."

"What of him?" Commarth asked. "Has he spoken to any Follower?"

Naergoth shook his head. "Nothing from him. He's in Shadowdale, as far as we know, seeking his chance to get at the girl."

"Shessair," another of the council mused. "Wasn't that the name of the mage our brothers-of-Art slew at the Bridge of Fallen Men years back, in the battle that bought them their deaths?"

"It was," Naergoth replied, "but no connection's yet apparent. Look you: We've at least three eyes in Sword Coast cities who share the last name of Suld . . . and none are related."

Naergoth nodded. "The price of getting this spellfire seems far too high. Others—the Zhentarim and other priests of Bane—avidly seek it. Yet 'tis we who've already paid a price, and I'm loath to turn away empty-handed. We can't afford *not* to take spellfire for our own. No one can. I expect much bloodshed yet." He looked around the table. "How we go about getting it I leave to you, Brothers!"

"Let the mages win it for us," said Zilvreen smoothly. "Waste no more swords—and especially no more sacred bone dragons—on this."

"Well enough," Dargoth agreed. "But spellfire or no, we cannot let this girl or the Knights go unpunished for what they've done. We've lost much treasure, two dracoliches, and the Shadowsil over this. The girl must pay. Even if we win her as an ally, she must die after we have gained her secrets and her power. This *must* ride over all."

"Well said, Brother," Naergoth responded. There was a murmur of agreement around the table. "We're agreed, then—for now, we let our Brother mage handle this affair?"

"Aye, 'tis his field," came one reply.

"Aye, 'twould be folly to do otherwise," said another.

"Aye—and if he comes not back, we can always raise other mages to the Purple."

"Aye to that, too!"

"Aye," the others put in, in their turn.

So it was agreed, and they rose and left that place.

⊠ ⊠ ⊠

The hour was late; all through the Twisted Tower, candles burned low. In an inner room of Lord Mourngrym's chambers, there was much discussion over the remains of dinner—in low tones, as Lady Shaerl slept in her chair at one end of the table, and Rathan Thentraver dozed over one arm of his seat.

"Have you a place in mind?" Jhessail asked as she leaned drowsily upon Merith's shoulder, their eyes gleaming together in the candlelight.

Narm shrugged. " 'We hunt our fortune, where'er,' as the saying goes. The Harpers said to seek High Lady Alustriel in Silverymoon."

"Would you have some of us ride with you?" Lanseril asked. "There're greater evils in this world than those you've fought."

"With all respect, Lord," Shandril said softly, "no. Too long have you watched over us, and spilled much blood on our account. We must make our own way in the world and fight our own battles—or in the end, we'll have done nothing."

" 'Nothing,' she says," Torm sighed to Illistyl, rolling his eyes. "Two dracoliches, a mountaintop, and a good piece of Manshoon of Zhentil Keep—and 'nothing,' she calls it! Scary; what if she tries 'something'?"

"Hush, you," Illistyl said, stopping his mouth with a kiss. "You're a worse windbag than the Old Mage himself!"

"Why, *thank* ye," came a wry and familiar voice from the room's far darkness. Narm saw the battered old hat first, perched atop the staff that Elminster wore. As the wizard's bearded face came into the light to regard them all, the smallest of smiles played about his lips. He looked last at Narm and Shandril. "Ye might go to the Rising Moon for a night, at least. 'Twould be a kindness to Gorstag. He's been worried over ye."

Shandril met Elminster's gaze, and silent tears rolled down her cheeks.

Narm took her in his arms, but her tears still fell. "Don't cry, beloved. You're among—"

"Hush her not," Merith said gently. " 'Tis no shame to weep. Only one who cares not, cries not. I've seen what befalls those—Florin and Torm, at this table—who cry inside, to hide it from others. It sears the soul."

Jhessail nodded. "Merith's right. Tears don't upset us, only the reasons for them."

"Cry here, Lord," murmured Shaerl in her sleep, patting her own shoulder. " 'Tis soft, and listens to you."

Mourngrym looked faintly embarrassed.

Torm grinned. "You see?" he said to Illistyl. "You could do that for me . . . you've the shoulders for it!"

She slapped him fondly.

Shaerl stirred and frowned. "Oh, 'tis that game this night? Well, my lord, you'll have to catch me first, I assure you."

Chuckles rose around the room. Mourngrym leaned over and lifted his lady gently from the chair. Still lost in slumber, she clung to his neck and drew her legs up across his chest, settling herself with murmurs of contentment.

Mourngrym turned to them, Shaerl cradled in his arms. "Good even, all. Shaerl should be in bed—and so should we all."

"Now, where were we?" Elminster asked moments later, settling himself into a chair that looked as old, shabby, and worn as he. "Oh, aye . . . thy plans for the future!"

The slow, disbelieving shake of Narm's head was eloquent.

Shandril fixed the wizard with tired eyes. "I suppose you'll tell us to steer clear of battles, or we'll be dead in a day."

"Nay." Very clear blue eyes looked deep into hers. "Ye two'll be given no such choice. Ye must fight or die. But think: One mistake is enough when disputing with those who wield Art. Remember that!" His gaze shifted to Narm. "Ye too, Lion of Mystra. If ye find thyself facing a mage, stand not to trade spells with him. Throw rocks and run right at him—unless he's too far away to reach. Then run away and find a place to hide—where ye can grab more rocks. Simple, eh? Before ye laugh, recall how thy lady first struck down Symgharyl Maruel."

"Hundreds of winters, eh?" was all Narm said.

Shandril awakened, in a cold sweat from being pursued through a ruined city by a black-winged devil. It had cornered her at last and reached for her, leering with Symgharyl Maruel's cruel, smiling face! She sat bolt upright, gasping.

Florin sat nearby with Elminster, talking in low tones through the blue haze of the wizard's pipe. He leaned over, concern on his ruggedly handsome face, and laid a soothing hand on her arm.

She smiled gratefully and held to his arm as she sank back down beside Narm, who slept on, peacefully.

Florin gently wiped the sweat from her forehead and jaw.

Shandril drifted off to sleep while still smiling her thanks. The next thing she knew, morning had come.

Jhessail was laughing with Merith over hot minted tea. Sunlight shone down warmly. The Knights, variously clad, lounged on couches or walked quietly about. The clear tones of a horn floated up from somewhere below, where an unseen guard blew his delight at a fine morning.

Shandril looked around at the old stone walls of the chamber and said both fiercely and mournfully, "I'm going to miss this."

"Yes," Narm agreed, hugging her. "You seemed ready to sleep forever!"

Shandril hugged him back. "You're mine, now!"

"A-aye," Narm managed, within her arms.

"Not for much longer, if you break him like a clay cup," Torm said dryly. "They're more useful, you know, when they're whole . . . back and arms able to carry, and all. . . ."

Shandril burst out laughing. "You're utterly ridiculous!"

" 'Tis how I get through each day," Torm told her earnestly.

It was much later when she realized he'd spoken the sober truth.

"Well," said Florin. "Here we part." He nodded at the weathered stone pillar just ahead. "Yonder's the Standing Stone."

The stone rose watchful and defiant out of the brush, overlooking the fields to Mistledale and south toward Battledale. Florin pointed. "Down that road lies Essembra. Take rooms at the Green Door. It once had a talking door, but we took a fancy to it, so now it swings at the tower." He grinned. "In all the excitement, we forgot to show it to you."

The white horse under Shandril snorted and tossed its head.

"Easy, Shield," Florin soothed. "You've barely begun!"

His words made a sudden lump rise in Shandril's throat. She turned in her saddle to look back. Past the pack mules on their reins, past the watchful guards who rode with crossbows ready, back to where the Knights rode with an ever-grumbling Elminster. She'd miss them all. She felt Narm's hand clasp hers hard, and fought down tears.

"None of that," Rathan ordered her gruffly. "All this sobbin' robs an occasion of its due grandeur."

"Aye," Lanseril agreed. " 'Soon you'll be too busy staying out of trouble to cry, so acquire the habit now. Remember: Mourngrym serves his best wine at Greengrass; we'll be looking for you, some year."

Narm nodded. Shandril was too busy sniffing.

"Go, now," Torm said gruffly, over his shoulder, "or we'll be all day a-weeping and a-saying farewells."

Rathan urged his large bay forward and took the hands of Narm and Shandril. "Tymora ride with ye and watch over ye. Think of us when downcast or cold—for happy memories can warm and hearten."

Torm stared at his friend. "Such bardic soft and high glory. You've not been drinking, have you?"

"Get on with ye, snaketongue, to the nearest mud and fall into it," Rathan told him kindly, "and mind thy mouth drinks deep."

"Peace, both of you," Jhessail chided. "Narm and Shandril should be well away before highsun, if they're to make Essembra even two nights hence!" She turned to the young couple. "Stay on the road. The Elven Court's not the safest place in Faerûn."

"Let not fear or pity stay your hand, either," Florin said gravely. "If you're menaced on the road, let fly with spellfire before hands are upon you. Too close a swinging sword can't be stopped by spell or spellfire."

"Oh, aye . . . one last thing," Elminster said. "This illusion will make ye look older, and a trifle different save to each other's eyes. 'Twill wear off in a day or so, or ye can end it anytime, each of ye affecting only thyself, by uttering the word 'gultho'—nay, repeat it not *now*, lumpheads, or ye'll ruin the magic. Let me see. . . ." He drew back his sleeves, sat back on his placid donkey, and worked magic upon Narm and Shandril.

The Knights drew their horses around in a respectful circle. When it was done, they edged closer for careful, critical looks.

Narm and Shandril failed to see the slightest difference in each other's appearance, but it was clear they looked different to the eyes of others.

"Go now," Elminster said gently, "or ye'll be seen. We shall ride north toward Hillsfar with illusions of ye for a time to confuse any who seek ye, but those who pursue ye are not weak-minded. Go now, swiftly. Our love and regard go with ye." His clear blue eyes met theirs fondly as they turned their horses and with a wave, spurred away.

Looking back as they thundered south along the road, tears stinging their eyes, Narm and Shandril saw the Knights sitting their saddles, watching. Florin raised to his lips something that flashed silver in the sun. They rode over the first rise and lost sight of the Knights, but the clear notes of his war horn rang out in farewell. He was playing the *Salute to Victorious Warriors*. At the inn, Shandril had heard bards perform it to crown their performances and leave everyone awed, but never had she dreamed it might be played for her!

"Will we ever see them again?" Narm asked softly, as they slowed.

"Yes," Shandril answered, with eyes and voice of steel, "we *shall*. Whatever stands in the way." She brushed hair out of her eyes. "Now, we must look after ourselves. If I must slay with spellfire every jack and lass so eager to take it, so be it. If all Faerûn expects 'Lady Spellfire,' I shall *be* Lady Spellfire."

Narm nodded, face somber.

Shandril spread her hands. "I'm afraid I can't laugh at devils and dracoliches and mages and men with swords the way Torm does. They just make me angry and afraid. So I'll strike back. I hope you won't be hurt . . . but I fear much battle lies ahead."

"I hope *you* won't be hurt, my lady," Narm answered, as they rode on. "You're the one they'll be after."

"I know," Shandril said softly. "But 'tis I who'll have spellfire ready when they find me."

⊠ ⊠ ⊠

The road was lightly traveled that day. Narm and Shandril saw no one else heading south, and only a few merchants bound north, who rode ready-armed but nodded and passed without incident or ill looks.

Great old trees of the Elven Court rose on both sides of the road. Between them and the road itself, a forest of stumps rose from the ditch like the gray fingers of buried giants; the remnants of saplings cut by travelers as staves and litter poles and firewood. Narm watched these narrowly as they rode, half-expecting brigands to rise from them.

No such attack came. The hours and rolling hills passed. They rode mostly in silence until the sun glimmered low and the trees laid dark shadows across the road.

"We should find a place to sleep, love," Narm said at last.

Shandril nodded. "Yes, and soon . . . we're almost at the Vale. A cursed place. Let's stop here—at that height, ahead—and hope none find us."

When they reined to a halt, and Narm swung down, the aches in his thighs made him groan and stagger. "Tymora watch over us!" His horse swung its head around to see what was the matter. He patted it reassuringly as he looked around and listened.

"Water, down there," he said after a moment, pointing.

Shandril swung down into his arms. "Good, then," she said lightly, kissing his nose as he set her down. "You fetch some while I tie the horses, O mighty mage."

Narm growled in the manner of Rathan and unhooked the nosebags from their saddles.

Somewhere nearby a wolf howled. Overhead, as daylight faded and moonlight began, a black falcon came silently to a branch above Shandril and perched there, watching.

⊠ ⊠ ⊠

They awoke in each other's arms on the hard bed of their canvas tent laid on mossy ground. Birds called in the brightening morning, but it was still damp and misty among the trees. A beautiful place, but somehow . . . unwelcoming.

Sitting up, Narm thought he glimpsed through the tent flap elven eyes far off in the tree gloom, regarding him steadily. When he blinked, they were gone. Hmm. The elven kingdom might have gone from these woods, but the hand of man hadn't tamed what was left behind—yet.

Narm felt more comfortable once his hand was on the hilt of his drawn dagger, beneath the cloak that covered their shoulders and throats. He turned to Shandril, who smiled through tousled hair, sleepy and vulnerable.

"Good morn, my lady," he greeted softly, rolling over to draw her close.

"And to you, my love. 'Tis nice to be alone for once, without strangers attacking and guards watching over us always, and Elminster fussing about . . . I love you, Narm."

"I love you, too," Narm said quietly. "How lucky I've been to see you in the inn and then be parted—only to find you deep in ruined Myth Drannor. I would have come back to the Rising Moon someday when I was free of Marimmar, only to find you long gone!"

"Aye," Shandril whispered against his chest. "Long gone and probably dead. Oh, Narm . . ."

They lay in each other's arms for a long time, warm and safe, unwilling to rise and end this feeling of peace.

From the road, a dull thudding of hooves came up through the trees, followed by the creak of harness leather.

Shandril sighed and rolled free of Narm. "I suppose we must get up." Long hair tangled about her shoulders as she rose to her knees, pulling the cloak about her against the chill. "If we stop in Essembra only to buy feed for us and the horses and hasten on, eating as we ride, we could camp on the southern edge of the forest this night. I want to be away west of the Thunder Peaks before the Cult of the Dragon and Zhentil Keep and anyone else know we've left the Knights. Come, now—you can kiss me more later!"

Narm nodded a bit mournfully and glanced out the tent flap. Mist drifted through the trees, and the horses patiently chewed leaves. Narm scrambled up to dress. Every step made him wince; his thighs were raw from yesterday's ride.

Tugging on his belt, he emerged, and then stopped abruptly to listen. He could have sworn he'd heard a chuckle, but there was no one to be seen. All was quiet from the road, too.

He shrugged and went to the horses, glancing back often at his lady. He never saw the black falcon winging low among the trees, heading east for the long flight home.

In falcon shape, the Simbul chuckled and shook her head.

They were good folk . . . children, still, but not for much longer.

She had other concerns, too long neglected, to see to now. Perhaps they'd be killed—but then again, it was entirely possible they'd do the killing, no matter who of Faerûn quarreled with them.

Farewell, you two. Fare you *very* well.

The lonely queen of Aglarond flicked raven-black wings and rose into a brightening sky.

They made good time across the Vale of Lost Voices, a strangely still valley of huge, dark, soaring trees. It was sacred to the elves. Men whispered that something unseen and terrible guarded it . . . something that destroyed axe-wielders and great mages alike, and left no trace. The elves of Cormanthyr had buried their fallen among these trees—and folk who dared to dig for treasure interred with them vanished in the mists and were not seen again.

Narm and Shandril and travelers who passed them said not a word while crossing the Vale. It was choked with the largest trees they had ever seen, some as big around as Elminster's tower. In the gloom under their lofty leaves, where boughs met high above the road, the light was eerily blue. In the forest distances, mists coiled slowly, and faint glowing lights drifted and danced. No one strayed from the road while traversing the Vale.

They left it at last, Shandril shivering in relief as they crested the steep rise of its southern edge.

"The Lost Dale, they call it in Cormyr," Narm said in a low voice. "Forever lost to men."

Shandril looked at him. "They say in the dales that every elf of the Elven Court would have to be dead before one tree of the Vale could be safely cut."

"But I heard from more than one trader that all the elves are gone now."

Shandril shook her head. "No. I saw one in the woods as we came down to Storm Silverhand's pool. She waved to Storm and slipped away." She peered back into the dark Vale, and then into the smaller, sun-dappled trees around them now.

"That's far from here," Narm protested.

"Think you so?" asked Shandril very softly. "Look there, then."

Narm followed her gaze. Ahead, on the mighty branch of a shadowtop that towered above the road, a motionless figure in mottled green-gray stood. It was an elf, leaning easily on a bow that must have been a head taller than Narm. He watched them expressionlessly. His eyes were blue and gold-flecked flames, proud and serene.

Shandril bowed her head to him, smiled, and spread empty hands. A little uncertainly, Narm did the same. A slow nod was their only answer.

The horses carried them past. Neither Narm or Shandril looked back. It was some time before she murmured, "A moon elf, like Merith."

"A possible enemy, unlike Merith," Narm said grimly. "We must watch our every step." He peered ahead. "The trees thin. We must be nearing Essembra. I can see fields."

Out of those fields, a caravan rumbled toward them: a dozen wagons pulled by oxen and surrounded by hard-eyed outriders with crossbows at their saddles. The wagons bore no merchant banner and passed without incident.

Well behind the caravan rode a family on heavily laden draft horses, leading strings of pack mules. They were led by a single excited youth whose halberd dipped and swung alarmingly as he rode to challenge them. "Way, there! Way, if you be not foes! Declare yourselves!"

Narm stared at him in silence.

The halberd lowered menacingly. "Declare yourselves, or defend yourselves!"

"Ride on in peace," Narm replied, "or I'll turn your halberd into a viper to bite the hand that holds it!"

The boy recoiled, his horse dancing uncertainly as its rider tried to draw his blade wrong-handed. "If you be a mage," he said shrilly, backing away as Narm and Shandril rode steadily on, "give your name, or face swift death!"

Beyond, Narm saw hand crossbows raised ready, and calm, wary eyes above them. He dared not hesitate.

Narm drew himself up in his saddle. "I am Marimmar the Magnificent, Mage Most Mighty. I and my apprentice here would pass you in peace—but offer us death, and it shall be *yours!*"

Beside him, Shandril burst into muffled giggles. With an effort, Narm kept his composure as the boy cast him a frightened look—and hastened by. Narm nodded pleasantly and stared straight ahead as he passed the family and their mule train, almost managing to hide a smile that kept creeping onto one side of his face.

"Sarhthor?" Sememmon peered into the crystal ball. Its magic was always difficult to focus at first. In its depths he saw an expressionless, elegantly bearded face.

Sarhthor looked back fearlessly, and effortlessly forced the link between them into clarity.

Sememmon tried to hide his irritation at the other mage's easy mastery of Art.

"Well met," Sarhthor purred. "I've searched the dale; Elminster and the Knights have just returned, riding south from Voonlar. The girl with spellfire and her consort mageling are no longer in Shadowdale, so far as I can determine."

"Not in Shadowdale?"

"Not. They *may* be here in hiding, but I doubt it. No Knight nor any Harper has gone anywhere out of the ordinary. The folk of the tower know only that 'Lady Spellfire' left two nights ago."

"Two *nights?*" Sememmon almost screamed. "They could be almost anywhere!"

Precisely why I'm returning to you, as soon as possible, Sarhthor thought flatly, letting the crystal carry his mental message. "Who's that with you?"

"*With* me?" Sememmon frowned. "I'm alone!"

"You are indeed—*now*. A moment ago, an eye floated above your left shoulder—the ocular construction of a wizard eye spell. A spy. Guard yourself, Sememmon."

Sememmon turned angrily from the crystal to stare wildly about the chamber. "Show yourself!" he thundered, casting a quick spell. Dweomers—the auras of familiar objects imbued with Art—glowed all around. The faint traceries of spells, too, shone in his field of revealed magic . . . but all were spells he knew about. There was no sign of any intruder.

Sememmon turned back to the crystal ball, but it was dark. No one waited at the matching globe any longer. Sememmon cursed the shadows, but they did not answer.

The sun sank low in the west as Shandril and Narm passed a skin of hot spiced tea between them. They rode contentedly, bellies full of warm roast phledge, the plump ground-partridge of the woods, smoky-tasting and delightful in a thick pea gravy. No one had seemed suspicious of them at the inn Florin had recommended.

"How do you feel, Shan?" Narm asked, not meeting her eyes. "About the spellfire, I mean. Does it . . . change one?"

A little startled, Shandril looked at him with something like pity. "Yes . . . but not in the larger sense. I'm still the Shandril you rescued from Rauglothgor." She hesitated. "I'm still the Shandril you love."

There was a little silence as they regarded each other.

Then the attack came.

Shandril sensed something was wrong an instant before the boulder struck Narm's shoulder and his head flew back. The jarring made her bite her lip. Narm whirled about, his arm striking her head solidly as he spun, toppled, and fell.

Stunned, Shandril stared at the huge, mossy boulder as it sank slowly past her to hang in the air above Narm's head.

He lay crumpled, unmoving. The boulder was large and dark—and over it, behind the grassy bank, stood a man in robes. He grinned at her without humor, his eyes glittering black and deadly.

Wild fear rose and choked her.

19

The Crushing of the Soul

I have known the crushing of the soul that defeat brings, and the burning, sickening pain of deep wounds—and would not have it otherwise. Such dark things make the bright spots burn the brighter.

Korin of Neverwinter
Tales Told by the Warm Fireside
Year of the Blazing Brand

"Make no sound!" the man in robes warned. "Speak not. Cast no spells. Use no spellfire, Shandril Shessair—or I'll let the rock fall on your husband's head!" His eyes bored into hers. "Think not to trick me or take me unawares, for I'm no such a fool—and yon stone can hardly miss its mark!"

Shandril sat in her saddle, cold fear trickling down her spine. She stared at this enemy mage, wondering who he was. How to win free? her mind screamed. How to win free?

"I am Malark," the man said with cold pride, "of the Cult of the Dragon. I come for revenge, and I *will* have it!" His eyes flickered. "Get down off your horse slowly, and stay just where you land, or your husband will die."

Shandril did as he commanded, never taking her eyes off his.

He watched her with the cold patience of a snake. "Lie down. Slowly. To your knees, and then upon your belly, arms stretched to the sides. Touch no weapon!"

Shandril did so, heart sinking as she pressed her face into the dirt road.

"Good. Spread your arms and legs—slowly. Do not try to rise." His voice was nearer.

Shandril obeyed, wondering how much she'd have to endure, and silently gathered spellfire.

Malark walked around her, staying at a safe distance.

Angry warmth filled Shandril's chest and throat. She glared at a tuft of grass, and it began to smolder. She hooded her fire hastily and held herself ready. Tymora, aid me!

"You've cost us much, Shandril Shessair. The Shadowsil, the sacred wyrm Rauglothgor, his lair, the fortified tower above it, all his treasure, the sacred wyrm Aghazstamn, many devout Followers—the worth of all these, you owe us. The price you will pay is your spellfire—and your life in service. Yours, and your husband's. You will serve or die. *Lie still!*" The cold voice above Shandril began a spell.

Gods aid me, Shandril thought. What will become of us? There are no Knights here to rescue us, now. . . .

Malark's cold chant ended in a sudden squeal and gurgle.

Shandril, waiting to absorb his spell, rolled over in breathless haste. If that rock fell on Narm . . .

But Narm was safely to one side, in the grip of a grinning Rathan Thentraver. The wizard Malark stood staring at her, his eyes very dark and very large. Torm grinned over his shoulder. In the thief's hands were the ends of the waxed cord that had choked off Malark's spell in midword. The wizard hung from the cord now, his face terrible, fingers clawing at his throat. As she watched in dawning horror, those fingers grew feeble, Malark's eyes rolled up into his skull, and he sagged.

Torm held the cord tight as he lowered Malark to the ground. "Well met," the thief said cheerfully. He drew his dagger in one fluid motion and beckoned Rathan with a jerk of his head. "His purse, quickly, before he's fully dead . . . these damned mages all have spells to trigger mischief at their deaths."

Rathan bent to work. "Ho, Shandril—thy lad's all right!"

Shandril stared at the boulder, sunk deep into the grass, and shuddered.

"Nothing but a rag and a few coppers," Rathan reported.

"His boots," Torm directed, still holding the cord tight. Malark's face was so twisted, dark, and terrible Shandril looked away.

"Is he—dead?" she asked weakly.

"Nearly. I'll cut his throat in a moment. . . . Then, Lady, 'twould be best to burn the body completely, or some Cult bastard will raise him to tail you!" Torm turned professional eyes on the boots. "Try that heel."

"Hah!" Rathan said in satisfaction, holding up six platinum pieces. "Hollow, indeed!"

"Hmmph," Torm said, wrinkling his nose. "No magic? Scarce worth all this trouble. Have off his robe, Rathan, and we'll cut his throat and be done with it."

"His robe?"

"Aye, his robe. Where he conceals the components for his spells, a few extra coins, and the gods know what else. Come on, my arms grow weary!"

"They do? Pretend they're around a wench, and ye'll have no trouble," Rathan told him gruffly, tugging off the mage's robe. He stepped back, surveying the wizard's body as Torm laid it down with both ends of the cord in one fist and a long, wicked dagger in the other.

Torm grinned at Shandril. "Not unimportant, are ye? Malark, one of the rulers of the Cult of the Dragon, and an archmage. Watch out, now: There're lots of other rats like this one in Sembia, and one in Deepingdale, too. . . ."

"Yes," Shandril replied, her voice a whisper as sharp as a sword. "*Korvan*."

Rathan nodded. "Aye, that's the name! Ye've been warned, then? Good. Well, ye're doing fine thus far!"

"Fine," Shandril said bitterly, watching Torm free the cord and slash with cruel speed. Her gaze fell on Narm, who still lay silent in the grass. "Oh, yes. Fine indeed."

Rathan sighed and went to her. "Look, little one, Faerûn can be a cruel place. Men like this have to be slain—or they'll kill thee. Nor is there any shame in defeat at his hands—this one could've slain any of us Knights in an open fight." He enfolded her in a bear hug. "Ye wouldn't be thirsty, perhaps?"

Shandril's shoulders shook helplessly, her tears overwhelmed by laughter. She laughed a long time and a little wildly, but Rathan held her tight. When at last she was done, she raised bright eyes. "Are you finished, Torm? I think I'd like to wield a little spellfire."

Torm nodded and stepped back. Shandril raised a hand and lashed the body with flames, pouring out her anger. Oily smoke arose almost immediately, and the horses snorted and hurried off in all directions.

Torm and Rathan let out despairing cries and ran after them.

Narm rolled over, groaned, and asked faintly, "Shan? Wha—why'd you do that? Am I not to kiss you?"

"They could be *dead* by now!" Sharantyr said angrily. "I ride patrol for a few days and return to find you've put your toes to the behinds of the nicest young people I've met! One struggles with half-trained Art, and the other bears spellfire every mage in the Realms would slay her to gain or destroy, and both are mad enough to seek adventure—only days married, too! Where's your kindness, Knights of Myth Drannor? *Where* is your *sense?*"

"Easy, Shar," Florin said gently. "They joined the Harpers and wanted to walk their own road. Would you want to be caged?"

"Caged? Does a mother turn out her infant because it's reached twenty nights? *Alone*, you sent them!" The furious ranger turned on Elminster. "What say you, Old One? Can they best even a handful of brigands? Brigands attacking by surprise in the night? Speak *truth!*"

"I've never done aught else, when it mattered. As to the fight ye speak of, I think ye'd be surprised!" Elminster drew out his pipe. "Besides, they're not alone, not by now. Torm and Rathan rode after them."

Sharantyr snorted. "Sent the sharpest lances, didn't you?" She paced, hair swirling, and drew a deep breath. "Well enough. They're not unprotected." She folded her arms and leaned back beside the hearth. "Gods spit on my luck. I wanted to say farewell, not just ride away and never see them again."

"They'll be all right, Shar," Storm said gently, "and they'll be back."

"Sharantyr raises a good point," Lanseril said from his chair. "The wisdom of sending them alone, with only a rescue force hurrying along behind, can be questioned." He raised thoughtful eyes to Mourngrym and Elminster. "I take it you considered their slipping away, while we rode a distraction to Hillsfar, a good risk?"

Elminster nodded. "It had to be. Think on that, Sharantyr, and be not so angry, lass."

"They passed the Vale without loss or upset," Merith put in. "I heard from one of the People watching the road."

Sharantyr nodded. "And since then?"

Illistyl spoke up. "I scryed Torm and Rathan yestereve. They were cutting across country southeast of Mistledale, and had met with no one then. I'll try them again tonight."

"Soon?"

"Aye . . . you can watch, if you like. You too, Jhess, if you have no greater game afoot." She looked meaningfully at Merith, who grinned. "We might need your spells if there's danger or alarm."

Jhessail chuckled. " 'Tis a good thing none but the gods look over your shoulders to see all we—and Narm and Shandril, gods smile on them—get up to! 'Twould make a long, confusing ballad!"

Elminster scowled. "Life's seldom as clear-cut, smooth, and easily ended as a ballad." He put his pipe in his mouth with an air of finality. The fire crackled and flared in the hearth. The Old Mage stared into the flames and muttered, "She's so young to wield spellfire."

"He lies within," the acolyte said, hastening back from the door.

Sememmon thanked him curtly. "Open it."

The acolyte stood in silence—and then glided reluctantly forward and swung wide the heavy oak-and-bronze door.

Sememmon motioned him through. The acolyte nodded and entered, face impassive. The wizard followed, through thick stone walls, into a vast chamber that glowed an eerie blue.

This was the center of the Black Altar, the Inner Chamber of Solitude, where one was said to be closest to the god. The High Imperceptor's forces had not penetrated this far, though Sememmon felt much satisfaction at the extensive damage. Bane's priests would be awhile recovering their cocky strength.

Perhaps never, Sememmon thought, if certain misfortunes befall them now . . . while weak and disorganized.

He came fully into the chamber, and such thoughts ceased.

Vast and dark above him hung a beholder, its great central eye gazing down in wise, dark malice.

The acolyte darted back behind Sememmon, the door clanged, and a heavy bar crashed into place.

Sememmon was imprisoned, and this eye tyrant was not Manxam. Sememmon cursed inwardly as he approached, his cloak concealing nervous fingers on the hilt of a useless dagger.

The floor of the chamber was polished black marble. In the center of that vast, cold expanse rose a black throne—a throne the High Imperceptor hadn't sat at the foot of for many a long year. It was gigantic—a seat for a giant. The seat of a god. It was occupied.

Red silk splashed across the black stone. Fzoul Chembryl lay asleep on a bed across the seat of the god's throne, recovering after the frantic healing efforts of underpriests. A rope ladder allowed them to ascend to the spot.

Sememmon approached, uncomfortably aware that the beholder was moving with him, floating directly overhead, its great unblinking eye staring down. At long last the beholders were making their own bid for mastery over the Zhentarim.

A deep, rumbling voice from overhead said, "You've come to discover death, Sememmon the Proud—and you've found not Fzoul's death, but your own!"

Sememmon broke into a run.

The dark body above him sank lower. In a breath, the eye tyrant would be close enough to turn him to stone, charm him into obedience, or perhaps simply pursue him about the chamber like a trapped rat, wounding him repeatedly. In the end it would use the eye that destroyed . . . and there'd not even be dust left of Sememmon.

He ran as he had never run before, diving frantically around the edge of the throne, where its great central eye that foiled all magic could not see. He began casting an incendiary cloud. He hadn't the right spells for a fight this grave. . . .

Buy time and cover, he thought. Use a dimension door to teleport above it, and then paralyzation—or, no, magic missiles now! Or . . . ah, gods spit upon it all!

Raging, Sememmon finished his spell weaving. He sprinted along the back of the throne, nearly tripping over the ring of a trapdoor he'd have needed the brawn of five acolytes to lift. Reaching the corner, Sememmon gasped and steadied himself. To hurl magic missiles, he must see his target—and if he could see the beholder, its eyes could see *him*. He tensed himself to take a rapid peek, and—

There was a flash and a roar, and the floor heaved, throwing Sememmon to his knees.

Up, get up!

Reddish spots danced before his eyes. He couldn't tell up from down.

"Well met, Sememmon," said a dry, coldly familiar voice.

Sememmon looked up into the calm gazes of Sarhthor and Manshoon. The High Lord of Zhentil Keep was robed in his usual black and dark blue, and he looked amused. "You can get up now. It's gone." He flexed his fingers, from which tiny wisps of smoke curled.

Swallowing, Sememmon found his voice. "You've returned! Lord, we've missed you, indeed—"

"Aye. No doubt. I've watched you—and seen the, ah, troubles with Fzoul. Slay him not. He's needed."

They strode briskly together across the marble floor to the doorway Sememmon had entered by. The door lay in blasted, twisted shards of metal.

"Sarhthor," Manshoon explained briefly.

The three mages went out through strangely deserted halls and sought the starlit night. Wordlessly they walked out of the Black Altar, past dim piles that had already begun to stink—the bodies of those fallen in the strife between Fzoul and the High Imperceptor—and proceeded straight to Sememmon's abode. The two dark-robed mages left Sememmon there.

"Cheer up," Manshoon told him. "You'll have your chance to fight the others for all this"—he shrugged and looked around at the dark spires all about—"someday. I can't live forever." With that he turned on his heel and was gone down the cobbled street into the night, Sarhthor at his heels.

Sememmon stared after them in the faint light, fear like cold iron in his mouth. When would Manshoon feel a certain Sememmon had lived long enough?

Bereft of cheer, he muttered the pass phrase, made a certain gesture, and passed within. Unnoticed, the little eyeball that Manshoon had sent to spy floated in with him, too.

⊠ ⊠ ⊠

"We just happened to be riding this way," Rathan said gruffly. " 'Tis an open road, is it not?"

"No," Shandril said with a crooked smile. "You came after us to protect us. Did you not trust Tymora to look after us?"

The burly priest grinned. "Of course Tymora watches over ye. Am I not an instrument of Tymora's will?"

"Is that why you moved a sleeping man and left all the fighting and dirty work to me?" Torm said. "Not a copper's worth in his robe, too."

" 'Dirty work,' is it? Who took off his boots?"

"I thank you both," Narm said, "despite your feeble attempts at humor. Again my lady and I owe you our lives. And our horses, too, it seems. Your spell even took away my headache."

Rathan grinned. "If ye want it back, I can lend thee Torm. . . ."

Torm gave him a sour look.

Shandril giggled. "I don't think that'll be quite necessary, Rathan. I *have* a man to drive me beyond endurance."

Narm looked hurt until Shandril winked.

Torm was delighted. "Leave Narm with Rathan, to learn to ride and fight and worship, and *I'll* ride with you! I'm witty, agile, clean, quick, and experienced. I know lots of jokes, and I'm an excellent cook, so long as you're partial to meat, tomatoes, cheese, and noodles all cooked together. I'm fully conversant with the laws of six kingdoms and many independent cities, and I'm an excellent gambler." He batted his eyelashes at her. "What d'you say? Hmmm?"

Shandril gave him a look that could have melted glass. She asked Rathan, "Is there *nothing* you can do about him?"

"Oh, aye," Rathan agreed. "Ye can give him first watch, so we can all get some sleep. Narm and I'll sleep on either side, close against ye, so ye won't have to worry about him getting cold and wanting to, ahem, snuggle up!"

"Ah hah," Shandril agreed dubiously, rolling her eyes—but flopped down onto her bed without hesitation.

Rathan grunted and lowered himself slowly to a lying position, rolling his cloak up as a pillow. He lay on the grass fully clad, without bedding or blanket, grasping his mace. He nodded as if satisfied, and soon was snoring. His boots twitched now and then.

Torm winked at Narm and reached out to pinch the priest. His fingers were still inches away when Rathan opened one eye. "Ye can forget pinching, stroking, and tickling honest folk—or even we who sleep in the arms of the gods. Just see that the fire stays high."

Narm fell asleep chuckling.

Morning sunlight broke over the rolling hills and fields of Battledale and northern Sembia—and found Rathan Thentraver warming water for tea over the dying fire.

He looked around at his sleeping companions, got to his feet with a grunt of effort, and clambered up the bank to look about. The land was bare of all but grass, rolling and empty. Nodding, Rathan tucked his mace under his arm and sat down.

He cleared his thoughts of all but Tymora, as he tried to do every morning. Opening his heart, he prayed that the two young folk—aye, Torm, too, bebother him—would see only Tymora's bright face until they had reached Silverymoon and befriended Alustriel.

Everyone needs at least one safe journey—and these two more than most, because of spellfire.

Looking across the twisted blankets to Shandril's sleeping face, Rathan thought about her weeping spellfire and lashing out with it and tearing open her tunic to pour it faster on a foe. He'd not want to carry such power, not for all the gold in the Realms. . . .

He sighed. If they'd ridden a bit slower, that snake of a mage might have had her yestereve. So close—a matter of breaths. How to nursemaid a lass who could blast apart mountaintops? They'd be running into trouble soon enough, these two, and they'd need someone.

Rathan sighed again. Ah, well, some things ye must leave to Tymora. He got up and began to make tea. Soon they'd be wanting morningfeast, too.

He looked at the sleepers, and a smile touched his lips. Why wake them? The younglings needed a good, long sleep when they were guarded and could relax. Let 'em sleep. He peered south toward the river Ashaba, but it was too far away to see.

We'll ride with them until they're up at dawn tomorrow, and then turn back, Rathan thought. If Elminster is half the archmage he pretends to be, surely he can hold Shadowdale together *that* long.

Scratching under his armor, Rathan opened the pack that held the food. Another day, another dragon slain.

"Will ye *never* be done scratching and scribbling?" Elminster demanded. "Ye're not writing an epic, ye know!"

Lhaeo turned calm eyes on him. "Stir the stew, Lord Mighty Mage."

Elminster snorted, shifted his unlit pipe from hand to mouth, and began to stir.

"You miss them, don't you?" the scribe asked softly.

The Old Mage stared angrily at Lhaeo's back. "Aye." He set the ladle down and sat on the squat section of tree that served as a seat nigh the kitchen table. " 'Tisn't every day one sees spellfire destroy one's spells as if they were smoke—or see the high-and-mighty Manshoon put to flight by a young girl."

"A thief, she said she was—or at least, she joined the Company of the Bright Spear as a thief."

Elminster snorted again. "Thief? She's as much a thief as ye are. If we had a few more thieves like her, the Realms'd be so safe we'd not need locks! Which reminds me . . . locks, and locked-away books, that is: Candlekeep. Alaundo. What did old Alaundo say about spellfire? We must be getting close to that prophecy, so 'tis no doubt Shandril he's talking about!"

Lhaeo smiled. "As it happens, I looked up Alaundo the last night Narm and Shandril spent here. Under the jam jar on the uppermost scrap, I've copied the relevant saying. If a certain 'war among wizards' has already begun in Faerûn, 'tis next to be fulfilled."

Elminster fixed Lhaeo with a hard glance, but the scribe went serenely on with his writing. "What're ye *doing*?" Elminster demanded. "There ye sit, scribbling, while the stew thickens and burns. What *is it?*"

"Stir the stew, will you?" Lhaeo asked innocently. Before the Old Mage's fury could erupt, he replied, "I'm noting down the limits of Shandril's power, as observed by you and the Knights. The information may prove useful," he added very quietly, "if she must ever be stopped."

Elminster slowly nodded, looking very old. "Aye, aye, ye've the right of it, as usual. But not that little girl. Not Shandril. Why, she's but a little wisp, all laughter and kindness and bright eyes—"

"Aye. As Lansharra once was," Lhaeo told the piece of parchment before him.

Elminster sat like a statue, and there was silence for a long time.

Lhaeo finished his work, blew on the page, and got up.

Elminster still sat unmoving, his eyes on the fire.

Wordlessly Lhaeo reached over the wizard, slid a scrap of parchment out from under the jam jar, laid it before him, and turned to see to food. Perhaps four breaths later, he heard the Old Mage's voice behind him, and smiled to himself.

" 'Spellfire will rise, and a sword of power, to cleave shadow and evil and master Art!' " Elminster read it as though it was a curious bard's rhyme or a bad attempt at a joke. " 'Master Art'? What did Alaundo mean by that? She's to become a mage? She's not the slightest aptitude for it—and I'm not completely new to teaching Art, ye know!"

"I've found Alaundo's sayings make perfect sense after they've happened," Lhaeo said, "but help precious little beforehand!"

"Ahhh, stir the stew!" Elminster grunted. "I'm going out for a pipe!" The door banged behind him. Lhaeo grinned.

The stairs creaked as Storm came down them barefoot, silver hair shining in the firelight.

"Leave the stew," she said softly to Lhaeo. "It's probably been thrashed into soup by now, between the both of you."

Lhaeo smiled and put strong arms around her. "Let's go back upstairs, before he returns for a flame to light his pipe. Haste, now!"

The bed creaked as they sat on it, a scant instant before the door below banged open.

Outside again, Elminster puffed, peered at the Twisted Tower through aromatic smoke, chuckled, and hummed his favorite of the tunes Storm had composed. One didn't survive so many winters without noticing a thing or two.

They rode south that day on a road busy with wagons rumbling north out of Sembia. Hawk-eyed outriders and shrewd merchants looked them over, and the scrutiny made Narm and Shandril uncomfortable.

Torm had acquired a mustache from somewhere about his

person, and brown powder of the sort used as cosmetics in the Inner Sea lands. He rubbed it skillfully about his eyes, jaw, and cheekbones until his face seemed subtly different. Riding in silence for the most part—a mercy on his companions—he affected a soft, growling voice when he did speak, and kept to the rear.

Looking back, Narm could see the glistening whites of Torm's eyes darting in the shadowy gloom of a cap that hid his face. The mage gathered that Torm was too well known hereabouts to ride openly.

Rathan paid such cautions no mind. He rode easily before Shandril, speaking of the kindnesses and spectacular cruelties of the Great Lady Tymora, and occasionally pointing out a far-off landmark or the approaching colors of a merchant house or Company of the Inner Sea lands. He addressed her as Lady Nelchave, and occasionally compared things to "your hold, Roaringcrest."

Shandril answered in vague murmurs, trying to sound bored. In fact, she was enjoying riding in the comfortable security of Rathan and Torm, with a guided tour of the countryside.

Torm and Rathan preferred to lunch in the saddle without halting. Shandril found it fascinating to watch them fill nose-bags with skins of water and lean forward to hang them carefully about the necks of their mounts and mules, after first letting each animal taste and smell the contents. They deftly passed bread, cheese, and small chased-metal flasks of wine about. Torm even produced four large, iced sugar rolls, probably pilfered from a passing cart. Shandril wondered if he had endless pockets, like Longfingers the Magician in the bards' tales.

A light rain squall came out of the west in the afternoon and lashed them briefly as it passed overhead. Torm nearly lost his mustache, but regained his high, sly spirits. He danced about on his dripping horse, firing jests, rolling his eyes, and mimicking the absent Knights.

The day passed, and the road fell steadily away. In high eventide, they came to Blackfeather Bridge, where the road between the Standing Stone and Sembia crossed the river Ashaba. There

Sembia maintained a small guard post of bored, hardened men armed with crossbows and pikes and bearing the Raven and Silver banner of Sembia.

The guards looked long and coldly at the four travelers. A cleric of Tempus and a silent man in maroon robes stood off to one side and watched steadily. Narm's throat went dry, but he tried to keep his face impassive. Dragon Cult and Zhentarim agents could be anywhere—and everywhere. Narm was certain Rathan was recognized, but nothing was said, and no one barred their way.

Two hills later, as the sun sank, Narm could see no pursuit. Still, his uneasiness persisted, and he wasn't surprised when at sunset Rathan led them wordlessly westward off the road, continuing until it grew too dim to ride safely.

"This seems as good a place as any," Rathan said gruffly, waiting for Torm's nod. "Ready watch tonight. If ye must go off to relieve thyself, Shan, go not alone!"

Torm began stringing a webwork of black silk cords in an arc around the campsite.

The Knights seemed to share Narm's foreboding. Narm and Torm had barely drifted off, long after an exhausted Shandril, when there came the thud of someone tripping amid the silk cords.

Rathan whirled, hefting his mace from his knees, and let out a warning bellow that must have echoed clear across the Dragonreach.

The attacker rose with a stream of soft curses, sword drawn—and others came behind him.

Narm rolled upright with frightened speed.

Torm was up and away into the night like a vengeful shadow.

"Defend thy lady, lad!" Rathan roared over one shoulder as his mace struck aside attacking steel. Two foes faced him, with a third rushing up. The first of them fell.

In a stumbling rush, Narm reached and stood over Shandril, who was rolling over drowsily.

More men with blades came out of the night.

Another attacker fell, and Narm saw the glint of steel as Torm leaped onward to deal death again.

Someone rushed right at Narm, steel gleaming in the moonlight. The man wore dark leathers and waved a hooked saber, an unlovely smile growing on his face.

Coolly Narm cast magic missiles at the man's eyes, and then drew his dagger and braced himself. Glowing pulses of magic swooped and struck. The man gasped, stared at nothing, staggered, and went to his knees. Narm set his teeth and leaned over to finish the job. Blood wet his fingers, and he felt sick as he looked around for new dangers.

A second man sprinted out of the night, teeth clenched and blade high. Narm ducked aside as he'd seen Torm do and stabbed at his assailant. The blade gashed a wrist. The man cursed, stumbled, and fell on his side—and Narm pounced. Into the throat—gods, it was so hideously *easy*. Narm swept that thought away and peered around for other perils.

There were none. Torm dispatched another foe from behind—the man stiffened and groaned.

Rathan was chatting jovially to those he slew. "Do'ye not realize what moral pain—nay, spiritual agony—striking thee down causes me? Hast no consideration for my feelings?" The heavy mace fell with a crash. "More than this, aye, ye—uhh!—grrh!—wound me. Instead, of challenging me in—ahhhh—the bright light of day, before men of worth to bear witness, with a stated—hah!—grievance, ye seek to do dishonor on my poor holy bones in the dark of the night! At a time when all good and—ahhh!—lucky men are abed, with better—unghh! —things to do than cracking skulls! Don't ye agree—ahh!—*now?*" Rathan's last opponent fell, twitching, jaw shattered.

Torm looked up. "The horses like this little. We'd best move them, and us, in case others lurk. Narm, is your lady awake?"

Shandril answered, "Yes." She shuddered involuntarily at the sight of his bloody dagger. "Must you enjoy it so much?"

Torm looked at her. "I don't enjoy it at all," he said quietly. "But I prefer it to getting a knife in the ribs!" He bent and wiped his blade on something that Shandril mercifully couldn't see, but he did not sheathe it. "Shall we ride?"

"Walk, pigeon-brain!" Rathan rumbled, "and lead the horses. Who knows what we'd stumble into if we rode? See to these, will ye? I want none alive to tell our names and route, and this mace is not so sure as a blade."

"At once, Exalted One," Torm said with sarcastic sweetness. "Mind you don't forget any of our baggage. I'll just see if our late friends were carrying anything of value."

Rathan nodded. "Mind more don't come upon ye while ye're slavering and giggling over gold!"

In quiet haste, they gathered their gear and led their mounts and mules into the night. Narm and Shandril followed Rathan west, pace by careful pace, over rolling ground.

Torm caught up. "I saw no one else following, but listen sharp, everyone!"

"It seems I'll be doing *that* the rest of my life," Shandril whispered bitterly.

Torm put his head close to hers. The faint light of Selûne caught his teeth as he grinned. "You might even get used to it—who knows?"

"Who, indeed," she replied crisply.

"Not much farther now," Rathan said soothingly from ahead. Loose stones clacked underfoot, and then he added in quiet satisfaction, "Here—this'll do!"

Shandril fell into sleep as if it were a great black pit . . . and she never stopped falling.

⊠ ⊠ ⊠

Lady Spellfire awoke with the smell of frying boar in her nostrils. Narm had just kissed her. Shandril murmured her contentment and embraced him sleepily. He smelled good.

Nearby, a merry voice said, "Works like a charm. Can I try it? Shandril, will you go back to sleep for a moment?"

Shandril sighed. "Torm, do you *never* stop?"

"Not until I'm dead, good lady. Irritating I may be, but I'm never dull."

"Aye," Rathan rumbled. "Thou art many things, dullard, but never dull."

"Fair morning to you both." Shandril laughed.

"Well met, Lady," the priest answered. "Thy dawnfry awaits

. . . simple fare, but enough to ride on. We were not bothered again in the night, but ye'd best watch sharp today. 'Twill not be long before those bodies are found."

Narm looked at the grassy hills. "Where exactly are we?"

"In the hills west of Featherdale," Rathan supplied. "Turn about; see ye that gray shadow, like smoke on the horizon? Arch Wood. Between here and there lies an old, broad valley with no river anymore: Tasseldale. I'd not go down into it. Though 'tis a pleasant place with many fine shops and friendly folk, 'tis also full of folk to avoid. Keep to the heights along its northern edge. There, ye'll meet with no more than a shepherd or two and perhaps a Mairshar patrol. Tell them—they police the dale and always ride twelve strong—that ye're from Highmoon, Shandril, going home, with this mage ye met in Hillsfar. Call thyself 'Gothal,' or something, Narm. Stick to the truth about Gorstag and the inn, and ye'll fare better. Give no information to any others until ye meet with the elves of Deepingdale!"

"Elves?" Shandril asked, astonished.

"Aye, elves. Know ye nothing of Deepingdale, where ye grew up?" Rathan's voice was incredulous.

"No," Shandril told him, "only the inn. I saw half-elves when I left with the company, but no elves!"

"I see. Know ye that the present lord of Highmoon is the half-elf hero Theremen Ulath, so don't say the wrong thing." The burly priest rose and pulled on his helm. "Now eat. The day grows old!"

They ate, and all too soon all was done. Rathan sighed and said heavily, "Well, the time has come. We must leave!"

He turned on his heel to look southwest. "One day's ride should take ye to the western end of Tasseldale, in the Dun Hills. That's one camp. Keep watch—sleeping together's for indoors. Peace, Torm, no jests now! Another day's careful ride west—just keep Arch Wood to the left of ye, whatever else ye come upon—will bring ye to Deepingdale. Ye can press on after dark once ye've found the road, and make the Rising Moon before morn. All right?"

They nodded, their hearts full.

"Good then," Rathan went on in gruff haste, "and no weepin', now." He held out a wineskin to Narm. "For thy saddle!" He fumbled at the large pouch at his hip, brought out a disc of shining silver on a fine chain, and hung it about Shandril's neck, kissing her on the forehead. "Tymora's good luck go with ye."

Torm stepped forward. "Take this and bear it most carefully—'tis dangerous." He held out a cheap, gaudy medallion of brass, set askew with glued cut-glass stones on a brass chain of mottled hue that did not match the medallion. He put it around Narm's neck.

"What is it?" Narm asked, wonder and wariness in his voice.

"Look at it," Torm replied, "but take care how you touch it."

Narm looked. About his neck was no cheap medallion, but a fine, twist-link gold chain. Upon it hung two small, golden globes, with a larger one between.

"This is magical," Torm warned. "Keep it clear of spellfire or any fiery Art, or it may slay you. You—and only you—can twist off a globe and hurl it. When it strikes, it bursts like a mage's fireball; mind you're not too close. The larger globe is of greater power than the others. They work without need of spell or commands. Keep these safe; you'll need them, probably sooner than you think." He patted Narm's elbow awkwardly. "Fare you both well."

The Knights mounted, saluted with bared blades, tossed two small flasks of water to Narm and Shandril, wheeled their mounts, and galloped away. Hooves thundered briefly on earth, and faded. They were gone.

Narm and Shandril looked at each other, eyes bright. "We really are alone now, love," Narm said softly. "We've only each other."

"Yes, and that will do!" She kissed him, spun away, and leaped into her saddle. "Come *on!* The sun waits not, and we must ride!"

Narm grinned at her and ran to his own saddle. "Spitfire!"

Shandril raised her eyebrows and obediently spat fire in a long rolling plume that winked out just in front of him. The horses snorted in alarm. "Ah yes, spitfire indeed—but also thy lady." She tossed her hair from her eyes, lifted her chin, and commanded, "Now—let us *away!*"

Away west they sped, leaving trampled grass and happy memories.

⊠ ⊠ ⊠

Stars shone clear and cold outside the upper room of Elminster's tower, but he saw them not. He gazed into a twinkling sphere of crystal on the table before him, and therein saw a red-carpeted chamber hung with tapestries of red and silver and gold, lit by a fine, roaring fire. A lady in a tattered black gown sat at a table and looked back at him.

"Well met, wizard, and welcome," she said, with the faintest of smiles.

"Well met, Lady Queen and mage. Thank ye for allowing this intrusion."

"Few enough call on me, Old Mage, and fewer still without intent to harm or hamper. I thank you."

Elminster inclined his head politely. "I've further thanks for thee this night, Lady. Thank ye for protecting Narm and Shandril these past few days. I'm most grateful!"

The Simbul gave him a rare smile. "My pleasure, again."

There followed a silence ere Elminster asked carefully, "Why did ye aid them, when the maid's such a threat to thy magic, and therefore the survival of Aglarond—and ye?"

"I know the prophecy of Alaundo and what it may mean—and care not. I like Shandril." The Simbul looked momentarily away, and then back at the Old Mage. "I've a question for you, Elminster. Answer not if you'd rather not. Is Shandril the child of Garthond Shessair and the incantatrix Dammasae?"

"I'm not certain, Lady, but 'tis very likely."

An eyebrow lifted. "Not certain? Did you not hide the girl and shelter her as she grew?"

Elminster shook his head very slowly. "Nay. Not I."

"Who, then?"

" 'Twas the warrior Gorstag, of Highmoon."

The Simbul nodded. "So much, I've also come to suspect. Thank you for trusting to answer me openly. I promise you, Old Mage, I'll not betray your trust. Shandril's safe from my power—unless the passing years change her as they did Lansharra, and she becomes too great a danger to leave unopposed."

"That's my present burden," Elminster said heavily. "Such a fall must not happen again."

"What, if I may ask without giving offense, will you do differently this time?" The Simbul watching closely, eyes very dark.

"Leave her be," Elminster replied grimly. "She'll choose her own path in the end, and that choice may be clearer and happier—if not easier—if I sit not upon her every act, and bestow advice on her every thought." Elminster met the Simbul's gaze. "The Harpers can protect her nearly as well as this old wizard, unless I lock her in my tower . . . and I couldn't do that, even had I so cruel a heart."

The Simbul nodded. "That's the right road to ride. 'Tis good I needn't force you to take that route."

Elminster smiled sadly. "Good, indeed, for such an attempt would likely destroy ye."

The Simbul regarded him soberly. "I know." Impulsively she leaned forward and whispered, "I've never doubted or belittled your power, Elminster. You take a sly and self-effacing way, playing the befuddled old fool—even as I take beast-shape to prowl and hide. But I've seen what your Art has wrought. If ever I stand against it, I expect to fall."

"I did not disturb ye this night to threaten ye."

"I know," the Simbul murmured, rising. "Will you allow me to teleport to you now?"

"Of course, Lady," Elminster replied, "but why?"

The Simbul let fall her tattered gown. Beneath it was a webwork of thin black silk strands reaching from her throat to cuffs at her wrists and a broad cummerbund. It was a garment that covered little.

Many small, twinkling gems winked out only to shine more brilliantly when the Simbul reappeared beside Elminster. Unsmiling, she stood amid the dark clutter of his books and papers and spread her hands almost timidly, offering herself.

Elminster gaped for some very long moments before he deliberately composed himself and smiled. "But Lady, I've seen countless winters," Elminster said gently. "Am I not too old for this?"

She stopped his lips with slim white fingers. "Those years will give us something to talk about, wizard and Witch-Queen," she said. She was slim and very light in his lap, and she leaned forward in a smooth, soft embrace. "I would tell you something," she whispered, as Elminster's arms went gently around her. "My name, my true name, is—"

"Hush, Lady," Elminster said, eyes moist. "Keep it safe. We'll trade them soon, aye. But not now."

Tears came. "Ah, Old Mage," the Simbul said into his chest, "I've been so lonely. . . ."

Lhaeo, who'd come silently up the dark stairs with tea, the pot wrapped in a thick scarf to keep it warm, stopped outside the door and heard them.

Without tarrying to overhear another word, he set the tray down carefully on a table nearby and went softly downstairs again for a second cup.

As he went, he wondered, what's the weight of secrets? How many can a man carry? How many more can a woman or an elf?

It was dark outside, but in the little cottage near the woods, candles flickered and a hearth fire blazed. A woman at the cauldron straightened as they entered. She was no longer young, and her clothes were simple and much patched.

"My lords!" she gasped, alarm falling from her face. "Welcome! But I've nothing to feed you—my man won't be back from the hunt until morn."

"Nay, Lhaera," Rathan rumbled kindly, embracing her. "We cannot stay, but must hasten back to Shadowdale. We've an urgent errand for thy daughter, and I'd renew Tymora's bright blessing on this house."

Lhaera looked at them in wonderment. "With Imraea? But she's scarce six—"

Torm nodded. "Old enough that her feet reach the ground."

He was promptly interrupted by the precipitous arrival of a

small, dark-haired whirlwind who fetched up against his legs, laughing. As he reached down to embrace her, she danced back out of reach.

"Well met, Torm and Rathan, Knights of Myth Drannor. I'm pleased to see you."

Both Knights bowed, and Rathan answered, "We're also pleased to see thee, Lady. We come to discharge our duty to ye; are ye in good health and of high spirits?"

"Aye, of course. But look how beautiful Mother is since you healed her! She grows taller, I think!"

Torm and Rathan regarded the astonished and smiling Lhaera.

"Aye, I think you're right. She *does* grow taller," Torm said solemnly. "Send word when she grows too tall for the roof, and we'll help you rebuild."

Imraea nodded. "I'll do that." She eyed Torm. "You are making me wait, Sir Knight. Is my patience not well held? Am I not solemn enough?" She fairly danced. "Did you *bring it?*"

" 'Tis not an 'it.' 'Tis a 'he,' as you are a she," said Torm severely, opening his cloak to pour something soft and furry into her arms. Silver and black fur surrounded great, glistening eyes. It let out an inquiring meow. Imraea held it in wonder as it stretched its nose out to her.

"Has it—he—a name?"

Rathan regarded her gravely. "Aye, it has a true name, which it keeps hidden, and a kitten name. But ye must give it a proper name, the name ye can call it. Choose wisely. The kitten will have to live with thy choice."

"Aye," Imraea agreed. "Tell me, please, its kitten name, that I may call it so while I think on so important a choice."

Lhaera smiled broadly.

"Its name," said Torm with dignity, "is Snuggleguts." He dropped a shower of gold into her hand.

"What's *this?*" Imraea stared in wonder at the nine large coins.

"Its life," Rathan replied. "Thy kitten will need milk and meat and fish and much care, and to be kept warm. Ye, or thy parents, must buy those things. Ye must take the mice and rats it kills, thank thy pet without disgust or sharp words, and bury them. 'Tis thy duty. Know ye, Imraea, that the gods gather back to themselves cats and dogs and horses even as they do ye and me. There's no telling when Snuggleguts may die. So treat him well and enjoy his company, but let thy kitten roam free and do as he will. And remember: Each time ye see thy pet may be the last."

"I *will*. Oh, I thank you both. You are kind, you two Knights."

"We but do the right thing," Torm replied softly.

"Aye, that you do," Lhaera said to them. "And there's few enough, these days, who take the trouble to."

20

Revelations at the Rising Moon

By night dark dreams bring me much pain—but always comes, after, bright morning again.

Mintiper Moonsilver, bard
Nine Stars Around a Silver Moon
Year of the Highmantle

They rode steadily west. Narm peered about constantly, expecting attack, but Shandril found this forest friendlier than the Elven Court. She could see through thick tangles of trunks and gnarled limbs into deep, hidden places. Vines hung in soft-furred arcs from one branch to the next. Ferns grew thick on the ground. Shandril shook her head in wonder at man-shaped clumps of moss and trees as large about as cottages. Narm saw only danger, possible ambush, and concealing shadows . . . but as the day grew older and no attack came, he too began to enjoy the road to Deepingdale.

"This is beautiful," he said as they crested a ridge. Sunlight streamed down through the trees, lighting a small clearing as if it was afire.

"Yes," Shandril said. "I've never really seen these woods before, though I lived just a day's ride hence." She sighed. "I wish I'd never known spellfire and could just go home with you now—instead of fleeing half a hundred power-mad mages."

"Why not stay in Highmoon? You have the power to slay half a hundred power-mad mages!"

"Maybe . . . but I'd lose the dale and my friends and even you. Powerful mages always destroy things around them. They work worse devastation than forest fires and brigands! Sometimes I think life would be much simpler without Art."

Narm smiled. "I said that to Elminster, and he said not so. If I could see the strange worlds he's walked, he told me, I'd understand."

"No, thank you," Shandril replied. "I've troubles enough in this one!"

The road rose through a leafy tunnel of oaks, out into a clearing. Narm and Shandril rode close and quiet, looking for danger. Tiny, whiplike branches fallen from trees above lay amid the dead leaves and tangled grass and ferns. They seemed faerie fingers waiting to clutch or snap underfoot. Silence reigned. They rode on, and still no attack came. Nor did they meet travelers on the road.

Shandril frowned. "This is eerie. Where *is* everyone?"

"Elsewhere, for once," Narm said. "Be thankful, and ride while we've the chance. I would be free of the dales, where everyone knows of us; your spellfire can't triumph forever."

Shandril shivered. "I've thought about that. Thus far, we've been *very* lucky. We've also fought many who knew not what they faced; ere long wizards will strike at us with spells crafted to disable me or foil spellfire—and then how shall we fare?"

Narm sighed. "Ah, Shan, you moan a lot! Adventure, you wanted; adventure you have. Did you hear Lanseril's definition of adventure, at that first feast in Shadowdale?"

Shandril wrinkled her brow. "I did overhear it—something about being cursedly uncomfortable and hurt or afraid, and then telling everyone later that it was nothing."

"Aye, that was it." They rode over another rise with still no sign of other travelers. " 'Tis a long way to Silverymoon," Narm added thoughtfully. "D'you remember all the Harpers Storm named, along the way?"

"Yes. D'you?" his lady replied impishly.

Narm shook his head. "I've forgotten half of them. I wasn't born to be a far traveler. Nor did Marimmar's teach me to be one."

Shandril laughed. "I'll bet. If much of the Realms is as beautiful as this, I won't mind the trip ahead."

"Even with a hundred or so evil priests and mages after us?"

Shandril wrinkled her nose. "Just don't call me 'Magekiller' or suchlike. Remember: They come after me. I've no quarrel with them."

"I'll remind the next dozen corpses," Narm replied dryly. "If you leave enough for me to speak to, that is."

Shandril looked away and said very softly, "Please don't speak so of the killing. I hate it. Never, never do I want to become so used to it that I grow careless of my power. Who knows when this spellfire might leave me? Then, Narm, I'll have only your Art to protect me—think on that!"

They rode down into a dell cloaked in lush green moss. Pools of water glistened under dark and rugged old trees.

Narm looked around warily. "Aye. I think of it often!"

⁂

"It seems this Shandril's fated to grow old unhindered—by us, at any rate," Naergoth said dryly to Salvarad when they were alone at the long table. "Is there any other business?"

"Aye. The matter of your mage. He was destroyed in Shadowdale—how, I know not—but know this: Malark perished at the hands of Shandril Shessair."

"You're sure?"

"I watch closely, and others watch for me. All told, we miss little."

Naergoth looked at him expressionlessly. "What have you seen in the way of mages to take Malark's place in the Purple?"

"Zannastar, certainly. You could even give him the Purple now; we've but the one mage among us."

"Why Zannastar?"

"He's competent at Art, but better than that, he's biddable, something Malark was not."

"Aye, then. Who else?"

"The young one, Thiszult. Wild—quiet but reckless. He could be dangerous to us, or brilliant. Why not send him, alone and in secret, after spellfire with half a dozen warriors? He'll either bring it back or get himself killed—or learn caution. We can't do ill by this."

"Oh? What if he comes back with spellfire and uses it against us?"

"I know his true name," Salvarad replied smugly, "and he doesn't know anyone has learned it."

Naergoth almost smiled. "Send your wolf, then. Perhaps he'll succeed where others have failed—ours and those of Bane and Zhentil Keep. The gauntlet this girl runs will bring her down in the end, though we pay richly for it in blood."

Salvarad nodded. "Yes. She's only one young maid, and not warlike at that. We'll have her by and by, spellfire or no. I mean to have spellfire, too . . . but if we take her alive, she's mine, Naergoth!"

Naergoth raised an eyebrow. "You can have women much easier than that, Salvarad."

"You mistake me, Bladelord," Salvarad replied coldly. "The power she's handled . . . does things to people. I must learn certain things from her."

Naergoth said, "Then why not go after her yourself?"

Salvarad smiled thinly. "I am intrigued, Bladelord. I am not suicidal."

"Others have said that, you know."

"I know, Naergoth. Some of them even meant it."

⁂

Night caught them in the woods. Narm and Shandril drew their cloaks against the cold and rode on. Mist rose among the trees.

Narm watched it drift and roll. "I don't like this. An ambush would be all too easy. . . ."

Shandril nodded. "All the wishing in the world won't change that. We're not far from the Moon; travelers who left it midmorning expected to make Tasseldale by night." She looked into the soft silence of the trees. Tangled branches hung still and dark. Nothing stirred, and no attack came.

Shandril sighed. "Come!" she said, spurring her horse into a trot. "Let's get there. I want to see Gorstag again."

The fire burned low in the hearth, and the taproom of the Rising Moon grew quiet as the last few guests went up to bed.

Lureene quietly swept up fallen scraps, and Gorstag made the rounds of the doors. She heard his measured tread on the boards in the kitchen, drawing nearer, and her heart rose. They'd have time for a kiss, perhaps. . . . She smiled in the glow of the dying fire.

Gorstag, who carried no candle when he walked alone by night, came into the room. "My love, I would ask something of you this night."

" 'Tis yours, Lord," Lureene said affectionately, reaching for the laces of her bodice. "You know that."

Gorstag coughed. "Ah . . . nay, lass, I be serious . . . ah, I mean—oh, gods look *down!*" He drew in a deep breath and approached her in the gloom. Quietly and formally, he said, "Lureene, I am Gorstag of Highmoon, a worshiper of Tymora and Tempus in my time, and a man of some moderate means. Will you marry me?"

Lureene stared at him, her mouth open, for a very long time. Then she was suddenly in his arms. "My lord, you need not . . . marry me! 'Twas not my intention to—ah, trap you into such a union."

"D'you not want to be my wife?" Gorstag asked slowly, his voice rough. "Please tell me true. . . ."

"I'd like nothing more in all Faerûn than to be your wife, Gorstag."

His smile was like a flash of sunlight, and his arms tightened about her.

"I accept," Lureene added, gasping for breath. "Kiss me, now, don't hug the life from me!"

Their lips met, and Lureene let out a little moan of happiness. Gorstag held her as if she were a fragile and beautiful thing. They stood together among the tables as the front door of the inn creaked gently open. A cool breeze drifted in about their ankles.

Gorstag turned, hand going to his belt. "Aye?" he demanded, before his night-keen eyes showed him who had come.

Lureene let out a happy cry. "*Shandril!*"

"Yes," said a small voice. "Gorstag? Can you forgive me?"

"*Forgive* you, little one?" Gorstag rumbled, striding forward to embrace her. "What's to forgive? Are you well? Where have you *been?* How—" Outside, there was a snort and a creak of leather. In midsentence Gorstag said, "But you've horses to see to! Sit down, sit with Lureene, who has a surprise to tell you. I'll learn all when I'm done!"

"I'm married, Gorstag," Shandril blurted. "He's—Narm's with the horses."

Gorstag threw her a surprised look but never slowed his step. By the light of the fire, Shandril saw tears on his cheeks . . . and then he was gone.

Lureene threw her arms about Shandril. "Lady Luck be praised, Shan! You're back and safe! Gorstag's been so worried, but now . . . but now—" She burst into tears and held Shandril tightly.

Shandril felt tears of her own stinging her eyes. "Lureene . . . Lureene . . ." she managed, voice breaking, "We can't stay. Half the mages in Faerûn are after us, and we're a menace to you even by being here!" Fearfully, she stared at the tavern maid. She was touched that Lureene had missed her so—she'd always thought the older girl must find her tiresome. Would Lureene's regard be swept away by fear?

Lureene met her gaze and smiled, shaking her head. "Ah, little kitten, you've been hurt indeed to fear these doors shut to you. If to see you again we must entertain a few thousand angry mages, entertain them we shall, Gorstag and I, and think it a small price to pay!" She laughed and hugged Shandril again. "Ah, Shan, thank you, thank you! You've made Gorstag so happy! He's like a youngling again—did you not see him stride to the door like a young buck? You've made him happy . . . as he's not been since you left."

"But we must leave again on the morrow. How—?"

"He'll understand, Shan. He knows you're not ours anymore—I don't doubt he's taking the measure of your man right now! It's just that he didn't know what had befallen you! Could you not have left a note, or some word?"

Shandril sobbed, pouring out all the fear and regret and homesickness of the days since she'd fled.

Lureene held her, rocking her wordlessly, until tears gave way to shuddering breaths. She kissed the crown of Shandril's bent head. "Be not so full of sorrows, little kitten. I'm most grateful to you!" The body in her arms made a bleating, questioning sound. Lureene hugged her more tightly. "Gorstag was so upset over you one night that he couldn't sleep. I comforted him. He'd never have permitted me to do as I did, if he'd not been so in need—and he'd never have asked me to be his wife."

Shandril looked up, hair in disarray across her reddened eyes. "He did? *Gorstag?* Oh, *Lureene!*" Her tears were happy this time, and she hugged the tavern maid with bruising force.

Lureene fought for balance and thought, ye gods, if this is what adventure does for a woman . . . A woman? Shandril? But—aye! She is a woman now.

This was not the girl who'd slipped away from the kitchen. This was a lady with a lord of her own—and something else, something beyond the weapons worn so easily at hip and boots. . . . Shandril had a quiet confidence, of power hidden, but none of the arrogance of many adventurers who came to the inn.

"Shandril, what's happened to you?" she asked quietly.

Shandril gave her an almost haunted look. "Oh . . . you can see it so clearly?"

Lureene nodded. "Aye, but I know not what 'tis!" She raised a hand to Shandril's lips. "No . . . tell me not, if you would not. I needn't know."

"But you *should* know. 'Tis not something easily believed, though. I hope Gorstag will be able to tell me more about why I have it."

Lureene grinned. "Then it can wait until after you've soaked your feet and eaten. I'll wake Korvan."

"No!" Shandril said sharply. "No, please. Wake him not. I can't trust his cooking—no offense to you—for my own good reasons. I'll cook, if you'll have me!"

Lureene frowned. "Did Korvan . . . bother you?"

" 'Tis not that," Shandril said. "*Please* trust me, and wake him not! I'll tell you, but 'tis better not to rouse him!"

"Then I'll not leave your side while you're here unless Gorstag or your man's at hand to protect you," Lureene said firmly. "You can tell me what you like after you've rested. Come to the fire."

Shandril let herself be led to a warm high-backed chair. Lureene poked the fire into new flames, set fresh wood on it, and went for a bowl. When she returned, Shandril's head had fallen onto her shoulder, and she was asleep.

⊠ ⊠ ⊠

Narm held the bridles of both horses, his body tense—ready to flee if need be. He peered into the moonlit mists, but could see or hear no creature moving in the silence.

"Wait," Shan had said. "Come after me only when you've stood so long that you grow cold—and if you wait that long, come carefully, ready for war."

Narm shifted nervously. Was he cold enough?

There was noise within. The door Shandril had entered by was flung wide. Out strode a burly, craggy-faced man with gray-white hair and eyes wet with tears. He stretched out a strong arm to Narm. "Well met, and welcome to my inn! I'm Gorstag. You're Shandril's Narm?"

Narm squarely met his gaze and swallowed. "Yes. I was here almost two months back, with the mage Marimmar. Shandril's told me of you, sir; I'm at your service."

Gorstag chuckled. "Well, you can serve by leading one horse round to the stables with me!" He set off with a horse and three mules in tow.

Narm followed into a warm, strong-smelling barn, where a sleepy boy on night watch unhooded a lantern and fetched water, brushes, and feed. In companionable silence, they set to work.

"You know the Art?" Gorstag asked gruffly as they bent to the same bucket.

Narm nodded. "I was trained in Shadowdale. Shan and I've come straight from there"—he drew in a deep breath—"where we were wed under Tymora!"

Gorstag's head snapped up. He turned, a looming shape against the light.

Narm felt suddenly shy under this old man's stern, clear eyes. He said no more, brushing Warrior, who nickered appreciatively. Pivoting from the horse's flank back to the bucket, Narm found his gaze caught and held by Gorstag's stare. Stepping back, Narm still said nothing.

After what seemed an eternity, Gorstag stalked over to the first of the three mules. "Tell me how you met Shandril Shessair."

Narm studied the innkeeper's broad shoulders. "I saw her first here, and . . . liked what I saw, though we never spoke. The next morn, I left with my master, and we made our way to Myth Drannor."

Gorstag's arms stopped their rhythmic brushing, and then, in silence, resumed.

"We met with devils, and my master Marimmar was slain. I was rescued from the same fate by the Knights of Myth Drannor, who patrol there. Later I returned to that ruined city and saw Shandril from afar. She was the captive of a cruel witch-mage, the Shadowsil. I tried to free her, calling on the Knights for aid. We ended up in a dracolich's lair, a cavern that collapsed during a mighty battle of Art. Shandril and I were trapped together. We thought we'd never get out, so . . ." Narm paused in embarrassment, studying the mule. "We came to care for each other. I love her. So I asked her to marry me."

Gorstag nodded and chuckled. "Aye. 'Twas the same for me." He made a clucking noise, and the stable boy instantly reappeared. Gorstag nodded at the beasts and told him, "See to them all . . . the very best of everything, as if a fine lord and lady rode them!" He waved to Narm to follow him out, and then turned back to the boy. "Because they do."

As they walked through the misty, moonlit night, Gorstag said, "My house is yours, but you seem in much haste. How long can you stay?"

Narm hesitated. "We must leave on the morrow, sir. Many have tried to slay us—Shandril—these past few days, and will try again. We dare not tarry. Elminster told us to be sure to call on you, and Shandril insisted, too, but there's danger to us in stopping, and we want not to bring it upon you."

The innkeeper's brow furrowed. "Can you say more? I'd rest easier, Narm—and call me Gorstag, mark you!—if I knew where and why the little girl I reared is riding, who'd do her ill . . . and why."

"I've not the right to answer you, Gorstag," Narm replied. "Only my lady should speak on this. I can say that those who pursue us follow different causes, but are powerful in Art. Therein lies your peril—and Shandril's secret."

They went inside to find Lureene regarding them with a warning finger to her lips. She knelt by a chair before the fire. Narm raced forward. Behind him, Gorstag smiled at that.

"She sleeps," Lureene said as Narm bent anxiously near.

Shandril moved her head and murmured something. They all came close to listen.

"Narm," she said. "Narm, we're here. We're home. Wait here. . . . Wake Gorstag. . . . Come carefully, ready for war. . . ."

Narm kissed her cheek, and in her sleep she raised a hand to pat his head. Then, suddenly, she was upset. "She went for you," Shandril cried faintly. "She went for you, and there was not *time!* I *had* to burn her!"

"Shan, *Shan!*" Narm said urgently, shaking her. "It's all right . . . we're safe."

"Yes . . . safe," Shandril replied, awake now and looking up at him. "Safe at last." She kissed his hand. Her gaze turned to Gorstag, who stood looking gravely down at her. "I *am* sorry. I'd no wish to be a trial to you; I should've told you where I'd gone. I was a fool."

Gorstag smiled. "We all play at being fools, betimes. You're back safe, and naught else matters."

Shandril thanked him with her eyes. "We can't stay, I fear.

We're fleeing far too many to vanquish or avoid if we stand here. We must ride on in the morning."

"So Narm said—*and* said 'twas for you to tell us why. Wilt do so, lass?"

Shandril said, "Have you ever heard of spellfire?"

Gorstag nodded sadly. "Your mother had it. I rode with her. Oh, lass . . . oh, Shandril! Beware the cult!"

Narm said ruefully, "If you mean the Cult of the Dragon, we've fought them too many times already."

Gorstag's eyebrows shot up. "Aye, I do." He'd been about to say more, but froze when he saw Shandril gaping at him, flame flickering in her eyes.

Fighting for calm, she asked in a voice that was almost steady, "Please, Gorstag, who were my parents?"

"Elminster told you *not?*" Gorstag asked, gaping. "Your mother was my dearest companion-at-arms. We adventured together, long ago. Dammasae the incantatrix; if she'd a surname, I never knew it. She was born in the Sword Coast lands, but would never talk of herself."

"Are you my father?" Shandril asked softly.

Gorstag chuckled. "No, lass. No, though we were the best of friends, Damma and I, and often held each other by the campfire. Your father was Garthond—Garthond Shessair—a powerful mage by the time he died. I never knew where he was born, but in his youth, he was apprenticed to the wizard Jhavanter of Highmoon."

"A moment, if you will," Lureene said gently. "This grows confusing. Pour ale, Gor, and tell your tale a-proper. If you ask question upon question, Shan, it grows as tangled as a box of old twine."

Shandril nodded. "You've told me the two things I wanted most to know. Unfold the rest as you see best, and I'll try not to break in." She waved her hands in sudden anguish. "By the gods, why didn't you tell me all of this *before*? *Years* I've wondered and worried and dreamed. Why didn't you *tell me?*"

"Easy, lass." Gorstag grew solemn. "There were good reasons. Folk sought you even then and asked me where you came from. I never wanted to tell you a lie, girl, not since I first brought you here. Oh, you had wise eyes from the first; I couldn't say false to you. I knew these same prying folk asked you and the other girls questions when I wasn't about. If you knew the truth, they'd have tricked it out of you. So I said nothing and let the rumors of my fathering you pass unchallenged and waited for you to be old enough to tell." He looked down at his hands. "Sorry I am that you had to run away to find yourself, and freedom. The fault was mine, not to have seen your need sooner and made you happier."

"No, Gorstag," Shandril said. "As the gods bear witness, I've had nothing but good from you, and I blame you not. But tell me of my parents, please! I've waited so long. . . ."

"Aye. Here's the backbone of the tale. Jhavanter and your father Garthond fought the Cult of the Dragon in Sembia and hereabouts, several times. On the eastern flanks of the Thunder Peaks, Jhavanter held an old tower that he called the Tower Tranquil. Garthond dwelt there with Jhavanter, and then alone after cult wizards destroyed his master. Garthond went on with his Art—and went on fighting the cult."

Gorstag gestured with his tankard and started to pace. "At every turn, he'd work against them, destroying any he could catch unprotected. He grew in power, though the cult tried to slay him every tenday or so. One day he rescued the incantatrix Dammasae from them—they had her drugged, bound, and gagged in a wagon, on the way to their stronghold."

Gorstag strode about the taproom, his voice low but his eyes bright. "Dammasae had adventured with me and others before and become known for a talent she had—a power that she wanted to develop by practice and experiment. She could absorb spells and hold their force as raw energy within her. She could use that force to heal and to harm—as blasts of flame that seared flesh, stone, even spells . . . so it was called spellfire. The cult snatched her to learn the secrets of spellfire, or at least compel her to use hers for their own schemes. No doubt they seek you now for the same reasons."

"That," Shandril agreed, "or my destruction. But please, Gorstag, say on!" To know her life at last! She almost sobbed with eagerness, and Narm put his arms around her.

Gorstag took down his axe and lowered himself into a chair facing hers, laying his great weapon on a table beside him. Then he turned his chair to better see the front door. Narm and Lureene glanced at it as if howling cult wizards might burst through in the next instant . . . but the night was silent. Beyond the windows, moon-dappled mist drifted.

"Well," the innkeeper continued, "Garthond rescued Dammasae and protected her . . . and worked magic with her . . . and they came to love each other. They traveled much and pledged their troth before the altar of Mystra in Baldur's Gate."

He peered into the depths of his tankard, found it empty, and set it aside. "Here I speak of guesswork—my own, Elminster's, and of some others. We believe a cult mage, one Erimmator—none know where his bones lie—cursed Garthond in an earlier battle-of-Art. The curse bound a strange creature called a 'balhiir' from another plane of existence"—Shandril gasped, and Narm nodded grimly—"in symbiosis with Garthond. Perhaps 'twas a cult experiment to learn the powers of the offspring of a spellfire-hurling incantatrix and a mage 'ridden' by a balhiir."

Narm nodded. "I fear so . . . but what happened after they were wed?"

"Why, the usual thing betwixt man and maid," Gorstag said gruffly. "In Elturel they dwelt quietly. In due time a girl, one Shandril Shessair, was born. They returned not to the Tower Tranquil and the dales, where the cult waited in strength and the danger to their babe was great, until she was old enough to travel. Eight months, that wait was!"

Gorstag shifted in his chair, eyes distant, seeing things long ago. "They rode with me. East, overland . . . and the cult was waiting for us, indeed. Somehow—by Art, likely—they knew, and saw through our disguises. They attacked us on the road west of Cormyr, at the Bridge of Fallen Men."

Gorstag shook his head and added quietly, "Garthond was thrown down and utterly destroyed, but he won victory for his wife and daughter, and for me. He did not die cheaply. He took nine mages down to darkness with him, and three swordsmen."

He stirred, and turned his head to look at his onetime kitchen maid. His eyes shone in the gloom. "He was something splendid to see that day, Shan. I've not seen a mage work Art so well and so long, from that day to this, nor ever expect to again. He shone before he fell!" The old warrior's eyes were wet as he stared at memories.

"Dammasae and I were wounded—I the worse, but she could bear hurt less well. She carried less meat to lose and twice the grief and worry—for she feared most, Shan, for you. When the cultists fled or were slain, we rode swiftly to High Horn for healing. Dammasae had some doctoring there, but she needed more: the hands and wisdom of Syluné. We did not reach Shadowdale in time."

Gorstag made a little sound in his throat that might have been a sob, but his grim voice was steady and quiet. "Your mother's buried west of Shadowdale, on a little knoll on the north side of the road—the one west of Toad Knoll. A spot holy to Mystra; she appeared there to a Magister once, long ago." Gorstag looked at the flagstones. "*I could not save her*," he whispered, old anguish raw in his voice.

Shandril leaned toward him, hands reaching out to comfort.

"But I *could* save you," the warrior added, setting his jaw. "And I did that." He caught up his axe and hefted it, as if he'd hew down the gods themselves if they came through his front door.

"I took you on my back and went through the woods from Shadowdale south to Deepingdale. 'Twas in my mind to leave you with elves I knew and try to get into the Tower Tranquil to get something of Garthond's Art and writings for you, but elves I met told me the cult had plundered the tower. They blasted its cellars, making great caverns to be the lair of a dracolich—Rauglothgor the Proud—whose hoard had outgrown his own lair."

Gorstag sighed. "So I counted on being unknown to the cult—few who had seen me ride with Dammasae and Garthond lived to tell the tale—and came openly to Deepingdale. I used some gems I'd amassed to buy a rundown inn and retire."

He waved a hand at the taproom and growled, "I was getting too old for rough nights on cold ground, anyway. Few of my companions-at-arms were still alive and hale, and an old warrior who joins a band of young blades is asking for a dagger in the ribs." He shook his head. "I brought you up as a servant, Shan, because I dared not attract attention. Folk talk if an old retired warrior lives alone with a beautiful girl-child. I had to hide your lineage—and, as long as I could, your last name—for I knew the cult would come if they guessed."

He waved his axe as if it weighed nothing. "That fight at the bridge—they could've slain us all by Art from afar without so high a cost, if all they'd wanted was us dead. No, they wanted *you*, girl, you or your mother." He clenched his fist and told the roof beams fiercely, "And I let them have *neither*! 'Twas the greatest feat I ever managed, down all those years of acting and watching my tongue and yet trying to see you brought up proper."

"They've kept nosing, all these years, the cult and others. I suspected your Marimmar, Narm, of being one more spying mage—who knows, now? Some were fairly sure, but had no taste for fighting rivals to death for you unless you truly were the prize, so they only watched to see if you'd show some of your mother's powers. I dreaded the day you would. If 'twere too public a show, I might not have time to get you to the elves or the Harpers or Elminster."

The innkeeper shook his head. "I was wary of the Old Mage, too—for 'tis great wizards who fear and want spellfire most. Even if I'd time to run, I might not have the time to get Lureene and the others away. The cult might well burn this house to the ground and slay all within, if they found us gone. Some days I was like a skulking miser, seeking plundering foes under every stone and behind every tree—and in the face of every guest!"

Chuckling, he said, "Now you're wed, and I'm to be wed. You went to find yourself because I would not tell you who you were. You've come back, with all my enemies and more on your trail, and you wield spellfire—and I'm too old to defend you!"

"Gorstag," Narm told him firmly, "you *have* defended her. All the time she needed it, you kept her safe. Now all the Knights of Myth Drannor must scramble to defend her! She drove off Manshoon of Zhentil Keep and wounded him perhaps unto death! My Shandril needs friends, food, the occasional warm bed, and a guard while she sleeps. But if others give her those, 'tis not *she* who needs defending!"

Shandril laughed ruefully. "There you hear love talking. I need you more than ever, now. Didn't you see how lonely the Simbul was, Narm? I'd not be as she is, alone with her terrible power, unable to trust anyone enough to relax among friends and let down her defenses."

"The Simbul?" Lureene gasped. "The Witch-Queen of Aglarond?" Gorstag, too, looked awed.

"Yes," Shandril said simply. "She gave me her blessing. I wish I could've known her better. She's so lonely that it hurts to see her. She has only pride and great Art to carry her on!"

In a far place, in a small stone tower beneath the Old Skull, the Simbul sat up in the bed where Elminster lay snoring. "How true, young Shandril," she said, tears in her eyes. "How right you were. But no more!"

Elminster came awake, and his hand touched her bare back. "Lady?"

"Worry not, Old Mage," she said gently, turning with eyes full. "I'm but listening to Shandril speak of me."

"The lass? You're linked to her?"

"Nay, I'd not pry so. A magic I worked long ago lets me hear when someone speaks my name—and what they say after, for three breaths. Shandril's speaking of me now, and my loneliness, and how she wished to know me better as a friend. A sweet maid; I wish her well."

"I, too. She's at ease and unhurt, judge ye?"

"Aye, as much as one *can* judge." The Simbul regarded him impishly. "But you, Lord! You are most surely at ease and unhurt. Shall we see to changing your sloth into something more . . . interesting?"

"Aaargh," Elminster replied eloquently, as she tickled him. "Have ye no dignity, woman?"

"Nay—only pride, and great Art, I'm told," the Simbul said, her skin gleaming silver in the moonlight.

"*I'll* show ye 'great Art'!" Elminster said gruffly, reaching for her—an instant before he fell headfirst out of the bed in a wild tangle of covers.

Downstairs, Lhaeo chuckled at the ensuing laughter, and began to warm another kettle. Either they'd forgotten him, or thought he'd gone deaf—or his master had ceased to care for the proprieties. About time, too.

He began to sing softly, "Oh, For the Love of a Mage," because he was confident Storm was busy far down the dale and would not hear how badly he sang.

These are the sacrifices we make for love, he thought.

Upstairs, there was laughter again.

"It grows early, not late," Gorstag said, as Shandril's head nodded into her soup. "You should to bed, and then you both stay and sleep as long as your bodies need, before you set off on a journey fated to be long indeed, with no safe havens."

"We've not told you all yet, Gorstag," Narm said quietly. "We've joined the Harpers, and we go to Silverymoon to the High Lady Alustriel, for refuge and training!"

"To Silverymoon!" Gorstag gasped. "That's a fair jaunt for two so young, without a warband escort! If I were but twenty winters younger! Still, it'd be a perilous thing. Stay with caravans for protection! Two alone *can't* survive the wilderlands west of Cormyr, no matter how much Art they command."

"We'll have to," Shandril told him in a grim, determined voice. "But we will take your advice and stay with caravans . . . and if you don't mind, we will sleep tomorrow through. Foes or no foes, I can't stay awake much longer."

"Come," Lureene said, "to bed, lass! In your old place in the attic. Gorstag and I'll sleep there too, by the head of the stair, the other side of the curtain. I'm not leaving you alone while you're here."

"Aye." Shandril pushed against the table to rise.

In the dark passage that led to the kitchen, cold eyes regarded the four folk in the taproom for one last instant ere turning to flee into the dark.

So the wench had returned, had she? Certain ears would give much to hear speedily of this. . . .

⊠ ⊠ ⊠

"Gorstag?" Lureene asked sleepily. "Happy, love? Put that axe down at hand here, and come to bed."

"Aye," Gorstag replied. "There's something I must find first." He ducked into the darkest corner of the attic, at the end beyond the stairs, and dragged aside a chest bigger than he was. Then he reached to the base of a roof beam, and part of it came away in his hands. He took something from a small, heavy coffer protruding from the length of wood, and then replaced everything.

Bearing whatever he'd unpacked, the innkeeper came back across the broad boards of the attic floor to the curtain. "Narm? Shandril?"

"Aye, we're both awake. Come in," Narm replied, from where they lay.

Gorstag did so, lowering something by its chain to Narm. "Does your very touch drain items of Art, Shan, or only when you will it so?"

"Only when I call up spellfire," Shandril told him, peering at the pendant. "What is it?"

" 'Tis an amulet that hampers detection and location of its wearer. Keep it, lass, and wear it when you sleep. Only try to take it off when you must use spellfire, or you'll drain it. Wear it now, and you may win a day of uninterrupted rest tomorrow. I only wish I had one for each of you—but the necromancer whose neck I cut it from wore only one."

Narm chuckled. "You should've looked for his brother."

"Someone else'd slain him already," Gorstag replied with a grin. "It seems he liked to torment everyone with summoned beasts. Someone finally grew tired of such claws and fangs, went to his tower with a club, threw stones at the windows until he appeared—and then bashed his brains out. The someone was eight years old."

"A good start on life," Narm agreed with a yawn, and put the amulet about Shandril's neck. "This has no ill effects?"

"Nay, 'tis not one of those. Good night to you both, now. You've found the chamber pot? Aye, 'tis the one you remember, Shandril. Peace under the eyes of the gods, all." Gorstag ducked back through the curtain.

Lureene grinned at him, indicating the empty bed and the great axe on the floor beside it. "Now close the bedroom door, love, so the gooblies can't come in and get us."

Gorstag looked at the trapdoor. "Oh, aye." He closed it, dragging a linen chest over it. "There. Now—to sleep, at last, or 'twill be dawn before I've even lain down!"

Clothes flew in all directions, and Lureene was rolled into a bear hug and kissed with delicacy. She chuckled and patted his arm.

"Good night to you, my lord," she said softly, and rolled over. She had barely settled herself before she heard him begin to breathe the deep, steady draws of slumber. Once an adventurer, always. . . . She fell asleep before she finished the maxim.

⁂

When Narm awoke, sun streamed through the small, round windows, and the curtain had been drawn back. Lureene sat on a cushion beside them, mending a pile of torn linens. She looked at Narm and smiled. "Fair morn. Hungry?"

"Eh? N-n-no . . . but I could be." Narm sat up.

Shandril lay peacefully asleep, the amulet gleaming on her breast and Narm's discarded robe clutched in her hands. Narm smiled and tugged at it. A small frown appeared on Shandril's face. She held to it and raised one hand in an imperious, hurling gesture. Narm flinched back, but no spellfire came.

"Shan," he said quickly. " 'Tis all right, love. Relax. Sleep."

Shandril's hands fell back, and her face smoothed. Still deeply asleep, she murmured quite distinctly, "*Don't* tell *me* to relax, you . . ." and trailed away into purrings and mutterings.

Lureene suppressed a giggle into a sputter, and so did Narm.

"Aye, we'll let her sleep," the mistress of the Rising Moon said kindly. "There's a pot of stew on the hook over the taproom hearth—untouched by Korvan's hands, mind. I've bread and wine here. Go on . . . I'll watch her."

"Well, I—my thanks, Lureene. I'll—" He looked about him.

Lureene chuckled and spun around until her back was to him. "Sorry. Your clothes are over there on the chest, if you can live without that robe Shan's so fond of."

"Urrr . . . thanks!" Narm scrambled out of the bed and dressed. Shandril slept peacefully on. Lureene gave him a friendly pat as he started downstairs. He was still smiling as he went past the kitchen—and came face to face with Korvan.

The cook and the wizard came to a sudden stop perhaps a foot apart, and stared at each other. Korvan had a cleaver in one hand and a joint of meat in the other. Narm was barehanded.

Silence stretched. Korvan lifted his lip in a sneer, but Narm stared calmly and silently straight into the cook's eyes. Korvan raised the cleaver. Narm never moved, and never took his stare away from Korvan's own.

Suddenly Korvan cursed, backed away, and ducked into the kitchen.

Narm promptly strode into the taproom, where he greeted Gorstag as though nothing had befallen in the passage.

Elminster had been right. This Korvan wasn't worth the effort. A nasty, mean-tempered, blustering man—all bluff, all bravado. Another Marimmar, in fact.

Narm chuckled. He was still chuckling as he went back past the kitchen door. There was a crash of crockery from within, followed by a ringing clang—as if something metal had been violently hurled against a wall.

21

A Sunset for Several

Mind you do your dying right. Most of us get only one chance at it.

Mintipor Moonsilver, bard
Nine Stars Around a Silver Moon
Year of the Highmantle

Thiszult cursed at the sun. "Too late, by half! They'll be out of the dale and into the wilderness before nightfall! *How*, by Mystra, Talos, and Sammaster, am I to find two children in *miles* of tangled wilderness?"

"They'll stay on the road, Lord," one of the grim cult warriors told him.

"So you think!" Thiszult snarled. "So Salvarad of the Purple thinks, too, but I cannot believe two who've destroyed the Shadowsil, an archmage of the Purple—not to mention two sacred dracoliches—can be quite so stupid! No, why would they run? Who in Faerûn has the power to match them? More likely, they'll creep quietly about the wilderness, slaying whomever they come upon, while the rest of us search futilely, until we're all slain. I *must* reach them before dark—before they leave the road."

"We cannot," the warrior said simply. "The distance is too great. No power in the Realms could—"

"No *power?*" Thiszult fairly screamed. "No power? Hah! That which I bear is power enough!" He reined in sharply and cast his eyes over the mounted warriors in leather. "Ride after us, all of you—to Deepingdale, and the Thunder Peaks! If you see my sigil—thus—on a rock or tree, know that we've turned off the road and follow likewise."

"We?" asked the warrior.

"Aye—Thiszult the Overly Demanding and *you*, since you doubt my power. Trust in it now, for it's all that stands between you and spellfire! Now dismount—no, leave your armor behind." He touched the gaping cult swordsman and spoke a word. Warrior and mage vanished in a silent instant.

The other warriors stared. One of the riderless horses reared and neighed in terror, and the other snorted. Quick hands caught bridles.

"Stupid beast," a swordsman muttered. "Why'd it take fright?"

"Because the smell of its rider is gone," an older warrior told him sourly. "Gone—not moved away, but suddenly and utterly *gone*. 'Twould scare you, if you'd any wits. A stupid beast? It goes where you bid and knows not what waits, but *you* knowingly ride to do battle with two children who've destroyed dracoliches. . . . So tell me now: Just who is the stupid one?"

"Clever words," was the bitter reply, made amid many rueful chuckles.

Another veteran asked, "You think we ride on a hopeless task?"

The answer was a nod. "Not hopeless, but I've seen many young and overclever mages—like the one who just left us—come to a crashing fall. This latest Grandly Rising Wizard has no more wisdom or power than the others."

"What if I tell Naergoth of the Purple your doubting words? What then?" snarled the warrior he'd rebuked.

The old swordsman grinned. "Say such, if you will. 'Tis my guess you'll be adding them to a report of Thiszult's death. I've served the cult awhile; I know something of what I say." His tone was mild, but his eyes were very, very cold. . . .

The other warrior looked away first.

They rode on in grim silence, seeing neither mages nor gouts of spellfire. For that, they were every bit as happy as the horses beneath them.

A wild-eyed Shandril buckled and laced at the head of the stairs. "We must away," she panted to Narm as Lureene helped her kick on boots. "Others come . . . I dreamed it . . . the cult, and others! Hurry and eat!"

"But . . . but . . ." Deciding not to argue, Narm ate stew like a madman, wincing as he burned his lips on hot chunks of meat. On bare feet, he danced about Shandril.

Lureene took one look at him and fell back onto the beds, hooting in laughter. "Forgive me," she gasped.

Shandril fastened her belt and started down the stairs.

Narm halted her with a firm arm to the chest. He handed her the bowl of stew.

After a moment of straining against him, she rolled her eyes and spooned it into her mouth. With a murmur of pain, she burnt one lip and sat hastily on the steps.

"You two!" Lureene hooted. "I doubt I'll ever again see a mage of power so discomfited! Whooo! Ah, but you look funny, gobbling like that."

"You should see me casting spells," Narm said dryly. "When did she awake?"

"Scarce had you gone down when Shan sat upright, straight awake, and called for you. Then she scrambled up all in haste, crying that she'd dreamed of foes fast on your trail."

Narm said ruefully, "She's probably right."

"Did your Art have the desired effect?" Sharantyr asked.

"Yes," Jhessail responded, passing a hand over her eyes. "This dreamweaving's wearisome; no wonder Elminster was so reluctant to teach me. Yet I think I scared Shandril enough to get her moving!" She sank back in her chair. "Ah, me . . . I'm ready for bed."

Sharantyr rose. "I'll get Merith."

Jhessail shook her head. "Nay, nay . . . 'tis sleep I need, not cuddling . . . you've no idea, Shar: 'Tis like a black pit of oblivion. I'm so tired. . . ." With that, the lady mage of the Knights drifted into her pit and was gone.

Sharantyr found a pillow for Jhessail's head, drew off the mage's boots, and wrapped her friend in a blanket. Then she drew her sword and sat down nearby, laying the bare blade ready across her knees. After all, it had been overlong since Manshoon had worked mischief in Shadowdale.

In haste, they kissed Lureene farewell, thrust the empty bowl into her hands, and were downstairs and out through the taproom into the sunshine before they drew breath.

In the inn yard, Gorstag stood with their mounts and mules harnessed. The packs lashed to the last two mules bulged suspiciously here and there. "Bread, sausage, cheese, hand casks of wine, pickled greens, a crate of grapes and figs, a coffer of salt, some torches . . ." Gorstag said briefly. "The gods watch over you." He enveloped Shandril in a crushing hug and swung her up into her saddle. "Carry this," he said, and pressed a bottle into her hands. "Goat's milk . . . drink it before highsun tomorrow, or it'll go bad."

He turned like a swordsman whirling from a kill in battle, shook Narm's hand in a bruising grip, took him by both elbows, and lifted him into the saddle. He thrust a small, bright disc of silver into his hands. "A shield of Tymora, blessed by priests in Waterdeep long ago. May it bring you safe to Silverymoon."

He stood looking up at them. "You're in haste, and I was never one for long gods-go-with-ye's. So fare you well in life—I hope to see you again before I die, with you both as happy and hale as now. I wish you well, both of you!" He stretched up to kiss them both. "You've chosen well in each other." Then he patted the rumps of their horses to start them on their way, and raised his fist in the farewell salute warriors give to honored champions.

As they turned out of the Rising Moon's yard, Shandril burst into tears.

Gorstag stood like a statue, his arm raised in salute. He stood so until they were out of sight.

When Lureene came down, she found her man muttering prayers to Tymora and Mystra and Helm. She put her arms around him from behind and leaned against the might of his many-muscled back.

He trembled as he left off praying and began to cry.

It was dark in the meeting chamber of the Cult of the Dragon. A single oil lamp flickered on the table between the two men.

"You really think this boy-mage can defeat Shandril, who's destroyed our best and most powerful?" Dargoth of the Purple snarled.

"No," Naergoth Bladelord replied. "And so another of our bone dragons pursues her right now."

"*Another* dracolich? We haven't many more Sacred Ones to lose!"

"True," Naergoth said, his gaze growing colder. "This one went of its own will. I compelled it not, nor asked it to go—but I did not forbid it, either. One does not forbid Shargrailar anything!"

Dargoth looked at him, mouth dropping open. "For the love of lost Sammaster! Shargrailar the Dark flies? Gods preserve us!"

"They'll hardly start doing that after all this time," Naergoth answered dryly, reaching to extinguish the lamp. Darkness descended.

Suddenly they were in a place of fragrant vapors, pots, and knives. The cult swordsman snorted unnecessarily, "A kitchen!"

At his words, the cook standing with his back to them whirled from his bloody cutting board, cleaver rising.

Thiszult smiled coldly. "So pleased to see us, Korvan?"

The sour-faced cook struggled to regain his composure; hatred, envy, fear, and exultation chased rapidly across his mean face. "Why, Thisz—"

"*Hush*—no names! How long ago did the wench leave? And what's our way out of here?"

"Outside, t-to the back of the inn, yon door," Korvan replied, with only a slight stammer. "Or, to the front: that door, turn right into the taproom, then left across it to the front door. She and the boy-mage left but ten breaths back. You'll be able to catch them if you—"

"Have horses. Where're the stables?"

"Around the side, that way. There's a good strong black and a stouter but slower bay, and—"

"The cult thanks you, Korvan. You'll receive an appropriate reward in the fullness of time." With a snap of his cloak, Thiszult strode into the passage, the warrior at his heels. The swordsman drew his broadsword.

"Korvan," Lureene whispered as she came out of the open pantry, eyes dark with anger, "do you know those—those folk?"

The cook stared at her, white-faced—and then raised his cleaver and went for her. Fury and determination twisted his face.

Lureene cast a tin of flour at that snarling face and fled into the hall and the taproom beyond. It was empty. She ran across it, dodging between tables and burst out the front door.

Before her, Gorstag stood with his hands locked on the forearms of the swordsman. They stood straining against each other, the warrior's sword shaking as he forced it up to strike. Behind them, the dark-cloaked mage spurred out of the yard on their black gelding.

Lureene ran as hard as she could, sobbing for breath.

The front door of the Rising Moon banged open. Korvan emerged—her death.

Lureene ran on, sliding desperately, knowing she had to warn Gorstag before Korvan's cleaver could reach him.

The two men were only ten paces away . . . six . . . three . . .

Gorstag dropped to one knee and pulled hard on the swordsman's wrist. The sword lunged harmlessly over and past him. Gorstag sprang up, his fist driving into the warrior's throat.

Throat, neck, and man crumpled without a sound.

Gorstag whirled in time to catch Lureene about the shoulders and spin her to a halt. "Love?"

Lureene pointed, frantically. "Korvan! He serves the cult! Look *out!*"

The cook put on a last burst of speed, hacking at them.

Gorstag pushed Lureene away to one side and leaped away to the other. The cleaver found only empty air between them.

Korvan looked wildly at both targets—too late. Fingers of iron took him by the neck from behind. Staggering, the cook lashed out, only to have his cleaver-wrist deftly captured and twisted. Korvan let out a little cry and dropped his weapon from burning fingers.

Gorstag wrenched him around until they were face to face. "So, *first* you molest my little one . . . and now you'd slay my bride-to-be! You threaten me with steel here in my own yard, and you serve the Cult of the Dragon . . . in my own kitchen." His voice was low and soft, but Korvan twisted in his grasp like a hooked fish, face white to the very lips.

"This has been coming for a long time," Gorstag added slowly, "but at least I've learned something about cooking."

The hand that held Korvan's wrist darted to the cook's throat, whip-fast, and twisted mercilessly. There was a dull crack, and Korvan of the cult was no more.

Gorstag let the body fall into the mud and turned to Lureene. "Are you hurt, my lady? Is there fire or ruin behind you in the Moon?"

Lureene shook her head, wide-eyed. "No, Lord," she whispered, close to tears, "I'm fine . . . thanks to you. We're safe!"

"Aye, then," Gorstag said, and he looked down the road. The dust of the mage's furious exit still drifted. "But will Narm and Shandril be? Find me the fastest horse, while I get my axe."

Lureene stared at him in horror. "No! You'll be slain!"

"Leave my friends to die because I did nothing?" Gorstag's face was like iron. "Find me the fastest horse!"

Lureene rushed toward the stables, tears blurring her sight. "No. Oh, gods, *no*." But this morning it seemed that the gods were as hard of hearing as usual. . . .

Gorstag bolted back out of the inn, his axe in his hand. Frightened guests followed to gawk. In the yard, he found a grim-faced dwarf on a small, weary, and mud-spattered mule.

The dwarf came to a halt before the glowering innkeeper and rolled down out of his saddle with practiced ease. Using his broad dwarven axe as a walking-stick, he leaned heavily on it as he limped over to Gorstag and peered up.

"Well met. You're Gorstag?"

The innkeeper was looking grimly toward the stables, whence an empty-handed Lureene staggered, face stricken. "Aye, that I am."

"Have y'seen a companion of mine, the adventuress Shandril? She waited on tables here, once," the dwarf growled. "I hear she rides with a young mage, now, an' hurls spellfire!"

"Aye. I have," Gorstag snapped, his axe lifting warningly. "Who then are *you*, and what's your business with Shandril Shessair? My daughter!"

"I'm come in all haste from Shadowdale," the dwarf replied, looking up at him with a glare as harshly steady as his own. "From Sharantyr, Rathan, and Torm of the Knights of Myth Drannor I heard where Shandril was headed, and followed. I'm sent by Storm Silverhand of the Harpers and Elminster the mage, and bear a note to tell you to trust me in this. Here, read it! Now tell me where Shandril is, man, for time draws on and my bones grow no younger!"

Gorstag grinned and snatched open the parchment. "Not so sour, Sir Dwarf. Life's less a trial to the patient!"

"Aye," the dwarf replied, "for most of them lie dead. *Tell me where Shandril is!*"

"A moment." Gorstag looked from the parchment to Lureene, and saw that she was shaking.

"Dead," she whispered. "All of them. Every last horse and mule and ox. Lightning still crawls around the stables. Damn all wizards!"

Gorstag put his arm around her, and held the parchment out so she could read what was written, too:

To Gorstag of Highmoon,

By these words, well met! The bearer of this note is the dwarf Delg, a sword-mate of Shandril in the Company of the Bright Spear, after she left your house. He serves no evil master and bears Shandril no ill will. Trust us in this—he has submitted to all our tests of Art in this regard, and it is true. The Cult of the Dragon destroyed the company, and it was thought only Shandril survived. This Delg, left for dead in Oversember Vale, made his way to the shores of the Sember, where he was found by elves and taken to priests of Tempus. While they were healing his wounds and praying for guidance as to what task they should set him in return, Tempus himself spoke, saying that Delg's task was to defend the girl who wielded spellfire against seeking swords. So he comes to you for aid.

Your part in defending Shandril is done, valiant Gorstag; we tend Dammasae's place of rest and remember. Aid this one as best you can, and you will be honored greatly. You shall have then in your debt,

Elminster of Shadowdale and
Storm Silverhand of Shadowdale

Gorstag read the letter, frowned a little, and looked up at Delg. "You've missed them. They rode west from here some short time ago, now. A hostile mage follows close behind."

"Hinges of the Nine Hells! This is no time to be standing about *reading!*" the dwarf growled, hobbling back to mount his mule. "Up, and go like the wind . . . she's in trouble again, and in need of old Delg!"

Gorstag glanced dubiously at the exhausted mule.

Delg saw that look. "I make haste in my own way. Fare thee well, Gorstag. Leave this chase to me, and stay by your lady. 'Tis the greatest adventure you can have." He grinned and rode away, raising his arm in a warrior's salute.

Gorstag returned it, and stood like a statue watching him go.

Lureene stroked his arm thoughtfully and said nothing.

After a time Gorstag looked away from the road. "Well, mayhap we'd best go in." His stride was slow and reluctant as he turned his back on the yard with its two sprawled corpses.

Most of the staring guests fell away before him. One opened the door and ducked inside. They followed in a general flood, anxious to be away from their host and his blazing eyes.

All save one. A priestess of Oghma, who'd said almost nothing since her arrival hours ago, glided forward to block Gorstag's way. "The letter, Goodman—I must see it."

The innkeeper's glare had teeth in it. "No."

"Goodman Gorstag," the priestess purred, golden fire kindling in her eyes, "I must insist. Refusal would not be wise."

"You serve the Binder, and so should respect bindings," the innkeeper growled. "This is one such; leave me be."

The priestess stabbed out one arm to snatch at the letter—an arm that shouldn't have reached that far.

Gorstag fell back in astonishment.

"*Give me the letter*," the Oghmanyte snarled. "*Now!*"

Gorstag's face darkened. "Don't command me in my own inn. I'll not—"

Golden flames leaped into a bright glow in the eyes locked on his. "*Enough!* Doom is upon you, fool human!"

Both of her hands reached for the parchment. Arms snaked past to curve behind him, darkening swiftly. The face drooped into nightmare, the holy crimson vest melted away into a glistening black bulk and—

Lureene screamed her horror.

Gorstag tossed the letter to the winds and used both frantic hands to swing his axe up—and then down. Hot blue and wine-red gore spattered him. He snarled in fear and swung again, hacking as hard and as furiously as ever in his life. He danced to one side in case those tentacles—a flailing forest of them—sought to strangle him from behind.

A droning, whistling cry arose from the nightmare thing. Tentacles severed. Rubbery innards cleft.

Drenched with its stinging gore, Gorstag kicked and sliced

and roared his defiance. He suddenly stood staring across much-riven darkness into Lureene's terrified eyes. White and trembling, she held her tiny belt-knife in her hand—at the end of an arm that dripped gore clear up to the shoulder.

Gorstag gave her a grin. " 'Tis dead, Lady." He lifted his axe in celebration. "We've done it! One less hunter after Shan!"

He looked down and gave one tentacle a hearty kick. The smell of death was sharp, like a cask of wine gone bad. Everywhere, dark fingers of blood spread across the churned and trampled mud. "Hmmph. I was going to ask you to fetch a stew-pot, but somehow . . ."

Lureene didn't smile at his crude joke. She shook her head, eyes large and dark. "Oh, Shan. What *else* is chasing you?"

Gorstag shot his lady a glance and asked, "Are you well?"

Lureene nodded, her face pale but with a hint of a smile. She put Delg's letter into his hand, and put her hands on her hips. "Of course, but there's a little matter of corpses lying about, and its inevitable effect on our trade. . . ."

Gorstag growled and went to put away his axe and find a shovel. He carried the letter very carefully in his hand, and looked at it again as he went.

A glowing sphere sank toward an ornate tabletop, darkening as the will that had driven it wavered. The noble lady of Waterdeep who'd been staring so fixedly into its depths reeled in her chair, aghast. Had the servants heard her scream?

"No," Amarune of the Blood of Malaug gasped. "*No!*"

Her daughter was dead. Trembling with grief and fury, she sprang from her seat. The chair crashed to the carpets. She strode across the room to snatch aside a rich blue curtain.

Sintre gone forever!

The tall painting beyond was enspelled to glow, but she tore its knights-courting-ladies scene aside to lay bare a plain stone door that it had hid.

She almost snarled the words that would unlock the door and let her pass without awakening death. Thin lines of blue fire formed and receded. She snatched open the door. In the tiny, seldom-seen chamber beyond waited a hoard of enchanted things, weapons enough to shatter a dozen backcountry inns and scores of idiot innkeepers! Why, she might not stop slaying until all the dales were lifeless slaughter-fields, with nothing left but vultures and crows!

Sintre, gone forever!

It had taken years upon years of scheming and lovemaking and poisonings and daring thefts to amass all this magic from fools of Faerûn—and now, by the Shadows, she'd use it to work many dooms! Sh—

Amarune came to a sudden halt in midstride. She wavered precariously for a long, gaping moment.

There was a man sitting on her magic—a gaunt man in none-too-clean robes, who had a long white beard, a hawk-sharp nose, and blue-gray eyes that, meeting hers, were fierce and sad.

"*Who*—?" she almost sang in astonishment.

"Ye may call me Elminster; many do. But ye'd do much better to listen before ye shriek anything more. . . ."

Amarune gazed at him in frozen silence. She'd heard of Elminster, oh yes, and . . .

"Dhalgrave did not issue his most infamous decree for nothing," the wizard told her mildly. "He spoke so because I offered him the same choice I'm now giving you: Dwell hidden among humans, doing them no harm, and live—or slay and meddle overmuch, and die."

She swallowed, very much as a high lady of Waterdeep should, and shook her head. This man knew of the Great Shadowmaster and his Dark Decree?

"I know who ye are, Amarune," Elminster continued, his eyes steady on hers, "and have known who ye are for some years. Yet ye've dwelt here no worse behaved than most, save perhaps thy gaining of these pretties—" Her enspelled things clattered and chimed as he dug one long-fingered hand through them, held it up, and let them trail back onto the gleaming, glittering heap. "—no less worthy of living in Waterdeep than the bulk of thy neighbors. Yet the time has come for a certain truth to be made plain between us. If ye lift a single tentacle against any creature of

Faerûn hereafter, I will come for ye—*after* telling Dhalgrave and all of Shadowhome who ye are and where ye are. Then we shall all have good hunting . . . and our kill shall be Amarune."

The tall, trembling lady stared at him, eyes golden and terrible. Then she knelt. Sliding slowly forward until her breast and chin scraped the flagstones, she reached out her empty hands, crossing one over the other at her wrists. Her forearms darkened into glistening tentacles, and with deft care she knotted them together, in the Malaugrym gesture of abject submission. "Wizard," she hissed, the smell of her fear sharp in the small chamber. She gazed pleadingly at him. "Command me."

Elminster rose with a small grunt of effort, and rubbed one hip, producing a lit pipe out of nowhere. "I'll go now and even leave ye all of these toys, despite the butchery ye must've done to gain some of them. Go not to Highmoon, and do nothing against any being in the Realms . . . and I'll let ye live to enjoy them awhile longer."

They gazed at each other, she tearful and trembling, he calm and implacable. She saw sympathy in his eyes.

"Avenging thy foolish children will but bring ye more pain," he added quietly, puffing on his pipe. "Lonely ye may be, Amarune—and wronged and long hunted . . . but ye live here as a high lady, and that's more than most folk in this world can dream of. Enjoy what ye have and try to be content—for if ye reach for more, ye'll lose all. This, I swear."

His figure faded. Magics gleamed *through* him in the gloomy chamber. "I'll watch for ye, Amarune—not just as thy keeper . . . but if ye'll have me, in time, as thy friend. I'd rather see ye laugh and be happy than have to slay ye. Remember that." He was gone, his last words left behind.

Amarune rose in tentacled fury, hissing. She lashed the air in rage and pain and loss, but when she sank down to the floor on her knees and wept, her sobs might have been those of any bereaved mother of Waterdeep. Black tentacles became slender white arms. With them, she cradled one silver-sheathed wand as if it were the most precious thing in the world. . . .

In time, she fell silent and rose empty-handed. She closed the door on the gathered glowing death and the faint smell of pipe smoke . . . and went to ring the servants for wine. Much wine.

Shargrailar the Dark circled high above Thunder Gap. Cold winds whistled through the spread, bony fingers that were all that remained of its wings. Shargrailar was the mightiest dracolich in Faerûn, perhaps the most powerful there had ever been. Its eyes were two white lamps in the empty sockets of a long, cruel skull. It looked down on the world below with the cold patience of a being who had passed beyond the tomb and yet could fly. It flew lower, watching and waiting.

So a human female dared to destroy dracoliches? Death must find her. Lucky she must have been, and her victims young fools. Still, she must die. Armed with spellfire, she was headed toward Shargrailar's lair. Interesting.

Like a silent shadow, Shargrailar glided among the clouds, peering at the tiny road called the East Way. It had been a very long time since Shargrailar had been interested in anything.

Thiszult rode hard, hauling savagely on the reins. To call up his special magic, he had to pass the maid and her mageling and get ahead of them—or find a height above their camp to keep them in view. It would not do to miss them now, or to get too close and warn them.

He thought furiously as he rode. He wore no insignia and rode alone. He displayed nothing to tell Faerûn he was a mage, nor that he wished anyone ill. Yet, he was riding in brutal haste—dangerous, as the road climbed into the Peaks. His speed would warn anyone that all was not right—especially this couple, wary of foes.

Thiszult slowed his mount, cudgeling his brains for a plan. In darkness they could easily evade him. Yet, one had to sleep. They would halt to camp. Perhaps then would be the best time to attack—but only if he was close on their trail, yet unseen. Yes, that—

A man stepped out of the trees right into his path, and Thiszult's horse reared.

"What *fool—*" the startled wizard started to curse, wrestling to keep his seat.

The man smirked, eyes calm and golden and very, very cold. "There's a Realms-shaking overabundance of idiot wizards riding Faerûn today. Hunting spellfire, I presume? With all your best blasting spells burning holes in your brain?"

Shocked, the cult mage stammered, "W-who are you?"

"Architrave, I am called. It's always nice to know the name of your slayer, don't you agree?"

Black tentacles stabbed out like sudden spears.

Thiszult twisted back frantically and fell head-over-heels from his saddle. Rolling furiously, he found a tree to get behind, and another to claw his way along until he was upright. Gasping, he whirled.

The mocking man had become a black, surging wave that rolled over his horse. Wild-eyed, it snorted, bucked, and lashed out with its hooves. Black tentacles closed around its neck with lazy grace, twisting.

Thiszult muttered the only spell his terrified mind could think of, to take him away from here. The dying horse rolled once more atop the black thing. Its tentacles lanced through the air toward Thiszult.

He finished the spell, and it snatched him up into the sky. A single black tentacle streaked after him, but he soared frantically aloft, racing on toward Thunder Gap.

In his wake, tentacles fell, a dead horse was flung free, and a glistening black bulk raged and coiled in a silent, quaking storm. Becoming a small, obsidian-hued dragon, it leaped into the sky and snapped its still-flowing jaws experimentally thrice. Flapping powerful bat-wings, a trifle unsteadily, the false wyrm arrowed west in the wizard's wake. This was no day for mercy.

Delg's head snapped up. Something had flashed past him, low above the trees—too large to be a bird—something that had lacked wings . . . a man?

Whoever or whatever it was had been going fast and hadn't been witless enough to soar above the open road. Delg could see nothing of it now through the trees ahead. Another wizard, after Shandril?

Well, why not? Wasn't it time for every last dragon and leviathan and many-headed *thing* in all Faerûn to join the chase? The dwarf shook his head and rode on, thinking of Burlane and Ferostil and Rymel, all dead now, never to laugh with him again. . . . Mayhap he'd join them soon. . . .

Kicking his mule into reluctant hurry, he watched the road ahead, his axe ready.

❖ ❖ ❖

Shargrailar looked idly in its wake, past the few wisps of cloud, back along the road to—

Another dragon? So small, and as black as seawater on a still night, but coming like a summer storm, cleaving the air at great speed. The dracolich eyed it, feeling fierce exultation, and dipped one of its wings to whirl and dive.

What mattered who this wyrm might be? Now it would be Shargrailar's latest kill. Too long had it been since he'd pounced on something worthy of the effort, too long . . .

When it saw its doom, it had time only to acquire a look of terror in its strange golden eyes. Then Shargrailar gave it death, literally plunging through it in velvet silence, raking with razor-keen claws and biting with long bone fangs to tear it to wet scraps and cantles. Casting them away, the dracolich whirled again and soared westward, as if nothing had befallen.

Behind it, unregarded, the riven wyrm fell, dwindling as it tumbled. Smoldering tentacles feebly clutched at the uncaring air . . . and Architrave of the Malaugrym struck ground in a series of wet, spattering crashes.

Shargrailar flew on. Ah, but that had felt good. Now to the puny humans. They could not be much farther west, unless—

Ah! There below, on the road. Two human riders with mules . . . one female . . .

Silently Shargrailar descended, skeletal head peering. Yes . . .

yes, this must be her. And if not, what matter? What pair of humans could hurt Shargrailar?

Like a gigantic arrow, the great dracolich plunged out of the sky. *Silent death comes for you morsels. . . .* As it descended, Shargrailar could see that the she-human was beautiful. It opened bony jaws wide to give her death. Silently, patiently . . .

A bright net of stars blossomed in the shade of a roadside tree. Motes fell away, drifting and darkening. A slender figure stood amid the smoking gore and tangled, twitching tentacles. Her white hand darted down, stretching impossibly long, to pluck something from the heart of steaming Malaugrym flesh.

A dull, dark gem was cradled to a breast that trembled with sobs. "You *fool*, Architrave. I *warned* you!"

Blue fire flashed. Another net of stars whirled up to enshroud the weeping woman and flared to snatch her back to a tower in Waterdeep, before a certain Old Mage could catch her.

Stars faded and were gone, leaving only tears.

Magusta watched those stars dwindle. She laughed, gloating. "So they both earn themselves the fate of fools."

Her brother shook his head. "Who was the woman? Kin to us, or some human she-wizard?"

"Someone who wanted a magic trinket back, not one of the Blood—or she'd have tarried to do the usual things." Magusta turned away from the whirling brightness of her scrying spell. "With them both dead, we've all Faerûn to ourselves to play in—thanks to the Dark Decree. So long as we watch out for Elminster."

Stralane's eyes flashed. "I believe I'll pay that Old Mage a visit to test his vaunted vigilance and magical might. It could be that he dodders or has dwindled to half the mage he used to be. If I take a suitably innocent human guise, there'll be little danger. After all, he's only human."

Magusta shrugged. "Your peril, Stralane. I'd stay far from that wizard and keep him busy with meddling humans whom we set a-striving with a whisper here and a murmur there. . . ."

Her brother snorted. "So you forge your own cage and climb eagerly in! Not me." He strode away—and then turned, his tentacles curling toward her. "Or are you playing a darker game, Sister? Are you going to snatch spellfire for your own the moment my back's turned?"

Magusta shrugged again. "Hardly. See what that seeking earned Sintre and Architrave? More than that: Two score Zhentilar ride hard after the spellfire maid right now." She turned back to the scrying-sphere. "I wouldn't want to miss watching the fun that'll befall."

"Zhents? I thought they were Dragon Cultists!"

"The dragon lovers were riding down little Lady Spellfire, too—but the Zhents butchered them even as Architrave was dying." She turned the sphere so he could see its other side, where tiny warriors rode hard along a rising road. "Thunder Gap's going to be a crowded place soon."

"Someone follows us," Narm said, peering back over his shoulder.

"Some*one?*" Shandril asked him. "One? Alone?"

"Yes . . . a child, or someone short, on a mule," Narm said doubtfully. "An odd traveler to ride alone through wilderlands!"

"Well, 'tis an open road—it can't be unused, by any means!" Shandril turned in her saddle. Behind them, the land fell away in gentle hills to dark woods and Deepingdale. Peering, she thought she could see the Rising Moon, or where it must be. Tears touched her eyes—and then she saw bony death gliding coldly down out of the sky.

"Narm!" she screamed, kicking heels to her mount and climbing onto its neck in wild urgency. "Get *down!*"

Narm looked—and saw. He frantically tore Torm's gift from his neck and threw it away.

Shandril had one glimpse of his white face before the world exploded.

"What in the name of the Soul Forger was *that*?" Delg stood openmouthed in his stirrups as the great skeletal bulk arrowed down out of the sky. 'Twas like a dragon, but . . . 'twas a skeleton! 'Twas . . . oh, by the lode-luck of the Ironstars, it must be one of those dracoliches Elminster spoke of!

Delg swallowed and sat down in his saddle again. "I'm getting too old for this sort of thing. . . ."

No dwarf stood a chance against that! Nor, he thought grimly, did little Shandril, even with fire magic and a boy who could cast spells.

The mule had slowed to a walk. Delg booted it mercilessly in the ribs, waving his axe so that it flashed in the sunlight.

"*Get* you going!" he snarled into its ears. "I'm late for a battle, and they'll be needing me, never fear!"

Thiszult flew low over the trees to one side of the road. The wind of his flight whipped past his ears. He had to find them and get ahead of them. Soon . . .

There was a flash and roar of flame ahead. Startled, Thiszult veered to one side, rising for a better look. Were they in a fight? This might prove even easier than he'd thought!

A vast, dark skeleton wheeled in the air. Thiszult gasped. A Sacred One! But how came it here? And who was it?

He'd never seen one so large and terrible before! As he stared at the dracolich, its cold orbs met his own, and it turned toward him. Its skeletal jaws looked somehow amused.

Blue-white lightning leaped and crackled from the great dracolich's maw.

Thiszult had no time to protest that he was an ally. It struck. All his limbs convulsed. He was dead, mouth open to begin his speech, even before Shargrailar's bony claws struck his body and tore it apart. His secret, long-guarded magic fell to earth, lost in the endless trees below.

⊠ ⊠ ⊠

Far away, Salvarad of the cult sighed and turned from his scrying font. Thiszult would never take the Purple now.

⊠ ⊠ ⊠

Shandril rose grimly. The stink of cooked horseflesh was strong; faithful Shield had lived up to her name. Shandril's arms tingled, but she was unharmed. The dracolich's flames had poured strength into her. . . . But how had Narm fared?

She ran across the smoking road, seeking him. Lightning cracked overhead, but she did not look up. Where was he?

A heart-twisting, blackened tangle of horse's legs and smoldering mules met her gaze. She swallowed and ran forward, peering anxiously into the smoking slaughter.

"Narm! Oh, Narm!"

He had no protection against dragon fire. He could well be dead, and their child would never know its father. . . . None of that! *Find* him, first!

There he was, moving weakly, half-buried under scorched baggage. He was alive! Oh, gods be praised!

Shandril crashed down on her knees beside him, tearing aside smoldering straps and scorched cloth. Narm moaned. His hair smoked, and the left side of his face was black and blistered.

"Oh, Narm! Beloved!"

Cracked lips moved. Lids that no longer had lashes flickered open. Watery eyes met hers, lovingly—and then looked past her and widened.

"Look out, love!" Narm hissed hoarsely. "The dracolich comes!"

Shandril looked up. The legendary Shargrailar wheeled directly above them, vast and dark and terrible. Though it was only empty bones, the undead creature was awesome. Shandril shivered as she gazed at its fell might. Soaring lazily, it turned and dived down the sky.

"Run, Shan!" Narm croaked from beneath her. "Get you hence! I love you! Shandril, *go!*"

"No," Shandril said, through threatening tears. "No, Lord, I'll not leave you!"

Great bony jaws opened, above.

Shandril lay gently atop Narm's blackened body, shielding him as much as she could. Narm groaned in pain. She braced herself to lift her weight off him. "I love you."

As the roar of the dracolich's approaching flame grew in the air, Shandril put her lips to Narm's and gathered her will.

Searing flame swallowed them.

"Clanggedin aid me!" Delg muttered. His mule bucked under his aching thighs.

The road ahead was one great smoking ruin. A cone of flames had just raked it—and in a moment the swooping dracolich would be above. The mule bucked again.

"Oh, *blast!*" Delg burst out. He found himself somersaulting forward through the air. His frantic grab for the saddle-horn missed. At least he still had hold of his axe. He tucked it close against him so it wouldn't be chipped in the hard landing.

The mule's saddle was empty when raking claws swept the poor beast skyward, rending and tearing.

The dracolich let out the first angry sound it had uttered in many long years—a long, loud hiss of frustration. Shredding the mule as if it were a rotten rag, Shargrailar wheeled. Destroying foes had never taken this long before.

Once more . . . just one last dive . . .

In the heart of the inferno, Shandril strained to draw in the dragon fire that ravaged Narm's helpless body. Through their joined lips she felt the fierce energy flowing; sluggishly at first, then faster and faster. Gods, the *pain!*

Her lips were seared as if by hot metal; tears blinded her. Her tormented body shuddered. Bright agony clawed and snarled through her. She held fast to Narm until the last of the flames swept over them and were gone.

Energy flowed into her. Narm's own life force streamed into her; she was draining him to death!

Hastily she broke their kiss and stared down at his slack, silent face. His eyes were dark, unseeing. Oh, Narm! She'd no Art to heal him!

What had she done?

Bitterly, Shandril felt the surging energy swelling within her. Her veins were afire; she was bloated with more than she could hold for long. The *pain* . . .

Into her mind came Gorstag's voice, telling of her mother: ". . . to heal or harm . . . !" Heal! Could she heal as well as burn?

She gathered her shaking limbs, lay tenderly on Narm again, and set her lips to his. Closing her eyes, Shandril willed energy to flow out of her gently . . . slowly, like cooling water. . . .

Energy flowed into Narm. She willed it into him, fiercely, and *felt* his feeble heartbeat strengthen. He moved under her, struggling to speak.

Shandril shed fresh tears as she poured more energy into her beloved. Let him be once more whole and strong and—

Bony claws raked agony across her back.

Shandril was torn free of Narm and flung to the road beyond by Shargrailar's angry strike. Pain almost overwhelmed her. She shrieked aloud, flames gouting from her mouth.

Ohhh, Tymora, the pain!

She had ignored another bolt of lightning from it as she healed Narm—but the great dracolich could slay her with claws as surely as if she had no spellfire.

Pain tore at her. She twisted and thrashed in the dust of the road. She could feel her blood pour out. Blood, blood . . . she'd seen more spilled this tenday than in all her life before, and she was heartily *sick* of it. Well—now she could do something about it!

Shandril opened her eyes and looked for the dracolich. A fierce anger filled her, and exultation rose to join it. . . . She could heal! She could use spellfire to aid as well as to slay!

Crawling on hands and knees, Shandril saw Shargrailar sweep down again, eyes glimmering at her from its cruel skull, claws outstretched.

The onetime thief of Deepingdale met that chilling gaze and laughed.

From her eyes, flames shot forth, two fiery beams of spellfire that struck the bone dragon's eyes.

Smoke rose from its skull—and Shargrailar screamed. Bony wings sheared away to one side.

Shandril laughed in triumph, and a white inferno of flames roared from her mouth into the blinded dracolich.

It reeled in the air, blazing, and crashed to the ground.

Ignoring its snaps and thrashes, she turned to finish Narm's healing. As she crawled back to him, she bent her will to heal herself. Soothing relief spread across her torn back, and the pain faded.

Narm's skin was cold under her fingers, and he lay unmoving. Shandril poured energy into him . . . but the fires in her were much lessened. She shouldn't have healed herself . . . she had too little left—and the dracolich was still dangerous. It wasn't wasting spells on her any longer, so she couldn't gain more spellfire. Oh, Tymora! Was her luck always to be bad? No, it could be fatal, just once—now, perhaps—and all her worries would be over.

Shandril scrambled up, looking wildly around for the dracolich. If it clawed her now . . .

She heard a strange smashing and splintering sound. Peering cautiously over the smoking mules, she saw an axe rise and fall in Shargrailar's shuddering rib cage. Bone chips flew. The dracolich had already lost its wings and two claws, and was trying feebly to turn its head to blast its attacker. The bones of its neck were smashed in two places, and smoke rose from its blackened skull. A hearty kick sent more pieces of bone flying. The descending boot was planted firmly on one of Shargrailar's claws ere its owner chopped brutally downward.

"Delg!" Shandril cried in happy astonishment. Racing toward the burly dwarf, she laughed and cried at once. His gleaming axe hacked tirelessly on the dracolich's splintered bulk.

Through whirling shards of bone he grinned at her. "Well met, Shan! Long days pass, and you've gotten into trouble, as always . . . only this time you're in luck: Delg's here to lay low your pet!"

Shandril swept him up in a happy embrace, clear off his feet. She let out a whoop of effort and staggered to set him down again. "Delg! Delg, I thought all the company were dead!"

The dwarf nodded soberly before his fierce grin came again.

"Aye. So did I," he told her, beard bristling. "But I've found you at last."

"Found me? Do you know what's *happened* to me? This dracolich's but the latest. Scarce a day passes without someone trying to slay us because of . . . that which I wield."

"Spellfire, aye, so they've all been telling me."

"All?"

"Aye, Elminster an' Storm an' the Knights an' Harpers an' all. I rode the legs of my mule a few finger-widths shorter following you! You've become important indeed, lass, in less time than I've seen most heroes and legends rise." The dwarf waved his axe. "So let's see this spellfire again, before we move Narm somewhere safer."

"Well enough," Shandril said, and waved at the dismembered dracolich. "Do you know this one?"

"Never seen it before I buried my axe in it. Does it matter?"

"No, I suppose not," Shandril replied, and let fly with roaring spellfire that blasted Shargrailar's flopping skull to bone shards. As the smoke died away, Shandril looked at Delg, saw fear lurking in his eyes, and shrugged. "I'm not safe to be near, these days. So much killing, since first I left the Moon . . . Is butchery what all the legends are built on?"

"Aye," the dwarf said gruffly. "Didn't you know?" He stomped toward Narm. "Let's drag your lord a good distance from all this carnage and see what we can salvage before sunset."

She walked beside him. " 'We'? You'll come with us?"

"Aye, if you'll have me along on your bridal journey an' all." The dwarf looked embarrassed. He squinted up at her almost defiantly, hands twisting on his axe. "We're friends, lass. I'll stand true by you an' your lord. Few enough such you'll find, mark you . . . an' one needs little more in life than good food an' good friends. The company's gone now, all save for you . . . so old Delg'll ride with you." He swung his axe onto his shoulder. "If you make it to Silverymoon an' are sick of me, we'll part ways. I hope you won't be . . . 'tis a trial indeed, when you be my age, befriending pretty girls anew. Folks get all the wrong ideas, y'see."

The old dwarf handed her his axe. "Hold this, while I carry your mage down the road apiece. Easy, lad, you'll feel better soon enough; I know, I've lived through battles enough to tell. Come, the sun waits not for all my talking!"

Nor did it, but it was a happy camp that sunset.

In the morning, the dwarf walked with the young couple as they headed west into the mountains. It was a clear day, and the green dales spread out behind them as they climbed to Thunder Gap. All was peaceful. A lone black falcon soared high above in clear blue air. The day passed with no attack nor hurling of spellfire.

Delg told Narm fierce tales of Shandril's daring with the company, and Narm told Delg of the struggles in Myth Drannor and Rauglothgor's lair and how his Lady Spellfire had blasted apart the mountaintop. The dwarf looked at Shandril with new respect, chuckling, "I'll not ask you to hold my axe, next time!"

Near sunset on the heights, they turned and looked back over the marching trees. The road dwindled down, down from where they stood to Highmoon, hazy in the distance.

"Who could know, looking at it, that this beautiful land could be so dangerous?" Narm asked quietly.

Delg smiled and said nothing.

"Never mind," Shandril replied, putting a hand on her man's arm. "We found each other, and that's worth it all."

They turned and walked into the evening together. As soft stars came out above them, they thought of many mornings to be shared ahead and were very happy.